"…The Scourge of Man will captivate readers and compel them to see the arid climates of their souls even more. It's deft and balanced, utterly engaging."

-Readers' Favorite Review

THE SCOURGE OF MAN

OF MAN

BY ZORAN OBRADOVIC

ISBN: **069294155X**

ISBN-13: **978-0692941553**

www.TheScourgeOfMan.com

This book is dedicated to my family and friends whose support made it all possible

PROLOGUE

She held his hand tightly as they walked back to her home. Her eyes looked up at him, then at the distant lights that brought her comfort. She asked him what happened to the man who took her away, but in a few soft-spoken words, he assured her the man wouldn't harm her again. Being six years old, she didn't understand much of what unfolded recently, but she trusted him as her fears subsided with each step.

For the first time in over two years, she felt a father figure next to her—someone who would protect her and make sure she was all right. The growing joy in her heart made her forget almost all the troubles she had just gone through. All that she cared about was going home.

As they approached the lights of a high-rise building and her home was a stone's throw away, he stopped and knelt right next to her.

"You're going to be okay," he said, still holding her hand. "Your home is right there." He glanced at the building, but her eyes stayed on him in quiet confusion. "You'll be safe there."

Pointing to the four men in uniform standing at the entrance of the building, he gave her instructions. "See those people there? You need to tell them who you are and what happened, and they'll take care of you. They'll take you to your mom."

"Aren't you coming with me?" she asked in a soft voice.

"Don't worry, I'll be watching you all the way," he responded as her eyes looked down in sadness.

She hesitated at first, but after a few moments, she let go of his hand and started walking. She looked back at him as he smiled and raised a hand in a goodbye. He kept his promise and watched her all the while she slowly and reluctantly approached the men in uniform. They in return seemed surprised to see a young child out that late. One of the men knelt down and started talking with her.

The man in the distance kept his eye on her until he felt confident the men were being kind. Then he walked away. Within a few moments, two of the uniformed men went out with their flashlights to investigate who had brought the little girl; however, the man they were looking for was nowhere to be found. It was just the darkness of the night and the sounds of the wild nature around it.

CHAPTER 1

Two years earlier, Vincent sat in a wooden chair and stared at the blue wall ahead. He felt the uncomfortable restriction of the handcuffs as he reached to scratch the side of his head. The police officers around him seemed relaxed doing their work, while the environment spoke of chaos and disturbance.

It seemed just another day at a police station in Brooklyn, New York, but to Vincent it was anything but ordinary. He couldn't believe he would ever find himself in such a place, even less with handcuffs on his hands. It was a mistake, he felt, and just waited for the officers to conclude that and let him go home.

In the unfortunate set of circumstances earlier in the day, he forgot to take off the airsoft pistol strapped to him when he went to do laundry in the basement of his building. The pistol, even though just a low-powered air gun firing plastic pellets, apparently appeared as the real thing to his older neighbor, Margaret. It also didn't help that he had fresh red stains on his white T-shirt from his new healthy diet that included raspberries. Margaret promptly ran out of the room, to Vincent's bewilderment. Then a few minutes later the police came in.

The airsoft pistol was a present from his friend Mark as a farewell gift when he moved to New York City from his hometown of Niagara Falls six months earlier. Vincent was a big fan of the classic westerns, and the airsoft seemed like a nice gift even though it resembled a much newer pistol than the Colt '51 used in the movies.

Vincent had never fired a real weapon before and thought he would rarely use the pistol Mark gave him, but for the past four months he spent a lot of time re-enacting the scenes from his favorite movies as he battled depression and various addictions that drove him to New York City in the first place. He became quite good at shooting "the bad guys" in his apartment, but now he sat in a chair designated for the lawbreakers with an ounce of worry and a ton of amusement about how he had gotten there.

Two hours later Vincent reflected on the whole ordeal while walking home on a hot July day. Even though it seemed inevitable the police would let him go, he was still glad they took it easy on him once they realized it was just an airsoft pistol he carried and released him from the police station. What baffled him the most was how clueless he felt about what went on until the police had him on the floor and in handcuffs, taking his pistol away.

He didn't feel upset at Margaret. After all, he should have been more careful; the toy did resemble a real pistol. Instead, he felt glad it was a nice day and another opportunity for him to go running in the evening. He remembered how in the past he wouldn't have been so calm about an unpleasant event like this, but rather resentful for days. Recently, however, he seemed to have changed and didn't feel bothered at all.

For the past four months he had managed to quell and avoid his depression feeders while doing something he felt was more productive. For a few years he had battled an unexplainable dispiritedness that sapped motivation out of him, left him dark and gloomy, caused him to drink frequently, compelled him to watch pornography and even use drugs, all the while hanging out with the wrong crowd and alienating the ones who cared about him. He felt old and forgotten, yet he was only in his late twenties.

Moving to New York City only helped in the beginning, but once the initial excitement dissipated it was back to the same old struggle. He recalled a day in March when he hit rock bottom and found himself on the bare floor of his bedroom, with no energy to get up, crying out to God, "I've had enough of this bullshit!" At that moment he knew it was live or die, and he had to choose.

Whether it was a divine intervention or his own willpower he didn't know, but the next time temptation called to him, he decided not to pick up the bottle. Instead, he picked up the airsoft pistol and challenged himself to shoot the various targets he set up in his apartment. He shut off his computer and started jogging around his new neighborhood. He began cooking his own meals and even turned to meditation. He did this regularly and called it *a path to recovery*.

He felt happy for the first time in a while and desired to reach the point where he would completely change for the better, perhaps reach a state of Nirvana, and become a new person. This *path to recovery* seemed to be doing the job, even to the point of being more forgiving of others. He headed into a direction he didn't quite know, but it felt right. He saw hope, and it was a welcome sign. Just like the bright sun ahead of him, this newfound optimism was making his path clear, and he couldn't imagine it going wrong.

CHAPTER 2

The next morning, Vincent woke with a renewed motivation. He didn't snooze at all and rose from his bed a few seconds after the alarm went off. He felt a little tired, shaking off the deep sleep, but he definitely felt more energy coming in. The commute was the same as always—busy and packed. It didn't matter to him. He was used to it by now.

Exiting at the Times Square station, he walked three blocks south and into his office building. He worked his way through the maze of small cubicles and placed his rucksack on the dark red carpet, which reminded him of a giant blood stain. He said a few "good mornings" to his neighbors and then placed headphones in his ears and started to work.

The workday started off the same as always, but with a little more excitement knowing that by tomorrow evening all the long hours would pay off with the completion of a project. Everyone on his team got into full swing. There wasn't any chitchat going on, only military-style discipline. Management seemed surprised that no one complained much. Vincent wondered if they had considered giving out higher than usual bonuses as a sign of their appreciation.

At around 11:30, a bit of chatter started around the cubicles. At first Vincent ignored it, but by quarter to noon, he became curious. People talked about something going on in the news. Something was grabbing everyone's attention. Vincent usually checked news websites in the morning, but for the past two weeks, he hadn't had the time to pay much attention.

Five minutes later the managers came out and appeared curious as to what was going on with all the workers. Vincent asked one of the colleagues in the next cube if he knew of anything, but the guy shrugged and said, "I've got no idea."

Next, he looked over at the managers in their offices as they talked among themselves, then at the TV in their office, but he couldn't tell what they were looking at. Soon he saw them pick up the phone. Within a minute, the voice on the intercom directed everyone to the conference room.

Crammed into the main conference room with all his colleagues, he saw a large projector screen with some news station on it. The head manager quickly addressed the employees.

"Hey, guys, please remain calm, but it was brought to our attention that something is going on you need to learn about. Please pay attention to the news and remain quiet."

On the screen, he saw maps of Europe, Asia, the Americas, and various speakers and experts talking about what was going on. Everyone seemed to be guessing and puzzled about how to explain it, but this only confused him more.

Next, the newscasters announced that as of noon, Eastern Standard Time, all flights in the United States had been canceled, and Canada and Mexico would follow soon. The faces in the room showed bewilderment. Many seemed worried. More news came out about off-duty hospital staff being called back to work.

"This is some serious shit," a voice came from the crowd.

Vincent tried to put all the pieces together, but he remained puzzled like so many of his colleagues. The news station had a difficult time running its broadcast in a coherent manner, so his coworkers switched the channel to another news station. This one seemed no better, but after five minutes the statement that would clarify things a bit came out.

"If you're just joining us for this major breakthrough news, we'll attempt to best explain what's been going on around the world. Starting approximately fourteen hours ago, there has been an outbreak of what we can only refer to as a global illness. We don't know what this illness is, but many experts doubt that even an airborne virus could spread so quickly.

"Some of the symptoms include extreme body aches, dizziness, cough, sore throat, and fever. The World Health Organization is still trying to estimate how many people have been affected. There are only a few reports that the illness has claimed lives; however, if left untreated, some experts warn that due to a large number of victims, this could turn into a deadly illness for many."

Everyone in the room appeared in a state of shock. Something like this couldn't be happening. It was hard to grasp that malady, as if it had come from a horror movie—all of a sudden so many people were affected, and the illness was spreading so fast. No one knew what it was, and that was frightening.

At first the room was quiet, but then people started talking, trying to make sense of it all. Vincent heard a few people wonder whether it could be a terrorist attack. Doubtful, Vincent thought, since it seemed to have spread almost evenly throughout the whole world. Someone even mentioned a zombie apocalypse. Many laughed at this, but a few remained serious as if they considered that a possibility.

Either way, no one had reported anything about zombies yet. At one point when the defense minister came on the news, the anchor asked this very question. The minister chuckled for two seconds and then replied that a zombie apocalypse was highly unlikely, but the truth was they didn't know what this illness could be or how it had happened. All they knew was that it had a resemblance to yellow fever. Incidence of a terrorist attack was also low on the list, but at this point everything remained on the table.

Two hours later, no one did any work. The cubicles were empty. Computer screens showed either unfinished documents or various corporate screen savers. Everyone from the company clung to their cell phones and the news station in the conference room. The supervisors ordered pizza for the hungry folks still glued to the news screen who had skipped their lunch. On the other side of the room, the head managers debated what to do.

Somehow, the major project due the next day still seemed to be on managers' minds, yet the world had a much greater problem at stake. By three o'clock, the news reported the first estimate of affected people in the world around 450 to 500 million—already by far the biggest pandemic in world history. Based on this information, the managers decided to let everyone go home while instructing them to keep an eye on their work email regarding work the next day.

Vincent knew the commute home would be tough. It appeared as if everyone were trying to leave Manhattan at once. Walking to the subway, he realized he wouldn't be home anytime soon. The trains were packed, and lines to get in were long. He decided to stop at a small coffee shop and wait for the rush to die down.

He sat there and wondered how long he would linger before he attempted to go home again. As for the spreading illness, he didn't know what to think. He had yet to witness someone actually getting sick. Perhaps he was the lucky one.

If the reports were true that the illness was similar to yellow fever, the only option was to hydrate, stay in bed, and call an ambulance if things got too bad. Finding an available ambulance seemed unlikely, though, considering the estimates of how many people had gotten sick.

After two hours of drinking decaffeinated coffee, Vincent decided to go home. It still proved difficult, but he managed to board one of the trains that would later drop him off a mile from his apartment building.

When he finally made it home, he decided to call his mom and dad. Unfortunately, the cellular providers, most likely overwhelmed by the volume of calls, couldn't let his call through. He turned on the TV and learned that the virus, illness, whatever it was, had spread to approximately 1.5 billion people worldwide.

In the U.S. alone, there had been cases reported in all fifty states. New York City had definitely been mapped as one of the affected areas on the East Coast. It appeared very difficult, if not impossible, to quarantine this epidemic. Nothing seemed to be known about it—what it was, how it developed, or how it spread.

The illness affected the globe so swiftly that it made many experts believe that it had started spreading at least a week before, and now it had entered its acute phase. Scientists were apparently scrambling to learn as much as possible, but in the meantime, they could only give advice to people: stay hydrated, stay away from crowded places, and avoid traveling at all costs.

The new list of symptoms included fever, headache, nausea, dizziness, muscle aches, and red eyes and face. By quarter to ten that night, the news hit a new low when it reported that more than two-thirds of all cellular users would not be able to make calls or texts, urging people to use email and online messaging applications.

Even these mediums had delays, as it seemed the Internet providers and their servers had a hard time keeping up with the volume of users and messages sent out. Vincent dialed his parents' phones every few minutes over the next two hours to no avail. Around midnight, he wrote an email stating he was fine and asked how they were doing. He went to bed with hope they were all right.

At three in the morning, he woke up with a sickening nausea.

CHAPTER 3

Vincent rose from his bed, and before he could make it to the bathroom, he started vomiting. The heaving was so violent that it shocked him. When he made it to the toilet, he felt a little better. Returning to the bed, he laid down, unsure what had just happened. Then a few minutes later the sickening nausea made him get up to vomit again.

Within a few minutes he was so weak that he found it challenging to make it back to the bed. Finally, under his covers, he felt a little better, but then an odd discomfort came over him, and he began turning from side to side trying to find a comfortable position.

Nausea quickly returned, and he made another trip to the bathroom. A pounding headache and muscular aches followed as Vincent stumbled back to his bedroom in pain. He did this routine ten times in the next three hours before he realized he was too weak to even make it to the bathroom anymore.

In his delirious state, he somehow remembered the instructions on the news station to stay hydrated. He doubted he would get any better if he didn't get some liquids into his body. So the next time he was on his way from the bathroom, he decided to go to the kitchen instead.

It proved a difficult ordeal. Even though the kitchen was a short distance away, it became hard to progress even a few feet without keeling over to the floor. When he finally managed to get to the kitchen on his hands and knees, he reached out to open the fridge door and found it incredibly tough.

Damn it all! he screamed inside. He didn't have enough strength to open the fridge.

He grabbed the door with both his hands and leaned back with all his weight. The door swung open as he fell back. Slowly, he mustered all his energy to grab a cold vitamin water bottle. Leaning back against the open fridge, he mustered more energy to open the bottle and take a sip.

Within ten seconds of taking a sip, the nausea kicked in and he vomited again. Exhausted, he propped himself to a sitting position against a kitchen cabinet and rested this way for a few minutes. He felt a little better this way. Then he took another sip.

"I have to do this!" he told himself. "I have to stay hydrated."

After a few minutes, he felt he could attempt his way back to bed. He grabbed the bottle, leaned against the fridge door to close it, and then slowly started making his way back to bed. Every time nausea came over him, he stopped moving, sat on the floor, and rested. It took him almost fifteen minutes to cross twenty feet.

Once in his bed, he took another sip and tried to sleep, but he found it difficult. His muscles ached no matter what position he put himself in. It didn't help that his headache didn't let go or that from time to time he experienced hot flashes, and the same with the nausea.

Vincent didn't try to make it to the bathroom anymore. If he felt like vomiting, he would do it in the small garbage can he had next to his bed. He simply had no energy to keep going back and forth between the bedroom and the bathroom, but he promised himself that every time he felt a little better, he would take a sip of the vitamin water to keep himself hydrated.

After two hours in his bed, he heard the cell phone ring. He knew the phone was somewhere in the room, maybe on the computer table at the other end, or perhaps in his sports coat in the closet, but it was nearly impossible to muster enough energy to find it and answer the call.

Even though the phone seemed to ring for a long time, he couldn't figure out where it was coming from. Any noise in the room disoriented him. He could barely tell where the window or the bedroom door was. It seemed as if he slowly spun in his bed one way and the room the other. The only upside was that at this point the nausea and vomiting were becoming less frequent.

After a long while, Vincent finally fell asleep, which didn't last long, but it was much needed. When he woke up, he burned with fever. He felt nauseous as well, but it was the fever that dealt the hardest blow. He forced himself to sip on the vitamin water as often as possible.

Again, his stomach started churning, making him want to vomit. He hadn't done it in a while, and the combination of everything made him feel worse than before—the fever, nausea, headache, and muscle aches were occurring all at once.

He felt everything come down on him, the full weight of it all, and this was the big climax. But he didn't give a damn whether it was the climax or not. All he wanted to do was put something cold on his hands because they felt incredibly hot.

Laboriously, he got up to go to the bathroom, stumbling around the room and pausing frequently to try to keep his balance. Just as before, it was a slow trip, and it took him forever to make his way through. Once he arrived at the bathroom, he collapsed to the floor. He propped himself over the toilet and vomited, and then he collapsed again.

As he lay there next to the bowl, he wondered how comfortable it would be to give up and die. He felt all he needed was to close his eyes and let go. All that kept him alive was the miniscule energy running like a thin thread in his mind telling him to keep going. But all he had to do was let go of it, and his life on earth would be over.

Dying was as easy as making the decision to do so. All the worries, troubles, hardships, conflicts, struggles, past embarrassments, and current hardship would disappear and bother him no more. All he needed was to give in and give up.

Vincent was about to slip into a dream. He could see it peeking through his mind as a blurry vision of a river making its way between two withering trees in the distance. The dying grass by the river looked inviting to rest on; however, that little dose of energy still in his mind kept him awake and felt incredibly precious. He was in a dilemma, but time was running out, and soon it would choose for him.

This is what it means to be on the verge of death, he thought, to feel its breath in my face, to have the choice to touch it or postpone the engagement for another day.

With all the suffering he had gone through in the past day, getting to that final rest almost seemed understandable, yet he felt guilty giving up, as that cardinal sin of life still remained unacceptable.

"It wasn't meant to be easy," he tried to convince himself.

"Mercy, God," he pleaded. "Could you please spare some mercy that's left over?"

Mustering all his energy, he leaned over the bathtub and turned on the cold water. Placing his right hand underneath, he felt immediate relief as the cool drips flowed down his arm. He slowly brought his hand to his face and touched it, feeling a greater sense of relief.

Even though it didn't last long, the water gave his mind a chance to think more clearly, and he was now more resolute to keep on fighting and staying alive. Standing back on his feet, he looked at the mirror. He appeared so pale that he could barely recognize himself. His ash brown hair appeared like a wig on a mannequin. Taking a slow, deep breath, he started making baby steps on the long journey back to his bed.

Lying on top of the covers, aching from everything, he started to see things in front of him. He wasn't sure whether he was dreaming or not, but in his dazed state he saw the bedroom wall missing and the streets at his level. Slowly, shining red blobs appeared from every direction. The people on the street tried to dodge them, but each person touched by a blob fell to the ground vomiting.

He felt he needed to do something to help, and looking around his room, he saw the air pistol next to the computer desk. He pictured himself grabbing the pistol and shooting at the blobs, which when hit would pop like a balloon.

He kept doing this in his hallucination for a while, and after some time, he snapped out of it. Thinking he needed to sip more vitamin water, he reached for a bottle and opened it, spilling some on himself, and drank nearly half of it. After this, the hallucinations left him alone.

For the next twelve hours, he would fall asleep for short periods of time and continue shooting at the blobs in his dreams. Sometimes he did all right; other times the volume of blobs made it difficult to shoot them all, and even those he shot reappeared. It frustrated him, and he would sweat, toss, and turn in his bed.

In one particular dream, the blobs spread through all of New York City. He partnered with his friend Mark and Leon Alastray, a protagonist from one of his favorite movies, *Guns for San Sebastian*, to fight them, but he was the only one with the pistol.

Mark and Leon encouraged him, telling him to keep fighting, and he felt the need to protect them. They ran all around the city, through the familiar and unfamiliar places, away from the blobs chasing them through the streets, buildings, parks, and subways.

A bystander who seemed unfazed by the blobs calamity asked them, rather nonchalantly, "Where are you going?"

"What's the difference?" Vincent replied by quoting a line from the movie. "A man goes from a place of his birth to the place of his death."

Soon enough, the blobs started losing their strength and slowed down. No longer chased, Vincent stopped to rest, only to realize he had lost Mark and Leon. The rest of his dream he spent looking for them, even if it meant going deep into dark alleys and buildings and facing more blobs. He just wouldn't give up.

"I have to save them," he said and kept running.

CHAPTER 4

Sometime in the early morning of the third day of his illness, Vincent woke up and felt his mind was clearer than before. He knew he needed to take this chance to drink as much vitamin water as he could. Going through four bottles by this point, he felt it was a good sign; he was keeping himself hydrated.

On the other hand, the headache and the pains in his muscles and bones bothered him. Perhaps because he didn't hallucinate, he ached more. He still felt exhausted and wanted to go back to sleep, but he promised himself to drink at least half of the bottle before he could let himself fall asleep.

Lying in bed, sipping on the bottle and staring at the ceiling, he realized he hasn't eaten anything but a few crackers in over two days. That thought alone made him hungry. He knew he couldn't rely on crackers alone; he needed something more nutritious. Getting up, he felt stable on his feet. "This is another good sign," he said to himself. Making his slow way to the fridge, he found a slice of pizza.

"I guess this will do. It's better than anything I've eaten in a while."

Before he took a bite, he started worrying the pizza could upset his stomach and soon after he would be in the bathroom vomiting. That was the last thing he wanted to do, so he decided to eat a few crackers first to ease his stomach into eating a heartier meal. Even though it took an hour to eat it, he thought it was the best slice of pizza he had ever had.

Soon Vincent felt a little more energy, and his headache wasn't as bad. He didn't want to get over-confident, but he hoped the worst was behind him. For the remainder of the day he remained in his bed resting and sipping the vitamin water while thinking about his situation. When it became dark in the apartment, he found his way back to the kitchen and grabbed three slices of cinnamon bread. He felt these, too, were the best slices he had ever had.

That night, and for the first time in three days, he slept without interruption. It was a long sleep. His body was so greatly exhausted from battling the illness that it needed a rest like no other.

When he woke up, twelve hours had passed, and he felt much better than before. His muscles didn't ache much. The fever had gone down, and he was glad the headache had disappeared. He experienced no nausea at all, and the hunger pangs came back. Once again this was a great sign, he thought, as an appetite meant he was getting better. As usual, he hydrated himself with a few sips and then walked to the window.

This was the first time he had looked outside in over three days, and he got an eerie feeling because he saw barely any activity. His neighborhood was always full of people during the day, and now it looked virtually empty.

He couldn't quite grasp what day it was. He had a hard time remembering the first day he had heard about the pandemic or the night he fell sick. Trying to satisfy his hunger, he went into the kitchen and ate four slices of cinnamon bread. Sitting at the kitchen table, he slowly started recalling the recent events. It was the fourth day since he had left work, so it must be Monday. He remembered his cell phone and immediately called his mom and then his dad. No one answered.

He left messages saying he was all right and that he hoped they were, too. He turned on the TV and found that the stations emitted the same message as before: a list of things to do if one caught the illness. Those included not panicking, staying in your home, and keeping hydrated. He flipped through all the stations, but all were the same.

Vincent went online and found that all the news sites were dated at least a day or two ago. The most recent stated that the pandemic has infected eight in ten people in the United States alone. He found no statistics from around the world but assumed it was just as bad.

As a desperate measure to identify the cause of the illness, some experts had turned to the genetic and biochemical testing of the blood of the victims. For the first time, there was some understanding of what was going on. They had identified some disorder in the victims' DNA that had resulted in hyperactivity of certain proteins.

This, in turn, resulted in the illness, but the mystery still remained what had triggered it in so many people all of a sudden. Some had speculated that it was always there in the human genes but turned off, and something had all of a sudden triggered it. It seemed as if human genes had a code specifically left behind to go off at a certain time.

"Was this a ticking time bomb?" Vincent questioned quietly.

The more he read, the less he could believe it was true. He had a hard time accepting that this was somehow preprogrammed into his genes, that it was always there, and that something, somehow lit the spark worldwide. It was as if nature had said enough with the humans and God had answered its prayers. Whatever the cause, the illness had humbled the most advanced creature on the planet to its knees.

For the rest of the day Vincent lay on his couch surfing the web on his laptop and reading up on whatever news he could find. Every now and then he called his parents, without luck. He would take a half-hour nap here and there and then go back to the laptop and cell phone. As the sun set and it became dark in the apartment, he felt depressed. He hoped to hear something different, but nothing seemed good, and it didn't help that the news wasn't being updated.

Trying to rationalize the information he gathered online, he thought that perhaps the illness wasn't as deadly in itself, but because such a large number of people had gotten sick, there was barely anyone to help them out. The sick would have to take care of the sick, and remembering the state he was in just a day ago, he could barely help himself, much less anyone else. What if people couldn't do the simple task of hydrating themselves? That would unfortunately result in the deaths of many.

At quarter to ten, he turned on the TV and saw something different. It broadcasted on every channel. A gentleman came on in front of a blue screen and prepared to read something. He had a stern look, and Vincent realized the message wouldn't be good.

"Fellow citizens. As you know, the world is facing a pandemic of biblical proportions. The government of the United States has employed many subject experts. Scientists and the researchers are working hard to provide you with the best information on how to battle this. You're not forgotten.

"Information is being gathered and analyzed on possible antidotes to this problem, but the most effective solution is yourself; remain calm and don't panic, stay hydrated as much as you can, and don't try to leave your homes. Hospitals cannot help you. Please leave the TV or radio on, as we'll provide you with important information that may help you and your loved ones. God bless you all."

The world was collapsing in front of his eyes. The nightmares rehearsed in many religions and various end-of-the world scenarios were finally coming alive. Struggling to sleep that night, he tossed and turned, not due to the body aches, but because his mind wouldn't rest. Sometime in the middle of the night, Vincent's cell phone rang. It was his dad. Vincent, so glad to hear him, leaped out of bed.

"Dad! Dad! How are you?" he asked excitedly.

Unfortunately, the voice on the other line was quiet with many pauses in between sentences, and Vincent knew his dad wasn't in good shape.

"Your stepmom is sick," his dad said in a quiet voice resonating with worry. "I tried to reach . . . I tried to reach your uncle, but there wasn't any response."

"Dad, you have to stay hydrated," Vincent responded loudly. "Both you and Claire, stay hydrated. That's the only—"

"I tried to reach your uncle," his dad cut him off. "I'm worried . . . about him . . . Your stepmom . . . she's sick."

Vincent felt so sad when he realized his father wasn't listening to him and kept repeating himself. As the conversation progressed, he started making less and less sense with his words. It became obvious that his father was delirious with fever.

A memory of his dad, when Vincent was a young kid, came to him. He remembered how strong his dad looked and how safe he felt with him no matter where they went or how scary the storm was overhead. It seemed, at that time, his dad could answer any of his questions. Now he sounded confused and scared.

Vincent tried to tell him to stay strong and drink water, not to give up on himself, but his dad continued rambling about random things—trees growing out of concrete, burning barrels, and spider webs. The conversation lasted about ten minutes, until his dad couldn't talk anymore and said a quiet goodbye.

"Dad!" Vincent called to him loudly. "Stay hydrated, drink water, you must-"

Before he could finish the sentence, the call disconnected. Realizing this could be the last time he would speak with his father, Vincent started crying. He felt the need to help him, but he didn't know how. He could barely walk from his bed to the kitchen, a mere twenty feet, without getting winded, and his dad lived over four hundred miles away.

Sitting on the bed and staring at the floor, he started feeling guilt for not spending more time with him in the past few years. Regrets forced more and more tears, and he couldn't do anything about it.

When the tears stopped, Vincent felt alone. He wanted somebody now more than ever. He dialed his mom but reached her voicemail again. This time he left a long message telling her he loved her very much and if he could be there to help her he would, but he didn't know if she would ever get the message.

Everything seemed to be slowing down, dying, or dead, deserting him on every side. This was the lowest point of Vincent's life he could imagine. Desperately looking for something different, he turned on the TV, but he saw the same news as the day before.

Having run out of vitamin water, Vincent filled the empty bottles with the water from the sink and sat on the couch forcing himself to eat a slice of bread. He stared out the window into the darkness of the night as the misery danced all around him to the painfully sentimental blues.

CHAPTER 5

The next three days went by slowly for Vincent. Physically, he got better, but emotionally he remained a wreck. He still couldn't get a hold of his mother, and there was nothing new on the television, radio, or any website. All information he could find discussed different methods people could help themselves and their loved ones recover from the illness.

To make matters worse, the weather was overcast with dirty clouds and light rain; it was just enough to make a person appreciate life a little less. There was modest activity on the streets. A vehicle went by from time to time, but that was pretty much it. Even the birds remained quiet, as if shaken by the sudden silence of the mighty human species.

It appeared that at least eighty percent of the human population was bedridden, and the other twenty tried to keep the most necessary services running, like water, electricity, and gas. The Internet ran well, as there was plenty of bandwidth available with fewer people using it. Cellular communications remained spotty, though. Increasingly, the calls wouldn't complete even though the signal strength appeared strong.

Although Vincent didn't eat much during this period, he worried about running low on food. He was never the kind of guy to stack up on food to last a few weeks, but more for a few days. He did luck out, though, because he had bought a big bag of Jasmine white rice and had some cans in the cupboards from the time he first moved in. Nevertheless, he knew that it wasn't going to last long, and white rice wasn't very nutritious anyway. He knew sooner or later he would have to find a way to get more food.

Though he felt strong enough to make trips around his apartment, he was far from making a trip down the street and to a store, which he knew was most likely closed anyway. Even though he was improving slowly, he still suffered occasional headaches and fevers before going to sleep. He hadn't vomited in a few days, but nausea came and went from day to day. Muscle aches remained the more common of symptoms but became more tolerable primarily because he became accustomed to them.

It was a Saturday and the tenth day since he had become ill. The United States government announced via TV and radio that anyone capable of physical work should report to the nearest fire hall, police station, or hospital in their communities.

The goal was to help distribute food and electrolyte-infused water to the many people who had no means of getting it. The new estimate released was that nearly ninety percent of people in the U.S. alone had become ill, with increasing numbers of people in immediate danger of dying.

The food distribution was a desperate measure, but it was all that could be done at the time. No vaccine existed, or medication, and there seemed no need for quarantine. The sick people needed the most basic nutritional needs, and the government could at least try to provide that.

Without the adequate labor to do it, the government relied on all hands available. With many of the healthy and capable people making sure the electrical grid, gas, and water remained operational, they desperately needed people for this task. All that volunteers had to do was come to the nearest station or hospital, and they would be provided with tools and instructions to help out with the effort.

They would be given a map with a route to go with other volunteers to help bring food and electrolyte-infused water to each apartment building or house. In other words, they'd be knocking on every residence on their list of neighborhoods and letting people know they had left them a package with food and water. A package could last a single person approximately ten to fourteen days and hopefully save many lives.

Over the next three days, Vincent thought a lot about volunteering. He wasn't in great shape after his own battle with the illness, but with so many people in need, he wanted to help, to make a difference. In his building alone, he calculated, resided at least five hundred people, and if he could help them, he might as well.

On the following day, he became resolute on volunteering. Not once did someone knock on his door from the relief effort, and he was down to half a cup of rice. This time he simply had no choice. Strong enough or not, he had to make it down there. He braced himself for a tough task ahead, ate the remainder of the rice, and went out.

So far so good, he thought. I'm not feeling dizzy or exhausted. He took his time, though, making short steps at a fairly slow pace.

"One step at a time," he kept telling himself.

Three blocks away, he saw a truck. He assumed it was full of food and electrolyte-infused water, rolling by with four guys inside. The truck made a right turn and out of his sight. He wondered which neighborhoods they were headed to. He doubted it was his.

Approaching the fire station, he saw around a hundred and fifty people gathered outside. A line of ten to fifteen trucks came into the station, and another line of trucks got ready to leave to deliver food.

Just as he crossed the street, he heard someone say, "Looking to volunteer, buddy?"

"Yeah," Vincent replied, feeling a little startled.

"All right, come over here."

Crossing the street, Vincent met the tired-looking man with glasses who pointed to a big guy with a notebook in his hand. "Okay, he'll tell you where you need to go. Hey, Pete, got another one here."

The big guy looked at him. "Great! How are you feeling? Can you lift fifty pounds?"

"I haven't in a while, but I can try."

"All right, let's put you in with these guys." He pointed to a large U-Haul truck. "You'll go to Prospect Heights."

Within a minute, Vincent found himself loading the truck with relief packages. It was a quick process, but unfortunately for him, it took its toll. After a few minutes, he felt tired and slowed down.

"Feeling all right?" a shorter black man who looked to be in his fifties asked.

"Yeah, it's been a while," Vincent said as he took a moment of breath. "Still recovering, you know. I'm not hundred percent yet, but I think I'll be fine."

"Oh, wait, you were sick, too?" the man asked with a surprised look.

"Yeah. Isn't close to ninety percent of the population affected?" Vincent replied, puzzled at the man's question.

"Well, yeah," the man said, "but all of us here are the lucky ones who haven't gotten sick, at least not yet. You're the first guy I know who was sick and isn't bedridden. Are you sure you're fine?"

"Yeah, I'm a little short of breath, but I feel strong." Vincent looked at the man wondering what he had missed while he was recovering in his apartment. "So, you're telling me you haven't come across any other people who got better, or at least are getting better?"

The man replied with a straight face, "Not really. I'm impressed that you did. Someone took good care of you."

"I . . . I actually had no one look after me. I just got through it somehow, but it was tough."

The man leaned back in bewilderment. "Well, that was God, son," he reasoned. "Unless someone is looking after you, I don't think anyone will survive here."

The sound of this made Vincent's stomach churn. He hoped that most people were slowly getting better like he was, not dying or already dead. The thought made him think of his parents, especially his mom. He hadn't heard from her at all. His father wasn't doing well, but at least he was able to hear from him. He feared the worst for his mother.

Thoughts of his friends from Niagara Falls crossed his mind as well. He wondered how they fared in this great calamity. Maybe they didn't get sick at all. Or perhaps they did but got better like he did. Or maybe they fell among the majority and were on their last breath.

Vincent learned the short man's name was Mike, and he was their truck driver. Mike seemed a kind and hardworking character, focused on his work without complaints. Vincent delivered the packages with two additional people: another guy and a girl.

After the truck was filled, they were on their way. It seemed the government had sent people in groups of four, while providing them with gloves, some basic gear, and a GPS route to take. Mike handled the truck with ease, and even though he was older and smaller than the people next to him, he looked stronger.

The guy sitting next to him was Nathan, a white man in his late thirties, somewhat overweight, wearing glasses with thick dark frames. Next to Nathan was Taylor. She looked to be in her late teens and some kind of a racial mix of black, Hispanic, and white. She looked athletic and shy.

On the drive, Vincent learned that Mike and Taylor had been helping with the relief effort since they first announced it a week before. The veterans of the effort, they looked exhausted from doing it fourteen hours a day each day. Nathan was on his second day and looked a little fresher.

"There are a lot of people dying out there," Mike said, scratching his short beard. "I'm not sure how much this will help, but we ought to do as much as we can."

Mike took a brief pause while dodging randomly parked cars on the street. "It's easy for any of us. Many loved ones have been lost, but we've got to keep on fighting. The Lord said this would come, and it did. Now we have to do what's right, help as best as we can and know how to. Can't give up now."

It seemed to Vincent that it was tough for Mike to give encouragement in such times, but anything was still better than nothing. Nathan, on the other hand, kept on making excuses about why he couldn't have helped more days. He apparently took a break of a few days since he had first come to volunteer. The excuses sounded bogus, and no one seemed to care about what he said. Taylor didn't say anything. It seemed to Vincent that she may have lost someone close, and he didn't want to bother her with questions.

Mike, on the other hand, kept talking. "We need as many people as we can get to help with this. Every second counts, man. Every life counts."

When Nathan and Taylor learned that Vincent had recovered from the illness on his own, they had a hard time believing him. It was the first time Taylor had opened her mouth and asked a few questions. Just like Mike, neither, apparently, knew many people who had recovered, and doing it alone seemed a miracle.

This appeared to give them hope that maybe it was possible more people would get better, including their loved ones. Taylor asked how he did it and what his "secret" was to beating the illness. Vincent, unfortunately, didn't have much of an answer to that.

"I tried to stay hydrated and forced myself to eat. I slept a lot. To be honest, I think I was just lucky."

"It was the Lord's will," Mike added, "and if he helped you, I'm pretty sure there are plenty of other folks he'll help as well. We just have to do our part."

There was practically no one on the road besides an occasional relief truck. When they arrived at Prospect Heights, Vincent had regained much of the energy he had lost filling the truck. He was aware, however, that he had to take it easy or he would become another burden. The question was, how could he take it easy if those offering aide were doing twelve to fourteen hours on average of hard labor?

Damn, he thought, did I do this too soon?

When they got out of the truck, Mike opened the map on his cell phone. "All right, folks, let's see. Taylor, why don't you go with Nathan into those buildings and cover section-area 223. That should probably be good for the day."

He turned to Vincent. "Now, you and I will cover these buildings, and that will finish up the rest of 224 and probably a good deal of 225."

They grabbed their walkie-talkies since they still couldn't trust that the cellular communication wouldn't go out, Mike's cell phone, the address sheet printed on a piece of paper, a pen, latex gloves, a mouth cover, and two wheelies, and started loading it with boxes of food.

Mike started explaining to Vincent, "All right, man, let me show you how we do this. See the routes they gave us?" He zoomed in on one of the section-areas. "They have these neighborhoods that were assigned to each day. Now, we can't always get the entire area finished in a day, which means we need to come back the next day and complete it."

Mike pointed to the address sheet next. "These are the addresses for each area we're assigned. It helps us keep track of what we've covered."

He paused for a second. "Now here are the rules; we have to visit every single residential address in the neighborhood we're assigned to, regardless of whether we think someone is in there or not.

"When we come to the door, we knock and state that we're from the national relief agency and want to leave them some food and water they may need. We do this three times. If no one responds, we move on to the next address."

"Okay, I wish this would actually help someone," Vincent responded with obvious doubt in his tone.

"Listen! We've got to try everything," Mike responded, "and since this is your first time doing it, I have to warn you, we aren't supposed to go into any homes . . . but I do if I suspect someone is in there and can't come to the door."

Mike shook his head. "You'll see some messed-up shit. It's never good to see an old person dead, but I'm talking about kids, babies, and young folks like you. Our job is to distribute food, and it's tough, Vincent, when you have to leave someone behind you know ain't gonna make it."

Vincent was quiet for a few moments and then asked, "How many living people do you come across?"

Mike scratched his beard. "Um, that's tough to say. Maybe one or two a day now."

"After visiting how many addresses?" Vincent asked again.

"Two to three hundred," Mike answered.

"Then this is practically meaningless what we're doing. There has to be a better way," Vincent said distraught.

"If it saves one person, I think it's worth it," Mike replied.

The first building they went to was four stories high and had eighteen apartments in it. No one answered at any of the doors. Vincent saw Mike try a lot more than three times at each apartment. He yelled, banged on the door, and sometimes tried to open it.

There was nothing but eerie silence. Mike listened carefully, leaning his head against each door, as if hoping someone would say something or make a noise. They completed building one. Vincent, already winded, slowed down but kept pushing on. He wondered how they would tackle a building the size of his, especially if they couldn't use the elevators out of fear the electricity would go out.

After five hours, they had made it to eighty addresses. Roughly half of them had their doors unlocked. Either they were empty, or their residents were already dead. What Vincent saw no one could have prepared him for; it was an awful sight. In one apartment he saw a mother lying on the floor next to her baby's cradle. The baby was still. The father was in the bed. All were dead.

In another apartment an older gentleman keeled over in a bathtub in a dark bathroom. Vincent didn't know he was there until he turned on the lights. In the apartment across the hallway they found three kids, six or seven years old, peacefully lying in their bed, all dead. Their mother lay in the hallway face up with open eyes and no pupils, and their father on the floor in another bedroom face down with vomit dried up all around him.

None of the dead bodies looked like he would imagine, with

blood pooled to the lowest part of the body and decomposition in the process. Instead, they appeared extremely pale and stiff, as if made of wax.

In one apartment they came across a little dog. It didn't make a sound when they entered and quietly watched them with its sad eyes while sitting next to his owner's head. Vincent was surprised that it didn't bark or make any noise when they yelled and banged on the door. All the dog did was lean its head on the owner's cheeks and continue to watch them.

Overcome by the scene, Vincent felt speechless.

"It's best we leave the dog alone," Mike said. "Like so many others in the city, he'll eventually realize his owner is gone and move on. We, on the other hand, should only focus on humans. After all, no other creature has been affected but humans."

Mike signaled for a break. Vincent nodded, and they went outside. Mike opened one of the food boxes, taking out some food for Vincent and himself. They kept in contact with Nathan and Taylor, who were on their sixty-third address.

"How'd you get over that illness man?" Mike asked. "Was there anything that pushed you through it? Did you take anything that made a difference?"

Vincent replied, "It may sound simple, but I think the defining moment was when I was at my weakest and lowest. For some reason, I didn't give up. It was as if something gave me this tiny desire in my heart that it was worth living. I guess it was hope. That's all I can say."

"I believe you," Mike said. "Hope is all we have to live on—to know there's some kind of higher purpose to all of this. That's why I won't give up on the next person we come across. They're so precious now. Most of the world is dead, so whoever we can find is worth more than anything."

Over the next five hours, they visited seventy more addresses. Unfortunately, there was only silence. Noticing Mike's dedication to reach as many people as possible, Vincent tried hard not to slow Mike down, even though he tired quickly.

After about thirty minutes, they got into a six-story apartment building. It had twenty-four apartments, and halfway through Mike came across an apartment that had a jammed door. It would open only a few inches, and Mike was adamant to investigate whether anyone was alive inside.

To Vincent this seemed futile, as it looked like another apartment where they would find a dead person or no one at all. He was about to start convincing Mike to move on to the next one, but after seeing him push against the door so hard, he let him.

After a few strong thrusts, Mike managed to open the door. Inside, in the hallway, they came across a young woman. She couldn't have been more than twenty-five, and to Vincent's shock she was still breathing.

"This one is alive!" Mike said excitedly.

She was unconscious and in bad shape, but she was alive.

"I won't leave her like this," Mike said. "We won't come across many more who are alive, and if we leave her this way she will for surely die."

"What do you think we should do?" Vincent asked, thinking that calling an ambulance wouldn't work.

"We're going to take her with us," Mike said, brushing the sweat off his eyebrows. "That's the least we can do. Someone can look after her and see if she can get better. We're wasting our time if we don't do more to help her, and you know we won't save anyone just by leaving them food. Help me take her to the truck."

They tried to wake her before picking her up, but it proved difficult. She barely opened her eyes a mere millimeter before closing them again. They knew she was dehydrated to the point of death. Calling an ambulance would have been great, but as Vincent predicted, they didn't bother with it because they knew it wouldn't have come.

They immediately called Taylor and Nathan back.

"We're done for the day," Mike notified them over the radio.

Nathan seemed pleased, while Taylor questioned him as to why so early.

"We need to bring a young woman to the truck," Mike explained. "She's about to die, and there is no way we're doing nothing about it."

At the station, the fire chief didn't appear overly happy they had brought the young woman.

"There's absolutely no one who can take care of her," the chief argued. "If others start bringing sick people back, it would be a burden we can't handle. In this city alone, there are millions who need help, and if she looks like she's not going to make it anyway, why waste time? Let's focus on those who can."

"I couldn't let her die," Mike persisted. "She's the only one alive we've come across today. Have one of the medics administer an IV line with normal saline, and I'll take care of the rest."

The chief reluctantly nodded, and they immediately rushed her to one of the makeshift ambulances. Mike's care for the girl impressed Vincent. He hadn't come across many people in his life who seemed so determined to help a stranger.

"Listen," Mike said and pulled Vincent aside. "I can't let her stay at the station. After the IV is done, she'd be on her own, which basically means a death sentence."

Mike walked up to one of the policemen. "Here," he said, and handed him some documents. "These are the documents we found on that girl. I'll take care of her, and I want you to know that I'm taking her with me."

The policeman shook his head and put the documents aside. "If you want to save her, then save her," he said. "I hope you're doing it for the right reasons."

Mike nodded without trying to explain any further. Then he signaled to Vincent to help carry the young woman to his SUV. As they got her inside, they noticed people gathering around the fire chief, who stood on some kind of a makeshift podium. They knew he was going to make some kind of an announcement, so Mike told him to check it out.

The fire chief began to speak. "Listen up! The government is canceling the relief effort starting tomorrow. We aren't really saving any lives by dropping food at people's doors anyway. It was a desperate effort, but this isn't working out anymore."

Everyone stared at him in silence.

"So, go home," the chief continued. "Take care of your loved ones or whomever you want to take care of. Take as many of these packages with you as you can, but don't fight over them. That's the last thing we need. There's plenty for everyone."

He paused for a second as he gathered some air into his lungs. "The government wants you to know that you aren't alone. They're working hard on keeping the most basic things running, like water, electricity, and so on. Keep your TVs and radios on, and wait for the next announcement."

He looked down for a few moments. "I'm sorry guys, I don't know what to tell you. This is the apocalypse as we know it. Take care of yourselves and your loved ones, but don't ever, I mean ever, lose decency. When we come out of this, we'll need to stick together. So, don't lose what makes us civilized. We'll all need it."

There was silence at first. Then it slowly broke as people started talking among themselves. They seemed not to know what to do next.

"Go home and do what?" someone from the group asked. "Aren't we more useful in doing something? Maybe helping out in some way with the electrical grid and other things? The country is so short of healthy people there ought to be plenty of work for us. Why would they send us home?"

"Listen folks," one of the doctors on staff came out, grabbing everyone's attention. "This illness isn't over."

Silence overtook the crowd again.

"Just because you didn't get sick in the last two or three weeks doesn't necessarily mean you won't. I get reports every day of new folks getting sick. Even my own wife got sick this morning, and she was fine until then.

"She had the same symptoms and everything. It looks like it's a matter of time that we all get it. The best you can do is get together with your family, stock up on fluids and food, take care of each other, and not lose the will to live. I'm going to pack up myself and go home to take care of my wife."

"I don't get it," someone in the crowd said. "How can this all be in our genes? In absolutely everyone's genes?"

"Imagine it this way," the doctor started explaining. "All the living organisms are like programs or machines. Genes are like the instructions manual on how to build these programs and machines. They make us different from that of a pigeon.

"Luckily for the pigeons, they didn't have something tell their genes to all of a sudden make them all sick. We did. Something, someone, God, nature, or both, triggered it in us. How this happened, we have no idea. It's beyond us, and that's the best explanation we have."

The people remained quiet for a while and then started going for the relief packages. Many who had cars brought them over. One guy even tried to drive off with a relief truck, but the others stopped him and a fight broke out.

While this went on, another group of people took off with a truck. It quickly became dangerous standing there, as decency among the people quickly broke down into savageness. Soon enough, a few gunshots went off.

"People!" the fire chief yelled. "God damn it! Didn't I say there's plenty for everyone? What the hell is wrong with you all? Stack your cars if you want, but don't take it all. If I see one more guy trying to drive off with a truck, I'll shoot the motherfucker!"

This calmed the situation somewhat while people hurriedly grabbed what they could. Mike and Vincent stacked Mike's car as much as they could and left.

"You should come with me, man," Mike said. "We'd be better off together." He paused for a few seconds. "I have nobody left. The Lord took my wife and kids already. All I got is this girl now. We'd be better off together."

Vincent thought about it for a moment. He still wanted to go back to his apartment as if it still mattered. He wanted to take something with him—clothes, documentation, cell phone, anything that would make him feel he wasn't empty handed.

Something still held him back from leaving his apartment, almost as if he was abandoning his family. He wanted time to think of what to do, and his apartment felt the most comfortable place.

"Just give me your address," Vincent replied as they pulled up to his building. "I want to gather some things. I don't want to lose them. I can find you if you give me your address."

"All right, but I don't think you should wait too long. This world isn't looking good. You've seen how quickly people turn into monsters," Mike warned him.

"I won't wait long," Vincent replied as he left Mike's car with a box of packages. Mike nodded and then watched as Vincent walked toward his building. Before he disappeared behind the entrance door, Vincent turned around and waved back. Mike's worried face shot a sense of sorrow through Vincent, as if they had just said their last goodbye.

Walking up to his quiet apartment, Vincent had an eerie feeling that it was a bad idea. The whole world was caving in around him. It seemed that everyone was about to die in the next few weeks, and he would be left alone because he chose not to give up, or perhaps because he was unlucky. As he glanced at the deserted streets from his window, he remembered how different it appeared a few weeks before when he made his runs through them.

He also remembered how stressed he and his work colleagues were to finish all their projects in time. How pointless that seemed now. The thoughts of his coworkers started roaming around his head. Were they all right? Were they going to make it, and even if they did, would they be on the casualty list in the next few weeks?

Look at all these apartments around me, he thought. Thousands, millions of people. In my wildest dreams I wouldn't have imagined something like this happening. So much talk about the end of the world. No one needs to preach about it now. No one will make money off it either. Money won't matter. All the spoils and riches people worked so hard for mean nothing now. The whole world had changed, basically in an instant.

CHAPTER 6

Less than a week after the relief effort was canceled, the government ordered the shutdown of all power generating plants, petroleum and oil refineries, gas delivery systems, and any utilities that could cause explosions, fires, and poisoning of the ground and water.

The reason was simple; since there wouldn't be enough skilled workforce left to take care of them, the least they could do was spare the remainder of humanity from dealing with nuclear fallout and various other disasters put in place by man.

If the first wave affected eight out of ten people, the second one seemed to have affected the remainder. Even though it ranged in severity, no one seemed to have been spared; basically every human being on the globe became ill at some point within four to five weeks of the onset. No one really knew if more waves had hit; after the second it was pointless to count. The destruction of the civilized world was complete.

There were no more countries or governments. No more armies or war. No more economies and wealth disparity. No more law of man. All that remained was nature and the law of nature as God intended it.

During daytime, the illusion of humanity still haunted the streets.

Everything seemed to have been left in place waiting for its residents to come back. At night, though, the world was plunged into darkness, and quiet roamed the depths of its once glamorous cities.

The survivors, few and far between, had made it, but scarred, scared, and still hiding in their manmade caves waiting for something or someone to come and pull them out. Like fish out of water, they were left to dry in the new world, losing the title of the most dominant and conquering species on the planet. Crushed and subdued by the higher power in less than six weeks, they were in no mood to state their claim over the land anymore.

In the meantime, while the angel of death made its rounds with new waves of illness, Vincent remained in his apartment building. He had enough food for a few weeks from the packages he had brought. Also, being the only survivor in his building, he had plenty leftover food from his deceased neighbors. Having regained much of his strength, he felt the need to go around his apartment block to look for other survivors.

To his surprise, the dead bodies didn't decay as he had expected them to. Their flesh turned into grayish dust and slowly withered from their bones. No worms feasted on them, and he didn't smell any terrible stench that came with the bacteria breaking down the organic matter. He desired to investigate it further, but then he came across two people still alive and in bad shape.

His priorities immediately changed, and he brought them to the apartment next to his to nurse for them the best he knew how. Inspired by Mike's care for the girl they had come across, he felt he should do the same.

The victims, a husband and wife, Vincent thought, seemed delirious, running a high fever and feeling extremely weak. They could barely speak. He grabbed some IV bags from the fire hall, as there was no one there to stop him, and tried to administer to them.

He knew that this was the best way to hydrate them, but he had never done it before.

He tried to be careful to make sure he did it right. He had heard before if he injected them with air it would kill them, so he made sure he knew what he was doing by reading the instruction manual on it, but it was to no avail. The couple didn't seem to be getting any better. No matter what he did, their condition didn't improve. They both died within a week. With this, he ended his search for survivors.

About a month after the electricity went out in Vincent's apartment, he heard loud explosions in the distance. Apparently the government shutdown of various services couldn't prevent all the disasters from happening. Some petroleum refineries still found a way to burst into flames, which thickened the air with the smell of burning oil.

Soon small fires ignited sporadically throughout the city, with some growing large enough to consume entire buildings. Much of the city was spared, however, and unusually cold and wet weather helped the situation.

It was early November, or three months since the illness had hit the globe and wiped out most of the human population. Survivors had started to come out of their apartments and hiding places to reach out to one another. One would find one, then two would find one, three together would find some more, and eventually larger groups formed. Soon enough, someone who understood how to use a radio broadcasted messages across New York City and elsewhere.

The broadcast stated, "Please come down to 5th and 59th Street in front of the Grand Army Plaza and Hotel. Other fellow survivors will be there."

The messenger hoped that someone would turn on a battery-powered radio and listen to it. Likewise, groups tried to post flyers around the city with the same message. The few groups that had banded together in other parts of the city spread it around to others, and eventually most of them ended up at The Plaza Hotel.

Vincent read a flyer about a group gathering at a small hotel near the cruise terminal in Brooklyn. He couldn't believe it at first and went to check it out. Already thirty-five people, of varying age and race and former social status, had gathered there. Much like him, they seemed glad to see another reasonably healthy human being.

The youngest was a girl in her mid-teens and the oldest a man in his sixties. Approximately two-thirds were men. Everyone looked worn and dirty. No one seemed to have taken a shower in weeks. They didn't talk much at first, but there was already some order established.

Vincent hardly believed he would see anyone again, so this came as a nice surprise to him. Shy at first, he reserved to small talk only, but soon enough he started breaking down his barriers with the sheer desire to socialize more and make some sense of their situation.

Quickly, he learned that a guy by the name of Rick appeared as the de facto leader. He was a young white man in his early twenties. Tall and big framed with light blond hair, he reminded Vincent of a football linebacker. He was an imposing figure—not just in appearance but in how he talked and carried himself.

It became clear to Vincent why everyone was listening to Rick. He was the least shy of all, and since no one took the job of the leader, Rick swiftly stepped into the role.

"I'm from Huntington, Long Island," Rick explained. "That's not too far from here—maybe half an hour drive east of Brooklyn. After my family and friends died, I didn't know what to do. I was so upset and angry I just ran out of the town. I went west and eventually came across a few guys who were as lost as I was. When we came to Brooklyn we met a few more people and decided to settle down, gather more survivors, and help each other through this."

The guys Rick referred to seemed to be around him all the time. Closer to him in age and demeanor, Vincent imagined they would have popped their collars and acted like punks before the illness struck. Some people at the hotel thought they had been Rick's friends before, but that didn't turn out to be true. With the exception of a mother and a daughter, no one else there knew another person before the illness had struck.

For the first few days with the group, Vincent tried to adjust to the new environment. Being on his own for a while, he got used to doing things his way. Now everyone was expected to work as a team, and that's what Rick was trying to accomplish.

It became obvious that sticking together was much safer and more practical than being alone. Just the sheer experience of having someone to talk with was good enough a reason. Vincent quickly conformed to the change and was glad to be a part of a team.

Rick kept telling people his thoughts on how they could organize and make sense of the new age. Sometimes he did this even to the point of boredom, but it was effective because it gave them a purpose. Unusually cold weather was at hand, and it had started snowing already. The temperatures had dropped, and there was a serious need to get working on accommodating everyone. This was primarily what stepped up the adjustment of everyone into one cohesive group. There wasn't much time to be apprehensive. Every capable person had to work on getting the essentials: water, food, warmth, medicine, and sanitation.

Everyone chipped in with ideas, and a small democracy formed. They chose to stay at the hotel, as it appeared the logical place for them to make their base. It was a small building, but perfect for them. It had enough space and necessary rooms for all to feel comfortable. The main lobby and a few other larger spaces in the hotel could quickly heat up with wood-burning ovens so that the entire group could stay warm as long as they aired it out well.

Luckily for them, they had a gentleman who was familiar working with these kinds of stoves and even went about getting one from an antique store a mile away. There was also plenty of space for them to store water, food, and medicine. The only problem was teaching people how to be sanitary. Everyone's hygiene was different, and getting thirty-six people to follow the new rules was a challenge.

Their hotel quickly started transforming into a suitable place to withstand the cold weather and provide them the necessities for survival. It was nowhere near the three-star hotel experience it would have been in the pre-apocalypse world, but they made it comfortable. This achievement brought them some pride and satisfaction of creating something. It had come out as they had planned it.

Vincent had been with the group only a week, but he felt he had been there much longer. He got to know everybody to some extent, and it reminded him of the time right before the illness struck, when his coworkers and he had to work together to get their projects done. It was hard work, but there was a sense of togetherness, and that made the work much more bearable.

CHAPTER 7

Living with the group, Vincent started getting a little better picture of the characters involved. Even though everyone seemed generally friendly, he became close with two guys: Aran and Marcus. Aran was in his early thirties. He had moved from Columbus, Ohio, to Brooklyn two years prior because his uncle offered him a job at a car mechanic shop for a pretty decent wage.

Aran looked like a handy man while working at the hotel, and Vincent didn't doubt his uncle had a good mechanic in him. He was tall and skinny with lanky but somewhat muscular arms. His mother was Asian and his father black, and he carried the traits of both well. He had a mild demeanor and didn't talk much to people, but he didn't shy away from working with anyone. Others in the group thought of him like a soldier. He didn't complain; instead, he did the work asked of him.

Marcus was a lot more talkative. He didn't mind voicing his opinion, in his smooth voice, on various things, but he didn't complain either. He, too, would do what was asked of him. He had just turned thirty-five when Vincent met him. A black man from Fayetteville, North Carolina, he spent much of his adult life traveling around for work.

"I was a salesman of all sorts," Marcus explained. "I rarely stayed at any job more than two or three years. I lived in over ten cities and got to know many people, but now, just like you, Vincent and Aran, I don't know anybody, and I highly doubt I will see anyone from the past again."

He, too, was tall and slim, but not as tall as Aran, who pushed six feet five. Next to them, Vincent appeared almost a half foot shorter and looked like a point guard next to the center and power forward in a basketball team. Nevertheless, they worked well together and spent much of their free time sharing stories about their past lives.

Vincent quickly got into the routine of doing his work for the group. Much like all the younger and stronger members, he was responsible for the heavy-duty stuff, which included scavenging for food around the neighborhood.

December was at hand, and everyone expected it would get colder and snowier, so they might as well gather as much food and amenities as possible. Unfortunately, the snow thickening and lack of someone to clean the streets hampered their efforts going out there.

In the first days of scavenging for food, Vincent experienced what the world really looked like now that its most dominant species had been reduced to an insignificant bunch. He had already seen how dark and ghostly the city looked without electricity and how the silence rang against the numb ears used to urban noise, but he hadn't gone into any buildings since he had come across the two unlucky souls on the verge of death.

Now he frequently entered various buildings, apartments, stores, and stations and noticed the stench created by trapped gasses of the remainder of rotten foods and bacteria still feasting on them. He had seen some places infested with creatures he thought had come straight out of hell, but they were just flies, maggots, ants, beetles, roaches, and various rodents all joining the great feast.

The scenes appeared pretty disgusting, but others were outright dangerous. The toxic air created by all the decomposition would make people faint. Soon enough, they all knew to be more careful when entering any one place.

Even though the group had no great need to investigate subway stations, perhaps only for the snack stations, they found out that most of them had flooded anyway. Much of the air there was toxic as the sewage backed up into the system, and the methane gas collected like it did in many grocery stores.

The sewage didn't spare the Hudson or East Rivers either. Much of it now freely flowed on the surface. Occasionally they would come across small packs of dogs that, like them, scavenged for food and water. With their masters gone and lucky enough to escape their household prisons, they would band together just like humans, trying to survive the coming winter.

Birds, on the other hand, were adapting much better. Used to scavenging and familiar with danger, they patiently picked off the tiny bits of food that were good enough for them. Many of these birds gathered energy to head south to a much kinder environment to meet the birds already there, but not the pigeons. They would stick around for the winter.

Vincent and his new colleagues searched mostly after bottled water and drinks, canned goods, and some rare unspoiled foods like snack cakes. Any medicine or vitamins were always good. Finding batteries of any kind was a major plus as well; there was still plenty of technology that ran on batteries.

With little effort, they found a small generator and fuel to light the lobby in the evening, but only for a few hours at a time. This wasn't the Stone Age; it was a post-apocalyptic modern age, different from the way many movies and video games had presented it. It was a make-the-best-of-the-leftovers age, and New York City offered a lot. A city of nine million reduced to a few hundred, perhaps a thousand, left a lot of things that its dead owners didn't need anymore.

On his trips, Vincent was joined by Marcus and Aran. They

shared their views on other people in their group and also on Rick and his closest friends who rarely left his side.

"They sure spend a lot of time together," Marcus said. "I wonder if in high school they were the kind who only hung out with the cool kids."

"They for sure seem like it, don't they?" Vincent replied.

"That's not a good thing for our group, though," Marcus explained while brushing snow off his gloves. "I'll give them the benefit of a doubt, but they need to be more inclusive of everyone. Show them that they care. A simple 'how are you?' would go a long way. This isn't the time for creating little cliques and divisions among the few survivors that are left."

"I wonder if they have ever thought of that," Vincent said as he briefly remembered the time in high school having faced similar situations.

"I'm pretty sure they have, Vincent, but it quickly gets eclipsed by the rewards of being more special than others. It's a part of human nature. In this case being with Rick means they in a way rule the rest, too."

"That's sad." Vincent shook his head. "You would think they would change their way of thinking after what they have gone through."

Marcus quipped, "People's minds are the last thing to change, and also the most difficult because they are greedy. Trust me, I would know. I was a salesman for many years."

Aran nodded in agreement.

"What do you think about all this, Aran?" Vincent asked to get some conversation out of their quiet companion.

Aran seemed to think for a few moments, and then he said in his deep voice, "People need to look at the big picture."

"I couldn't argue with that," Vincent replied, happy that Aran had actually said something.

"I think that's good advice," Marcus added. "As a matter of fact, I think that's the best advice I've heard in a while. I wonder how many people truly know what that means? Anyway, let's head back before I freeze to death."

At the hotel, the older and weaker members of the group organized the findings of each scavenging party into respective storage areas and prepared food for everyone, which much of the time meant distributing cans and water bottles to people.

Vincent was in his third week of living with the group, and that nice team picture was becoming tainted by the unraveling of some of the bad characteristics in people. He initially noticed it in their leader, Rick. Vincent could tell that he was a smart guy, but he was far from being well rounded.

At first, Vincent thought, it was because Rick hadn't socialized in a while, but the longer he thought about it, Rick reminded him of a former high school bully. That leadership characteristic that makes people appreciate their leader quickly dissipated as Rick showed that smarts didn't compensate for his lack of experience.

Whereas before Rick asked people to do things, he now ordered them, and that didn't sit well with many, especially Marcus. He told people how they should organize to get food and water without taking the democratic process into consideration—in other words, without asking for others' opinions.

Not much time passed before some people started feeling Rick wasn't the right man for the job and began murmuring among themselves. Marcus, for one, felt Rick missed some important subjects in his language, such as giving people hope things would be all right or showing them compassion by asking if anyone needed medicine or help with anything.

Aran, on the other hand, gave Rick a little more credit, primarily for gathering the people, but he, too, didn't appreciate the bossiness of his character, especially Rick's four closest friends who acted with more and more authority. They become almost like the ruling class in the group, ordering people around and helping out less with the actual work.

One day, while everyone warmed themselves in the lobby, a conversation developed in regards to their group's future. People seemed to wonder if they should stay there or go somewhere else.

"I'm telling you, guys," Rick argued. "This is a good spot. We can make this work. We just have to keep an eye on where to get the food and fresh water. It's our base, and if you come across anyone out there, bring them over here. I'm telling you, they'll like it."

"I think we should post more flyers around. This way we can spread the news about where we are," an older gentleman said.

"Yeah, that's a good idea," Rick replied with excitement. "I tried to get flyers out as much as possible, but we should definitely do more."

"Has anyone gone to Queens?" a soft spoken and usually shy, middle-aged man with glasses asked. "I know it's kind of far, but I came across a flyer today as I was looking for food about a group of people inviting everyone to the Fairfield Inn near Queensboro Plaza. They said they had food, water, and medicine anyone needed."

Rick's face quickly changed from excitement to stiffness. "Yeah, I came across those guys when I first started gathering people, but they ain't good." He shook his head. "They seemed sketchy to me. Kind of like they were former thieves or something. I couldn't trust them."

"Oh, really? How come you never told us about them?" a freckled blonde lady, asked.

"I didn't want to risk you guys going over there. I don't think it's safe." Rick continued shaking his head. "Like I said, they rubbed me the wrong way. They told me some stories I didn't like."

"What kind of stories did they tell you?" Marcus asked.

Rick looked at Marcus, clearly displeased at having to answer the question. "It was something like how they wanted to gather all the medicine out there, to kind of force-invite other groups to join them. It all seemed sketchy to me. Like they wanted to get me and the guys I was with to help them do that, you know, get the drugs and spread the word to others. They were pushy, too. So, we gave them a clear idea that we weren't interested."

"I don't understand," Marcus asked again to Rick's irritation. "What was making them seem so sketchy to you?"

"You know. When we told them we weren't interested in gathering their medicine, one of the guys got into my face, telling me we had to do this and that. I just had enough and threw the guy down, made sure he understood not to mess with us or tell us what to do. They just seemed like a bunch of jerks, ordering people around. They didn't appear willing to help."

Marcus nodded as if he had heard enough from Rick.

Later that day Marcus pulled Vincent aside and told him he thought Rick was a typical bully. Perhaps he had legitimate reasons to turn down the other group, but the way he talked was stereotypical of someone who was willing to dish out orders but not take them.

Also, not telling them about the group in the first place only made Rick look like he had tried to hide it.

"It's highly doubtful, in my mind, that Rick avoided mentioning this to protect us," Marcus explained. "These are all negative signs, Vincent, and I think it's time to start thinking about our next move."

The next day Marcus, Aran, and Vincent went out scavenging for goods as usual.

"I think we should go check out Greenpoint to see what's over there," Marcus proposed.

"Isn't that way up there close to Queens?" Vincent asked.

"My point exactly. Let's go see if we can come by some people from that infamous group that Rick so dispraised."

"I'm not so sure," Vincent said with doubt in his voice. "Isn't it kind of far to do that now?"

"It's only a few miles at most," Marcus justified. "Plus, we have plenty of daylight left."

"It would be pretty tough to trek there in deep snow," Aran added.

"Come on, guys." Marcus looked at his friends in disappointment. "Where is that young blood in you? You have gone through a lot worse than some deep snow. I really think we should check it out. Otherwise, we might regret it later."

After thinking about it for a few minutes, Vincent and Aran agreed to go for it. After all, Vincent thought, they may end up being decent people, and if that turns out to be the case, they could quietly tell everyone back at the hotel, short of Rick and his posse.

The three of them sat down in a deserted coffee shop, looked up a map, drew their path to Queensboro Plaza, and took off on their way. Unfortunately, within the first half hour, Marcus stepped into a deep pothole covered by snow and rolled his ankle. This made it impossible for him to continue, and Aran and Vincent ended up carrying him back to the hotel.

"God damn it!" Marcus was furious. "Why in the world did this have to happen today?"

"Hey, it could be worse," Vincent tried to comfort him, but his words didn't seem to appease his friend.

"Yeah, it could be. You could be carrying me back to Rick and his God damn minions. Oh wait, you are bringing me back there!"

"Listen, man," Aran added. "I know what you're saying. But you're not the only one. They annoy us, too."

When they got back, one of the women, a former paramedic, took care of Marcus's foot, which was badly swollen. The cold weather didn't help, as he also ended up with some frostbite, although nothing serious. Rick and his posse weren't helpful either; instead of saying something comforting and showing they cared for his well-being, they made fun of him for being clumsy and getting injured. Marcus, in turn, seemed even more determined to check out the Queens group.

CHAPTER 8

As a few more days went by, Vincent and Aran started feeling the same as Marcus. They got tired of Rick and his posse's behavior. On one occasion one of the guys smacked Vincent upside the head because he spilled a jug of water, and Aran was verbally insulted in front of the whole group when he had made his dinner portion a little larger than usual.

At first Rick stepped in and acted as an authoritative figure to calm the situation, but soon he joined in on the fun by making offhand remarks. Vincent saw Rick as a weakling looking for approval of his posse by letting them have more freedom. One time, though, he acted sternly toward one of his guys by smacking him when he felt the guy insulted a girl Rick had an eye on. Regardless, Vincent and his two friends had had enough, and they were determined to check out the Queens group.

Marcus recovered slowly, and it didn't look like he'd be able to walk for miles through snow any time soon. Vincent and Aran thought it would be a good idea to find a vehicle to transport all three to Queens, but Marcus seemed doubtful.

"You've seen the streets," Marcus said. "They're littered with cars, trucks, and other things. On top of that, the snow is deep. There's at least two, three feet out there. You'd need a pickup truck, and even then, how are you going to start it? You'd need a car battery and keys."

Marcus made a good point, but Vincent counted on Aran, being a car mechanic, to do his magic in starting a vehicle. The battery, according to Aran, shouldn't be a problem because there were many at various auto shops just sitting there. Starting without keys would be a little trickier, but he thought he could manage.

Therefore, the next time Aran and Vincent went out to scavenge, they looked for a vehicle. They didn't come across many pickup trucks, and those they did wouldn't start without keys. It quickly became frustrating, but as they were about to give up they came across a small crossover that happened to have the keys in it. The vehicle started on the first try when they placed a new battery into it.

"It's about time," Aran said in a monotonous voice.

"Awesome," Vincent replied excitedly. "Now let's go back and show it to Marcus."

Driving the crossover wasn't easy. It lacked a four-wheel drive, which made it difficult to drive in deep snow, and on top of that, as Marcus predicted, many streets were difficult to pass through due to other vehicles blocking the way. Nevertheless, they didn't give up. Even though they moved slowly, they did move.

Parking some distance from the hotel, not to attract too much attention, they went to pick up Marcus. As Marcus limped out of the hotel with them, they were excited at the thought this could actually work. As they approached the car, they couldn't have asked for a worse scene ahead; Rick's posse stood there checking out the car.

"Good job, guys," one of the guys said. "We just needed some car batteries. It would have helped if you had brought it a little closer to the hotel."

All three of their faces dropped with disappointment and no one made a sound. Then Vincent, seeing that they needed to say something to avoid drawing more suspicion, replied, "Umm, yeah, but the snow made it too difficult. The tires are bad, and no four-wheel drive made it tough. So we asked Marcus to come out and see what we could salvage."

"That's because you don't know what you're doing," the guy belittled them. "I would think at least Aran would know how to drive it."

That was the last straw, and usually mild-tempered Aran seemed to boil up inside. He got into the guy's face and clenched his fist. The guy backed off with obvious fear on his face, but luckily for him, Marcus quickly pulled Aran away saying it wasn't worth it.

"Well then," Marcus replied. "We'll leave the car to you since you know more about it. Then we'll see how you'll get it by the hotel without keys, as there weren't any. It was all Aran's magic."

The next day Vincent and Aran headed out looking for another car, but a heavy snowstorm had hit the city. The wind blew the snow so hard they could barely breathe or see anything in front of them. Barely fifteen minutes later, they had to call off their plan and return to the hotel.

Marcus didn't look so well. He had contracted a cold and was running high with fever. At first everyone became afraid that he had gotten the infamous illness, but many other symptoms were different. The paramedic ensured him that it was just a common cold.

"You should be fine," she said in a calming voice. "There is nothing to worry about. Keep yourself warm, drink tea, eat well, and take lots of vitamin C."

"Okay, I like the sound of that," Marcus replied with relief in his voice. "I just wish other folks weren't so scared. They are looking at me like I'm turning into a zombie."

"Don't worry. I'll explain it to everyone that this is quite common in winter."

Still, some people were apprehensive about Marcus's illness until they contracted it, too. Soon everyone started taking lots of vitamin C, Echinacea, and zinc, which they had plenty of, and drinking lots of tea.

One evening Marcus pulled Vincent and Aran aside and told them to leave without him.

"No, man, how could we?" Vincent objected. "We can't leave you behind looking like this."

"I'll be fine, guys," Marcus persisted. "I have to stay warm and drink this stuff. I definitely won't be okay if I go out into that cold, but you guys should go regardless. Don't worry about me. I know how to handle these guys. When I get better I'll join you."

Still, they hesitated for a few days, but as the snowstorm subsided, Aran and Vincent reluctantly agreed and said goodbye to Marcus.

"I hope you get better soon, Marcus," Vincent said, shaking his friend's hand. "If we don't come back for a week, know that the grass is greener over there, and come join us."

They packed lightly so that they didn't look suspicious and hoped if they needed anything else they would find it on the way. By making it appear that they were going out to scavenge, no one assumed otherwise. Looking over the map, they got a decent idea of how to get there, and the excitement encouraged them to proceed.

Almost right from the start it became evident that it would be a slow trip. Treading through the thick snow proved difficult, but worse was the cold and the wind. They also regretted not starting earlier in the day. As the night rolled in, they had barely covered half the distance they had planned.

Realizing they were too tired to proceed, Vincent and Aran called it a night in one of the apartment buildings across the Brooklyn Navy Yard Development. It was once a part of section eight housing. They were more than happy to call it their home for the night, but once inside, they realized how much they missed the warmth left behind at Rick's hotel.

They had bundled up for the cold temps they knew they'd experience on their walk. They paid a price for sweating, though. Their wet clothes became bitter cold, and they had to look around the apartment for other clothes to change into. They looked comical dressing in whatever they could find, but they felt warmer and could fall asleep. Outside, the late December showed no mercy.

The next day started off well initially, but it soon became just as tough or even tougher than the previous day. On top of that, it looked as if another snowstorm had brewed, and the already difficult passage quickly became nearly impassable. Aran and Vincent could barely walk two blocks before they had to seek shelter from the cold and wind, making their slow trip even slower. By the time the night approached, they had barely crossed half the distance of the day before.

To add to their struggle, they realized they had run out of food and had only a few sips of water left. This forced them to keep going until they came across some fruit cakes at a small, largely empty, mom-and-pop store, that were still edible, untouched in their packaging by any maggot or insect. It may not have been much food between the two of them, but it was by far the best fruit cake they had ever eaten.

The following day they finally made it to the Fairfield Inn. They couldn't believe that a mere five, six miles had taken them three days to cross. They approached the inn cautiously, wary of any unpleasant surprises, and then walked up to the door. It was definitely the place they had been seeking as they read the sign on the door, "We have moved to The Plaza Hotel at 59th and 5th Ave in Manhattan. All survivors with good intentions should go there. There is food, water, medicine, and safety. Hope to see you there."

They went inside the hotel and found some food and water the group had left behind. They were disappointed to find the place deserted, but at least they knew where the others had gone. Bundling up, they started making plans about how to make it to The Plaza Hotel the following day. They wondered what it was like and how many survivors had gone there.

Marcus came up in their conversation as they speculated how he was doing. They felt bad for leaving him behind and pondered if they would see him in The Plaza Hotel anytime soon. They doubted that Rick would encourage anyone to investigate much outside their own hotel.

Vincent and Aran decided to rest up one more day before heading to Manhattan. They didn't have to worry about food and water in this place, which made it more inviting for them to stay a while longer.

Also, Vincent had developed a cough. Neither could afford for him to become seriously ill, and there was no reason to rush. Therefore, they sat at the hotel, warmed themselves at the fire they had started in the lobby fireplace, and made conversation.

As they were eating lunch a couple days later, Vincent thought he heard some noises outside. As Aran went to investigate, a man at the entrance startled Aran so much that he leaped back and grabbed a can of tuna to throw at him.

"Whoa, guy! Calm down, I mean no harm," a skinny man wearing a messy gray hat said. "We just came to see if anyone was inside. We mean no harm."

"Who are you?" Aran asked, still holding the can of tuna.

"I'm James," the man replied as four more guys appeared by his side. "I'm just an old fellow with some folks waiting outside. We came to see if anyone was still here. We saw some flyers and wanted to make sure you guys were okay, that's all."

"Yeah, we're okay," Aran lowered his hand. "We got here a few days ago."

After a few moments of silence, Aran continued. "Um, we're not originally from this group—this hotel. We found it deserted. You read the sign up front. All of them went to Manhattan. What about you guys?"

"Well, friend," James replied. "That's where we're going, too. We heard the message on the radio, and a few of our guys checked it out. The place is good. It's safe. We tried to take busses there, but it didn't quite work out. The roads are terrible."

At this point Vincent came to the entrance and joined the conversation. Looking outside, he saw at least a hundred people waiting in the cold. They seemed peaceful and much like the group Vincent and Aran had left. They were of all ages and races, and there were some little children, too. Soon enough they all made their way into the lobby and the cafeteria.

"What's going on in Manhattan?" Vincent asked James, who turned out to be one of the leaders of the group, and unlike Rick, seemed kind.

"Didn't you guys hear anything about it?" James asked as he gobbled up some canned fruit. "It's been advertised over the radio for over a month now."

Of course, the radio, Vincent thought. How didn't we think of that before?

"I guess we didn't think there was anyone broadcasting considering that the electrical grid is down, but we should have known better," Vincent replied.

"Don't worry about it," James said. "Even though we got the

message, we hesitated for a while, too. You know, we weren't sure what the place was like, so we sent a few guys to scout it out. The next thing you know, they sent us a message via radio that the place is good."

"Well, it's better to be safe than sorry," Vincent replied. "Aran and I were going to take our chances."

"You'd be surprised," James added as he rubbed his unshaven cheeks. "We came across some folks who weren't so nice. Luckily, we had numbers on our side."

"Oh, really?" Vincent was surprised to hear this. "Were they some kind of thugs?"

"Yeah, they were thugs all right. They had weapons, too. Apparently some people had already started enjoying this lawlessness. It's sad, it really is. There aren't many people left, but as expected, you take the law out of them, and they turn into animals."

"Well, Aran and I are harmless," Vincent reassured James. "We haven't turned into savages, at least not yet. We'd love to join you guys to Manhattan if you don't mind."

"We absolutely don't mind." James seemed more than glad to accept them into his group. "You'll see we're a pretty nice and relaxed bunch. We even have a pastor, Jeff. He's a nice, uplifting guy. I think you guys will like him, whether you believe in God or not."

"As long as he's nice we'll like him," Vincent replied.

Vincent was glad to have run into this group because they did seem like a nice bunch. The next day they ventured out to Manhattan.

It was December 24th, and Pastor Jeff kept reminding people that even though this Christmas Eve was much different from previous ones, it was still Christmas, a time for everyone to get together in harmony.

A few kids with the group, still believing in Santa Claus, asked questions about him, and the adults played along. The older folks told Christmas stories as they traveled to keep their mind occupied from the cold, and Vincent saw what a stark difference it was from the group he and Aran had left. People smiled and looked forward to where they were going.

"Complaining won't get you anywhere," Pastor Jeff mused. "We're all struggling in this life, but we won't make any difference by grumbling about it. It'll bring you down and those around you. Stay positive and have hope."

As they approached the Grand Army Plaza, they noticed that the roads were cleared of cars and snow, some of the people standing around were wearing police uniforms, and The Plaza Hotel had lights on. It had been a long time since Vincent, or anyone from his group, had seen a large building lit up by electricity, and it was a beautiful sight. In a way it was a Christmas present to all of them, and the building itself was like a Christmas tree.

As they came closer, men dressed in police uniforms directed them where to go. Things seemed well organized, and that brought sighs of relief.

"Wow, look how many people are here!" Aran said excitedly.

"I swear, I never thought I would see this many again," Vincent agreed.

"I don't remember the last time I was happy to see a policeman," Aran added.

"And I never thought I'd be staying at The Plaza Hotel either," Vincent replied.

The policemen guided the group to the inside of the hotel lobby as the doorman counted their numbers: 124 people in total.

Everything seemed lit up inside, and that showed the grandeur beauty of the hotel. Everything looked even more amazing than it had before the apocalypse.

Once inside, everyone was required to write down their name, age, sex, and profession. Then they were guided to a large auditorium, where a speaker waited for them at the podium. It looked as if the folks at the hotel knew of their coming and had everything ready.

"Hey, guys, we're so glad to see you made it here. It really is a great feeling," began the middle-aged man with squinty eyes, white hair, and thick beard who addressed the crowd. He looked tired, yet his voice spoke of excitement as he spoke into the microphone.

"My name is Bill Loren. I'm one of the survivors who helped start this community at The Plaza Hotel. I'm a native of New York City, where I was a district attorney. I've lost all my family to the illness, and I know that many of you have, too. However, I'm a strong believer that we can make our lives better and move forward."

Bill took a quick sip of water and continued. "As you know, it's been a while since there has been some normalcy and order in everyone's lives, but here we are trying to do exactly that: bring back civility for all of us. We want to let you know that we can start the new chapter here—the chapter that perhaps can reflect onto the whole country or even the world."

Bill paused for a moment as he peered over the crowd. "I'll briefly go over the history as we know it of the past five or six months since the world was affected by this terrible illness. If you aren't aware, the name that has been given to it by the World Health Organization is the Scourge, or the Scourge of God. I'm not sure if we'll ever know how many lives it has claimed, but it's near to extinction. I think it's safe to say that more than ninety-nine percent have perished.

"We don't know how this illness started or where it came from, but somehow it was triggered within our genes. I don't know the scientific details behind it, but I do know that we are the survivors. How each of us has made it doesn't matter; what is important is that we're here. There's no government, no nation, or any countries as far as we know, but there's still some humanity left. We have another chance to make this world a better place."

Bill adjusted his glasses. "Here at The Plaza Hotel we've created a community, growing every day, that will give the survivors an opportunity to be part of the civilized world again. Imagine us like a small town; we have the government, a constitution, laws, and plenty of jobs.

"The laws apply to everyone here, and everyone's expected to be a productive member of this society. In turn, everyone will be provided a room, food, clean water, medicine, warmth, and safety. We don't force anyone to stay here. It's not a prison; it's an opportunity for you to find a purpose in a safe and civilized world.

"Some of you may wonder why we chose The Plaza Hotel here in Manhattan as our staging ground. The city, as you may argue, is not an ideal place because of the dangers it poses, and you know what? I agree. However, the city also provides the benefit of being home to as many goods as we stockpile before we leave.

"The hotel has a lot to offer if you think about it. Also, it's a famous landmark equipped with generators, fuel, and utilities much like a cruise ship. This is not a permanent stay, but it will give us time to get ready for a longer lasting place. Plus, we want to gather as many survivors here as we can before we make the move."

Blah blah blah. Where are these rooms to sleep in? was all that Vincent could think about. He had heard about the rooms, and his mind became fixated on them. After all, his body still ached from the exhaustion of the trip and the cold he had contracted.

After another forty-five minutes of Bill speaking, two gentlemen handed out pamphlets that further described what this community was all about. Then everyone got on their way to their assigned rooms.

Vincent and Aran received the keys to a room on the sixteenth floor of the hotel. It was small but nicely decorated with two twin-sized beds. Apparently, most of the floors below had already been filled with other survivors. It was by far the most beautiful hotel that Vincent and Aran had ever seen.

Vincent was no stranger to the fact that before the Scourge, this was arguably one of the most expensive hotels in the city. Now both of them were staying there basically for free. Even though The Plaza Hotel didn't have all the amenities as back in the day, it still carried a mountain of breathtaking charm.

The only caveat was that no one could use the elevators because they required too much power. For those who were staying on the higher floors, as was the case with Vincent and Aran, it was a bit of a climb. As for the lights in the hallways and rooms, Vincent read in the pamphlet, all used efficient lighting that automatically turned off at eleven in the evening. Then only the most necessary turned back on at seven in the morning. The rest would turn on at seven in the evening when it was too dark to navigate around. All the clocks in the hotel kept in synch, and to Vincent's surprise, his wrist watch was off by only two minutes.

Even though it was still a little chilly in the room, he was glad it was much warmer than at the Fairfield Inn. Once he got under the covers, the comfort overtook him and he fell asleep within minutes.

CHAPTER 9

Grand Army Plaza was located on the southeastern corner of Central Park. On the northern end of that plaza stood the large statue of General Sherman riding a horse. In the center was the snow-covered Pulitzer fountain, and right across rose the iconic Plaza Hotel, resembling a large castle done in French Renaissance chateau style.

Vincent wondered if anyone could have imagined, before the Scourge, that one of the city's most luxurious hotels would now house not the rich, but the beat-up group of survivors, and possibly the center of the new civilization in North America.

Over the next couple of days, he learned that the survivors referred to the hotel and its community as "the campus" because the rooming style resembled a college campus; men and women shared their own rooms and floors. The few who broke that law were parents with children and married couples. Either of these was uncommon.

No weapons were allowed on the campus besides those carried by the campus police, and the police strongly enforced that rule. Vincent also learned there were about two thousand people from New York and other states, even as far as Georgia and Tennessee, who had joined the campus in the past two months. They had all heard about it over the radio and figured it was better for their small groups to join a larger community for the protection and resources it offered than to stay alone.

Vincent also learned a little about how the campus originated. It started with Bill and five other members. As the U.S. government shut down the grid and various other services back in August, they banded together thinking of what the new world order would look like. It became obvious by that point that the survival rate was miniscule and the collapse of the civilized world was inevitable.

Their apparent desire was to bring civility to that new world. Without the government, law enforcement, and sense of community, the survivors would quickly turn to their instincts, which wouldn't have separated them much from animals or the days of the Wild West.

As they made their plans, four of the original planners succumbed to the Scourge. It was then up to Bill and his close friend Paul to continue creating the community. Originally they had planned to stage it somewhere outside the city, but as it became evident that it would take a lot more time, they opted for the beautiful and iconic Plaza Hotel.

It also helped that Manhattan was a relatively easy place to get around because the streets were laid out in a grid—12 long avenues going north-south, dissected by 218 streets going east-west. At first they had gathered only a few dozen people via flyers from all around Manhattan, but once they started broadcasting via radio, that number grew to hundreds, then past a thousand. Less than four months later, they had hit two thousand.

The community they hoped to create was based on some kind of a large family structure where people cared for one another and didn't do work just because they had to, but because they wanted to help their community grow. They knew this dreamlike picture wasn't going to be easy to paint, and they weren't naïve to believe it would happen overnight either.

Bill and Paul carefully drafted their constitution and tried to make it as fair and relevant as possible, while borrowing heavily from the U.S. constitution. A leader was elected once a year. This was the case with the nine councilors who advised him and managed the officers of various campus departments, which the working members of the campus made up.

Vincent and Aran quickly started embracing the new life at the campus. They enjoyed having a clean, relatively warm, and comfortable place to sleep and a safe and organized community that gave them a sense of a civilized world. And they didn't have to deal with Rick and his posse bossing them around.

Waking up and knowing they didn't have to deal with some juvenile attitudes made their day much better right at the beginning. Even though Vincent was an accountant by trade, he was given work doing all kinds of chores around the hotel, and he liked it. At least it wasn't boring, he thought, as each shift brought something new to work on.

Aran, on the other hand, received more mechanically inclined work due to his past experience. He fit right in and expressed to Vincent that it was almost too good to be true. People seemed happier here; perhaps they, too, had left something behind and here felt a sigh of relief.

With each new day they met someone new as more people joined the campus. It was an unusually harsh winter, yet almost every day someone new came in. Strangers were everywhere of all ages, races, statuses, and creeds, but as an endangered species they quickly accepted one another.

One day Vincent came across a familiar face.

"Mike, is that you?" Vincent asked, astonished to see the good-natured man again.

"Oh, my good Lord, Vincent!" Mike, who looked younger and more spirited than Vincent remembered, responded excitedly.

Even though they shared a short history together at the relief effort, it was as if they were a family. After all, in this world where rarely anyone knew anyone else from before the Scourge, they were considered longtime friends. They embraced each other.

"Mike! Man, I'm so glad to see you. You have no idea. You're the first familiar face I've seen since . . . well, since the last time I saw you. How have you been?" Vincent could not hide his excitement either.

Mike put his arm around Vincent. "Vincent, I'm good, my friend. I've gone through hell, but I'm good, and boy am I happy to see you. I got a lot to thank you for. You helped us survive."

Not quite sure what to make of the last statement, Vincent felt glad to see Mike looking healthy. "I mean, I'm not sure what I did, but man I'm happy to see you're alive and well."

Mike responded, "Remember how you told me you got over the Scourge of God? You had the will, my friend. You fought for your life when it was so easy to slip into blissful death. It was your story that inspired me. That's all I needed; It gave me inspiration. I fought for my life. I fought for her, too. And now I have a daughter."

"Well," Vincent said, feeling embarrassed by the praise he received, "whether it was my story or not, I am happy for you. Wait, did you say you have a daughter now?"

"You don't remember her, Vincent, do you?" Mike asked with a smile. "Her name is Elysie, and she's the girl we rescued."

Vincent thought for a few seconds. "Oh, my God!" Vincent started recalling the girl he had come across with Mike at the apartment with the jammed door. "Now I remember. It's been so long. I thought she wouldn't have—"

"But she did," Mike interjected, "and I feel thankful for your helping me that day."

"Where is she now?" Vincent asked, curious what happened to the young lady he thought would never make it.

"She's over there." Mike pointed out a black-haired girl talking with another girl fifteen feet away. Vincent looked over and immediately was struck by her dark hair, eyes, eyebrows. Her slender body gave the impression she was taller than she really was, and her face made him wonder if she was Asian, Samoan, or some kind of mix.

"Mike," Vincent spoke as he stared at Elysie. "I wouldn't have recognized her in a million years."

"I can't blame you," Mike replied. "When we found her, as you know, she was in rough shape. She was so pale and sick, barely breathing. She was on the verge of death." Mike paused as he gazed at his new daughter. "But God had mercy. You know, if it wasn't for her, I wouldn't be here."

Mike looked back at Vincent. "While she was still recovering, I got sick, and man it was rough. Yet she still found the strength to nurse me back like I was her father. We barely knew each other, and we were already like a family."

Mike called Elysie over. "Bye, Joanna," Elysie said to the other girl as she turned around and looked at Vincent and Mike together and smiled. Vincent, struck by her smile, still couldn't believe it was the same person he had seen five months ago.

Her full lips teemed with color. Her dark eyes had so much life in them, and for a moment he thought Mike had lied to him and this was another person. As she approached, he could appreciate her smooth, olive-skinned face adorned by her smile. Like a resurrected body risen from the dead, it took strong faith to believe she was the same person as before.

"Elysie," Mike said. "Let me introduce you to a good friend of mine, someone I've told you about."

Her eyes opened wide. "This must be Vincent," she said excitedly as she hugged him. "I never thought I would actually meet you. Mike told me how you guys found me. I can't thank you enough for saving my life."

Vincent was flattered and embarrassed. Her arms around him felt surreal. It had been a long time since anyone had hugged him. As a matter of fact, he couldn't even remember the last time. Soon a strong sense of guilt came over him as he remembered how they had discovered her and how it was Mike who had tried hard to break into the apartment while Vincent had backed off thinking no one was in there, at least no one alive. Her true savior was Mike, her new dad.

"I'm speechless." Vincent shook his head. "I can't believe it. I never thought I would actually meet you either. You look, um, different. I'm so glad that you made it." He put his hand on Mike's shoulder. "Actually, that both of you made it."

"And we're glad to see you," Elysie said as she grabbed Vincent under the arm. "We have a lot of catching up to do. I want to know how you got here. It's remarkable that we've met each other."

Vincent was full of excitement having seen Mike and Elysie. He had a lot of respect for Mike, as he, too, looked to him as a father figure. After all, he was about the right age, and seeing how Elysie turned out, he had even more respect for him. Instead of pawning her onto somebody else, he actually took it upon himself to take care of her. Maybe it is indeed God or something divine, Vincent thought, that can bring a man so close to a stranger in such a difficult time.

Going back to their room for the night, Vincent told Aran, "It's so surreal, man. Elysie was in such horrible shape. I never would have recognized her the way she looks today. She was so close to death that day. I doubted she would make it, and look at her now."

"It's miraculous how people can change," Aran responded.

"All I can tell you, Aran," Vincent gazed at the marble steps in front of him as they climbed "is that she was definitely lucky to have Mike there that day."

CHAPTER 10

As days turned into weeks, Vincent got into a comfortable routine of living at the campus. Work shifts ranged from seven to nine hours a day, while they rotated five or six work days a week. He had one hour lunch break per shift and was guaranteed three meals a day at the cafeteria. Everyone at the campus had a total of twenty-one meal passes per week.

The portions were usually small, but much better than nothing, and people mostly got used to them. Meals normally contained some kind of canned goods: meats, fish, vegetables, and fruit. For the side, they usually had rice, oatmeal, cornmeal, jam, or peanut butter with crackers.

As for drinking, purified water remained the norm, but powdered milk and various kinds of powdered juices weren't rare either. Alcohol was allowed only on Fridays after dinner. Everyone twenty years of age received two drink passes per week, which could be spent on a bottle of beer, a glass of wine, or some kind of mixed drink. Fights and inappropriate behavior were not tolerated and were usually punishable by revoking the drink passes for up to two months. This wasn't common.

As Vincent's work duties changed, he would sometimes go scavenging into the deserted parts of the city to gather various goods. For example, one week his supervisor sent him to look for various batteries. This included practically anything holding charge: AA, AAA, 9 volt, car batteries, UPS units, and even solar panels.

Going out into the streets, he learned how raccoons had adapted to the new environment. He would find them in many buildings he entered, almost as often as roaches and other bugs. What surprised him most was how they got into various places even he and his colleagues would have a difficult time breaking into. Remarkably, apartments in high-rise towers weren't safe from them.

Vincent looked at these animals as cute and mischievous little bandits, not shy to steal anything they could get their hands on. Sometimes he would work right alongside them grabbing whatever he needed at the time. They didn't seem to mind, and neither did he. That all changed one day when someone at the campus got sick and the symptoms pointed to the rabies virus.

The person died, and soon these cute little guys weren't so adorable anymore, especially when the campus doctors informed everyone that the raccoons were the most common carriers of the virus. If the raccoons weren't afraid of humans, there was a chance they weren't afraid of anything, and for a reason.

Since then everyone going out became much more careful when entering deserted buildings. The last thing anyone needed was to contract rabies, having survived the Scourge. Scavenging was, however, still uncommon because of the bad weather. The winter was harsh, mid-February, and a new wave of snow had hit the city, making it difficult to traverse the streets. It was also during this time that the campus was barely seeing newcomers. Everything was slowing down, but that came as a good thing for the campus to regroup, having acquired so many new members.

In late February, the weather lightened up a little, and people started going out scavenging out of sheer stir craziness. Around this time, word spread that various buildings in the city were cursed and haunted, and others were said to be dangerously unsafe and on the verge of collapsing.

Targets of these stories didn't spare the super modern, strikingly tall, residential towers right in the neighborhood of the campus. When the explosion of built-up gasses blew out the windows on the thirty-fourth floor of the JDS Tower, it reinforced this thought.

This tower, which had an ultra-slender height-to-width ratio of 1:23, looked like a fifteen hundred foot needle pricking the sky, which amazed people even before the Scourge at how it had stood without toppling. The campus folk who happened to witness the explosion thought it was about to break in half and ran for their lives.

Even though the same folks considered the JDS Tower an architectural marvel of design and skill of its builders, now they viewed it as a dangerous and unstable death trap. Soon these fears spread to other towering buildings in the neighborhood: the Nordstrom Tower, the tallest one in midtown Manhattan at 1775 feet, and the 432 Park Avenue tower a few blocks down from the JDS Tower.

Even though these structures were much more stable than people thought, their incredible height and apparent evidence provided by the recent explosion proved powerful enough to keep many away from venturing close to it.

Vincent, on the other hand, didn't buy into these superstitions and spent most of his free time with Mike and Elysie. Aran joined them as well from time to time when his shift allowed him to, which was usually around dinnertime. The four of them got along well. The various discussions and jokes made everything lighthearted, and any bad news felt a lot more bearable.

Since Vincent had no one else in the world, Mike, Aran, and Elysie became his new family. Because of the Scourge, everyone else had dusted away in millions of houses and apartments across the city, the country, and the world. Vincent felt fairly confident that he would never run into his parents or any of his family members again.

Perhaps, he thought, he may run into one of his distant relatives at some point, but this, too, seemed a long shot. His new family was right here. He missed Marcus and regretted that they had left him behind, but he hoped that at some point Aran and he would go back and bring him here.

As days went by, Vincent enjoyed the company of Elysie more and more. She brought a fresh outlook to his life. Any desperation, anger, confusion, or injustice seemed to wither away with one look at her face. It seemed simple, but he couldn't deny the effect. In the beginning he viewed her as a cute girl with attractive dark features, but she had become a beautiful woman with alluring character.

At times Vincent couldn't believe that he could be so affected by Elysie. He had never planned for any of these feelings to happen. It wasn't like he had aimed for her all along, but now he realized he was drawn to her regardless of what he wanted. It didn't hurt that she was attractive; she radiated some new womanly qualities that he wasn't quite sure how to explain. It unnerved him to be out of control like that.

Sometimes he wondered what it was about this situation that made him feel the way he did about her. Could it be as simple as her smile or the sincerity in her eyes? Did he appreciate the fact that she was down to earth and someone he could talk to about many things? Or that she didn't hide her flaws, which made her more like him? He didn't have the answers, but he knew he enjoyed being around her.

Originally, Elysie lived with Mike when they joined the campus, but soon they moved to different floors as per campus rules. She now lived on the tenth floor, and Vincent found himself there more and more frequently.

Sometimes he came down there with Aran and other times he ventured alone. In the evenings, when he climbed his way up to his room on the sixteenth floor, he frequently made an excuse to stop on the tenth to rest before continuing the ascent. He feared at times he would become an annoyance, but Elysie never seemed to mind his company, no matter how late in the day.

At times Vincent and Elysie found themselves talking about venturing into the city and exploring the urban jungle. It was, however, unlikely until the snow receded and the temperatures became warmer, but it gave them something to look forward to and in a way dream about.

Two months into knowing her, Vincent found out Elysie was a Native American from the Ottawa Indian tribe. She had grown up in Chapleau, Canada, a small, isolated town in the midst of a wildlife preserve in northeastern Ontario. When she was in second grade, she had moved with her parents, a younger brother, and a sister to a town outside of Columbus, Ohio, because her mother had gotten a job there, and her father had some family nearby.

Even though Elysie was only seven when this happened, she told Vincent what a stark difference Ohio was from her small birth town. There were simply a lot more people. The malls and advertisements that were everywhere excited her, but she missed the natural beauty that Chapleau offered. Even though people were mostly nice in Columbus, they lacked that connection with the natural world that her Ottawan people had.

Vincent was amazed at Elysie's story—not so much because it was drastically different from most survivors' stories, but because of the way she explained it. He liked the way she talked and described things—what she did with her hands and how her facial expressions changed.

He realized he was falling for her, and he wondered if it had become obvious to Aran and Mike as well. Mike never objected to seeing Vincent around Elysie because he always remained pleasant and friendly to him. Aran also seemed happy for his friend, perhaps slightly jealous, as he frequently told Vincent he wished to meet someone to be smitten by.

Elysie was drawn to Vincent as well. At first it seemed just as friends, but as time went by she saw something more. She was impressed by the fact that he was the only person she had heard of to have survived the Scourge all on his own.

Even though it probably wasn't true that he was the only one, the vast majority of survivors had someone else to thank for their continued existence, at least to a degree. Either they were initially helped in the hospitals or they were helped by relatives and friends who were around them, who, ironically, died themselves.

Elysie liked how humbly Vincent approached that fact, primarily because he didn't seem to realize how significant it was. To him, he was lucky. To her, he was unique.

She also thought Vincent was a bright guy. In his own way he was insightful and stimulating, holding himself well in conversations and coming across as quite knowledgeable when it came to numbers. Being an accountant helped that matter. Hearing how he liked to jog around Brooklyn discovering new areas made him adventurous. Talking about various places they wished to visit only reinforced this image.

Vincent had an adorable and sensitive side as well. He was shy about his attempts at writing poetry and usually kept his poems to himself, but she appreciated that he wrote them. He was also an attentive listener, showing he cared about her opinion. The times they would spend together increasingly made Elysie forget how badly the world was beset by the Scourge.

CHAPTER 11

The Ides of March arrived. Snow remained on the ground, but the temperature climbed slightly above freezing. It was a Saturday, and Vincent and Elysie had decided to venture out a little farther from The Plaza Hotel as they had talked about before. The trek wasn't easy as they headed into Central Park, but they didn't give up on it.

They had their mind set on Bethesda Terrace, where both of them remembered seeing an a cappella band in the past. Vincent recalled observing a homeless man tucked in a corner under the terrace while no one seemed to have any notice of him. The man had long hair and a beard, and his staring creeped Vincent out, which caused him to get out of there as fast as he could.

Elysie found that funny and told Vincent how he should never be able to get lost in Central Park because every lamp post has two pairs of numbers, the first pair indicating the closest street and the second indicating east or west—even numbers meant east and odd numbers meant west.

Once they got to the terrace, they felt a sense of accomplishment because neither was quite sure of the precise location. Bethesda Fountain no longer had water, but the beautiful terrace remained recognizable with its colorful walls and ceilings. A lot of snow still covered the ground, but at least it also hid the leaves and mud. As the sun rose high above them in the middle of the day, it was quiet—just the hum of the wind and an occasional bird song.

Vincent felt it was ironic that, around the same time a year ago, he had walked this very spot while exploring the city. It was much noisier then, with people talking, kids playing, and dancers moving to the music. That was normal then. Now there was a new normal.

After visiting Bethesda, Vincent and Elysie went north and managed to get inside the beautiful Metropolitan Museum of Art, also known as The Met. The museum was locked and boarded up, but some folks had managed to break in, leaving a small enough entrance for Vincent and Elysie to come through. They spent hours walking through various halls and rooms and marveled at all the magnificent creations of artists from around the globe and throughout history.

Filled with awe, and in agreement to come back here again, they left the museum and followed 5th Avenue up to 86th Street and turned right, or east. Along the way they came across a few people from the campus who either had ventured out for a change in scenery or were bringing something back to the campus.

They strolled past Madison Avenue and Park Avenue, checking out the once-expensive apartment buildings that the ultra rich used to call their home. Now they didn't even dare go in them because they feared coming across raccoons or dusty bones of their former owners. It was too nice of a day to see dead people.

Through conversation, Vincent learned that two years prior to the Scourge Elysie had moved to New York City to pursue her career in writing as a way of escaping her mundane life back home. Vincent couldn't judge her because his own motivation wasn't any more glorious. His was an escape from the depressive state he was in.

There was one place in particular Elysie did want to enter— a café on 3rd Avenue. She wanted to check it out because that was where she had started writing her short stories that had published two weeks before the Scourge.

The café stirred up some emotions for Elysie. Vincent could sense them, but he didn't want to pry too much. He wanted to let her make the decision about whether or not to talk about it. Elysie took in the scene, and soon they moved down south on 3rd Avenue looking at all the beautiful urban desolation. As it turned later in the day, they became hungry.

Stopping in one of the small market stores, they hoped to find some food. Walking in, they were surprised to see that there weren't as many bugs or rodents inside. The produce section was reduced to mostly unrecognizable leftovers, and the meat section contained nothing but a few bones here and there. Luckily for them, though, they found canned green beans and some lunch meat.

They went into McDonald's a few blocks down and ate on the second floor overlooking the street below. The large windows heated by the sun made it warm enough inside for them to take their jackets off. They talked about the ironies in the new age and how just listening to a can opening made them excited about eating unspoiled food.

"If I could thank one person right now," Vincent said, "it would be whoever came up with canned food."

Elysie chuckled and then responded, "I couldn't agree more."

"The process is pretty simple," Vincent replied as he watched her eat the green beans. "They pack the food into sealed airtight containers. Then they heat it to kill all the microorganisms. As long as it stays airtight, it's pretty much good for years to come."

"It's interesting that you know facts like that," Elysie responded, "but I'm glad you do. If I ever decide to can food, I'll need to have you by my side."

As the night approached, they headed back to the campus. They knew not to stay out past dark because the news of some gangs had already made it to the campus. Increasingly, the newcomers were telling stories of being harassed on their way to Manhattan.

It surprised Vincent that the miniscule remainder of the world population would try to hurt one another. If anything, this was the time they should all band together and help rebuild the new world, not cause more harm. The campus, even with its tiny population, was quickly becoming the most populous area on the East Coast. It was attracting people of all types.

As they made their way back to the campus, Vincent and Elysie were greeted by the lights of the elegant building, emanating a blissful sensation of safety. Even some of the street lamps in front of the hotel were on, illuminating the Grand Army Plaza. Most of the folks had already gone inside, and only a few policemen keeping watch could be seen at the entrance.

Moved by the occasion, Vincent asked Elysie, "Would you like to dance?"

Elysie seemed pleasantly surprised by the offer and accepted. Vincent reached around her coat and lightly moved her around to the sound of the wind as it gently grazed their ears. They danced like this for a few minutes. Then another couple joined them, and soon a few more.

Seeing this, two violinists walked outside and started playing "Skater's Waltz." Hearing the music, more and more people stepped outside, intrigued to find out what was going on. Some joined in the dance, while others looked on. Vincent felt like they were in the clouds as they gazed at each other's eyes, moved by the music. Bliss came over the crowd as they looked on, and a genuine hope for the new harmonious world seemed to develop.

When the music drew to a close, as if on a cue, the wind picked up, forcing everyone back to the hotel. Vincent walked Elysie to her room on the tenth floor, where they hugged each other and he gave her a kiss, wishing her a good night. On his way up to the sixteenth floor, Vincent thought about the magical day he had had. Then the lights were shut off for the evening, and he found himself following the fluorescent emergency lights back to his room.

CHAPTER 12

From time to time Vincent found himself staring at Elysie. She was so beautiful, for a thousand reasons. Every passing day, she seemed to blossom a little more, and he felt privileged to witness it. At times he would stop with all the mesmerizing and try to remember the previous disappointments of falling in love, but those negative feelings wouldn't last long. Being in love with Elysie just felt better.

She stood out like a jewel in the crowd, and he believed he could spot her from a mile away. Not only that, but he felt he had developed a sixth sense of knowing when she would come his way. Each time he sensed her presence, he started smiling right before she appeared in his line of sight. Then there she was, and he was pleased.

The following Saturday, after they had ventured into the city the first time, the temperature had risen to the high forties. Soon the streets of Manhattan were trickling with the melted snow. Birds began dominating the skies.

It seemed that there wasn't a single high-rise building that didn't bow down to the new rulers of the sky. The pigeons, doves, European starlings, house sparrows, gulls, hawks, and even shy bluebirds were making their presence known in their city.

In Central Park, campus workers had already started digging or driving wells to draw water out, the latter being easier and much quicker to do in soft soil.

Vincent and Elysie decided to venture out to the city again. She wore a white flower in her braided hair, which Vincent found endearing, but he didn't want to tell her. The flower made her long dark hair look even more beautiful. They ventured out east as before and soon found themselves exploring various market stores. Elysie liked to try out different clothes, while Vincent preferred to look at different gadgets.

They had had an uneventful day until they heard some voices coming from a block away. Elysie wanted to check it out, but Vincent felt uneasy about it. He still didn't like the stories he had heard from the folks on campus about their run-ins with bad people roaming around the city. Elysie got the better of him, though, because she had already started walking toward the voices. Vincent had no choice but to follow.

Less than a minute later, they approached the corner of 72nd Street. As Vincent reached to pull Elysie aside to tell her to check out the people before being spotted by them, they heard a voice saying, "Hey, I think I heard something!" followed by, "Hey, we know you're there. Show yourselves!"

Vincent and Elysie came out into the open and could now see who they were dealing with. About thirty yards away stood eight guys, ranging in age from mid-teens to about mid-thirties. They seemed to have been walking around the area, scouting or looking for stuff. Some wore backpacks, others nothing, but all carried guns. They looked rough, as if they hadn't eaten well for a while. They wore dirty clothes and definitely didn't belong to the campus.

"Hey, guys, have you been looking for The Plaza Hotel?" Vincent said, knowing full well these guys didn't particularly look interested in joining any campus. He could see them measuring him with their eyes and got a bad vibe.

Before they could respond, Vincent said, "We have a bunch of people around gathering many survivors. We have medicine, clean water, and lots of police." He said this to make them think police were nearby. He knew they probably weren't interested in him, but Elysie for sure. It was doubtful they had seen a woman in a while.

A short silence followed. Then the one who looked to be the oldest and their leader of the group replied, "Yeah, that's right. We were looking to see where you guys were."

Vincent didn't believe him. First of all, the flyers and the radio had stated the campus was at The Plaza Hotel, and it had given the street corners. These guys ought to be familiar with how the city avenues and numbering worked. On top of that, being on the corner of 72nd and 3rd Avenue, they had come too close not to realize where it was. They must have been moving around the city, without getting too close to the campus for whatever reason.

"Yeah, we got to catch up with one of the groups around the corner," Vincent said, looking for a way to get out of their sight. "But if you guys continue down this street, you'll hit 5th Avenue. Then just turn left and you'll end up at The Plaza Hotel."

The guys stood there as if waiting for something. They seemed unsure what to make of it all. Vincent turned to his left and yelled, "All right, be right over, give me a minute," to make him sound as if he was talking to someone these guys couldn't see.

He turned to the group. "Okay, down that way. Can't miss it. You'll see somebody, guaranteed." He walked up to the corner and out of their view.

Just as he got behind the corner, he heard one of the guys yell, "Hey! Hold up." Vincent motioned to Elysie to hurry up behind the corner, too.

Once Elysie was out of their sight, too, Vincent grabbed her hand and started running up the street. A few moments later, glancing back, one of the gang members appeared at the corner.

"Sons of bitches!" He motioned to the rest of the guys, who immediately took off in pursuit after them.

Running in the melting snow on the street littered with debris and randomly parked cars wasn't easy, but they were running for their lives. Behind them, about eighty yards away, they could hear the gang yelling after them, which only confirmed that these guys meant nothing good.

Vincent was glad Elysie was keeping the pace with him, but it didn't seem they were gaining much of a distance on the pursuers. Just as they were about to make a left turn behind a building, Elysie tripped and fell. Vincent quickly reached and pulled her up. At that moment they heard a gunshot, and a car window shattered right next to them. The situation had turned much more serious.

This came as a shock to Vincent and Elysie because neither had experienced another human trying to kill them, even less with a gun. This wasn't some kind of video game where people could simply respawn after they had been killed; this was reality. One shot in the right spot, and they were gone forever.

This only made them run faster, with the goal to get behind another corner and out of the gang's sight. A few more shots zinged by, and one grazed Vincent's right cheek, causing it to bleed. He felt a burning sensation on his face as he and Elysie slid behind a building.

At this point Vincent was beginning to feel fatigued, and Elysie didn't appear in any better shape. He knew they couldn't last much longer at this pace. Fortunately for them, their pursuers were also seeming to lose steam and resorted to firing more shots without aiming.

"Oh my God, you're bleeding!" Elysie cried out.

Vincent reached for his right cheek and felt the warmth of his blood.

He looked at his bloody hand and then said, "We've got to keep moving, Elysie."

They ran another street block before making a turn, expecting to hear more shots, but nothing came.

"Get behind me," he urged Elysie with a heavy breath. "I have to see if they're still behind us."

Pausing for a moment to catch his breath, Vincent quickly peeked behind the corner and saw the gang walking. They looked unsure about whether they should continue the pursuit having lost sight of them again. Vincent motioned to Elysie, who looked at him with fear in her eyes, to head down the street.

"Just keep going. They've slowed down. A little more and we're out," he assured her.

Vincent and Elysie pressed on and ran some more. Less than fifteen minutes later, they barely fast-walked.

"I think they're done chasing us," Vincent said wearily as sweat poured down his bloodied cheek. "They weren't running when I saw them. I think if we make another left, we should be all right at the park."

Looking exhausted, in fear, and out of breath, Elysie turned to him. "How, how do you feel? Are you all right?"

"Yeah, I think so. I'll be fine." He stopped and took a deep breath. "We've made it. We're safe, Elysie. We're almost at the campus."

As they approached the campus, he felt huge relief. People standing around knew something bad must have happened when they looked at Vincent's bloody face and quickly reached out to help him. They notified the police of what had gone down. The police expressed displeasure at hearing that the incident had occurred so close to The Plaza.

As Vincent received medical care, he described where they had discovered the gang and the last place he had seen them. The police, in turn, put on their gear and went out to investigate the area. Within an hour they came back, having discovered only the empty shells as the night closed in, forcing them to return. This only added to the fears around campus of the presence of dangerous people roaming the streets of New York.

From that point, anyone scavenging for the campus had two police officers accompany him. The days of Vincent and Elysie venturing out together became something they only talked about, not something they actually did.

CHAPTER 13

April ninth was a special day to Vincent and Aran, for on that day their good friend Marcus showed up at The Plaza Hotel. Vincent was overjoyed at the sight of Marcus. He still harbored some guilt at leaving him behind even though it was Marcus's idea for them to leave without him.

Marcus looked like he had lost about fifteen pounds, and on a skinny guy like him, that wasn't really a good thing. He still didn't walk straight due to his injury. Vincent thought that after four months Marcus's ankle would have healed. But a combination of Marcus's own neglect and various chores forced by Rick and his posse had considerably slowed his recovery. When asked how it was spending the winter with Rick's group, Marcus just replied, "It could have been worse."

Rick's entire posse accompanied Marcus, which was the downside. When they saw Vincent and Aran, they nodded and went their own way, as if they didn't care to see them.

"Man, I wanted to come here so bad and leave those dumbasses," Marcus explained, "but you know how bad the winter was, and I could barely walk. Then after a while I got used to their bullshit, so I guess it wasn't so bad."

"What changed Rick's mind to come here?" Vincent asked.

"Well, I'll tell you, but if you haven't noticed, we have fewer people now than when you were with us," Marcus replied. "Some left soon after you guys did, and then more in the middle of the winter. I'm not sure if they came here or ended up somewhere else."

Marcus looked around and then asked, "Do you remember the young girl Rachel and her older friend Diana?"

"Yeah, I do remember," Aran responded. He had taken to liking Diana before he left.

"Well, one of them had enough of Rick's boys constantly coming on to them, so they left. I think it was late January. Have you guys seen them here?"

"I do remember who you're talking about," Vincent said, "but I don't remember seeing them here."

"They were such sweet girls." Marcus shook his head. "I hope they made it here and everything is all right with them. When they left, soon enough more people left also. We were almost down to half the size. Then others started openly talking about leaving, too. Eventually Rick had no choice. Pretty much everyone left."

"That's funny, I don't remember seeing anyone here from Rick's group until today," Vincent said.

"Wherever they left, I hope they are all right," Aran added.

A little later Vincent told Marcus of his run-in with the gang and his fear that the people who had left Rick's group might have fallen prey to them. Neither liked the thought of what could have happened to them if they did. They avoided mentioning this in front of Aran because they knew he liked Diana.

About a week after Marcus joined the campus, another group of people walked in. There were twenty of them, mostly men, led by a guy named Neil. They said they had come from up north and heard about The Plaza campus over the radio when it finally dawned to them to use one. Neil said they had wanted to come down there much sooner, back in January, but they were halted by the winter and had to wait it out. They also carried guns with them, which wasn't welcomed.

Even though members could own guns, none could carry them on the campus premises. They had to keep the guns with the campus police and ask for them if they were going off-premises and needed them for self-protection. Neil and his people didn't like rule at first, but soon they realized they had no choice if they wanted to stay with the campus.

Neil looked to be in his early thirties. He was slightly taller than an average guy but wore boots that added an additional two inches. Even though he was skinny, he had broad shoulders with a fairly muscular body. He had a short military-style haircut and a few scars on his face and hands. He looked like he had involved himself in quite a few brawls in the past, some still bearing their mark on him.

Neil was always surrounded by five or six guys, but one guy Marcus nicknamed Neil's *Number One* because he would answer to no one but Neil. Even though Neil seemed to be a pretty smart guy, he was sometimes brash with people when he talked to them. Neil was someone who wasn't educated by an institution, but by the streets, and he had a solid master's in them.

Always in the center of attention in a group, Neil was like a leader of a pack of wolves. He reminded Vincent of Danny Zuko from the movie *Grease*, but much rougher around the edges.

Over the next three to four weeks, Vincent noticed Rick and his posse starting to hang out more with Neil and his group. Rick tried to keep his grip on his posse, but he also wanted to see what Neil was all about.

It had become evident to Vincent that Rick didn't quite measure up to Neil in leadership. He could tell that by everyone's body language in the group. They all faced Neil, and Neil did most of the talking, not Rick. Rick stood around just like the other guys in a circle around Neil.

Soon Vincent heard about some trouble that Neil and his group had started. They had made some people feel uncomfortable, and apparently it wasn't the first time they had done so. Some other folks came out and voiced that they, too, were made to feel uneasy.

Aran told Vincent that some of Neil's guys had brushed against him on purpose as he walked by them, as if they wanted Aran to turn around and start a fight. A few more incidents occurred, and soon the police became involved.

Neil acted as if they minded their own business and it was the other folks who were responsible for the trouble. The chief of police didn't like his excuses, and soon Neil's group was brought to the campus court to discuss their behavior.

"These guys are bad news, Vincent," Marcus said to Vincent one day. "I'm pretty sure some of them are former skinheads, and the Scourge didn't quite get it out of their system."

"You really think so?" Vincent asked, wishing it wasn't true.

"Yeah, I do," Marcus replied. "Look at them. See who they hang with, who they start trouble with, and it'll quickly become clear."

"They could be white trash with an attitude problem." Vincent remained in denial.

"They're trash all right," Marcus responded, "but I don't think their attitude is their only problem. I think certain folks around here are their problem."

Vincent looked around Neil's group congregating in the distance. "Damn. I don't like the sound of that. I wish that weren't the case."

"I wish it weren't the case either," Marcus added, "but the facts are there: all the people they've started trouble with are Asian, Latin, black, or Middle Eastern."

Vincent observed Neil's guys silently. He hoped Marcus had made a mistake in his judgment.

"I have a pretty strong feeling they're some kind of white supremacy clan or something," Marcus explained. "It suits Rick pretty well to hang with them since he never really liked me or Aran anyway."

The more Vincent thought about it, the more he realized Marcus could be right. Neil and his group didn't seem to pick arguments with many whites. Maybe it was a coincidence, but thinking that it could be true, fear immediately gripped him, and then anger. Most of Vincent's friends were nonwhite. It didn't matter to him what color they were, but Neil's group had already brushed with Aran. How much longer before they started something with Elysie?

Vincent thought, if they touch her, I'll kill them! He didn't know what he would do if one of them said or did something. He felt so helpless. He didn't have a large group of people who would fight on his behalf, but he wanted to react and defend her if they did try something. He started keeping Elysie away from that group of guys wherever they went.

CHAPTER 14

Unexpectedly on May 3, Bill Loren, the president and creator of the campus, passed away. Nine days shy of his fiftieth birthday, he suffered a stroke, and the hospital at the campus couldn't provide him with the necessary care to survive. A majority of the campus had high regards for him as a good and fair leader and were greatly saddened by his passing.

Bill had lots of plans that weren't realized—one being to start working on a more permanent location for the campus outside the city. He always regarded The Plaza Hotel as more of a staging ground and never planned to stay there more than one or two years at most. The island of Manhattan was no longer a good place to stay because its once-urban magnificence would deteriorate under the mighty force of nature to the point where it would be too dangerous.

Putting those worries aside, the campus quickly started working on electing a new campus leader to the office. Paul, a friend of Bill's, opted out of the race due to his own failing health, which pretty much left the election wide open. Anyone who had resided at the campus for at least a month, who was at least twenty-one years of age, was eligible to run for the office.

The councilors expected to see a few dozen applications, mostly from the officers they managed, but they never imagined that more than 120 people would file for the office. Almost immediately, campaigners started making various promises, then accusations of their opponents. People couldn't keep track of all the candidates, and within a week the councilors limited the number of people who could run for the office to 12.

They planned to interview each of the candidates and then select the top twelve they felt had made the strongest argument. There would be three rounds of voting. The first round would eliminate half of the candidates. The second round would do the same, and the last round would elect the campus leader.

The interview process would take at least a few days. Soon the candidates began roaming around the councilors to see if they could get a favor. Among those who applied for the office was Neil. He got a decent following going mostly among the younger white men, but he alienated all the nonwhites, which made up more than half the population, and it was too late to appeal to them.

Nevertheless, that didn't stop Neil from trying. The first obstacle he needed to get by was the interview. He was looking for a way to appeal to the interviewers. For the most part the councilors weren't too fond of Neil, but persistence seemed to pay off, at least with one of them, a councilor named Ed who gave Neil a chance to see what he had to offer.

During this time, Vincent and Elysie tried to make another excursion into the city. They couldn't have cared less about the whole election process and preferred occupying themselves with other interests.

On top of that, they hadn't ventured out since the run-in with the gang in March from which Vincent still bore the scar on his face. Their goal this time was the Museum of Natural Science. They figured that because the campus members went there frequently with the police, it would be a relatively safe area.

On the way to the museum, they came across a few folks on

utility ATVs, or all-terrain vehicles, zigzagging between deteriorating cars and debris, presumably carrying some equipment to the campus. They also discovered many small cracks in the streets and avenues, with some growing grass and flowers. In addition, there were a few small creeks running into the nearest subway station.

Walking these streets before the Scourge, they would have never imagined it becoming this way. They found it beautiful to see how life found a way to survive even in the streets once busy with innumerable cars and busses.

Vincent plucked one of those flowers and gave it to Elysie. She placed it on her black hair as they had a quiet picnic in the gardens of the museum while the campus echoed the noise of the election process.

They found the museum building hard to get into. Whoever left the place last made sure it was locked up well at every entrance. They saw where people had attempted to break in, to no avail. Slightly disappointed, they didn't manage to get in like they had at The Met. Instead, they decided to enjoy the beautiful and overgrown garden in front of the museum and agreed in due time they would come back and figure a way in.

While Vincent and Elysie enjoyed themselves, the interviews were taking place, and the campus had become much quieter than the previous week. The campaigns didn't matter until the councilors approved of the candidates. The candidates' focus was on passing the interview.

This interview process nearly resembled the old singing or talent competition shows. The councilors did come across some good candidates who had prepared themselves well, usually with prior experience in management or politics. Other interviews turned outright comical; some were campaigning only for attention and were denied within a few minutes of the interview. Most sought attention and some a way to get out of doing their regular chores.

When it came time for Neil's interview, forty-seven people had already gone ahead of him. The councilors were tired, as were those waiting to be interviewed. Neil went in, and after about fifteen minutes he stormed out. "This is a damn conspiracy, a bunch of bullshit!" he yelled.

People looked at him in shock. His posse started asking him questions, but all he said was, "This whole thing is a pile of shit! They already know who they want. It's pointless!" He turned around to the rest of the people who were there. "It's all rigged!"

While Neil vented at his posse, the 12 candidates were announced, much to the dismay of the other 108 candidates and their followers. The announcement came over the loud speaker, the message boards, and word of mouth.

The twelve candidates quickly went on campaigning, and the other unsuccessful candidates tried to buy their places with one of them. The campaign, in essence, came down to a number of debates.

Neil tried to align himself with one of the candidates in hope of gaining a position out of it. Without coincidence, this was the same one that councilor Ed supported. Rick, on the other hand, had been secretly trying to get his position with one of the opposing candidates while still hanging out with Neil and his posse. He still seemed to desire some kind of a leading position because his own posse had become more devoted to Neil, and his support had dwindled.

When it became obvious to everyone that he supported another candidate, Rick came to Neil and said, rather politely, that he supported someone else. Neil didn't seem upset. He acted as if it didn't bother him and largely ignored Rick. This, however, didn't seem to fool Marcus when he heard about it.

"I would be careful if I were Rick," Marcus said to Vincent. "He doesn't realize the kind of people he's dealing with."

CHAPTER 15

A few days later, Vincent, Elysie, and Aran hung around outside The Plaza Hotel when they heard Neil speak loudly to a group of people about Rick. He made fun of him, telling all kinds of embarrassing stories about him and how badly he had managed his group in Brooklyn. It seemed he did so purposely when Rick advertised his own candidate of choice nearby, and people laughed.

At first Rick looked to mind his own business, but Vincent wondered how long he'd remain passive. For too long he had been a bully who had never let anyone push him around. Now the tables had turned. Nobody from his days as the leader of the Brooklyn group supported him, and now Neil made a mockery of him.

Vincent thought that a proud guy like Rick could only last so long before he did something. Unfortunately, Rick didn't seem to realize that Neil had baited him. Neil tried to force Rick to make the first move, so then he could make his own.

Enraged, Rick turned around and went straight at Neil. "You got a problem, motherfucker? Huh? You got some problem with me?"

"Chill, man, we're just having a little fun here," Neil responded as Rick's face turned red with anger.

"Well, I don't like your fucking fun!" Rick raged.

"Hey, man, I'm just stating the facts," Neil responded nonchalantly. "Everyone here is saying that you fucking sucked as a leader in Brooklyn."

Rick looked at the people around him and noticed his former posse standing aside. He stared for a moment expecting a reaction from them, but they remained silent. He turned to Neil.

"You think you could have done any better, asshole?" He shouted, and people noticed something was about to go down.

"Get out of here, you dumbass bitch," Neil responded calmly, spitting to his side.

Rick appeared to have had enough. He got a step closer and swung wide with a right to strike Neil, who, being a much more experienced fighter, quickly stepped to the side and delivered a two-punch combination to Rick's head. Rick fell to the ground. People standing around were aroused and forgot about the message of peace and unity of the fragile human race. They started chanting, "Fight! Fight!"

Rick rose and charged at Neil full force to take him to the ground. Neil made a step back and kneed Rick right in the face. Rick's nose broke from the impact, and blood began pouring out.

"You had enough? You bitch!" Neil taunted Rick.

Rick looked confused. He couldn't breathe through his nose but still had rage in him. He swung two more times at Neil, almost blindly, but missed. Neil now had an easy time taking shots at Rick's face. After four or five shots, Rick stood dazed. Then Neil gave him a powerful punch to the ear, which knocked Rick to the ground and out.

It was all over. Neil had had his revenge. It was an educational beatdown not only to Rick, but to anyone in his group who had considered betraying him. Neil humiliated Rick and made him look like a fool. Campus police quickly reacted, arrested Neil, and took Rick to an infirmary.

Neil pled his innocence as the police took him away. He claimed he was attacked and was just defending himself. No one around denied it. After all, that was the truth; Rick had charged him time and again, and Neil had only defended himself, however brutally. Vincent had no doubt they would release Neil soon, perhaps with a stern warning to stay away from trouble.

This violence shocked Elysie. The media may have been full of violence before the Scourge, and she must have seen a lot worse in movies, but it was still different seeing the fighting in person.

Vincent took Elysie away from the scene to get her mind off of it. He couldn't help but feel sorry for Rick, though. Rick had bullied people in Brooklyn, but it still seemed wrong to be humiliated like that. Once Rick was the leader of a group of people; now he was a bloody mess with no supporters.

June third was a sunny day. The temperature hung around in the mid-seventies, and the city, even in its post apocalyptic light, looked strangely beautiful. Vincent gazed at the skyline in front of The Plaza Hotel, and it appeared peaceful.

The hotel felt, perhaps, a little too peaceful and serene. He explained it to Elysie as a sense of calm before the storm. Something didn't seem quite right, but he couldn't quite put his finger on it.

"It's the election day," Elysie said. "Maybe you're just excited about that."

"Yeah, maybe that's it," Vincent agreed, although he wasn't fully convinced. "I never paid much attention to it, but I guess all the talk and everything that's been going on has kind of caught up with me."

In the evening, after the last ballot had been placed, the counting began. Great tension filled the air, and everyone waited for the results. Even though Vincent didn't care too much about who might win, he hoped it wouldn't be the candidate Neil associated with.

Everyone seemed quiet and anxious. Even Neil showed signs of nervousness. He had his posse around him, but he didn't talk to them either.

The results came in and the winner was announced. Vincent smiled in joy, as did so many other folks. Neil pounded his fist in fury. He seemed more disappointed than the candidate he supported. That candidate congratulated the winner and went his own way, but Neil walked out of the auditorium with his posse complaining about the votes being rigged. The new leader celebrated with his own followers until it was time for everyone to head to their rooms before the lights went out.

CHAPTER 16

Lying in his bed, Vincent still smiled in gladness that the election hadn't gone Neil's way. He had a tough time falling asleep that night. After two hours, his mind relaxed. As he went into a dream state, he heard an alarm and woke up.

"What's going on?" he asked, looking around the dark room in confusion.

"I have no idea," Aran responded in bewilderment. "It woke me up a few minutes ago, but it was so faint I thought I was dreaming. Now it's gotten louder."

Vincent left his bed and walked into the dark hallway before he realized the alarm was coming from the stairs at the other end. He made his way closer to the sound as his neighbors exited their rooms with flashlights.

"What in the hell is going on?" he heard someone say.

Vincent carefully walked up to the guardrail and looked down the stairs, lit only by fluorescent emergency lighting. Then he heard someone yell, "Fire!"

He stepped back, and the first thought that entered his mind was Elysie. Was she okay?

"Hey, what's happening?" an anxious neighbor came from behind and asked.

"I—I think there's a fire on the floor below," Vincent stammered.

"Fire?" the neighbor asked again, as if looking for confirmation.

"That's what I heard," Vincent responded, before descending the stairs to investigate. Within moments he smelled the smoke. Just as he reached the floor below, a rush of people came toward him and pushed him aside. He fell on the stairs and hit his head on the side wall.

Thudding pain engulfed his head, and he heard buzzing noises. He closed his eyes, hoping it would go away, and then opened them to find himself alone on the stairs. He staggered up and started coughing as the smoke thickened. He ran up to his floor to find that panic had set in among his neighbors.

"You have to use the other stairs," he yelled, but people didn't seem to listen. All he saw were numerous flashlights franticly shining all over the hallway as people ran around, shouting and cursing. He ran up to Aran, who stood at the entrance of their room.

"This isn't looking good, Aran," he warned, breathing heavily. "We've got to find a way out."

Soon enough another form of light presented itself in the hallway. It was fire, and he had no idea how it had gotten to his floor so quickly, but it caused even more panic.

Vincent and Aran headed for the stairs at the other end of the hallway only to encounter a mass of people already rushing down as if being chased by a monster. They pushed each other trying to make their way through.

Below, the campus firemen, with flashlights, tried to climb the stairs while others attempted to guide the rushing people in a coherent manner. Unfortunately, this only added to the congestion and confusion as more and more people escaped down the stairs.

In the midst of the chaos, Vincent and Aran were separated, and soon Vincent decided to get off at the twelfth floor instead of battling his way with the rest of the people down the stairs. He went back twice calling for Aran at the stairs, but each time he did so, people rushed him as if he knew of a quicker way out. Soon he realized he had to look after himself and find Elysie to make it out alive.

Zigzagging through the hallways, he came across another staircase and hurried down to the tenth floor to find Elysie. Unable to read the room numbers in the near darkness, he opened each of them calling out for her.

The noise of the panicking people eventually receded, helping him hear better, but it seemed to no avail as he still couldn't find her. Either she had made her way out, or she lay unconscious somewhere, he thought. He felt guilty for passing her by the first time he met her, and he didn't want to make the same mistake again.

Going back and forth on the tenth floor, Vincent finally located Elysie's room and desperately went in seeking her. It was a larger suite that was turned into two rooms, and he checked every corner of it until he was certain there wasn't a living soul inside. His mind told him he'd done everything he could, but the guilt didn't go away.

With sadness he descended the stairs, battling the ever-increasing smoke presence. He hoped all his friends were all right, but especially Elysie. If he had to choose, he would give his own life for her. That critical test didn't come, but if he stayed in the hotel much longer, he knew he would be wasting his own life.

The top half of the twenty-story Plaza Hotel looked like a blazing furnace from the outside. The fire brigade didn't seem prepared for the scale of the fire and quickly found themselves overwhelmed. Even though many people who fled the building volunteered to help, there simply wasn't enough water or equipment to stop the fire from spreading. By the morning, the glamorous Plaza Hotel had largely been consumed by fire. It was becoming clear that there was no hope in saving it.

The Plaza campus was now without its beloved home. The survivors standing outside gazed at the horror and wondered what was to become of it all. As time went by, people gave in to their nerves and started demanding answers. Where were their missing friends? What were they going to do now? Where would they go now? Who was to blame for this?

When no answers came, it quickly became apparent that there wasn't strong leadership. With all the promises aside, the newly elected leader found himself in deep waters trying to act his part. He missed a few of his closest aides, and many folks around didn't seem to pay any attention to him.

The chief of campus police lay on the gurney, severely injured, and it didn't look like he was going to make it for long. The rest of the campus police tried to control the large crowd, but without their chief appeared like sheep without a pastor, as did everyone else. No one knew how many people remained trapped in the building or how many had been lost to the fire. They were homeless now.

In the midst of all the terror, Vincent found his joy as he embraced Elysie, who, much like him, had barely escaped down one of the stairs. His friends, Mike, Marcus, and Aran, were also safe. They had all gotten by without serious injury, and that was all that mattered to him. They could always rebuild the campus or find a new place to live, but they couldn't revive someone from the dead. The friends stuck together and emotionally tried to prepare themselves for the uncertainty.

Everyone seemed to have been caught off guard, and for a while the surviving councilor members tried to gather everything under control. A great deal of disagreement brewed among people, and shouting increased. One fool's actions ignited the mob, and soon fights broke out. The campus police became overwhelmed in an instant, and the councilors saw themselves in need of someone to help them.

Councilor Ed quickly reached out to Neil and asked for his aid. Neil objected at first because he had never helped control the crowd, much less assist police in doing it. Other councilors didn't seem too fond of hiring Neil for anything, but with the threat of the mob completely getting out of control, they reluctantly reached out to him as well.

As if he sensed some kind of opportunity all of a sudden, Neil changed his mind at the councilor's plea and got a hold of his own mob. They quickly went around breaking fights, usually with their own fists, and forcing people to remain quiet and listen to what the councilors had to say. This took a while, but with the campus police they eventually had everyone's attention. The people stood by and waited for the announcement.

It turned out that Bill Loren was somewhat of a safety planner, and he had taken into account a lot of what-if scenarios. One was precisely what to do in case a fire or other catastrophe destroyed The Plaza Hotel.

A half mile down the street, by the once heavily trafficked roundabout called Columbus Circle on the southwest corner of Central Park, stood their backup place: The Royal International Hotel and Tower, the former Trump International Hotel and Tower.

A well-known high-rise building, the Royal International was much taller than The Plaza Hotel, and much narrower. Whereas the Plaza Hotel resembled a castle, or a fortress, the Royal International looked like an office tower.

Unfortunately, there wasn't enough time to attend to everything adequately. Much like the *Titanic* had more passengers than the required number of lifeboats, so did the campus have a backup place inadequate to accommodate all the members.

The major problem was that the Royal International wasn't quite ready to be populated or big enough for more than two thousand people. Bill had people work on it for a couple of months before he passed away, but a vast majority of the focus remained on The Plaza Hotel. They had managed to get two backup generators working and store some food, water, and medicine. They had also planned to convert its large suites into multiple living quarters.

The work on the Royal International was done, however, without expectations of ever having to use it, and many things were overlooked. It was a fifty-two story building, and without using elevators, it was a nightmare to climb. Even with converting the suites, it would still be difficult to accommodate such a large number of people. The sanitation problem hadn't been thoroughly worked out yet either. Also, keeping the place air conditioned on hot summer days was a major issue. In any case, this was the best they had, and the new chapter of the campus had begun.

The Royal International was by no means as welcoming a place as The Plaza Hotel. The past ten months had taken their toll on the hotel, and obvious signs of deterioration were visible. At this point people didn't seem to care at all that they were downgrading their accommodations as long as they had a place to sleep.

They gathered at the circle in front of the hotel while a group of maintenance folks and engineers went in to make it somewhat ready for the rest of them. Neil stood on a makeshift podium and with a megaphone started to speak to the people. "Hey! Shut up!"

Some people seemed to have heard him and looked up, while the rest continued talking.

"I said shut up!" Neil practically yelled through the megaphone. A good majority of the crowd quieted down and paid attention to him then. "The councilors are going to speak, and you need to keep your mouth shut!"

Councilor Ed came up to the podium as Neil handed him the megaphone.

"Please folks, listen. I know it's easy to say this in times like these, but please calm down. It was a very difficult day for us all, and we understand what you're going through, but we need to be calm and patient. We're terribly sorry for everyone's loss, we really are, but to get to the bottom of this we need you to pay attention to the instructions."

Ed looked around the crowd. When everyone became silent, he continued. "This tower behind me, the Royal International Hotel, will be our new home, at least temporarily. It was our backup in case something happened to The Plaza Hotel, and it can be as good of a place as that was if everyone does their part. So please listen to what we have to say."

Another councilor came up to the podium and provided guidelines for everyone to follow to ensure a smooth transition to their new home. It reminded Vincent of the instructions provided when they first arrived at The Plaza Hotel. It offered stability and encouragement that despite what happened everything would be all right.

For the remainder of the day the councilors did quite well organizing the officers and various supervisors to help with making the whole process run smoothly. Their experience with running The Plaza Hotel had paid off, and soon things seemed to get into some kind of order.

Neil and his posse intimidated anyone who would be troublemakers, and that suited the situation. To many folks it seemed they overused their authority with force, especially toward the nonwhites, but no one tried to stop them.

To the councilors, Neil remained the one that the crowd respected, no matter how ruthless he seemed, and they needed his authority to enforce their own laws for the time being. What they planned to do with him in the future was not clear. The event was soon labeled as Ash Wednesday, since it happened on a Wednesday.

It became evident to everyone that the new hotel, despite being luxurious back in its day, had far fewer rooms than the campus needed. At 168 rooms and 158 condominium units, it was nowhere near what they needed to house everyone properly, no matter how they divided it.

They placed more people together than at The Plaza Hotel; in two bedrooms suites up to ten people would stay. Still, lots of folks had to sleep in the lounges, meeting rooms, or conference rooms because they had no other place to go. As in The Plaza Hotel, the elevators were off limits for the most part, and many had to climb twenty, thirty, or even forty floors to get to their rooms. Vincent, Aran, and Marcus ended up being the unlucky ones who had to stay in a small conference room on the forty-fourth floor.

"If the fire didn't kill me at the other place, Marcus grunted as sweat poured down his face, "walking up the stairs here will do the job."

CHAPTER 17

Three days after the campus relocated, the counseling body released the official casualty list of the fire disaster at The Plaza Hotel. Out of 2,228 members as of the day before the fire, 1,912 signed in at Royal International, so the presumed missing or dead was 316.

Material damage was substantial as well. The group lost many documents, medical supplies, and equipment of all sorts. Recovery efforts to retrieve anything of value hadn't been in full swing since fire still burned in some parts of the building. Only small groups went into the most accessible areas to recover items of value.

As days went by, people went full throttle to make the best of their new home. This included working on the lower floors of the large apartment buildings across the Columbus Circle to offload the population off Royal International. Walking up the many floors didn't befit anyone.

The weather became increasingly hot, and people searched for various ways to cool off. Many flocked to Central Park to hide in its shade in their free time. The grass and bushes grew wild on either side of the running and cycling paths, and the leafy trees provided shade. They avoided the marshy lakes because they brought swarms of mosquitoes.

To their surprise, they found foxes and white tail deer populating the park right alongside raccoons, who always seemed busy with mischief. People stayed there until late in the evening and only came back to their rooms to sleep.

The councilors, in the meantime, tried to recruit a large enough police force and minimize Neil's influence as the intimidating force. At first, Neil didn't seem to quite catch on to what they were doing, but as his role of the enforcer diminished, it became apparent to everyone he wasn't as important or necessary anymore.

For a period of time, Neil had a grim facade, as if he was lost in some kind of disillusionment. Everyone around him noticed his attitude change and talked among themselves about what was going on with him.

Marcus was quick to spot this and told Vincent, "I'd be careful around this guy. If he can't be the police, he's most likely going to cause trouble instead."

Before Neil could cause any serious trouble, an outbreak of a disease known as TD, or Travelers' Diarrhea, had spread due to the poor sanitation around the campus. As the medical crew did their best to give everyone unexpired Pepto Bismol and Imodium tablets, the rumors spread that one of the councilors may have orchestrated the fire incident at The Plaza Hotel, which many now believed to be haunted by the souls of those who died.

On three occasions, people ran out of there convinced they had heard and seen ghosts after they went in to scavenge the leftovers. Much of the populace vowed never to enter it again out of fear. The word also spread that some of the water wells had been contaminated.

Frustrated by the hot weather, the disease, and the story of the accused councilor, unrest quickly sprung up among the people, especially those who had lost their friends to the fire. The turmoil soon exploded into open and almost violent criticism of how things were handled by the responsible parties, and the councilors had to hold an emergency gathering to prevent any further unrest from breaking out.

At the meeting, the accused councilor tenaciously defended himself. The other councilors promised everyone they would investigate the matter closely and gather all the evidence to make the right judgment. In the meantime, the accused would be imprisoned, mostly for his own protection. Many people had a hard time accepting this delayed sentence. The rumor satisfied them enough to finally release their frustrations at someone. The campus police had barely managed to get the accused away before the people lynched him.

Neil, who Marcus suspected may have facilitated the story about the councilor, used it to reign his terror of accusations on all the councilors. At first he accused them of not telling people the truth while they were aware of who caused the fire.

When this gained him more followers, he raised questions about whether all the councilors were behind the fire incident. Even though not a shred of evidence to accuse any of them existed, the rumors did their job on people's frustration to cause a turbulent environment at the campus. This time, however, many people joined Neil's side, and not only the young white men.

They demanded the new councilors be elected. If anyone spoke about investigating the whole matter, they were ignored, and in some cases assaulted. The police appeared largely helpless to control the situation as more and more violence broke out. The young, strong, and foolish spread their terror, convinced no one would punish them. Those who tried to reason found more conflict than those who acted like animals. In turn, they increasingly found themselves resorting to violence as anger and vengeance brewed in them.

What happened next resembled a state of semi-anarchy. Violence quickly became rampant, and it didn't spare anyone. A few older gentlemen were severely beaten up. One of the officers working under the councilors committed suicide in a questionable manner.

Stories spread of rape and other sexual violence. Vincent witnessed Neil and two of his friends drag a guy into a room, where he could hear them beating him up, yet it seemed no one cared or anger consumed them too much to pay attention to the crimes. Neil only fed the situation and quickly grew into the wild man people would listen to. His brute power and that of his followers terrified many, including some of the police as they struggled to unite without the guiding hand of their deceased chief.

After a week of this, Vincent, Elysie, and their friends planned to leave the campus altogether. That seemed to be the obvious thing to do. The campus simply became too dangerous—far worse than what he had experienced with Rick's group in Brooklyn. It was a shame that the place that had once given the survivors hope to build a better future now resembled a broken-down society, a thug haven, order dictated by a gang-like existence.

The campus was pretty much finished. Inevitably, it would break down, then break some more, until it withered away into some smaller groups or gangs roaming the country like locusts feeding on whatever they could find. Vincent couldn't believe how quickly the campus had changed from a stable and civilized place he learned to enjoy so much to a barbarous and broken-down society.

Therefore, Vincent, Elysie, and their friends planned to go outside the city, somewhere in the vast country away from any major metropolitan areas, far away from Manhattan. They hoped to find another group of people who had managed to create a stable and safe community, but without someone like Neil trying to ruin it to gain his own power. Marcus suggested that westward or perhaps north to Canada would be the best direction to go. They would be homeless for a while, but at least they would have each other, and that's all that mattered.

CHAPTER 18

On the day Vincent and his friends had planned to leave the city, the folks protected by Neil organized a large rally. They invited everyone to gather at Columbus Circle, in front of the Royal International, to establish the great agreement on the new order of things at the campus. The councilors, who were basically helpless to make any difference on their own, had agreed this was perhaps the last chance to talk to the people and instill some sense into them.

Vincent had gathered whatever little stuff he could take in a rucksack for the long trip. The recent turn of events saddened him, but he was smart enough to know things wouldn't change for the better if a violent thug like Neil had any input into it, and it only looked like he would.

As he went to the medicine stockpiles, he managed to grab some of the most basic antibiotics and bandages that would be useful on a long trip. Before he met up with Elysie and the rest, he decided to use the bathroom.

The nearest one with lights was a bathroom he'd never been to before. When he stepped inside, the foul smell struck him, causing him to stop at the doorstep. It wasn't too uncommon to come across smelly bathrooms here, but this one seemed a notch worse than the others. He wanted to take a quick leak as fast as possible and get out.

As he took a few more steps inside, he saw Neil and one of his friends. They stood by a somewhat large bathtub filled with urine and people's excrement. It was obvious that the sanitation had gone badly wrong in this one. But something caught his attention as he peered a little closer. He saw a human hand sticking out of the tub as it made a single twitch, then nothing.

Vincent couldn't quite believe what he had seen. He stood motionless and in absolute shock. What had they done? A whisper of horror went through him of what the victim had gone through. The most horrible things ran through his head. He had never witnessed anything like this—something so cruel, humiliating, and wrong.

At first Neil and his friend, Number One, just stared at Vincent. Then Neil said, "You're all right. You're not one of them," as he motioned to the dark-skinned hand in the tub. They quietly walked past Vincent and out into the hallway, leaving him alone in the bathroom.

He stood there frozen for a few seconds as the stench of guilt for doing nothing and the feeling of powerlessness consumed him. He went over to the tub to pull the man out of it. As he lifted the body, it became clear that the man was dead. Vincent's life changed forever in that moment.

He walked out of the bathroom and his body shook. He stared blindly into space for a few minutes. Anger and rage at the injustice quickly consumed him. His head became hot as his hands became numb.

At that moment he knew what he would do. It was something he had never done before, but he must do it now. He set off for one of the rooms the campus police usually spent time in. Opening the door, Vincent found the room empty. The police either had gone to the rally or had left the campus altogether. It didn't matter. Feeling fire and rage, he left the room with a pistol and went to the rally.

Neil stood at the podium next to one of the councilors who was giving a speech, and his closest followers stood around him. Most carried guns because they were clearly trying to make a statement. It was the first time anyone outside the police was allowed to carry guns on the campus premises.

Some of the campus policemen stood there with him. It seemed that if they couldn't beat Neil, they might as well join him. None of it seemed to matter to Vincent. He didn't care for the guns or the people carrying them on the stage.

He walked to the front of the crowd. Those on the stage and those around him didn't seem to notice as Vincent pulled out the gun. A moment later a single shot broke the councilor's speech and Neil dropped to the ground.

A great silence doused the crowd. Neil's friend, the one Vincent had seen standing with him in the bathroom, reacted first. He reached for his own pistol hidden under his shirt, but Vincent noticed it, fired another shot, and killed him instantly. Neil's followers on the stage and those close by looked on in a state of shock.

Their leader and his closest aide fell down, side by side, in what seemed a single moment. Just as they had risen in power and seemed almost unstoppable, they had met the unthinkable end. The invincible leader was gone. Neil was the lion, the ruler of the jungle, the most dominant of men, but now a single shot had reduced him to lifeless flesh.

Vincent turned around and started passing through the crowd while in a daze, not quite realizing what he had done. Many people in the back couldn't tell who had pulled the trigger as he walked by. They only looked ahead in shock at what had just happened.

Soon the voices from the front started alarming everyone, "Murderer! Murderer! Arrest him!" Hearing this, Vincent started running as fast as he could. Nothing remained on his mind but the will to get away, not only from his pursuers, but from everything, including the truth of what he had just become—a killer.

He ran far up the avenue, the entire length of Central Park, and some more. His pursuers chased him, but the gap slowly increased between them. He didn't run so much to avoid being captured as to escape everything in his mind. Somehow he hoped his legs would carry him to that point.

Not knowing how to stop, Vincent zigzagged the streets with their obstacles, as most of the pursuers seemed to have given up. He ran far ahead, and it appeared at the moment his will to escape was stronger than anything chasing him. A gunshot changed that thought as a wild bullet missed him by a few feet and struck a stop sign ahead, causing him to freeze on the spot.

Vincent quickly turned around, raised his gun, and pulled the trigger three times in rapid succession. The bullets seemed to have met their targets, and the remaining three pursuers fell to the ground as if cut by a saw. He turned back and resumed his run. Not once did he glance back to see if people were still chasing him. He just ran. As if he was Lot running away from the destruction of Sodom, he didn't want to look back.

After two hours, Vincent's body started shaking. Snapping out of the running daze, he realized how exhausted he was. He came to a stop at the corner of 122nd Street and Riverside Drive, the area known as Morningside Heights, housing the empty classrooms of Columbia University.

Facing the sun half an hour from setting below the horizon, he bent over and clutched his knees. He hadn't even realized that he had been holding the instrument of death the entire time. He dropped it to the ground and closed his eyes. He could only hear himself breathe. Sodom was far behind him, but his thoughts were right there.

He didn't know how to feel. Confusion befell him. Was his life ending? Was it starting anew? What did he do back there? He wasn't even sure if he felt guilty. He only looked at the setting sun and wished so much that someone—even more that God—could hear him. Under his breath, he muttered.

"What did I do, what did I do, what did I do? Oh God, what did I do?"

His eyes watered with grief. "But God damn it if I was to let that scum get away with all those things!"

He took another deep breath and closed his eyes as tears came down his face. "I don't know anymore, but it still feels right. Forgive me."

Vincent sat on the ground and stared at the sun. His body slowly cooled off, and his thoughts calmed down, too. Soon the sun would be gone. His stomach started growling because he hadn't eaten since the morning.

He was supposed to eat with Elysie and the rest of his friends on their way out of the city. Well, that didn't pan out. Now he was starving. He looked around and wasn't quite sure where he was. He didn't remember being in this part of Manhattan before.

He tried to break into the small market stores hoping to find some cans, but it was to no avail. Most were locked with guardrails, making them difficult to break into. The only one he could get in had been looted before, and nothing edible remained. He started feeling a headache, and he realized he probably needed water a lot more than food; he couldn't remember the last time he had had something to drink.

He decided to go into the residential buildings. In the first one, all the apartments were locked, and he didn't have enough energy to break through the door. He went to another building and entered an apartment.

The first thing he saw were the dusty remains of a person on the floor, the casualty of the Scourge. He couldn't help feeling this was a grim sign. Nevertheless, he went straight for the fridge.

Besides the fungus still growing on some remnants of food, he found an unopened six pack of spring water. It briefly reminded him of his apartment in Brooklyn and how he had battled with the Scourge.

Next, he looked for some food in the cabinets but couldn't find any. Tired and exhausted, he lay on the couch and closed his eyes. He went to sleep hungry that night.

CHAPTER 19

The next morning, dazed Vincent spent a few hours looking for food and got lucky when he managed to get into one of the convenience stores and find some cans. There didn't seem to be much of a difference between a desperately hungry man and an animal when he came to scavenging for food. He ate with uncontrollable shaking and desperation.

After he filled up, loneliness consumed him, and he didn't know what to do. He couldn't go back, but he wanted to see Elysie so he could explain himself. What would she think of him now? She despised Neil and his followers just as he did. Maybe she wouldn't be so disappointed.

Who was he kidding? He disgusted himself with the thought. He was a killer! How could Elysie look at him the same again?

What about Mike, Aran, and Marcus? What would they have to say about that? Would they ever look at him the same? Would they understand what he had gone through? Could his action be possible to explain? Many questions ran through his head, but no answers.

That day courage left him, and it didn't return the following three days. After he decided he had had enough of desperation, he wanted to go back to reach out to Elysie and his friends. Walking back, he decided to take an unusual route, the one his instinct told him the fewest people from the campus would take.

All the way back, he thought of ways to find Elysie without coming out into the open. He thought the best he could do was to stand at a distance and watch. Maybe he would see his friends and somehow either signal or catch their attention; he hadn't quite figured that out.

When he made his way to a few blocks from the Royal International, he thought there wouldn't be a street he could go by without someone from the campus noticing him. He decided to go through the deserted nearby buildings instead. Trying to figure out the way through the maze of hallways and rooms eventually got him into the adjacent building and one step closer to his target.

It became a hard and a patience-testing task, but he managed to do it. He found himself in the building not far from the Royal International overlooking the plaza in the front. He sat there and watched.

Vincent could tell something was going on at the campus, but he couldn't quite put his finger on it. People were going in and out of the buildings, pockets of them forming outside, discussing something, and then going back in. Were they followers of Neil or someone else? He couldn't tell, but they looked uneasy in their mannerisms.

After a while he changed floors to get a higher and wider range of view. As the evening drew closer, he moved to a different building so he could look from a different angle. The last of the daylight hours slipped by, and he still didn't see anyone he wanted.

The next day he drew even closer. He found a spot in the building right across the Royal International. He remained extra careful since many of the campus folks frequented this building scavenging for anything of value. He moved as stealthily as he could, but it took a lot of time.

He eventually spotted a girl Elysie had befriended. He tried to remember her name. Joanna, he thought. They had all hung out together before, although not very much. She was in her mid-twenties, athletically built, with thin and curly reddish hair. He didn't know what her reaction would be if he approached her, but it was the best chance he had so far to find out what had happened to Elysie and his friends.

He watched her for a while, and when she came close enough to where he hid, he quietly called her name. At first she didn't respond, causing him to raise his voice a notch. She turned around and noticed him peeking behind a wall. She seemed startled and confused. When she reluctantly drew closer, she recognized him.

"Vincent? Is that you?" Joanna asked, whispering. "Oh, my God, it is you! You shouldn't be around here!"

"Long story, Joanna," Vincent replied. "I need to know what happened to Elysie."

"Oh, Vincent." Joanna shook her head.

"What? Tell me," he pleaded.

"She left two days ago with Mike and some other people," Joanna explained. "They couldn't stay here. Neil's guys were going to do something to them, and Mike didn't want anything to happen to her."

Joanna paused and turned around to make sure she wasn't suspicious to anyone. "She did leave you a message. She said they would go to a town called Parsippany, west of here, and probably stay there for some time. I think it's somewhere in Jersey."

"What about Marcus and Aran?" Vincent asked, worriedly.

"I'm pretty sure Marcus is still here," Joanna replied, whispering, "but I think Aran left with them."

That's what Vincent needed to know. Elysie, Mike, and Aran

were safe from Neil's thugs at the campus, but he still worried about Marcus. Even though Marcus had other friends there who would likely stand by his side, it wasn't farfetched for Neil's thugs to take vengeance on him, too. He said goodbye to Joanna and hurriedly disappeared among the buildings.

Vincent spent that night debating what to do. Should he stay there to make sure Marcus was all right or go after Elysie right away?

"How in the world could I help him?" Vincent asked himself. "Am I going to storm in with a gun and shoot more people if I see him in trouble?"

Because of this, Vincent's mind troubled him greatly. He didn't know what to do. He still felt rage and wanted to protect his friends, but at the same time he didn't know what would be the right action. The struggle and unrest in his mind made him feel nauseous. He wasn't going anywhere with it.

Curling up on the floor in one of the halls, making up the beautiful Lincoln Center of Performing Arts complex, he read the sign above him that said "Not for the privileged few, but for the many."

"Whatever you say, Mr. Rockefeller," he murmured to himself.

He didn't care about the place or the significance it once had as the venue where some of the world's finest performers amazed and inspired audiences of all walks of life. All he wanted was to forget the last few days of his life.

An image of sailing on a boat popped into his head as he stared at the sign above his head. It was a random thought, indeed, but it acted like an anesthetic. Before he realized, it eased his heart and mind, and soon he found himself basking in the warm sun sailing in his dreams.

CHAPTER 20

The next day Vincent left a message to Marcus via Joanna that he was all right and that he was on his way to Parsippany to meet with Elysie, hoping to see him there soon. He felt a little guilty leaving him behind again, but he reasoned that he had no other choice. On top of that, he didn't even know if Elysie was safe or whether she had made it to Parsippany.

It didn't seem all that unlikely for some gang to roam the outskirts of the city, making their trip much more dangerous. Aware of this possibility, Vincent's worst fear was that Elysie had run into a gang much like they had a few months earlier. He tried hard not to allow such assumptions to cloud his mind as he prepared for the trip.

Finding a map proved quite difficult because the world in the days prior to the Scourge relied on GPS devices instead of paper maps. Nevertheless, he found one in a small convenience store not too far from the Lincoln Center.

Reading the map, he learned that Parsippany was a large town in New Jersey close to the border with Pennsylvania, some twenty-five miles west of Manhattan. Once ranked as the best place to live in the state, now it was likely devoid of human residents other than a few stragglers like Mike, Aran, and Elysie and slowly rotting back to nature.

Vincent thought it would take two to three days to get there on foot, as he pictured Elysie would already be in the town. He figured if he tried hard enough he could get there in less than two days. After all, the weather seemed nice as August approached. It had been a full year since the Scourge.

Vincent looked at the pistol he carried and felt unsure what to do with it.

"Should I bring it along?" He wondered out loud. He viewed it as an evil instrument reminding him of what he had done not long before.

He reasoned that, no matter how much he hated the idea of using the pistol, it could come in handy if he ran into any trouble with people or wild animals.

"I would rather carry it and not have to use it," he concluded, "than be sorry I didn't have it."

It was early enough in the day, and he didn't want to waste any more time, even if it meant he would travel through the night. He wanted to get to Parsippany as quickly as possible, explain his actions, and maybe find some comfort among his friends.

Walking toward the Hudson River and examining the map, he tried to figure out the best way to get across. The Holland or Lincoln Tunnels, south of him, were dark and most likely flooded. Finding a boat or a kayak was an option, but he preferred to be on foot. George Washington Bridge north of him seemed the most desirable choice, so he decided on that route.

Food and water he would get on the way. He knew he could find canned food without trying too hard. Plenty of small convenience stores had canned food items, and it was likely that any apartment building would have some as well.

As for water, he worried a little more. The campus had purified water with various filtration systems, heating it and using purification pills. Now that he was on his own, he knew not to count on bottled water to be readily available, and he was aware how sick people could get from drinking contaminated water. Therefore, he put some thought into learning to purify water himself.

He remembered an older gentleman in Brooklyn mentioning some of the readily available filters could simply be clean towels or clothes. Pouring water through a couple of layers should catch much of the crud and various junk.

Next would be killing the microbes in the water, which the gentlemen insisted didn't necessarily need to be boiled, but kept at over 150 degrees Fahrenheit for a short time. This would save on time and fuel. Chlorination and iodine tablets, as well as high-quality compact filtration systems, worked well, but if they weren't available, using towels and heating the water should be the next best thing.

Vincent planned to find commercial purification tools. He thought they would work much faster than waiting to heat the water. In the meantime, however, he would trust the gentleman from Brooklyn.

Gathering all of his necessities in a new rucksack, he started moving toward the bridge. He felt like he was going hiking, and it brought memories of camping at Alleghany State Park, some seventy miles south of his home at Niagara Falls.

Vincent remembered how much he had liked nature before the Scourge. He'd wonder where the various trails were taking him. Those exciting nature walks would last a few hours before he would arrive back home. This time the trail would last a lot longer, but without the comfort of a home waiting for him at the end of the day.

After a long trek along Riverside Drive, while trying to remain stealthy, he approached George Washington Bridge. It was late in the day, and the sun was slowly fading on the distant horizon. It was the first time he had seen the bridge up close. Just under a mile long, the suspended bridge stood supported by two massive steel-plated towers. Straight up, he could see peregrine falcons nesting on top of the Manhattan side tower.

At almost a hundred years old, the bridge carried traffic at two levels. Even though it was empty now, it was still an impressive sight. Vincent wondered how little of the city he really knew. Before the Scourge, he didn't have much of an interest in seeing many landmarks in the city, but at that moment he found himself in amazement of the bridge.

It looked larger and more impressive than he had originally thought. The map showed a line; his eyes saw a great monument to human achievement. He must have seen it a thousand times in film, but actually being there was an overwhelming experience. Now he had to cross it.

Scouting the area, he wasn't surprised to see or hear no one else. He tried to be extra cautious, but he still felt like a novice. He wondered if someone was stalking him, watching his every move, toying with him before they attacked.

With too many thoughts going through his head, he decided to take the stairs, overgrown with foliage, toward a residential brick building overlooking the bridge. He climbed to the fifth floor, and to distract his worrying thoughts, he imagined how different the scene in front of him would have been before the Scourge. He pictured thousands of cars waiting to cross. Tonight, the bridge would hopefully get one walker across it.

When he felt a little more at ease, and the sun had completely set, he made a careful study of the nearby area under the moonlight. He wanted to scout out for the presence of others. He also had to make a choice about which level of the bridge to take. Both looked to have only a few abandoned vehicles scattered here and there, and while the top was nicely lit by the moonlight, the bottom provided better cover.

Therefore, he chose to take the bottom level, figuring to cross it in twenty minutes. Once again, he heard or saw nothing that caught his attention. Everything seemed to be quiet and peaceful. This put him at ease as he picked up his pace.

As he took a few steps on the ramp toward the bridge, he started feeling something that he couldn't explain. He wondered if he had experienced it before, but he couldn't distinguish it. It had come over him lightly, but it was unmistakable.

He felt it underneath what the regular five senses could perceive. It was something, perhaps, that the whole natural world, besides man, could feel. It was as if he had been numb to it his whole life but now had a tiny taste of it, and it gave him a unique understanding of the environment that surrounded him. Puzzled at first, he was unsure if he could trust it, but the more he let it sink into his being, the more he became aware of the things around him. He felt as if someone had taken a layer of a blurry screen off his eyes and mind, giving him a much better sense of his surroundings.

As he got closer to the Manhattan side tower, he heard faint voices. He stopped. In the distance he saw a glimpse of fire, right around where the tower stood. As he paid closer attention, he noticed an occasional figure blocking the light of the fire. His heart pounded, yet he still felt a duty to check it out.

Vincent walked slowly, trying hard to make out their voices and their conversation. He pondered what he should do if he found it necessary to fight. He didn't have much of a staging ground, cover, or confidence to proceed. However, he didn't turn back either. Instead, he hid himself in the darkness and observed.

The people he watched seemed immersed in their conversation. He could tell from their voices that most, if not all, were men. This was a bad sign. He learned from the campus police that the gangs in and around the city were exclusively men, with a few straggler women who were their toys, either forcibly or willingly. Their language alone confirmed they were up to no good.

Everyone tried to act tough, not only with how they talked, but in how they carried themselves or treated others in the group. There was definitely a hierarchy, and those of higher status seemed to have permission to muscle those of the lower status. It was much the same as a wolf pack.

One of the guys, a rough-looking person with messy hair flowing down his shoulders, stood out from the rest. Definitely of higher status, he didn't muscle anyone around him. Those who talked to him kept a slightly greater distance than they did with the others, respecting the space around him. When he talked, others listened.

This looked to be some sort of a den for them, but Vincent doubted people like this stayed in one place for very long. There were sleeping bags lying around, a small rollout mattress, rucksacks, cans, clothes, and various other goods. Vincent couldn't imagine why they would want to be there other than to control who crossed the bridge.

Vincent's eyes soon focused on a person who sat on the floor against the metal structure of the bridge with hands hugging at its bent knees. As his eyes adjusted more, he saw that it was a woman. He drew closer to get a better look at her. The more he observed, he could tell she was battered, with long curly blonde hair partly covering the right side of her bruised face. Her skinny pale hands were scarred and tied with rope to a chain, which was secured to one of the metal beams of the bridge. He guessed she was no more than thirty-five. Her eyes looked exhausted with no will to live.

Sadness consumed him, and he couldn't imagine what she had gone through, but he knew it must have been awful. He took great pity on her and wanted to help, but he didn't know how. He felt helpless and reached for the gun strapped to him. He remembered how easily he had shot Neil, Number One, and those who had chased him, but he wondered what had happened to his confidence now. I just can't, he thought. It would be suicide. There must be another way to help her.

Playing out various scenarios in his head, Vincent remained hidden in the darkness as the familiar sense of rage crept in, slowly taking over. But before the rage could consume him completely, he came to the conclusion that the best he could do was to wait for everyone to fall asleep and then sneak in and free the woman. If it came down to fighting, then he would set the rage free and take out as many of them as possible. One thing was for sure; he wouldn't leave her there that night.

As the night wore on, one by one, the gangsters went to sleep around the fires they had made as Vincent waited. A few of them approached and fondled the woman. She squirmed away, but they seemed too tired to do anything else. One guy smacked her hard across the face, went away, and lay on a bunched-up sleeping bag. Vincent pulled the gun out and nearly shot the guy but somehow managed to tell himself to just sit and wait.

After a while, when Vincent was confident all the gangsters were in deep sleep, he took a deep breath and carefully walked out of the darkness and slowly toward the woman. She appeared asleep, too. He didn't want to startle her, inadvertently causing her to make noise. So he picked up a small stone and threw it at her legs while a short distance away.

She didn't seem to respond, and he threw another. She opened her eyes and gasped when she saw him. He put his finger over his lips to let her know to be quiet. She just stared at him and seemed confused at what was going on. Vincent slowly approached her on his toes, all the while looking around to make sure no one else woke up.

When he came to the woman's side, he knelt down and once again put his finger on his lips. She just stared at him. He pulled out a Swiss knife to cut the rope, but she pulled away in fright. He stopped and then pointed to the rope that strapped her to the chain. He slowly approached her again, and this time she remained still while her eyes still indicated mistrust. He proceeded to cut the rope.

All of a sudden he heard some noise behind him. He immediately turned around and pulled out his gun. Just before he pulled the trigger, something told him to stop. The gangster who made the noise fifteen feet away slowly staggered to his feet, seemingly clueless Vincent was even there. Still, just a single heart pulse could have triggered the gunfight. Vincent watched as the gangster walked some distance away and then started urinating off the bridge. When finished, he walked back, slouched on the mattress, and went back to sleep.

Vincent let out a slow sigh of relief while his heart pounded in his ears. He put the gun away, turned around, and continued to cut the rope. The progress felt agonizingly slow, and he was becoming frustrated. A few times he had to stop to take a deep breath before his frustrations got the better of him. Even though it felt like an eternity, the rope was eventually cut all the way through.

Vincent signaled to the woman to get up and start moving. He held her by the hand, and both of them tiptoed between the sleeping gangsters as sweat poured down his face. Before darkness hid them completely, Vincent glanced back and saw the guy who had struck the woman earlier now sleeping comfortably. A sense of injustice powered through him like a lightning bolt, and he felt the desire to reach for his gun again, but before he could do anything the woman yanked his hand and he snapped out of it.

Within a few minutes they came down the bridge and walked onto the street looking back to make sure no one had followed. It seemed pleasantly quiet. They proceeded to walk a few blocks until they arrived at George Washington Avenue, a wide road leading to and from the bridge. There, they made a right, away from the bridge. With every street block they passed, Vincent felt more at ease. Still, he watched his every step and made as little noise as possible.

About a mile down, they came to another avenue, Broadway, and at this point Vincent motioned they stop. He felt exhausted, and having eaten little that day, fatigue was taking over.

"I think we are safe now," he said under his breath. "I'm too tired to continue any more. Let's rest in one of these apartment buildings."

The woman gave a quick nod in agreement. He walked into one of the nearby apartment buildings, and she followed. He used one of his small flashlights to find their way up the dark stairs. Luckily, one of the apartments on the top floor wasn't locked, so they made their way in.

Inside, the bathroom door creaked on their left, and in it on the floor laid the dusty remains of a Scourge victim. They closed the door and went into the living room. There they sat down on the couch. They didn't talk, but only stared ahead as if in a daze.

After a few minutes Vincent got up and opened the window to the living room to let some fresh air in. He turned around and saw the woman curl up on the couch and close her eyes. He switched off his flashlight, lay on the floor a few feet from her, and quickly fell asleep. The night was finally over.

CHAPTER 21

The sun's rays slowly crept up on Vincent's face through the window. He put his hand over his eyes, hoping it would be a comfortable enough position to continue sleeping. After a while it became obvious that it wasn't going to work out that way.

He slowly opened his eyes, still drowsy from sleep and the events from the night before. He looked up and stared at the window for a few moments. He could see the clear sky in midday. He checked his watch. It read well past three in the afternoon, however accurate that was.

Not that time mattered much in this world, but it still seemed comforting to keep track of it. Vincent felt they must have slept for twelve hours or more. He propped up and saw the woman sleeping on the other side of the couch. He looked at her and thought how exhausted she must have been to still be sleeping. After all, he had just had a long day, but who knew what she had gone through.

Vincent slowly got up to avoid waking her and then headed to the kitchen. There he drank some water left over from last night and freshened up with moist towelettes he had come across a few days earlier.

When he returned to the living room, the woman had woken up. She seemed groggy, and as soon as she saw him, she got into a

134

defensive position. Her reaction confused him, and he slowly lowered himself to the ground to her eye level. She eased up a bit but still emanated her discomfort with him.

"How do you feel?" Vincent asked in a soft voice.

She didn't respond and looked out the window.

He felt slightly confused by her reaction and tried again. "I never introduced myself. My name is Vincent."

She remained quiet.

Still confused by her silence, Vincent continued. "As you may have figured out by now, I'm not one of those people who's been hurting you. I'm from the Plaza campus you might have heard about, and I'm here to-"

"I'm Marie," she responded, abruptly.

Surprised by her sudden answer, he said the first thing that came to his mind, "Well, Marie, uh . . . are you okay?"

She gave a quick nod and focused her vision on the floor. Even though her silence slightly irritated him, Vincent didn't want to press her too much. He felt he needed to establish some rapport with her, make her feel more at ease, and figure out what to do next.

"I need to use the bathroom," Marie said and got up. "So, if you don't mind, I'd like to go to the next apartment to do that."

"Sure," he responded, glad to hear a little more from her. "Let me help you get in there."

The apartment next door was unlocked, so Vincent didn't have to do anything to let her in. He proactively closed the door after her to give her an understanding that he would respect her privacy, which was something he knew she didn't have while with the gang. The thought of that brewed up anger inside him. He wanted to enact justice on the gang and felt a little ashamed he hadn't done anything.

He remembered again how, a little less than a week ago, he had killed Neil and Number One and wounded or killed three more of his scum followers. Yesterday, however, he had acted like a sheep hiding from the wolves—defenseless, scared, with a thought of fleeing the scene. Now more than ever he wanted to be the wolf.

After ten minutes Vincent turned around from the gaze he had fixed on the building across the street and, startled, found Marie sitting quietly on the couch. He didn't realize she had come back, but now that she was there, he thought it was a good time to find out more about her.

"Hey, listen," he started the conversation. "I'm not going to try to pry out of you what you don't want to tell me, but I thought at least we ought to know a little about one another."

That started well, he thought, and just as he was about to continue telling her about himself, she broke her silence.

"I come from a small town north of Binghamton, west of here," she explained. "I'd pretty much lived there my whole life until, well, you know, everyone got sick and turned into dust. Most of the people from my town are gone, but some of us survived. We stayed there for a period of time, living from day to day, making ends meet the best we knew how."

She paused for a second and sighed. "One day we picked up a signal on the radio about the survivors gathering at The Plaza Hotel in Manhattan, like it was some kind of a refuge. A safe place. After a while, some of us decided to try to go there."

She sighed again as if to control her emotions. "When we got close to Manhattan we ran into the gang. We tried to fight back, but there were too many. They killed some, others ran away, and they captured me."

Marie stopped talking. Vincent, impressed that she had spoken this much, knew not to ask her any details. He decided to respect that and let her decide when she was ready to tell more of her story.

He felt obliged to tell her his story.

"Thank you for letting me know that, Marie. I, uh, I'm from Brooklyn. Well, actually I'm originally from Niagara Falls, but I moved to Brooklyn about seven or eight months before the Scourge hit, or the Scourge of God—that's what we call it at The Plaza Hotel. I got involved with some survivors from around Brooklyn, and we eventually made our way to The Plaza campus; that's what we called the community there."

He noticed that she was paying attention to him and felt better about continuing his story. "To be honest, it was a good place for a while. We had a good structure going, and it attracted a lot of survivors. We pretty much had everything a normal society would have. We had rules, good leadership, and each of us had our duties. Unfortunately, it also attracted some bad folks who decided to live by their own rules."

Vincent sighed and felt guilty about giving her the bad news. "But then a fire broke out at the hotel, and that's when things went downhill. Some people started causing trouble. It became a rough place.

"Things got a little ugly, and it wasn't safe for me to stay there, so I had to leave. Some of my friends left, too, while others stayed. I decided to find the friends who had left before me. Anyway, that's how I got on the bridge."

Vincent avoided telling her about killing Neil and the others. He doubted she wanted to hear that story after what she had gone through.

That day Marie and Vincent didn't do much, mainly because there wasn't much of a day left. Stepping out into the neighborhood, they focused on gathering the essentials and whatever small supplies they felt they needed. Vincent also came across a police car and grabbed two loaded pistol clips without mentioning it to Marie. They talked occasionally, almost just enough to avoid an awkward silence.

Even so, every once in a while they found themselves glancing at each other not knowing what to say. This awkwardness made Vincent think of Elysie and how easily he could talk to her. He couldn't remember ever feeling uncomfortable around her from the moment they had met, and now he missed her more than ever. He didn't think it would be easy, but the hurt he felt now cut deep into his heart. He shed a tear in secret so that Marie wouldn't notice and quickly brushed it away thinking of something, anything, other than Elysie. Otherwise, he knew he would be overtaken by emotions.

Vincent, slightly scared, didn't know what to do with Marie. She seemed so fragile, and he felt a great deal of compassion for her. He didn't have a plan on how to proceed. She had come into his plans unannounced, and it had changed things around.

He felt he couldn't offer her much of a future. He didn't think the campus would be a good place to take her if it resembled the one he left. Perhaps it would be worth reaching out to Marcus or Joanna to find out the situation there, but if it turned out to be just as bad, the only other option was to take her to Parsippany, which meant he and his friends would have to take care of her.

The next day Vincent woke up with the sun on his face again. He noticed that Marie wasn't there. He thought she might be using a bathroom in one of the apartments, but after half an hour he went looking for her.

After searching a few apartments, he started believing she had left him for good. He felt sad and wondered why she would just walk away. He thought he had treated her right, but maybe what she had gone through was too much and she needed some time alone. After all, he was a stranger to her.

Feeling sad and confused, he wanted to know she was all right. She seemed to be a good person caught in a horror story. Slowly, that sadness was joined by his desire to avenge her. Those on the bridge ought to be punished, he thought, and by God they'd better be soon.

Groggy with a sense of abandonment, Vincent walked outside the building. There on the steps he saw Marie, sitting and looking at the dandelions springing from a crack in the street. He didn't know what to say, but he felt relieved she was there. He quietly sat next to her and stared at the street.

After a few minutes of thinking, he spoke, "I can take you to the campus if you want. I'm going there to see a friend and maybe take him to Parsippany, but if the campus is in bad shape you can come with us."

She kept looking at the dandelions, and without changing her gaze, replied in a soft voice, "Yeah, that would be nice."

After a few moments she started to open up. "I, I don't know how to feel anymore. I'm not sure I even want to live anymore. My life, it's ruined. I don't see the point anymore. Why keep going? I had a family. Now they're all gone. Everything I had is lost. Why keep going?"

Tears opened up, as did her feelings. Vincent remained lost for words.

"I've had it with this life. I don't know what keeps me going anymore," she sobbed as more tears fell down her cheeks. "When will this be over?"

There was nothing he could think of besides showing her that he cared. He gently put his hand on her shoulder and said the only thing that came to his mind, "It'll be okay. You'll get through this. I don't know everything you've been through, but somehow I believe you'll be okay. All this will pass, and you'll find yourself happy again."

A little smile came across Marie's face, and Vincent smiled back.

He didn't know if she believed anything he said, but she brushed her tears aside, which gave him encouragement that somehow, however unlikely, she would be all right.

They made small talk about what made dandelions so captivating to look at, and the atmosphere eased some more. They ate food and made plans to head out to the campus the following day. She seemed ready to go that very day, but Vincent held it off. He told her he wanted to rest his back a little longer before they made their way down. In truth, he knew what he planned to do that night; he had some unfinished business to take care of.

As evening approached, Marie got ready to call it a night. Vincent knew he was about to get started, but he didn't want to give Marie any hints about his plans. Instead, he pretended he was getting ready to go to sleep, too.

For a few moments he debated whether he should mention something about what he was going to do. For all he knew, Marie would have agreed with him, but now that they had broken the ice between them, he felt obligated to keep her away from knowing his plans to avenge her. He waited for her to fall asleep, wrote a quick note and left it by her side, and then slipped into the night.

CHAPTER 22

It hadn't been long since Vincent's last dangerous encounter, but it felt a lifetime since he was in control. He felt he would need a whole lot of that tonight. He recalled the numbness to all feelings when he had shot Neil and others and how decisive his actions were.

Now he hoped to get that confidence back. He wasn't sure about the outcome, but that didn't seem to matter as much as doing something about the gang.

The thought of God judging what he planned to do came into his mind. He wondered why of all times God would enter his mind now. Perhaps he questioned his own actions and needed some assurance in what he was doing, or God was choosing to step in and knock on his conscience to encourage or dissuade him.

Nevertheless, he made himself believe his decision was right and there was no other option. Perhaps this was meant to be, and it was God's will. God would punish those deserving it. Silence means consent, he reasoned, and since he didn't hear a clear voice in his head, God must be consenting. Excitement overcame him, and he tried to place himself into the zone he needed to carry his actions.

As Vincent approached Washington Bridge, he became more observant of himself and the environment; his steps became more elegant and slow, his ears sensitive to the faintest sound, and his eyes sharper. The bright moon above appeared like the sun. It paved the way clear, and he got closer and closer.

All of a sudden he heard something unusual. Footsteps. Soon enough, voices followed. He hid and watched, and then the shapes began to appear. He counted six. They seemed to act a little too careless. They should know better, he thought, but then again, if no harm had come their way in a while, why would they worry? Vincent just watched, knowing there were more of them somewhere, around the corner, or most likely back at the bridge two or three blocks away.

They carried weapons and some supplies in their bags, and he could hear juggling of liquid from one of them. There was little doubt in his mind these were the guys from the bridge. Now he debated whether to attack now or wait a little longer. The shots would echo, and he was certain they would be heard on the bridge, alerting the rest of the gang, but if he waited too long and they got closer to the bridge, he didn't want to face more of the gang all at once.

Vincent wanted to strike them in smaller groups, not upfront like he did Neil and his Number One. That was stupid, he thought, and he had lucked out big time on that one. Now he wanted to be more tactical.

As the gangsters walked up Fort Washington Avenue, careless in their attitude of anyone or their surroundings, spread out wide on the street, Vincent quietly followed and then started feeling the intense fire inside of what he was about to do. Time seemed to apply a brake. His heart rate dropped, his breathing slowed, and his eyes got bigger.

The next moment two loud gunshots shattered silence. Before the gang knew what hit them, two of their guys fell to the ground. The first gangster to turn around opened his eyes wide in confusion and fright. Then another gunshot went off, and he, too, fell over. One gangster started running away, and the other went for cover.

Vincent immediately pressed forward.

By the moment the one hid behind a car, Vincent already had him in his line of sight. Two quick shots left the gangster slouched on the ground as he immediately went in pursuit of the last one.

Turning left on the next street, Vincent followed him into a dark, overgrown park, quickly closing the gap between them. He raised his pistol, but all of a sudden the gangster disappeared from his view.

Not sure if his victim had tripped, Vincent held from shooting. A quiet sigh came from the darkness a few yards ahead. Quickly, finding him on the ground, Vincent didn't hesitate to pull the trigger before his victim could fight back or plead for mercy. Another shot rang through the night, breaking the silence once again.

He pressed forward while reloading his pistol. At this time the intense internal fire released him, and he found himself feeling again. For a moment, he felt sorrow for the last gangster he shot, but the remorse was fleeting, as he forced his mind to think about his next move.

He headed toward the gang's den and knew they must have heard the gunshots. At that time, he wished he had some kind of suppressor or silencer to use with the pistol, but it was too late now. He had already announced his coming.

Walking the street, he came to the intersection close to one of the ramps going up to the bridge. He waited there for a few minutes, hidden in the darkness among the brick buildings, carefully listening to anything that may give him a hint what his opponents may be doing. The uncertainty of the situation assaulted his nerves, but he remained cool and observed.

A few moments later he heard someone coming from his right. About 65 yards away, he vaguely saw a few figures walking past his line of sight. They came from the lower level of the bridge, then onto the parallel street to his own.

Vincent couldn't tell how many there were at first, but he guessed no more than five. He figured there still must be some left on the bridge. These gangsters didn't talk at all. It seemed they were in a perplexed mood going to check out what had happened.

As they disappeared behind the building, continuing their way down the street, Vincent considered his two choices: either go after these gangsters first and then come back to the bridge, or vice versa. How many were left on the bridge, he didn't know, but he felt if he was stealthy enough that he could surprise these gangsters like he did the first group.

Quickly, and as quietly as he could, he hustled up to the street corner. There, he saw there were indeed five of them, perfectly lit by the moonlight some twenty yards away. They walked away from him. Pausing for a moment, he started feeling the fire burn inside him as desire for action quickly eclipsed any other thought.

Vincent followed them, first at a fast-paced walk and then into a run. As soon as one of the gangsters turned around and said, "Hey! Who-" Vincent fired. Shots echoed, and the fight was on.

The others turned around in shock and reached for their weapons. Vincent kept pulling the trigger at them one after another, shooting two more in the chest before anyone fired back. Managing to pull off a few shots, the gangsters looked too confounded to take a good aim.

Vincent kept moving and shooting, closing the distance between them even more. His mind didn't think about fear; it was either him or them. There was no going back.

He shot one more, while the last one jumped over the railings and ducked. Vincent quickly moved farther up and peeked over the railings, having outflanked his opponent. He saw the guy crouched on the ground, sticking out his gun over the railings, shooting aimlessly at nothing. Vincent took one shot at him, ending the fight.

All this had lasted no more than fifteen seconds, but the damage was lasting. Vincent was certain the remaining gang in the den knew something bad had happened. It was much too close, and much too loud, for them not to realize it.

A muffled radio noise came through on one of the fallen bodies. Investigating for a few seconds, Vincent realized that the gang on the bridge was trying to reach out to their comrades. It didn't surprise him to see them using shortwave radios like they did at the campus, but he didn't plan on answering just yet. He wanted to let them dwell in uncertainty as he jumped over the railings and started moving toward the bridge.

When he realized this path would take him to the upper level, he stopped at the point by the rails where he thought he would have a good line of sight of someone coming from the lower level. This, unfortunately, didn't turn out to be a good spot. He couldn't see much of anything due to darkness.

He moved farther up to the short median bridge, connecting the incoming and outgoing traffic on the upper level. He looked at the street below, which turned out to be another ramp going to the upper level. It seemed there were too many ramps and roads, and he didn't know where they all led.

This quickly put Vincent in a dilemma because he didn't have a clear plan on how to approach the rest of the gang. He had no idea where they would come from. The feeling of being exposed came over him. Thoughts ran through his head: Hide! Abort! No, keep going! Figure something out!

A familiar paranoia invaded his mind—the flashback of being chased with Elysie a few months ago. This time, he wouldn't let it linger any longer. He observed there were at least six ramps getting traffic to or from the bridge, but he didn't let it confuse him. He took a deep breath and carefully scrutinized his choices.

One of the ramps looping to the right of him looked to provide good cover of darkness leading to the lower level of the bridge and the gang's lair. It appeared to run parallel to the ramp those six guys got off, he thought, which meant they would probably expect trouble to come from there, not here. That should be my path.

Having decided on his way in, Vincent went back, got off the bridge, and found himself on a grassy area next to the ramp of his choice. He hopped onto the ramp and faced a dark tunnel ahead. He looked up and saw the little median bridge he had used. His fears were confirmed seeing how exposed he was up there in the moonlight.

He went forward into the dark tunnel. A cold wind came over his face, and he felt the chill. He couldn't make out what was ahead, but he kept listening as carefully as he could and kept moving.

On the right, he saw metal bars, much like those he expected to see in a jail. The light of the bright night peeked through them, and he felt a sense of abandonment from the comfort of this world. It was raw and unforgiving, a merciless rejection that devoured all hope. He shook it off as best as he could and focused on his task.

When Vincent moved up a little, he heard noises some distance behind him. He realized that some of the gangsters, if not all, had come to investigate the second shootout, taking the parallel ramp to the one he was on. It seemed pointless going after them because he could already perceive the lights of the den ahead of him. Now was his chance to attack the divided gang—first at the den, if any remained there, and then those behind him.

Moving a little closer, he saw two guys standing there talking around a fire lit inside a garbage barrel. They seemed uneasy, telling quick jokes to each other, while their laughter gave the nervousness away. One had a shotgun, and the other a fully automatic military-grade rifle.

They would jerk their weapons each time they heard any noise, whether caused by a restless bird, the creaking of the metal structure of the bridge, or the wind. Vincent stopped. A quick shot of fear went through him thinking they might have heard him.

So far, everyone he had attacked had been caught by surprise; he had the advantage, but these guys had their guns raised, most likely aware something bad had happened near the bridge. He thought of what element of surprise he could use now. Should he try to approach them pretending to be one of their own and then strike? Or should he sneak as far as he could, without being noticed, and then fire in quick succession?

Luckily for him, they stood in front of the light sticking out like sore thumbs, while he blended in the background. Other than that, all he trusted was his accuracy. Nothing else.

Vincent carefully looked beyond them but couldn't see anyone else. It was just the three of them, and he was glad they stood close to each other, making them much easier targets to hit. He raised his gun and aimed at the first one, then the second, in preparation of what he was about to do.

He then walked slowly toward them with his back against the railing. He made a few steps and stopped, a few more, and stopped. It surprised him that they still couldn't tell that someone was barely thirty feet away from them, but he didn't want to push his luck. When he reached a distance he thought would no longer conceal him, he burst forward, firing rapidly.

Barely having time to react, the two gangsters found themselves overwhelmed. Firing from left to right, Vincent killed the first one instantly, while the other fell over, badly wounded and helpless to fight back. He moved up to their fallen bodies while looking to see if anyone else was around. Assured he was alone, he put the injured gangster out of his misery.

Reloading his pistol, he turned around, took a deep breath, and then started moving down the ramp to seek the rest of the gang, still intently focused on finishing his job. Once again, he heard radio noise coming from one of the bodies; the others were trying to find out what had happened. They didn't get a response.

It was the third time the gang had heard gunfire and gotten no response from their friends. The gangsters looked at each other in shock and fear as they stood over the scene of the second shootout. They had never had anything like this happen to them. They had had run-ins with other gangs, but they had always managed to come out on top.

Now they had no idea what kind of killer or killers preyed on them. They quickly convinced each other that it was better to leave the scene than to face some unknown death sower, so they did. Less than two minutes later they came across the bodies of the first shootout. Now they were even more convinced they had made the right choice and hurried off.

At this point Vincent came down the ramp and onto the street. The intense fire inside him had withered away a bit, and in its place came second-guessing. He couldn't hear anyone, and he had no idea where the last of the gang was hiding. He started thinking they might be waiting for him somewhere.

Still moving forward, Vincent slowed down and then stopped. He monitored everything around him but heard nothing. The remainder of the fire left him at this time, while the silence became a little frustrating. He almost felt like he was on the stage of some sick play while the whole world watched.

After half an hour of moving up and down the ramps, on and off the bridge, with extreme caution followed by the deathly stillness of the night, he came to the scene of his second shootout.

Slowly, Vincent gained confidence that no one was around him other than the dead bodies of his victims, and he eased his posture.

THE SCOURGE OF MAN

He felt assured that the gang was practically destroyed. If they were still around with a will to fight, they would have attacked him by now. Still, he didn't let himself feel overconfident and frequently stopped and ducked at any sound he heard, just to be sure.

He went back to the gang's lair to investigate what they might have left there. The fire from the burning garbage barrels provided some heat, but the wind on the bridge caused him chills. He wondered why they would want to be up there with all the wind when they had the whole city full of buildings to sleep in.

He saw the two dead gangsters lying there, and the thought that he had shot and killed numerous people that night entered his mind. He felt a sense of wrong. He felt confusion. Things had happened so quickly. Perhaps in some sense it had been easy to end that many lives. But now he wasn't sure whether he approved of it all.

A few moments later Vincent came across the rope and chains where he had found Marie two days earlier. They appeared cold and brutal, hanging there from the metal structure of the bridge. Blood stains coated some of the rings. Sadness overcame him as he thought about what she must have gone through, and it justified his actions.

"Those bastards got what they deserved," he said to himself, angrily, yet it still felt a little odd. Somehow his actions didn't smell right. Something was missing, but he didn't want to try to figure it out tonight. His justice didn't feel great, just better, and it made a world's difference to him. Things will be different now, he thought in his heart. I may have found my purpose.

When Vincent got back to the apartment, darkness still consumed the streets. Marie lay steadfast on the couch in deep sleep. He took the note that he had left in case he didn't come back and instead carefully placed the chains as a gift for her—a sign of justice that her captors had gotten what they deserved.

As he quietly sat back on the wooden chair opposite the chains, he debated whether or not his bringing back the chains was a good idea. Marie could wake up and be reminded of the horrible past she had gone through. Thinking more about it, he realized that the chains would be the last thing she would want to see.

Again, knowing that her captors, or at least a majority of them, were destroyed, could be a good feeling—at least it was to him. He still had anger in his heart, but Marie was probably full of shock and sorrow. He found it too tiring to figure out the right thing to do with the chains, so he quietly took them off the table and put them away.

He leaned back against the wall and gazed outside the window at the moonlit night. He thought about nothing for a few moments, then lay down on the floor, closed his eyes, and fell into deep sleep.

CHAPTER 23

Waking from her sleep, Marie lazily walked up to the window and saw the light of the day. The bright, sunny day greeted her with patches of white clouds against an azure blue sky. It gave her a quick sense of bliss—something she didn't think she could feel again. However, she didn't want to be in it for long. The delight felt strange to her. There was no rationale for it, not after the horror she had gone through. Why then did she feel it? she asked herself.

Looking to the right of her, she saw Vincent sleeping on the floor. He lay motionless and silent and was barely noticeable. Only the rhythmic movement of his diaphragm up and down with each breath gave him away. Marie felt at peace seeing him like that, quiet and resting like a harmless little baby.

To her, he was a straggler, a mysterious one, but not the kind who seemed malicious. If he meant to harm her, he would have done it by now, she reasoned. Nothing could stop him because he was clearly stronger, yet he chose not to. She wouldn't put her guard down yet, but at least she wasn't worrying as much as before.

She freshened up and waited for Vincent to wake up. Half an hour turned into an hour, then two. She started feeling a little restless and went outside. She walked around the city block appreciating the chirps of the birds that made their nests in the trees and buildings, all the while keeping her guard for any humans.

When she returned to the apartment, Vincent still slept in the same position as before. This time she looked closer to make sure he wasn't dead and wondered why he slept for so long. After all, she thought, he went to sleep around the same time she did. Why, then, was he sleeping for such a long time? She debated on waking him, but Vincent moved his arm and slowly opened his eyes.

She quickly said, "Good morning, um, how are you feeling? Well, it's more like late afternoon. Do you feel all right?"

Vincent appeared dazed from his sleep. He looked at her and then at the sun, which peeked through the window.

"Oh, uh, oh man, I must have been out for a while," he said, groggily, while rubbing his eyes. "Umm, I'm fine. I must have been tired. How are you?"

"I'm fine," Marie responded. "I wondered why you were sleeping for so long. I didn't want to wake you because you looked like you really needed it."

"Umm, yeah." He cleared his throat. "I must have. I wonder what time it is. The sun looks like it's well past noon."

"Oh, it is," she confirmed, "but if you needed the sleep, I understand." She didn't want to sound like she was rushing him to get up.

He rubbed his eyes again and stretched his arms. He looked as if his muscles were sore, and Marie felt if it wasn't for her, he would have gladly gone back to sleep for another hour or two.

"I wonder if it's too late to go to the campus today," Vincent said, followed by a yawn. "We have about four miles. That can take us into sunset by the time we get there."

Marie stood silently. She wanted to go. She felt tired and restless of the place they were in. It almost didn't matter where they went, as long as they moved. Vincent looked at her for a moment and then walked to the window and stared outside.

"Actually, I think we should be fine," he added. "We can always find a place somewhere to spend the night."

This pleased Marie, even though she still had uneasy feelings about the campus. To her, those at the campus could be just as bad as the gang on the bridge. She trusted no one else, besides Vincent to a degree, and the idea of getting involved in some group of people she didn't know scared her.

"You said we should scout it out, right?" she asked.

"Yeah," he replied. He turned away from the window and looked at her. "I wouldn't just walk in there. I want to make sure it didn't deteriorate into some anarchist hell. I hope it didn't, but I don't know right now, and I feel it's safer for both of us to investigate."

Marie nodded in approval. "All right. I'm ready to go then." Reaching into her backpack, she took something out. "Oh, and I got you some food. Here, take it."

She handed him canned fruit. Vincent seemed pleasantly surprised that someone had given him food, thanked her, and took the can. He polished off the contents in less than two minutes, put his clothes into the backpack, and got ready for the trip.

Within twenty minutes they were out the door and on their way to the campus. They left behind an empty apartment and the blood-stained chains he hid in the bedroom closet, a symbol of enacted vengeance.

Early on, the trip seemed pleasant. They talked but remained alert to any dangers. Unfortunately, the air felt hot and the sun merciless, and as time wore on, their exchanges became less frequent, almost as if to reserve their energy to keep moving.

A few times Vincent thought he heard something, and both quickly hid away, but they didn't encounter any humans, only birds, occasional rodents, and a few stray dogs. He told her how he had snuck by the campus the last time, so he chose the same path today. The only caveat was that it would take a long time. Halfway through, he made a few modifications since neither had the energy to zigzag through all the buildings and streets as he had done before.

As the sun slowly set, they decided to find a suitable place to sleep before they continued the next day. Vincent suggested a high floor since there was much less chance of someone finding them there.

"The higher you go, the safer you are," he explained.

They came across a large building on West 66th Street and Columbus Avenue. It was a tall apartment tower, with large windows overlooking the juncture of Broadway and Columbus Avenue, as well as a good view of the Royal International, a quarter of a mile away.

They walked up eighteen stories, with a flashlight leading the way in the dark stairway. It was pretty much as far as their legs could carry them. Managing their way into one of the apartments, Vincent peered out the large window and took in the serene view of the Manhattan skyline in front of him, looking so peaceful and uncharacteristically natural in the last rays of the sun's day.

Even though they could have been higher, Vincent felt they were standing on top of the world. The vastness of the city below and the sky above absorbed him. Marie stood next to him and stared out as well. The birds perched on the ledges didn't seem to mind their visitors on the other side of the glass. The full colors and shades painted a sedate picture. Silence took over. No words needed to be spoken. This was beautiful.

The following day Vincent woke up before Marie. He looked outside and saw the peaceful city basking in the morning light. He also saw people. They were from the campus, and Vincent thought they must be going out to do some of the chores or something more sinister.

It had been less than a week since he had last seen the campus, which was in a turbulent state then, and he questioned how much of that had changed by now. It seemed like it had been months. Vincent felt like he was in an episode of "The Twilight Zone." Time couldn't explain actions or feelings, and he didn't know if he could tell the difference between a week and a month.

He felt hunger pangs, but he didn't want to eat before Marie got up. They had been sharing food so far, and he felt guilty taking something without her. It seemed unfair.

He kept looking out the window. He remembered the first nights he spent in Brooklyn, how scared he felt and how the evening sunlight danced shadows in his bedroom and brought him comfort. He imagined how scared Marie must be about joining the campus. He felt the same way when he moved to New York City. It wasn't easy for him, and he knew it wouldn't be for her either.

When Marie woke up, they had breakfast. He could tell she was nervous.

"Hey, don't worry," he reassured her. "You won't join the campus unless we're both sure it's safe."

She seemed to appreciate his reassurance, but she didn't say anything.

Coming down from the tower, they carefully bounced between different buildings, avoiding everyone in the path while checking them out. They wanted to see how people behaved and talked and what they were doing so they could get any idea of the current state of the campus.

The last time Vincent visited the campus, tension ruled the atmosphere. The campus itself barely held up as a community. Neil was gone, but his followers still roamed around, unsure what to do next. They showed fear, and sometimes those were the worst opponents to have.

This time, however, the people seemed a little more at ease. They weren't on edge like before, and it puzzled Vincent why that may be the case. Did someone with an iron fist put order in the place? Or did people vote on a new set of rules and luck out in getting the right people to implement them? Did the councilors convince the people, and most important, the disintegrating campus police, that the only way they could survive as a community was to follow their lead? He also wondered what had happened to Neil's closest posse. Did they leave? Were they driven out? Did they blend in?

That answer soon came about as he recognized two guys from Neil's posse walking around the campus. They, too, seemed at ease, but he didn't trust it. Perhaps his impression of the place was much better than it really was. Again, he thought, it was pretty bad when he left.

He hoped to see one of the people he could trust. There weren't many, since they had left already, but the one person he knew he could definitely trust was Marcus. Now he needed to find him and get his attention without being noticed by anyone else.

Vincent and Marie spent hours hiding out and looking for Marcus. A few times campus people saw them but didn't pay much attention. Still, Vincent didn't want to be seen. He knew if anyone took a closer look they would recognize him. Then who knew what would happen.

The evening drew closer, and they finally saw Marcus. He was hanging around with a few guys on Central Park Avenue, not far from the Royal International. He looked unhurt, which pleased his friend. Vincent feared that the racist Neil thugs who had mistreated nonwhites indiscriminately would take revenge on Marcus. They must have been well aware they were friends.

After all, Aran, Mike, and Elysie had left because of that fear, but there Marcus stood, with all four limbs, and not drowned in human waste as the person Vincent had seen not too long ago. He looked well enough and talked to other people. When the opportunity arose, Vincent wanted to send Marie to talk to him.

"You'll be fine," Vincent reassured Marie. "Marcus is my friend."

Marie worried but decided to go anyway. Walking out into the open, she mustered all her energy and slowly started approaching Marcus. As she drew closer, Marcus had a puzzled look and stopped talking to his companions. She quickly broke the stalled conversation he had with three other guys.

"Marcus, can I talk to you in private?" she asked. He appeared even more puzzled, and so did his companions. Somewhat reluctantly, but with intrigue, he walked over and carefully looked at her.

"I'm a friend of Vincent," she explained, quietly. "He sent me to tell you to meet him in an hour by 65th Street in the park, at the overpass. He'll be waiting for you there."

Marcus became quiet and seemed stunned by the information. Marie felt she didn't sound convincing enough and was about to speak again when Marcus asked, "How do you know Vincent?"

"That's a long story, Marcus," she replied. "But if you could please meet him there, alone, he'd like to talk to you. He said you're the only one left at the campus he can trust."

Marcus looked on quietly for a few moments and then softened up his posture. "Okay, yeah, tell him I'll be there. Oh, and tell him I'm glad to hear from him."

Marie left much quicker than she had approached, while Marcus looked after her as if to see where she would go, but Marie, well coached by Vincent, blended in and then disappeared.

As the sun went down, Vincent and Marie waited anxiously behind the overpass expecting Marcus to come from the front. Vincent wanted to make sure no one would see them. The fact was, he didn't have to worry much because as the sun set, people drew closer and closer to the campus. After all, it was around dinnertime, and if the campus functioned anything like it had a month before Vincent dispatched Neal into the afterlife, it still provided food at regular hours to its residents.

These were all good signs, and it made Vincent glad. It reminded him of the time when, with Elysie and their friends, he hung around the campus having conversations about everything and enjoying themselves doing nothing extraordinary, but talking, laughing, and taking in the evening sunshine in the quiet megalopolis.

Remembrances of the past made him nostalgic. His thoughts quickly changed to Elysie, and then he had to stop. It wasn't the same anymore, and it couldn't be. He wasn't the same, so there was no point in thinking about it; it only brought unnecessary pain.

Thankfully, he saw Marcus approach, and that brought him some joy. Marcus seemed nervous but kept his composure well. Vincent admired that about him and watched. Then when he was confident no one else was around, he quietly called to Marcus. It took a few tries to catch Marcus's attention, but then he came out in front of him.

The two friends looked at each other and then hugged. A quick flash of memories of them hanging out together emerged. So much had changed in such a short time, yet Vincent felt nothing had changed between them.

"I'm so glad to see you, man," Marcus greeted his friend, albeit quietly. "Are you all right?"

"Well, I'm in much better shape than I thought I would be," Vincent replied. "But it's really good to see you, too, man."

A brief pause ensued as Vincent struggled to tell Marcus what had happened to him in the past ten days since he had run away. He yearned to explain himself but now didn't know how to begin. After a few moments, he let out a sigh in slight frustration and started talking.

"Listen, Marcus, I'm going to lay out everything that has happened to me." He took another pause as if to make sure his listener was ready.

"After that fateful day I shot Neil, I just ran and ran. I broke down. I couldn't come back. I wanted to, but I didn't know how. It was too hard. When I finally got the courage to come back, I learned from Joanna that Elysie, Mike, and Aran had left the campus out of fear of what might happen to them. And I didn't blame them. It must have been difficult, and most of all, it was the right thing to do. I decided to go after them."

Vincent paused, trying to figure out how to proceed next. Marcus stood silently while giving slight nods with his head. He looked at Marie and noticed that she, too, was quiet. She stood there like a lost sheep, so helpless and without hope. He felt sorry for her. She was dealt such a bad deal of life, and it felt cruelly unfair.

He thought for a moment and then continued, "On my way to cross the Washington Bridge, I came across some gang. They held Marie captive, and I had to help her."

He looked at Marie again. He wasn't ready to disclose what he had done to that gang afterward. Not to her or even Marcus. He couldn't convince himself they would believe him anyway. He couldn't believe it himself, so he left it out, he figured, until an opportune time.

"Marie," Vincent looked back at Marcus, "needs a home. She's gone through a lot, and I thought maybe the campus, by some chance, could be that place. That's where I need you to tell me if it is or it isn't. When I left, it for sure wasn't."

Marcus nodded as if acknowledging the question. "Well," he said, then paused for a moment. "Things have definitely changed since I last saw you. What can I say, Vincent; a lot has happened here. Before you left, you know it was a hot mess. I thought a war was going to break out. Then you shot Neil and ran away . . . man, it was like a shock. People didn't know what to do. I didn't know what to do. It changed everything."

Marcus took a pause as if he had inhaled a cigarette he didn't have. "It was pretty rough at first, but it has since calmed down. It's definitely quieted in the last few days. But it's a good thing they didn't catch you. They were really after you, man, and it's good Elysie isn't around either. People were saying things."

As if sensing this had upset Vincent, Marcus changed his tone. "But I guess there are some signs of hope. New leadership has taken over. They seem to be all right. It looks like they're trying to get things back in order, like it was before."

Vincent wondered about this and then asked, "Would you say it's safer now?"

"They're working on it," Marcus replied. "It's not great, but it's getting better. Neil's gang is still around. They're definitely not as united as they once were, but they still cause trouble here and there. Most people, I think, are looking for some normalcy."

This didn't sound good to Marie. She didn't know anything about Neil's gang, but the word "gang" scared her, especially since they were residing at this campus. It also turned her off that Vincent had shot a person before he ran away.

Would she learn he shot even more people, she wondered? The time she spent with him didn't reflect that kind of personality. For some reason she had a hard time picturing him pointing a gun and shooting, even though he had pulled out a gun at the bridge.

Still, she wanted to respect him and give him a chance. After all, he did save her at his own expense, and she wouldn't forget that.

Vincent looked at the overpass as the rays of sunset said their last goodbye to the day. He did this to take a break from the dilemma he now found himself in. Should he let Marie join the campus now?

He hated being in the position of not knowing what to do—not so much for himself, but for Marie. He knew that if he came back, he would most likely be tried and found guilty of murder, if Neil's minions didn't get to him first. Then who knows.

This would be the right thing to do, if the campus society functioned as intended, and it would appease those who would call out the injustice. The campus needed to give the survivors a sense of order and a breath of justice, even though when he broke the law he was far from being the only one at the time.

Vincent may have taken out the bad guy, but he also acted on his own accord, which shouldn't be allowed. Everyone in the campus must follow the laws of the campus, and he had broken the law practically in front of everyone. He had no desire to join the campus anyway. Elysie wasn't there, and once he knew Marcus was all right, he would figure out what to do.

"How did things calm down, Marcus?" Vincent asked, trying to piece the time he was gone together. It was such a mess when he left that this "calmness" seemed almost unfair, even though it felt like he had opened a path for it.

"People didn't know what to do," Marcus restated. "At first, everyone talked about what had happened and who had done it. Neil's gang was after you, but that was just something to do in the midst of a shock. So what happened next was that some smarter people came forth who didn't have enemies, or at least not many, and they calmed the people down, as much as they could. It took a few days, but slowly they got the backing of the majority of the people, and then the councilors and the campus police."

Marcus walked over to a nearby bench, tried to brush off the foliage unsuccessfully, and then decided to sit down anyway. "You know it was a good thing that people were fed up. Neil was nothing but the breakup point in the campus, and you did the blessing that no one else dared to do at the time, though a lot of us wanted to."

"I'm not saying it's always the right thing to do," Marcus added, "but it may have saved the campus. Things quieted about a week after he was gone. Neil's posse was breaking down. You could see that some of them wanted to make things work. They got smarter and didn't act like they had before. Some have left, and others are still here."

"But what about you?" Marcus asked. "Are you going to Parsippany?"

"Umm, yeah." Vincent didn't like the question, mainly because he wasn't sure, but also because he could sense Marcus was probing him about his feelings toward Elysie, something he didn't want to ask himself. "I want to make sure you're good, Marcus, and that this place is good for Marie. Then I'll go."

"I'm good, man," Marcus replied. "I appreciate your coming back for me. It really means a lot. I've got what I need here, and if it ever gets too rough I know where to go. As for Marie," he gave a little nod, "she could join. It ain't a resort, but there's food, clean water, and shelter."

Marie, on the other hand, didn't look convinced, and for the first time she spoke up in a soft voice, pulling Vincent to the side, "Can I think about it for a little while? Do you mind?"

What's a little while? Vincent wondered without saying anything. He could see in her expression she wasn't ready to join the crowds of the campus, and he felt bad for her. The last thing he wanted was to put her through any more anxiety.

"Okay, I understand," he assured her. "We can give it some time before you feel comfortable."

Turning to Marcus, he said. "Hey, Marcus, give her a day or two to think about it. We'll be around in one of the buildings not too far away. I'll catch up with you when, well, when we know."

Marcus nodded in understanding. For the next half hour they talked about what they would do about food, water, and other things of necessity. They also discussed which of the buildings they would stay at.

This actually made it a little fun since there were so many choices, and they were acting more like tourists than refugees. It brought a childish feeling of adventure in Vincent to think about how even the most expensive penthouse in Manhattan seemed easily accessible to them.

They all laughed at the thought of how many millions of dollars people had spent for these residences and how outrageous the prices were, only to be freely given to anyone who wanted to walk in now. Ironically, the most expensive penthouse now was valued far less than a small and cozy apartment because the latter could be heated much quicker. Nevertheless, the elegance of a penthouse still had its appeal.

When all the luminosity had parted ways from the sky, they, too, parted ways, in agreement to meet up in a day or two and have Marie join the campus. Marcus went toward the campus, and Marie and Vincent left across Central Park to one of the buildings on 5th Avenue.

CHAPTER 24

Being on the eighth floor of a once ultra-expensive 5th Avenue apartment building overlooking Central Park still felt privileged. The tall, unruly trees and the overgrown foliage below gave Vincent a firsthand view in the moonlit night of the true desire of Mother Nature for the city surrounding it.

It made him think of the times when Elysie and he would watch the park from Elysie's room at The Plaza Hotel in the evening hours. Vincent's room faced other buildings, but Elysie's had a beautiful panoramic view of 5th Avenue as it stretched the entire length of the impressive jungle harbored by New York City.

They could see how this jungle, once bound and groomed by man, had unraveled itself in the early stages of its wild glory, and they wondered what secrets it was hiding. Questions like, "What will this new nature be like?" and "What kind of interesting new species would it eventually produce?" would keep them talking for hours.

They also wondered what else life had to offer them in this new world. Neither would have guessed things could change so drastically in a few months. How much more would the next few months bring?

The hope and excitement they experienced at the time made them believe they would still be with all their friends and each other and that things would have only gotten better. They would have moved with the campus to the new place outside the city, gotten used to the new life, and made more sense of the new society.

Who knows, maybe they would have even gotten married. The world was far from perfect, but they were discovering each other, and they couldn't have cared less about anything else. They were happy and in love.

Everything, however, was different now. Vincent's innocence had left him. The angel of revenge had come from within and spread its black and white wings, drawing a line between the guilty and the innocent. His friends seemed unreachable now, and his lover was gone.

Life now seemed sad, yet he still felt he had gotten something else in return that he didn't have before: a purpose. It made a difference, and it enacted justice. He no longer felt sorry for any of those who fell before him. They deserved it. He just never thought he would have been the one executing their deaths.

He wasn't necessarily happy about what he'd done. If he could trade it with the way things were before, he would have in a heartbeat. Now he was a man carrying a gun with deadly intentions. It was deadly for those he felt were the scum of the new earth, bound from the beginning of time to be destroyed because they rejected harmony and bowed down only to murder, theft, and rape. He thought he had done a good thing, but believing it proved much more complex. He would let time and God deal with that.

While Vincent had his own struggles to cope with, Marie's situation had to be dealt with. Within a day or two, they would have to make the decision about whether she would join the campus or not. There wasn't much of a debate; either she would join or she would be left somewhere hoping to make some sense of her life. Vincent, at this time, wasn't ready to head to Parsippany so that Marie could tag along.

Marie expressed to Vincent that she didn't feel comfortable being around many people at this point. If she joined the campus, she would have to make strides to integrate into the society. That would require her to meet new people, and she felt too fragile to try that.

Memories of Marie's time in middle school and her feelings of loneliness among all the kids surfaced. She didn't fit in well then. She was shy, and kids sensed that as a weakness and took advantage of it for their amusement. That time in her life left deep scars that resurfaced when she felt weak and fragile, as she did now.

Vincent seemed to understand Marie's struggle and tried to calm her fears by saying, "It will be all right. We'll do it at your pace."

She felt a little better afterward, but her stomach still churned at the thought of joining the campus.

After two days had gone by, Vincent wanted to check in with Marcus about how things were going at the campus and see if it was good enough for Marie to join. They caught up with Marcus in the same fashion as before. Marie got his attention, they agreed on a safe spot, and then they met, but this time the meeting took place much earlier in the evening.

Under the same overpass as before, Marcus and Vincent started with small talk to catch up on how the past few days had gone. Then Marcus told them of an incident in which someone was caught urinating in the drinks being served to the group of Middle Eastern folks. It was apparently the second time something like this had happened.

"Some of those Middle Eastern guys in return beat up that idiot and ended up arrested by the campus police," Marcus said, unenthusiastically.

"This, of course, caused more unrest among the people because the police had focused more on the offense of the Middle Eastern folks than on the one who had urinated in their drinks."

Vincent shook his head wondering who could do such a thing, causing unnecessary problems, especially now that things had seemed to get better.

Marcus continued, "It didn't help when rumors started flying that almost all the food and drinks served to the nonwhites were tainted by white people, which apparently the campus police overlooked."

"I highly doubt this is true," Marcus added. "As you know, the police and the kitchen staff are a good mix of all races, but to those who were angered by the events it doesn't matter. It is up to the leadership to calm the situation down."

"Unrest again!" Vincent rolled his eyes. "So stupid. Because of some idiot the whole place goes crazy again."

Vincent almost felt bored by the drama. He thought this would be the day that Marie would finally get a chance at a new life, but hearing of the recent events didn't sit well with him at all.

"Vincent, I would really like to stay with you longer," Marie interrupted all of a sudden. "I appreciate everything you've done for me, and I don't want to be a burden on you, I really don't. I just feel I need a little more time before I'm ready for this. I'm sorry."

This sudden interruption took Vincent by surprise. She must be terrified, he thought. He looked at her and once again saw in her eyes the delicate person with no one to protect her. He couldn't say no.

"That's fine," he said. "I mean, that's fine if you want to stay with me for some time."

Marcus silently nodded. Vincent felt as if Marcus was trying to figure out the relationship between him and Marie as something more than just companions by necessity. A sense of guilt came over him, and soon thoughts of Elysie invaded his mind. His face dropped as his eyes met the ground in disappointment.

He looked up and saw Marcus and Marie staring at him. Then he realized they must be wondering what brought him down all of a sudden. He shook off the thoughts of Elysie and straightened his posture.

"So, yeah," Vincent said and cleared his throat. "We will give it some time, however much is needed, before Marie joins. Let's hope things don't get out of control at the campus again."

Marcus and Marie agreed. The rest of the conversation seemed quick and without any of them having much to say. Marcus gave them a two-way radio in case they ever wanted to contact the campus in an emergency or if they just wanted to listen in on the broadcasted announcements. They parted ways more somberly than before, each for different reasons. Vincent felt each of them was disappointed at the turn of events.

Returning to their luxurious 5th Avenue apartment, Marie and Vincent were quiet. Deep down, he didn't expect to come back with her, but alone, figuring out his future. He anticipated that she'd join the campus, despite all her fears, and that he'd lose his only companion. In his mind, he prepared what that would be like so he wasn't caught off guard.

He thought he would go around "shopping" for an apartment, a place he would find suitable to call home while sorting things out in his head, and perhaps on the street. He had an idea of building a lair where he could store his weapons and any other equipment. He also thought it would be a good idea to get some books on martial arts and self-defense.

This would be useful because he only knew how to use a pistol. If it came down to some hand-to-hand combat, he would find himself unprepared, and knowing how to fight in case the pistol disappointed would be a good idea. He already had in mind finding some literature on Krav Maga. He had heard about this form of Israeli combat system before and became convinced it was great for self-defense.

Expecting that he would be alone for a while, Vincent had tried to excite himself about this new lifestyle even though he realized he would be cocooned from the rest of humanity. Only twice in his life he felt this way: once when his parents divorced and he had lost himself in his own imagination, and once when he had detached himself from much of social life in New York as he battled his depression and addictions.

All of that had changed now, or at least been postponed. Marie was back with him, and his expectations had changed once again. He didn't feel upset at her, but he needed a little time to adjust to the new outcome. This, in return, caused him to be quiet.

"Are you okay?" she asked.

"Yeah, I'm fine," he replied and kept staring out the window.

A minute of silence passed and Marie asked again, "Are you sure you're okay?"

"Yeah, Marie, I'm fine," he said, slightly annoyed she asked him again. He also didn't know how to tell her he needed a little time to think, alone. Then he came up with an idea.

"I need to find us some food," he said. "You can stay here and I'll go look. I could find us some tea as well."

He hoped she wouldn't insist on coming with him. Even though there wasn't much daylight left, they needed food, plus it gave him some time to think, away from the awkwardness of her questioning him if he was okay.

"Okay," she said and gave him a soft smile.

Her eyes gave away worry and discontent with the way things were. He noticed it, but his task was ahead of him already, and he felt he couldn't do much good staying there unless he got his thoughts together and brought some food.

"I'll be back soon," he said and went out the door.

He knew he didn't have to go far to find food. There were plenty of apartments and small shops in the area, and one of them was bound to have something they could eat that no one had looted yet.

He went from place to place that he could enter easily and grabbed a few items here and there. By now the sun had set behind the buildings, and it had become increasingly difficult to see anything deeper inside, so he resolved to get enough for a day or two.

After about an hour he headed back. When he walked into the apartment he found Marie sobbing in one of the rooms. He came over to her side.

"Hey, what's wrong?" he asked.

A few tears dropped from her face as she gazed at the floor in front of her bare feet.

"Everything. Everything, Vincent," she said, sobbing. "I'm not sure how to tell you. My life is completely gone. I don't have anyone in this world. Everyone is gone, and I feel so alone."

"Hey, you're not alone. You have me." He tried to comfort her, but she didn't seem to pay attention.

"Even before the Scourge my life was always tough," she continued. "I've always had it tough. My family was poor, and we never had much. You know, people pitied us, and I felt embarrassed. My dad died when I was young. I struggled with making friends and was a loner. I had a tough time with boyfriends, and sometimes they didn't treat me right. I didn't catch a break until I married my husband, Luke. He was a sweet man who was good to me, but a few months later the Scourge took him away."

Vincent stood speechless. He found himself staring at the floor by her bare feet like she did. He didn't know what to say, but he felt he had to say something. He thought her life was tough after the Scourge hit, but now from the sound of it, it was never easy.

Would it really make any difference or make her feel any better to know that most of her captors on the bridge were dead and she had gotten some justice? Would revenge make her feel better? He didn't think so.

It seemed too immature to consider that, he thought, and he doubted it would make her feel any better to know that side of him. Definitely not now. He felt stupid for even thinking it. He remained quiet for a few minutes more and then resolved to connect with her from his own experience.

As he was about to say anything, Marie continued. "And now the whole world is upside-down. I lost my loved ones. The few friends I had are all gone. The campus, I'm not sure I care about anymore, and I can tell that you don't want me here with you, and I just don't know-"

"Hey, hey," Vincent interjected, "I don't have any problem with your being here with me."

"But you don't want me here, I can tell."

"No, no. I'm not upset that you're here at all. I'm not. I don't want you to think that," he said, sternly. "I made these plans in my head. I was getting ready thinking you would be gone. I wanted to get myself prepared for being alone until . . . I just didn't expect this, that's all."

A brief silence ensued. Vincent looked on and ran his hand through his hair. "You know, I think I know a bit how you may be feeling now. Not too long ago I felt the world was going nowhere for me. Perhaps not like yours, but it was still a lonely world."

He sat next to her and put his hands on his knees and looked down. "I didn't have anyone special in my life. I did nothing but drink around town looking for nothing. I started hating my work because, well, I saw no point in it. I had no will to exert any energy. The money was all right, but I wasn't. I saw no inspiration in myself or anything that I did. It didn't help that I looked for quick fixes to escape into some ecstasy and then beat myself into depression for doing that. Everything fed my struggle."

He took a deep breath. "Then I decided to end it all. End all the misery that is, but I never thought of suicide. I never wanted to go down like that. For some reason, I actually liked life even then; it's just that it was fading fast. I wanted to end my person, not my life. Become a brand new one, with a new chapter."

Marie's sobbing slowed down. Vincent got up and walked to the window. "That's when I decided if I was going anywhere with my life I needed to start fresh. Brand new. I got rid of everything—the people whose lifestyles and influences made me more depressed, my attitude of not doing anything about it, furniture and clothes I never really used, the car I wouldn't need—and I was off to a fresh new start in a new city."

Marie now looked at him with more interest while brushing her tears away.

"You know," he said. "It was pretty scary to move to a big place without knowing anyone. It was exciting, that's for sure, but it was also scary. And you know what? That evil thing that holds you down, that hurts you and taunts you, doesn't really go away. It stays with you, dormant in the memory somewhere. It doesn't require anything. It just gets triggered, and it comes right back.

"But, Marie," he looked at her directly in the eye, "you know what really got me out of that state? It was the stubborn will to do something about it. I don't know where it came from. It was as if some wheels in my brain finally matched up perfectly, or God decided that I had had enough of suffering and steered my brain impulses to put my foot down and say 'that's enough.'"

Marie focused on Vincent fully. She had no more tears. Somehow, she didn't feel quite alone in this anymore. Maybe it was his story, or what he said, or perhaps she was tired of feeling sorry for herself, but his words seemed to do the job.

"It feels like it's been a while, but I remember running a lot during that recovery time," he said, paused for a moment, and then laughed a little. "I remember the first time I went out running. I got winded so fast that I could barely get back home. I don't think I even went a mile."

Marie chuckled as she imagined him huffing and puffing down some busy New York street. He looked at her and seemed pleased to see her laugh.

"Later," he continued, "I was able to go for miles and miles. The night before the Scourge I think I had my best run. It rained a little before I went out, but I didn't stop for two hours. It was a great run. It was just me, the streets, and the city lights, and I had no care in the world."

Marie pictured the city streets at night beautifully glazed by the reflections of the city lights of all colors. She saw a silhouette of Vincent crossing the intersections and continuing the length of a street, and then disappearing in the distance.

She saw herself running. No care in the world. Just running. Putting everything aside in her life somewhere in the street gutters and running. No worries, no memories, no burden. For the first time in a while she dreamed.

CHAPTER 25

A week went by, and mid-October weather brought its charm. The leaves had spread throughout the city and started changing their colors. Nowhere else was it more noticeable than in Central Park, which slowly transformed into a harvest heaven for many of its inhabitants.

Vincent and Marie slowly became more comfortable with their place on the outskirts of the campus. They did the everyday chores necessary for life and a few that would make their apartment more pleasant to live in. The temperatures still held in the high sixties, so they didn't worry about heating the place.

When they realized some campus folks were entering the building either to scavenge or for fun, it became apparent to them they needed to find a different place to call home. After all, they had all the luxurious apartments their souls could desire to choose from.

After a brief search, they both agreed that a condo in upper Carnegie Hill on 5th Avenue looked good. Located in a fifteen story building built in 1928, it was a classic example of the period.

The first time they walked into the condo, they saw an ad for the place *SPECTACULAR DIRECT CENTRAL PARK VIEWS! 6S and 7C have been masterfully combined to create a magnificent 5,118 SF, 7 bedroom, 6 bathroom duplex.* That was it; they were sold.

Vincent and Marie were much like college roommates, but living in an extremely expensive apartment that, before the Scourge, was reserved only for the ultra rich. They slept in separate bedrooms and used different bathrooms to make it more comfortable between the two and because there was simply so much space. Luckily, the toilets still flushed with adequate water poured down.

Vincent gathered all the stuff he had wanted when he expected to live alone—books, tools, ammunition, and a few pistols. He didn't hide the fact that he had weapons from Marie, but he also didn't discuss the truth behind it all.

"It's good to have them, just in case," he explained to her.

Marie didn't object. This was the Wild West, and she was well aware of the dangers. Vincent would stash all that equipment in his large, luxurious bedroom, while Marie would do the same with hers. The rest of the rooms were pretty much left unused.

"They're good to have in case someone needs to sleep over," they joked among themselves.

As time went by, their regular chores became a routine, and at the end of each day they usually relaxed and conversed about various things while overlooking Central Park from their living room.

Marie listened to Vincent with intrigue. As was usually the case, there was a lot more to the person than when first met. She also started having a small crush on him, yet her feelings were still tender to admit it. She became aware that Elysie was with him before he left the campus, yet he didn't like to talk about her much. She felt intrigued by that and tried in subtle ways to understand the entire situation.

Vincent found Marie quite well versed in psychology and philosophy. Their conversations about those subjects could stretch for hours at a time, with the two of them sitting and talking around a $2,000 South Cascade coffee table, many times well past sunset.

At times Vincent found himself noticing Marie's figure. He didn't realize for a while how attractive she was. For a long time, he saw her as a fragile victim who needed care, and for that very reason he felt guilty thinking of her in sexual terms. This also made him act oddly at times, being sweet to her one moment and then looking for his own space in the next. He still loved Elysie, but he felt attracted to Marie because she was the only woman around.

Marie seemed more at ease with him, and Vincent felt he could talk to her about almost anything. At times, while the daylight still reached deep into the apartment and they didn't have much to do, they would spend time reading books or working on a hobby in their separate rooms.

Vincent would practice Krav Maga moves he had read in a book, and Marie would play the harmonica she had found in the apartment. Vincent would shush her when she would play it too loud out of fear someone may hear it, but over time he became more drawn to the sound of it.

There was some unexplainable beauty in the music that the harmonica produced. He couldn't shake off the spell, and at times he would sit and listen to Marie from the other room wishing he could play it.

Marie, discovering his appreciation for the harmonica, offered to teach him a few riffs. She taught him an easy one, "Amazing Grace," and when he learned it, he eagerly called her over to listen to his new achievement. He made mistakes and played off pitch, but he had accomplished something new and felt happy about it.

In the evenings, they would, with greater frequency, gather at their favorite place in the living room in front of the coffee table, looking at the city skyline on the other side of Central Park and talk. Occasionally, they would turn on the radio Marcus brought them in case there was some news from the campus, but most of the times they found the announcements rather boring.

They kept in touch with Marcus about once a week. They wanted to know his situation and what was new at the campus. Pleased to hear things had gotten better, albeit slowly, they were glad that the campus seemed to be moving in the right direction.

Marcus, on a few occasions, visited their secret hideout and brought them sweets from the campus kitchen. This made Marie especially happy because she had a sweet tooth, and coming across such goods was becoming increasingly rare in the city.

One day in early November, Marcus announced big news: he had met a woman, and he would like them to meet her.

"I started seeing her during that troubled week after Neil was gunned down," Marcus said almost apologetically. "I didn't want to mention her because I wasn't sure what would come of it."

Marcus had protected the beginnings of their relationship in a manner similar to a person protecting a tiny ember when starting a fire, careful not to disturb it before that ember turned into flames and something significant.

Marcus seemed to care for this woman a lot, and he was mindful about how things were going between them before introducing her to his outlaw friends. He easily reassured Marie and Vincent that she would keep their secret safe.

Vincent felt pleased to hear that someone had entered Marcus's life and his friend was happy. At times this made him think of Elysie, but then he quickly tried to think of something else. Otherwise, he knew he would get too sensitive and slip into emotional hell.

When they finally met Marcus's girlfriend, they were a little surprised to find that she was white. After all, Marcus mostly had hung out with the black crowd, especially since the time Neil created racial tensions at the campus. So in a way this was nice to see.

Her name was Marlene. She was about the same age as Marcus, and she was sweet. She had a friendly personality—a soft contagious kind that people didn't even notice until they had fallen into deep friendship with her. Marie was excited to have a female friend she could talk to.

The four of them usually met at the apartment in the early evening, after Marcus and Marlene had finished their jobs at the campus. Each brought some food or drinks, and then they experimented at making a nice and enjoyable dinner. Sometimes they failed, and the food wasn't tasty, but most of the time they managed to make something good enough.

After dinner they would talk, laugh, tell stories, and play board games. On a few occasions Marcus and Marlene stayed overnight. The folks at the campus apparently assumed they had gone to spend the night for private reasons, and no one really questioned what they did as long as they got back to their jobs at the campus.

Marcus and Marlene supported this assumption by playfully denying it, which only strengthened the fact that they wanted time to themselves. Nevertheless, whenever they met they had a good time with Vincent and Marie, and the frequency of their visits increased from once a week to every few days.

CHAPTER 26

Every now and then, as the sun hid behind the buildings and Marie went to sleep, Vincent would stay up, ready to go out into the night. The joy of spending time with his friends also made him anxious about the people who were out there to harm others. A strong thirst for justice made him walk out there and want to do something about it, like he had at the Washington Bridge.

He learned from Marcus that there were a few renegades in small groups still preying on anything and anyone in the city, especially those who ventured far from the campus. Marcus worried for his friends. They didn't have the protection of the campus like Marlene and he did, but one thing he didn't know was that Vincent was in many ways more dangerous than the renegades in the city.

Vincent dressed warmly, packed his rucksack lightly, strapped two pistols, a silencer he discovered in a small studio apartment on one of his outings that fit the pistols, took a deep breath for a moment of rational thought, then headed out. It became easy for him to leave unnoticed because Marie's room was far from the main entrance. Also, there was more than one way of getting in and out of the large apartment, and he knew each one better than she did.

He went on what he called a patrol. His goal was to assist anyone needing help and eliminate those causing trouble. In his mind he was the sheriff of this Wild West town. He avoided open areas and wore dark jungle moc shoes because they were light on his feet and he barely made a sound walking. Even on the streets or hallways littered with broken glass and all kinds of degrading material, his steps remained quiet and serene.

He opted out of fixing himself an ATV or a motorcycle for three main reasons: the roads increasingly were becoming treacherous with debris, cracks, and large potholes; it created way too much noise; and much of the time he would be inside buildings anyway. Instead, he walked the streets of Manhattan, each time a different area and different set of buildings. He looked and listened for anything where he felt he was needed on foot—hunting for any creep or gang that he deemed was out to harm people.

Each time Vincent went on a patrol he felt less and less afraid of the dark. Even though he had a flashlight, he used it on low, and only when it was absolutely pitch black. That conserved the batteries, but it also challenged him in poor visibility to use his other senses.

Vincent noticed that he was starting to develop this sixth sense he had felt before. It was beyond his understanding, but it gave him confidence that he could perceive if something was out there that disturbed the flow of things.

This didn't always pan out too well. Vincent sometimes ran into things or knocked them over, and on one occasion he fell down some stairs in an office building. He thanked God that it wasn't a big drop and that he walked away with only a few bruises and scrapes and a whole lot of cussing. He realized the importance of weight balance. Only when he felt certain the next step was on solid ground would he shift weight to it, and he always kept one contact with a wall, whether with his back or his hand.

As he slowly sped things up in the dark, he learned that reaction time was crucial to correct himself as much as possible to avoid a mishap. He practiced this by quickly shifting weight to the last good step he had made, sometimes reaching out for something he knew was there to grab or tuck himself into a fetal position in case a fall seemed inevitable.

As he became more comfortable with handling the situation, he made fewer mistakes, and more frequently he walked deep into buildings to scout out their corridors, rooms, and floors. So far he hadn't come across anyone. No one seemed crazy enough to go in there anyway. It was just him, the night, and the city.

These patrols came with some unexpected surprises and discoveries. When Vincent ventured farther south of the island, in the financial district, he walked up to the roof of one of the high-rise buildings. Something drew him to get to the top. While he was up there, he found a small runway and a rusty World War One airplane. Who in the world would put a runway on a skyscraper? he wondered in amusement. Getting into the plane, he looked around its decrepit instruments.

For a moment he pretended to fly the plane above the city, zigzagging between the buildings. Two pigeons flew by him, almost mocking that this human thought he could fly. He didn't care; he had a good time discovering something new. In the same area of the city he came across a bronze clock embedded in the pavement. It stated *WILLIAM BARTHMAN SINCE 1884*. This is cool, he thought. The clock is actually still ticking! He wondered if it had ticked since 1884.

Not too far off, on Huston Street, he saw a statue of Lenin, the father of Soviet communism, with his right hand raised on top of a red brick building. Behind him was a giant clock. It faced Wall Street, as if it reminded the capitalists that their time was up as well.

In Lower Manhattan, he found African American burial grounds dating back to the first half of the seventeenth century, which was right around the foundation of the city. Then, while walking through Greenwich Village, he spotted Strand Bookstore. There were thousands upon thousands of books piled up in this building. Exploring the bookstore, he forgot his patrol duties and instead

181

spent the rest of the night browsing different titles with his flashlight.

On another occasion, he decided to patrol and explore the lower west side. There he came across a long-abandoned New York Central Railroad. This was an elevated railway, running a mile and a half through the Chelsea district, which was transformed into a walking promenade two decades before the Scourge. Now it stood empty, with a few raccoons and Vincent walking along, and, of course, the various birds that made the railway their meeting grounds.

There was one particular place that made Vincent feel quite strange. It was a vaulted area covered in some kind of interlocking tiles in Grand Central Terminal. No matter how quiet he tried to make his walk, he could hear every bit of every step he made. The noises were so evident, as if they whispered to him from every direction, sometimes right into his ear.

His sixth sense told him the place was relatively small, but the sounds didn't seem to agree. He thought for sure this place was a candidate for being haunted, and for the first time he wondered whether those ghost stories he had heard about were true. He made sure to exit as fast as he could.

CHAPTER 27

It was a moonless and dark night. Vincent had gone on one of his patrols when he spotted a light in one of the luxurious residential buildings in part of the city called Turtle Bay. He found it peculiar and went to check it out.

After a quick search through the building, he located the light in an apartment on the fourth floor whose door was slightly ajar. Quietly, he went in. He found three guys and three girls sleeping in the living room around a fire they had started in a barbecue grill.

They had pushed the Manhattan sofa against the wall, placed their barbecue grill on a metal plate close to the glass door of the balcony, and positioned themselves in the center of the room. They had the window slightly open, and he figured they hadn't gone to bed long ago since the fire still gave off a decent amount of light.

He watched them for a little while to make sure no foul play had occurred. They seemed pretty harmless—six rucksacks, sleeping bags, books, card games, some cooking pots, utensils, cans of food, and bottles of water. They looked young, in their early twenties. He thought for sure they had come from the campus and were enjoying a little getaway or vacation of sorts.

He labeled them tourists in his mind because they seemed a little too naïve to do something like this so far from the campus. It was still nice to see because it reminded him of when he used to take little excursions with Elysie. It also wasn't much different from what Marcus and Marlene did visiting his hideout. A light smile came across Vincent's face, and he left the group alone, gently closing the door behind him.

As he left the building, he thought how nice it would be to be one of them, just having a good time, enjoying the little things, exploring the new and strange world. Perhaps it was a bit careless, but the innocence of it all made it more interesting and fun.

As he quietly walked down the street, relaxed but still alert, he noticed something moving in the shadows toward him. He paused while his senses kicked in. He could hear vague voices. He spotted them, but they didn't notice him, and he immediately hid behind a nearby car.

Whoever they were, it sounded like there were more than two—maybe four or five. They whispered but rather loudly, as if they didn't want to be heard but were too excited to keep it down.

They started moving faster toward the building Vincent had just exited until they broke into a light run. At least one carried a gun. They went for the entrance not realizing Vincent was kneeling a mere ten feet away from them. As he tried to make sense of what all this was about, he looked up at the building, and it dawned on him.

"Shit! The light." He knew they were up to no good. "They must have seen it too. Now they're going after the tourists!"

He didn't have time to count all of them, but now it seemed there were at least seven or eight. Worst of all, he heard two of them cocking their pistols. The tourists had no idea what was coming their way. These guys weren't stopping by to say hi, that was for sure. He knew what he had to do, and he had to do it fast.

Vincent quickly looked around to ensure no one else was coming. Then he went after them. No more than ten seconds after the gang entered the building, he entered also. Since he was just in there, he knew which way they needed to go and quickly found them flashing their flashlights left and right looking for the entrance to the staircase. They had no idea he was behind them, and it helped that at least three went the wrong way, while the rest, unfortunately, found the entrance.

Within seconds the gang went through the entrance, rushing their way up. The three who went the wrong way turned around, said something to each other, and went for the staircase. As he watched this, an intense warmth came over him. He blocked out everything other than what was ahead and what he intended to do.

His eyes followed as they moved quickly, while their flashlights paved the way across the wet and dirty floor. They still had no idea he was in the hallway with them. They weren't human to him at that moment, only vicious beasts and targets for destruction. He knew this was his chance—divide and conquer, like he had done at the Washington Bridge.

Before the last three could reach the door of the staircase, he shot them in quick succession. One, two, three. The silencer did its part well enough, but the closest guy to the door managed to open it and let out a yelp before Vincent could silence him for good.

Vincent had no idea if the rest heard him, but he chose to take his chances and move forward. He opened the door and pressed onto the stairs. He could hear them at least two floors up moving at a steady pace. They must not have heard the last yelp, he reasoned, and kept climbing up.

By the time Vincent reached the second floor, the gang had reached the fourth. He heard one say, "Here, I think this is it!"

When he reached the fourth floor and peeked down the hallway, it disturbed him to realize they had already figured out the right apartment and went inside.

Damn it! he thought. What the hell am I supposed to do now?

He hoped to take them before they went in, but he now stood paralyzed for a moment. The intense sense of focus left him, and he didn't know what to do. All kinds of scenarios played out in his head. Should he wait outside and then ambush them, sneak in right away and attack them, or perhaps call them out pretending to be one of their friends and then attack?

He heard screams, and all the plans went out the window. The fight was on. He went straight for the apartment, pushed the door open, and went to the living room. In one corner of the room he saw the tourists at gunpoint, frightened and confused. In the other, five bearded gangsters yelled and pointed flashlights in their faces.

"I ain't tellin' you again," the shortest of the gangsters shouted. "Don't you fuckin' move! I swear, if one of you tries something, I'll shoot you in your fuckin' face!"

The tourists appeared petrified. They seemed to have no idea what had hit them. The girls cried, and the guys looked stunned and helpless. They tried to look away from the flashlights, but their captors had other ideas.

"Don't you fuckin' look away when I'm talking' to you, shithead! I said, don't you *fucking* look away!"

Vincent had had enough. He shone his flashlight at the gangbangers and then started firing rapidly. Within the blink of an eye, the two who stood closest to him grabbed at their chests, blood pouring over their fingers, and then collapsed to the floor.

The other three gangsters froze for a moment. The quickest one to react fired a shot in Vincent's direction but missed by a few feet. Vincent, while still shining his flashlight, quickly ducked and fired more shots. The gangster let out a gurgling sound, dropped his gun and grabbed at his neck, and then keeled over onto the floor.

One of the remaining two gangsters ran to the other side of the room and shot frantically, while the other rushed and tackled Vincent to the floor. He grabbed at Vincent's face, scratching him, but then he quickly lost his fervor and let go. In all the frantic firing, his comrade shot him in the back.

"Get him, Ray! Kill the motherfucker!" the one who shot him yelled, but his friend didn't react. Then, as if he got some courage, he walked over to shoot Vincent at point blank range.

At this, one of the tourists rushed and tackled the gangster to the floor and then grabbed at his gun. A shot went off and struck the wall above Vincent. The confusion ensued as lights from the flashlight went everywhere. The girls screamed, and one of them rushed over to help her friend. In the next few moments all the tourists went at the remaining gangster. They climbed on top of him and two more shots went off. Then the gun went empty.

Vincent got up from underneath the gangster who tackled him, grabbed for his flashlight, and pointed at the struggle going on a few feet from him. The last gangster was all but subdued now. One of the tourists grabbed the gun and struck him over the head until he stopped fighting back. Vincent watched for a few seconds until he felt confident they had him under control and then darted out.

The tourists, still crying and petrified, tried to figure out if this was only a horrible nightmare. They had no idea who had helped them, but whoever it was, he was gone. They were left shaken but unhurt, and with a story to tell.

CHAPTER 28

Things seemed only to get better at the campus. Each time Vincent, Marie, Marcus, and Marlene hung out, Vincent would see in Marie's eyes that she felt more and more comfortable with what she was hearing. She seemed to gain confidence in herself and slowly recovered from the emotional drama that she had gone through.

Marcus and Marlene had been a positive influence on her, and Vincent was glad to see rejuvenation on her face. He felt that she might even decide to join the campus sooner than he expected. The thought of being left alone brought him sadness. Even though Vincent knew the three of them would keep in touch with him, he felt he would forever be an outcast.

On one occasion, Marie accompanied Marlene to the campus to spend a day or two. It was a big moment for Marie to get a taste of what this famous and infamous place was like. They walked around Royal International, the headquarters of the campus, and a few other buildings close by that had become living quarters for many of the residents and where Marlene lived also.

They ate food together and talked about what it would be like if Marie joined. Marie was getting increasingly excited about it. She didn't, and couldn't, forget her past hardships, but at least this friend made her feel that the hardships had happened a long, long time ago. The doors were slowly opening for her to join.

When Vincent and Marie first started living together, he was careful not to get Marie too attached to him. He may have saved her and acted as her guardian, but mostly he was all she had. He thought she might get too dependent on him, and that scared him at times. He wondered if they would live like this for the rest of their lives, in their luxurious apartment, but away from the rest of society.

He may have changed from the moment that trigger released the angel of death from within him. He felt he wasn't the kind of person Elysie would want, but still he had her somewhere in his heart, no matter how hard he tried not to think of her. It didn't feel right for Marie to stay with him forever.

The moral question, his duty to justice, and most of all, his promise to take the matter into his own hands, wasn't something he thought Elysie could ever accept. That, however, didn't excuse him from his loyalty to her.

When Marie opted to stay with him longer than he expected, he felt it was out of his duty to protect her that he should allow this. When she seemed ready, he would let her go on her way. Now he didn't feel like that so much. As Marie pulled away from him, he felt more and more alone and secluded. He started realizing what he would miss if she went away. It felt unfair.

Everyone seemed to be going somewhere but him. Why did his life have to turn out like this? he questioned. Why couldn't he be like his friends? Why did it seem like he had to lose everything for justice to be served? Why always such a harsh sacrifice? Because of it, he felt sadder and depressed, and the only comfort he increasingly found was in his patrols.

December rolled in. The city had yet to see snow. That was a little unusual for the last few years; nevertheless, it was more than welcomed by its inhabitants. Occasionally, the northern wind teased them with its chilly fingers, but the sun gave its sign of hope that it wouldn't be as cold as the year before. Still ten degrees above freezing, it felt more like an extension of autumn instead of winter.

Marie packed her stuff in the bedroom. She was getting ready to visit the campus for the third time with Marcus and Marlene after their job duties. Vincent had just gotten back from his outing to get some supplies. He went over to her room and peeked through the door.

"Hey, how are you doing?" Vincent asked as he took off his jacket.

"I'm doing well, how 'bout yourself?" Marie responded, quickly, as she seemed immersed on deciding which sweater to bring. It made him feel a little bad she didn't even look at him, but he tried to ignore it.

"Hey, guess what I got?" He tried to bring some attention to himself. "I got us some hot cocoa mix! We could have hot chocolate tonight!"

"Oh, sweetie." She turned toward him. "That's so nice, but I'm going to Marlene's tonight. I thought you knew that?"

He did know it, but he chose not to remember in hopes it wouldn't happen. Either way he felt disappointed. His face dropped, even though he tried not to give it away that it bothered him.

"Oh, that's right. I totally forgot about that. That's cool. You and Marlene are really getting along. That's great. I'm glad to see that." A warmth of jealousy came over his face.

"Yeah, she's nice," Marie replied in almost a childish voice. "She really likes me, and I like her, too! We definitely get along well. I'm starting to like the campus, and she's going to show me more of it.

It's not that bad of a place at all."

Yeah, thanks to me, Vincent replied without saying anything. He continued audibly, "It's moving along. I'm glad to hear that. From what it was when I was there, it's definitely a better place."

He walked over and faced a large painting of a row of trees in their autumn colors adorning a walkway. "But you know how it is. Sometimes things are nice; sometimes they aren't. You never know with that place."

The last thing he wanted now was to praise the campus. He left it when it hit its lowest point, and now that it had rejuvenated itself with a new sign of life, he felt cheated in a way. He felt that his actions were the main reasons it had gotten better.

His patrolling work only made it safer. It hurt him knowing that he was no longer a member, always on the outskirts no matter how much good he did for it. He couldn't reap any rewards. The campus had taken his innocence, his love, and the majority of his friendships and social life, and now it was slowly dragging Marie away. He felt alone.

"What do you mean 'you never know with that place'?" Marie asked.

"You know, things aren't always going to be perfect," he explained, still staring at the large painting. "Not with a place like that. There's too much dynamic, but that's how it is with everything."

Marie's face dropped a little. Her anxiety seemed to rise, and he could tell.

Now he felt guilty that he made her worry. "But don't worry, that doesn't mean it won't be a great place. I'm just disappointed at how it was before."

Vincent found it difficult to keep his talk about the campus all nice and peachy when he didn't feel any of that positivity, and he didn't want to pretend. He wished he had someone. That he wasn't alone. Marie wasn't a bad companion. She was nice, polite, and thoughtful. He was going to lose her if he didn't do something.

"Oh, well, I'll be hoping for the best then." She gave him a smile and grabbed her rucksack. As she walked out of her room, Vincent grabbed her by the right arm. Her eyes opened wide and she seemed startled. He turned her around, looked into her eyes for a second, and then embraced and kissed her.

"Why-why did you do that?" she asked, with a surprised look.

"Uh, I don't know," Vincent stuttered. "I really like you, I . . ." He left the room.

He knew why he kissed her. He didn't want her to leave. He didn't want to be left alone since he wasn't settled with himself, his life, or his future. He would lose his only companion, and now he felt desperate to stop her, but he didn't know how. He didn't want to be the bad guy, but he also didn't want to be the good guy all the time. This time, he just felt confused.

Vincent went into his room and shut his door. Marie stood at the entrance of her room confused. The apartment remained quiet for another twenty-five minutes; then Marie realized she had to leave to meet Marcus and Marlene. She approached Vincent's door but stopped before walking in. She stood there for a few moments and waited to say something. All she could muster was, "Hey, Vinny, I have to go now. I'll be back Monday." Then she walked away.

Monday was two days away. He had plenty of time to think, alone. Saturday came, and the sky had a gloomy look to it. The sun hadn't peeked through the veil of clouds, not even for a moment. This was the strongest sign of the winter yet to come.

Vincent's mood was much the same. He found pleasure in

nothing but only hoped for the night to come to go out on his patrol. He thought, why not do the same in daylight? There was no one at home to notice him gone anyway. So he put on his gear and went out.

Slowly getting used to patrolling in winter clothes, he felt his movement restricted, but then again, so was everyone and everything else that might come along his way. He walked a lot and then found himself not patrolling so much as thinking about everything.

He ended up on 58th Street, not far from the East River in a four-story brick apartment building looking at the Queensboro Bridge. The view was a nice complement to what he felt he needed in order to think. There was space—lots of it—and a large metal structure overlaid on giant stone pillars, still standing, enduring the time and weather.

The structure had been completed at least a hundred years ago. Vincent admired its stability now, something that he yearned for in his own thoughts. He stayed there until darkness overcame the gray sky. Without a resolution, he headed back home desperately trying to see things in a better light.

When Marie returned two days later, they both behaved as if nothing had happened. They did their chores, but with less conversation and with more awkwardness, as if they had only recently met. To Vincent, this seemed strange.

How could she act as if nothing had happened? Then again, he tried to reason, he was acting the same way, so he guessed he couldn't blame her. He felt even more abandoned by her lack of interest in discussing the kiss. He became more irritated, disappointed, and lonely, and he fell deeper within his own abyss, far from seeing any light.

CHAPTER 29

Marie, on the other hand, was waiting for Vincent to say something about the kiss. She didn't know what happened. She liked him, but she had never received strong signals from him. Sometimes she thought those were her insecurities holding her back from the truth that he was maybe interested. Other times she thought he didn't want to be anything more than a friend.

She had a time clock in her heart. It ticked, and ticked, but it wouldn't tick forever for him. She knew eventually it would hit midnight, and then a whole new day would start. She still had a few minutes' time for Vincent, but she felt too confused now, too afraid to ruin the friendship they had. Vincent's despaired mood didn't help. If anything, it confused her even more.

About a week after the kiss happened, they were together, trying to get a fire going in a small oven so they could warm up. The temperature had dropped significantly over the past few days, and most of their focus was on staying warm.

Vincent had built a funnel system to redirect the smoke to the hallway to get their apartment aired out through an open window on the other side of the building. That way no one from the main streets could spot the smoke and discover them.

The system Vincent had rigged didn't work quite well that day, though. The smoke backed up into the room, and Vincent became agitated. Marie offered her help, but that backfired when she broke a piece of a metal he used to hold the funnel leading out of the apartment.

"God damn it! What the hell. Are you trying to help me or destroy this piece of crap?" Vincent fumed.

Marie lashed back. "Damn it all, Vincent! What's your problem? I didn't do it on purpose. You've been crabby lately. I was only trying to help."

Vincent sighed and walked over to the couch, dropped his tools onto the floor, and then sat and covered his eyes. Marie looked at him for a second and then sat next to him, gently putting her arms around him.

"What's the matter? What's bothering you, sweetie?" she asked.

"I don't know, Marie," he said, sobbing a little. "Well, I do know. It would be a lie to say I didn't."

"Is it about the kiss?"

"It's about everything," he responded, opening his eyes and raising his voice. "I see how happy you are with Marlene and visiting the campus, and I'm left all alone. I see everyone going somewhere but me. I can't even see myself going back to the campus, even though they're probably better off because of me."

He covered his eyes again. "I feel like I'll always be stuck this way, and it's hard. It's a lonely life. I kissed you out of desperation. I'm sorry. I felt so sad to see you go. I tried anything to stop you. I'm sorry."

Marie had gotten her answer. She was glad that Vincent missed her, but not that he was sorry he kissed her, and especially that it was out of desperation. She now knew that he longed for a companion more than a lover and that perhaps Elysie was still keeping him from opening up to her. Perhaps in time he would, but not now.

"Well, sweetie." She tried to forge all the right words to console him but at the same time mask her disappointment. "I wouldn't be that far. We would still hang out, and I'm pretty sure in time that you'll be able to rejoin the campus sooner than you think. I don't mind staying here a little longer if you need me."

She felt obligated to stay with him a little longer, especially because of what he had done for her. She couldn't leave him in this state, and there was a tiny hope that maybe another kiss would happen. Their chat seemed to brighten the atmosphere in the room, and they fixed the funnel system well enough for it to function again.

For the rest of the day things got lighter between them. It helped that Vincent had found some powdered eggs, which made them both ecstatic at the thought of having an omelet. They kept warm inside while talking.

"So, what were your impressions of the campus this time?" Vincent asked.

"I like it," Marie said enthusiastically. "I really enjoyed spending time with Marlene. She's a good friend. She and Marcus are great."

"That's nice to hear," Vincent replied, and Marie could tell he wasn't as enthusiastic about it. She assumed he felt slightly envious because he was left all alone, so she changed the subject.

"Oh, I heard an interesting story!" she said excitedly, hoping to get him excited as well.

"Really? What kind of a story?" Vincent asked.

"It's about a group of youngsters who were held up by this notorious gang," she explained. "They were about to get hurt really bad when someone attacked the gang and helped them out. Apparently all but one of the gangsters was killed, but no one knows by whom. These guys have been roaming around this area, and we've been lucky not to run into them. I guess there's someone watching out for-"

"Wait! What happened?" Vincent cut her off.

"Umm." She paused for a second. "Someone helped a group of people who were being attacked by a gang, and no one knows by whom. I'm just glad neither of us ran into them."

Vincent became silent while he stared ahead, as if in deep thought over what he'd heard. Marie was a little surprised by his reaction and wondered if it made him fearful of hearing stories about gangs preying on people.

"Hey, sweetie," she said, placing her hand on his shoulder. "I don't think you have to worry much. You're very good at spotting people in this city. I highly doubt any gang would sneak up on you like they did to those kids."

Vincent looked at her and gave her a gentle smile. "Yeah, you're probably right."

CHAPTER 30

Vincent wondered whether people at the campus felt sympathetic or edgy about what he had done. At the same time, he doubted there were many, if any, vigilantes risking their lives out there either. In a way he felt a little exposed and uneasy about hearing the news. He didn't want the attention.

Somehow, he felt it could easily backfire on him from ever having a normal way of life or joining the campus for that matter. Was he still hoping deep down somewhere that he could? Or was it his fear of forever being an outcast that produced such feelings in him? Again, this was the Wild West of the new era, and there wasn't much law outside the campus other than the survival of the fittest. Could they really look at him that differently?

Nevertheless, he didn't give any more indication to Marie that he wanted to know more about the story than she had told him. He felt pretty confident that she hadn't connected all the dots. She was only aware of him shooting Neil and his number one, nothing else. He avoided the subject, yet hearing of this did discourage him from going out patrolling for the time being. It didn't help that the temperatures had dropped to a mere twenty degrees Fahrenheit, a steep plunge from forty-two a week before.

Even though Vincent felt accustomed to the cold, he was concerned about getting frostbitten, especially when the numbing chill brushed his face, hands, and feet. It reminded him of the last winter when Aran and he had left the group in Brooklyn. He remembered how cold and snowy it was. They struggled through at least three feet of snow, but they made it to the campus. They were frostbitten yes, but they had made it. There he met Elysie, and everything changed for better.

He thought about how different he was now. Back then the deadliest thing he fired was an air pistol, but he hadn't killed anyone. Now he didn't quite know how many he had killed or wounded. Always to console himself, he repeated in his mind that it was the right thing to do; he had taken out the bad guys, the people who were ruining the new world and trying to prevent it from developing into a stable and harmonious place.

A week went by, and it was Christmas. Earlier in the day Marcus and Marlene had visited them, bringing some goodies from the campus. It had been a while since they had had freshly made bread and cakes. The campus had stocked itself pretty well with flour, sugar, cocoa, and most of all, some great cooks.

Marcus also brought them some good news; the campus had elected him to the council! This was great news indeed. There were still plenty of changes needed at the campus, and he could now play a more influential part in them. Marcus's election also brought a possibility, and hope, that Vincent could be pardoned for what he had done or at least given a much lighter sentence. This may have been a long shot, but it was still a possibility.

In the evening, as their visitors left, Marie and Vincent huddled close to the stove with some hot tea looking out the window and talking. Vincent started thinking that it has been a while since he had gone out patrolling. The night had a serene aura to it, and he didn't feel like going to sleep while something inside pulled him to go outside. He decided that tonight he would venture out a little, mostly to stretch his legs and do some thinking.

Marie had been asleep for at least an hour before he left the apartment. The streets looked cold and motionless, much like they had for the last year and a half, but the moon radiated its light stronger than usual, making it much easier to see than on most nights.

The snow dust gently danced across the asphalt and concrete, and it seemed to Vincent that he was the only living being for miles around. He glanced to the right and saw the lights of the campus, the only lights in the city. They looked like Christmas trees to him. This was one night the campus wouldn't curtail electricity, but let it celebrate the occasion.

He started thinking about how he hadn't really patrolled close to the campus for obvious reasons. This time, he thought, why not get a little closer. The lights made it attractive, and he felt drawn to it like a fly. He figured, with a little extra care, he wouldn't be spotted. Then again, even if he was, he would act as if he was a member of the campus. Who could identify him at night wearing all the winter clothes? On top of that, he reasoned, most people would be asleep.

He came to Columbus Circle in front of the Royal International tower and noticed how they had it decorated with Christmas lights and scenes. He admired how much this gave an image of the campus being stable and in harmony compared to when he had left.

This was the place where Neil had established his brutal authority but also met his demise. Now it had transformed into a peaceful symbol. It was ironic. Vincent saw four security guards inside the entrance to the tower. They seemed relaxed, waiting for their shift to be over.

He walked over to other buildings that had been turned into homes for the campus residents. He wanted to see how they looked up close, perhaps to give him inspiration for something, even though he wasn't a part of it.

He walked around, not bothering too much with the cold, his

mind elsewhere. This truly seemed like a blissful night. He walked a little more on Central Park West admiring the enchanted night when he heard some panting coming in his general direction.

Hidden in the darkness, Vincent stood still. Ten yards away a figure ran by. Its run seemed labored, more of a fast walk. It looked exhausted, and its breathing was increasingly heavy.

Vincent followed the figure on the other side of the street until it reached the Royal International tower. There, the lights from the tower revealed a man wearing a thick blue winter jacket and a woolen black snow hat. The man stopped, took a deep breath, and then went knocking on the glass door. The security guards let him in.

Vincent came in closer and looked through the glass window. He couldn't make out what they talked about, but it looked to him that the man who had come in running had informed the security of something important. He saw one of the guards use a two-way radio, while the others had a look of alarm. A minute later, two more security guards appeared. The other four guards and the man went outside and headed up the street running.

Vincent knew something was up and decided to follow them some thirty yards behind. He thought someone may be in trouble and he could do something to help. A few things quickly ran through his head—someone noticed a rabid raccoon or coyote on the campus grounds, someone was attacked by a gang, or a fire started in one of the nearby buildings. He focused on what was ahead and carefully followed the guards.

No more than thirty seconds after, however, he heard something come from behind him. Vincent turned around and saw a figure approaching fast. He tried to grab for his pistol, but it was too late; the person came at him and thrust a knife at his midsection.

Shock and pain triggered Vincent's response immediately. Without thinking, he threw two quick punches at the attacker's face. Staggering back with a bloody nose, the mysterious figure quickly found composure and hurled forward to thrust the knife again.

Still in shock and on impulse, Vincent kicked as hard as he could at the groin section, which made the attacker grunt and keel over. Raising his fist, he followed with a hard blow to the back of the head, and the attacker fell to the ground face-first.

His self-practice of Krav Maga had paid off, but not without a scratch. Even though the adrenaline had done its part initially, he now felt a sharp and steady pain in his midsection. His winter clothing had prevented the full blow of the thrust, but it still had pierced through. How much damage was done, he didn't know, but it didn't feel good.

The attacker seemed dazed with pain on the ground and, without giving him a second chance, Vincent put a bullet into his head. The silencer did its job and he, still shaking from the shock of the attack, looked up and prepared for any more attackers. In a frenzied manner, Vincent scanned all around him while sweat dripped down his face. The night seemed silent, and the guards he followed were out of his view now.

A few seconds later, down at the Royal International, he saw about ten figures closing in on the entrance of the building. He moved away from the body of the fallen attacker to the other side of the street where he felt more secure, and carefully observed what was happening at the Royal International.

He sensed more trouble, but he couldn't quite put his finger on it; who was the attacker, and why was he attacking? Who were those figures approaching the entrance of the tower, and were they working together with his attacker? Where did the security guards he had followed go, and was all this connected?

Trying not to breathe too hard, he decided to move back to the tower to get a better understanding of the situation. The pain in his midsection made every step agonizing. When he neared the tower, he stopped a stone's throw away and watched what was unfolding.

Two figures approached the entrance, while the rest hid themselves by the short concrete wall fence outside. They knocked on the glass door, motioning to one of the guards to come open it.

As the guard pulled the door open, the men rushed in, striking that guard to the head and pointing their guns at the other. They signaled the rest of the guys to come in. It was becoming apparent to Vincent what was going on; an organized group had just staged a diversion and attack on the campus.

A dilemma came over him. The pain in his midsection said *you're badly hurt, go home*, but his overwhelming sense to help pled with him to stay and do something. The logic sided with the pain, but the heart sided with helping out.

His heart and logic battled somewhere within him until a deep breath made him cringe with pain. This made him turn around and face the general direction of his home. He took a few steps, but then guilt came over him and he couldn't move. Turning back, he faced the tower.

"Ah, to hell with it," he told himself and moved forward.

Without any plan on how to tackle the situation, he hoped to God to adapt to whatever he would face. Moving a little faster, he stopped and hid himself behind the same wall fence as the attackers did. He peeked in and saw two of them holding one of the guards hostage while guarding the entrance to the tower at the same time. The rest of the attackers went somewhere inside the tower.

Vincent was convinced that his attacker was part of the same group. The gang had probably sent him to keep an eye on the security guards but then saw him. It seems plausible. Vincent planned to approach the entrance pretending to be that guy.

Vincent barely had any recollection of what the attacker looked like or if he resembled him at all. It was dark enough outside, and he figured the group wouldn't be able to recognize that he wasn't their friend, at least not right away. Vincent took a slow, deep breath and then went up the steps toward the entrance.

He purposely came at an angle to hide the gun in his right hand as much as possible. When the men guarding the entrance noticed him, Vincent waved with his left to open the door. They just stared back.

Shit! It's not working, he thought. Why aren't they opening the door?

He waved again, this time more energetically, and winced with pain. At this, one of the men holding the rifle went into the foyer to take a closer look, his face inches from the glass door. Vincent made a small step back and looked away, pretending to be on the lookout for the real guards. Then he waved his arm again. A moment later he heard the door open.

"Hey, what's going on?" the man asked with intrigue.

At this Vincent quickly turned around and fired two shots at the man's chest. The rifle dropped to the floor and the man fell backward. The other man raised his shotgun to shoot, but before he could pull the trigger, the guard who was taken hostage rushed him and knocked him to the floor. The shotgun slid down the floor until it stopped at the wall. Vincent quickly rushed in and shot the man in the head.

"Where's the rest of them?" he asked wildly.

"They went down to the basement," the guard whose eye had swollen answered. "I think they're after our medical supplies. They have Jeremy hostage!"

"All right," Vincent said, and then stopped to think about his next move. He knew the building well, but he felt far from confident he could take on all the attackers by himself. "Can you call some backup? I'm going down there."

"I don't think that's such a good idea," the guard answered. "They probably want the medicine, and they could kill Jeremy if they see you."

Vincent thought for a moment. He didn't want to stop the momentum of surprise; otherwise, it could get much uglier for everyone.

"Just call the backup," he replied, sternly. "I don't think your friend is better off if I stay up here."

Vincent didn't have much time to think, and this seemed the only plan he had confidence in. The pain in his abdomen shortened his patience for action. He left the guard calling for backup while he went down to the basement.

Carefully moving down the stairs, he felt the warmth of his blood coating his midsection. He looked down and saw a baseball-sized red stain on his winter jacket. The blood had seeped through, and a quick chill came over him with thoughts of his injuries. This was the first time he had sustained a knife injury, and it felt surreal to him. When he got to the bottom of the stairs he heard voices. Immediately, his entire focus changed. His thoughts now centered on the task ahead. His only goal was how to deal with them.

The attackers seemed to have separated into three storage rooms, stuffing their backpacks with whatever items they thought were useful or simply desired. Peeking into one of the rooms, Vincent saw three gray-faced guys minding their own business going through the cans of food and packing it in quickly.

Without much hesitation, Vincent crouched to the floor and fired three shots in succession, hitting and killing all three guys. No one in the other rooms seemed to have noticed. The silencer, once again, had done its job.

He went toward the second room. As he approached it, one of the guys with the face of a twenty-year-old suddenly came out, startling Vincent and himself. Vincent immediately raised his pistol and shot him. The young man fell to the floor, grabbing at his chest, gasping for air and toppling some of the nearby food boxes and cans in the process. The noise spread alarm among the rest of the attackers, and Vincent leapt for cover.

Within seconds a shootout was happening, the attackers firing from the two storage rooms they were caught in and Vincent from behind a metal container in the hallway. Bullets went flying, some hitting the walls and some ricocheting off metal objects, which made Vincent uneasy about his location. He dove for the room where he shot the three guys and fell on top of them.

Getting up, he quickly took the half-empty magazine out of his pistol and put a full one in. As he aimed to fire back at them, he heard one of the attackers yell, "We have one of your guys! I swear I'll kill him if you don't stop and let us out!"

Vincent thought about Jeremy, the guy they had brought down there with them. Trying to buy some time, he replied, "Prove it!"

"Prove what?"

"That you have one of our guys!"

Silence ensued for a few moments.

"I'm here! Please stop shooting," another voice came out of one of the storage rooms. Vincent had no way of telling if it was Jeremy or not.

"I want to see you!" Vincent replied again, unsure how to identify Jeremy.

"You've had enough proof!" the attacker yelled back. "I swear I'll blow his brains if you-"

"Bullshit!" Vincent cut him off. "What's his name?"

Silence.

Two more shots whizzed in Vincent's direction.

"Pssst!" He heard something from the other side of the hallway. Turning around, he saw three security guards a few yards behind him covering in the adjacent hallway—one on the left and two on the right. Farther behind them the guard with the swollen eye peeked behind the stairwell. They signaled to Vincent, *how many are there?*

He responded by pointing to one of the rooms and lifted two fingers, then at the other room and lifted three fingers. The guards asked again, "Jeremy?"

Vincent motioned with his hands that he didn't know what had happened to Jeremy, but he shook his head that he had a bad feeling about him. After another ten seconds of silence he tried again.

"Show me the hostage you have," Vincent requested of the attackers, "and we can work something out."

Silence.

He knew this was a bad sign. Jeremy was the attackers' only bargaining chip, and they refused to present him. Why wouldn't they reassure him that he was alive? Vincent questioned. Unless. . .

"We knocked him out!" the attacker responded. "He's unconscious. He can't tell us his name."

"Show him!" Vincent demanded.

Silence.

"All right," a somewhat reluctant response came back.

Slowly, Vincent started seeing a person's head appear on the floor. It seemed to be the guard. They pushed his head out into the open so he could be seen. He had a winter hat on and looked completely knocked out, but pale.

Vincent motioned to the guards to confirm it was Jeremy. Two of them nodded; the other two still tried to have a good look at him. Vincent noticed the hat was darker in one spot, and he didn't have a good feeling about it.

After a few seconds, he asked, "Take his hat off!"

"You've seen him," the attacker responded in frustration. "That's what you asked for. Now if you don't-"

"I want to see him without the hat!" Vincent cut him off.

"You've seen enough!"

"Take his hat off!"

"You want me to shoot him, motherfucker?" the attacker fumed.

"You do that, I guarantee you'll not come out of here alive," Vincent threatened. "Take his damn hat off!"

Silence.

"All right."

It wasn't all right. The next moment two attackers ran out of one of the rooms with guns blazing. They couldn't have been more than in their late teens or twenty years old.

They screamed and fired shots, barely aiming. Vincent and the guards fired back. Bullets went everywhere, but the shootout didn't last long. Without cover, the attackers were quickly gunned down. They lay motionless on the hallway floor, and then silence ensued.

"Whoever is left, you better surrender or you'll meet the same fate!" one of the guards yelled.

This wasn't something Vincent would have thought of. So far, his encounters were all or nothing, no prisoners. Soon enough, a voice came out.

"Okay, okay. We're coming out. Don't shoot."

The attackers threw their weapons and slid them as far as they could toward the guards, most of them getting stuck at the bodies of their fallen comrades. A few seconds later they came out with their hands in the air. There were three of them—boys just like the rest.

At this, the ordeal at the tower was over. Unfortunately, Jeremy had been shot in the head at some point earlier in the shootout. He was breathing, which seemed unknown to the attackers who thought he was dead. One of the guards immediately called for the campus EMS service.

Vincent then turned to the rest. "What about the other four guards who went out?"

Everyone was silent. The guards questioned their new prisoners about whether they had had anything to do with the runner who came in right before they attacked. All they kept saying was, "We don't know; it wasn't our plan."

They asked Vincent what he had seen, but he had a hard time concentrating on their question. The pain and blood loss in his abdomen made him feel nauseous and woozy, and he wanted to get out of there.

"There's no time to waste," he said under his breath.

"You don't look so good, man," one of the guards replied, worriedly. "You're bleeding!"

"It was just a graze, on the side," Vincent said, unconvinced anyone would believe him. "We've got to find out what happened to those guys!"

This was Vincent's way of trying to get out of the tower. He very well knew he was in no shape to go out looking for the other guards. He told himself he'd done all that he could.

The other guards insisted that the EMS team check him out, but Vincent responded sternly, "I'm telling you, I'm fine. We have to find the rest of the guards! They could be in serious trouble!"

At this he started walking as fast as he could up the stairs, breaking into a slight run, and then back to a fast walk when he realized he had no energy to run. A cold sweat came over him, and he started feeling clammy.

Two of the guards went out with him while the other two remained guarding their prisoners and waiting for the EMS to arrive. As soon as they had left the tower, Vincent suggested they split up. They didn't think this was a good idea, but he pretended he hadn't heard them and kept fast-walking, pointing that the four guards had gone down Central Park West Avenue.

The guards followed him for a short time and then surpassed him. When Vincent noticed they weren't paying attention to him anymore, he quickly turned to his right and entered the park, running as far away from them as he could.

No more than fifty yards away he had to stop, gather his breath, and continue walking instead. He increasingly felt tired and dizzy, and he barely had any sensation in his fingers and toes.

Only one thing circulated in his mind now—how nice the apartment would feel when he finally arrived there. The warmth of the fireplace, the cozy bed, the safety. The pain snapped him out of that thought and made him quiver. He dreaded the possibility of finding out that one of his vital organs had been injured. In that case, he would be as good as dead. It was a tough idea to swallow.

After an agonizing forty-five minutes trekking through the snow and frozen foliage of Central Park, and by feeling the numbers on lampposts indicating where he was in relation to streets, Vincent finally managed to get back to his building.

The silence of the hallway greeted him, which felt much better than the brisk wind that had started to pick up toward the end of his hike. Walking up the stairs took another twenty minutes. Once he reached his floor, he felt he had climbed Mount Everest.

His vision played tricks on him, as if he were buzzed on some heavy liquor. He would stop, close his eyes, take a slow breath, and then slowly open his eyelids to momentarily bring things into focus. He finally arrived at the place he had dreamed of in the past hour.

He entered the apartment in slow and labored steps, and to his surprise Marie was awake and sitting in the living room with a hot cup of tea in her hands. The fire from the makeshift fireplace was lighting the room, giving it a yellowish and warm appearance.

He didn't even care to explain what happened; he just went to her. She seemed startled at his pale and exhausted appearance. The closer he came, the wider her eyes became. She looked at his midsection and saw the dark stain on his jacket and a pistol strapped to his side.

"Vincent! What happened to you?" Marie asked worriedly as Vincent collapsed onto the couch next to her.

"It, it," he stuttered. "It's a long story. You, you need to help me."

He tried to unstrap his gun and take his jacket off, which now became clearly visible to be stained with blood.

"Oh my God! What happened?" she nearly shouted.

Vincent lay there and groaned.

Marie gently raised his head and looked into his eyes. "Why are you so bloody? Who did this to you?"

He didn't have the energy to talk, so he brushed her questions off with, "Later."

Marie started taking his clothes off and was frightened by the amount of blood. The wound was in the upper-left lumbar region, right at the bottom of the rib cage. About an inch across, it looked like a perfect line incision. The stained clothing and the freezing conditions seemed to have slowed the bleeding, but once Marie took off his shirt, the bleeding began to pick up speed.

Marie cleaned the wound with gauze and drinking water and then smeared it with antibiotic ointment and applied lots of gauze pads. This seemed to control the bleeding, and it brought some comfort to her efforts to help him. Then she wrapped his abdomen with a roller bandage to hold the gauze in place and gave him an antibiotic to take with lots of water.

Vincent looked exhausted and wanted to slip into a blissful dream, but she wouldn't let him. She didn't give him a reason behind it, but she woke him every time he dozed off. She fixed him some tea, which he sipped every few minutes. After a while, when he couldn't help it anymore, Marie let Vincent fall into a deep sleep.

CHAPTER 31

The next day felt a little warmer at thirty degrees Fahrenheit. The clouds still appeared heavy, but at least there was daylight. Marie had barely slept all night. She kept the fire burning and stared out the window with worry. Vincent slept until midday.

When he woke up, he felt pain in his abdomen, but there was something else. He felt rested. That was a good sign. If an internal organ had been injured or he had internal bleeding, he would have felt weak, cold, and clammy and might not have woken up at all. Instead, Vincent felt warm. Of course, Marie had covered him with many blankets and kept the room toasty.

The pain Vincent was experiencing felt harsh with each breath. He thought that the knife must have injured his rib, which would have prevented vital organs from being pierced. When Marie saw Vincent awake and coherent, he witnessed huge relief come over her.

She shed a few tears but kept herself from crying. She smiled and hugged him. Vincent could see how much he meant to her, and he felt a huge appreciation for her help. They were one for one in saving each other's lives.

That afternoon they ate some warm soup. Then the inevitable question came up. What had happened?

"Marie." Vincent took a deep breath and grimaced under the pain. "I'm going to tell you everything. There's no point in keeping any truth from you."

Marie was all ears.

"You're aware that I shot this guy Neil and his friend, and that's why I ran away from the campus," Vincent explained. "This is all true. It brought great change in my life. I'd never hurt anyone before then, but if you were to ask me to go back in time and change it, I don't think I would."

He grimaced under another breath and looked at the fire crackling in the fireplace.

"I made a promise to myself and to the new world that I wouldn't stand idly and see evil things happen around me. If I could, I'd do something about it."

Marie looked puzzled. Vincent continued, "After I discovered you at the bridge I actually went back there, Marie . . . and I killed them."

Marie stood silent. Her look was one of confusion and disbelief. "You shot the whole gang?" she asked.

"Most of them," he replied. "Some got away, but I don't think many did. It's something I felt I needed to do to prevent others getting caught like you had. And the story you heard at the campus, about the young folks being helped by a stranger when they were attacked? That was me. Then last night, I was around the campus, and a group of people stormed the tower to steal something— medicine I think. I was caught in it. That's how I was stabbed."

Marie looked away from him. "How long have you been doing this?"

"Not long before I met you," he answered.

"How? I never noticed you doing any of this. I've been with you most of the time since we met."

"I would go out at night," Vincent explained. "Not every single night, but some nights. I would wait for you to fall asleep, and then I would go out."

"I see," Marie said, as if she had been tricked. "That's why you were tired some days and would sleep late. I thought you were up late reading or simply needed lots of sleep."

She took a deep breath. "How many people did you kill?"

"I don't know." He hated the question. "Twenty, thirty; I haven't really kept count. That's not the point of this."

"Thirty!" she said loudly. "You killed thirty people?" Marie got up, shaking her head. "I don't believe this. I *can't* believe it. How could you kill so many people that you don't even know how many?"

"They're not people, Marie," he insisted, almost angrily. "They're monsters. They're those who chained you up. Who did . . . who knows what kind of things to you. You can't tell me they're people! They're the cancer in this tiny bit of population we have left. They kill, beat, and rape without mercy. Why would I give them any chance? They for sure don't give others a chance.

Vincent paused to control his breathing because it was causing him to hurt, and then he continued more slowly. "They don't want to be part of a normal society. They only want to destroy it, dwelling on anarchy and destruction. They want power and their own will exercised on others. Nothing more. Just like Neil did, and just like his friends did. They don't give a damn about anyone else. They're bullies. The Scourge freed them to do whatever the hell they want, and damn it if I will let them destroy the tiny bit of hope we have left in this world!"

Marie absorbed all that Vincent was telling her and for the remainder of the day remained mostly quiet. The revelation was too much. The thought of killing someone felt too horrid for her. Even though she went through a lot at the hands of her captors, she still found killing people fundamentally wrong.

No matter how much Marie hated some people for what they had done, she couldn't bear that Vincent was their killer. Perhaps if he did it out of self-defense she would have accepted it, but going out of his way to seek and destroy other human beings—that felt different. Her view of him changed drastically.

Marie didn't hate him, but she didn't feel strongly about him either. She was confused. Her admiration and the feeling of being drawn to Vincent was slowly leaving her, or at least being buried deep underneath the distress of what she had just heard. The sweet and innocent Vincent had vanished from her eyes.

The next few days Vincent slowly recovered. He could walk around slowly, but his pain prevented him from doing anything more strenuous. Marie cared for him, but she mostly did her own things when she didn't need to help him, and they didn't share much conversation anymore. Vincent felt hurt by her reaction to his revelation, just as he feared Elysie would have, and it only reinforced his belief that Elysie wouldn't accept him back either.

One evening Marie walked into his room and started to speak, to Vincent's surprise.

"Vincent," she addressed him in a soft tone. "I don't want you to think I'm angry with you. Actually, I appreciate that you told me the truth."

Vincent stood speechless, taken off guard by her statement. He thought Marie felt cheated by his sneaking out at night to go on his patrols, and especially by the work he did when he went out there. He thought she hated him.

"I still believe you're a good guy deep inside," she said.

Vincent didn't know how to respond. He looked at her green eyes and wondered if she was being honest with him. She had never lied to him before, he reasoned, so why would she start now?

"To be honest, Marie," he said. "I feared so much how you would look at me if I disclosed what I had been doing. I thought maybe you would see me as a monster. That's why I kept it to myself. I'm not proud of it. I just thought someone ought to do it."

Marie, silent at first, as if she contemplated the *someone ought to do it* part, responded. "Well, I'm not going to say I wasn't shocked when you told me. It was disturbing in a lot of ways. I didn't see your being like that. You're so sweet and . . . Well, I just didn't expect it."

Vincent felt disappointed. She had thought of him as sweet, but that probably wasn't the case anymore, and it hurt him.

Marie continued. "It does make a difference that you're after those monsters out there, and not just anyone. It's just hard to comprehend that you, you know, kill people. But I'll always appreciate what you have done for me. I'll never forget it, and I want you to know that."

That made Vincent feel a little better. He wasn't any other killer out there. He went after those who killed and tortured others. What he did made a difference, they both agreed. He felt glad he and Marie had had this talk because he didn't like the silent tension that had existed between them. Nevertheless, he also felt this was a preparation for something else, a revelation of her own, and she was coming clean about her feelings before revealing them.

After about a week, Marcus and Marlene came to visit. Vincent explained the injury as a bad slip on ice while scavenging for food, and Marie played along. The next day Marie broke the news to him that she would be joining the campus in two days. She had already made the arrangements with Marlene.

Vincent wasn't surprised. He knew that transition would come down the pipe, even before his own revelation. He felt sad more than anything. He felt like he had lost the care and affection of someone whose company he enjoyed and was now left to his own devices.

When the day came for Marie to leave, Vincent's expression looked like a puppy being left alone at home while his caretaker left for a party. It was just that this caretaker wouldn't come back.

As Marie started to leave the apartment, she turned around and gave Vincent a big hug.

"Thank you for everything, Vincent," she said, while a single tear fell down her cheek. "I'll come visit you."

Vincent could barely mutter any words and only hoped that the moment would end so that he could shed a tear of his own. To comfort him, Marcus and Marlene brought him some goodies from the campus and reassured him they would still keep visiting him.

After they left, Vincent stood quietly, looking out the window at Central Park. He didn't shed a tear as he thought he would. He bottled his emotions inside, and he breathed them out. He stared out the window well past night and then huddled underneath many covers on the couch and slipped into a dreamless sleep.

CHAPTER 32

Days went by. Vincent was all by himself. His plan to build a lair for himself could take place uninterrupted, without him having to hide anything from Marie. He could pay as much attention to the details as he wanted. He could gather as much equipment and training manuals as he could find, go out on his patrols as much as he wanted, whenever he wanted, without having to hide from anyone.

Now that he could finally do this, he didn't like it. He didn't feel good about it and didn't want it anymore. It felt unsatisfactory, unfulfilling, and unexciting. He had no one he could talk to, share ideas with, or share a cup of hot cocoa with. It seemed that there was nothing to hope for. He had no desire to do anything, and it started to feed his depression.

Marcus, Marlene, and now Marie would visit him from time to time, but it wasn't the same. He wasn't the same. Marie wasn't the same. Things had changed too much between them, or at least that's how it felt for him. Marie didn't seem to have disclosed his secret to anyone, and that remained the only thing he felt glad about.

Marie still seemed to care for him, but more at a distance. Vincent wondered whether it would have made any difference if she *had* told anyone. Would anyone bother at the campus? The guards he helped on Christmas didn't seem to have recognized him. Perhaps some of Neil's loyal posse would still like to have their revenge, or maybe they, too, couldn't have cared less what happened to him.

The weather added to the gloominess of Vincent's situation, so he did the only thing he could since he couldn't move much: he forced himself to read. He had all the time in the world for that. He got rid of the radio he and Marie used to listen to, partly out of resentment for not being part of the campus but mostly because he felt there was no need for it. His situation didn't seem to be much different than being stranded on some isolated island.

Picking up the harmonica Marie purposely left behind, he mastered "Amazing Grace." Then, desiring to learn something new, he started messing around with the harmonica version of "Ravel's Bolero" he once heard years ago. He had no notes to go by, so he improvised the best he could from his memory. As a result, it turned into his own song.

Weeks went by, and the monotony of the winter bore in. Luckily, he had recovered well enough from the stabbing to step outside if he wanted to; however, it wasn't easy. It definitely took some wind out of him to walk down the stairs of his apartment building. He took it easy, though, regaining his strength and stamina.

At first Vincent didn't have much motivation for his patrols, but then one day that changed. He came across a small studio apartment where some middle-aged man had trapped a young girl for his erotic pleasure. Vincent took pleasure in putting a bullet into his brain and taking the young girl back to the campus. After that incident, Vincent started going out more. He found himself more motivated and started feeling a sense of purpose to his outings again.

When he was on one of his patrols, making his way through a rundown corridor of a building, he got that feeling of being watched. He stopped in his tracks and froze as his heart skipped a beat. He thought he was stealthy, yet someone still had spotted him.

His feeling of overconfidence was replaced with insecurity. He closed his eyes for a moment and listened, desperately trying to pinpoint the location of his stalker. He deciphered nothing at first; then he felt a slight disturbance in the environment. He didn't hear it, but he felt it. Vincent couldn't explain how, but it revealed his stalker's approximate location to the right of him.

Vincent turned slightly to the opposite side pretending he didn't sense anything. Secretly, he slowly reached for his pistol, ready to make a quick turnaround and fire if he had to. His muscles were geared and tingled for action.

"You won't need that, son," a voice came from the darkness. A gravely low sound put a stop to his action. He turned around and looked but could see nothing.

"All right," Vincent said while keeping his hand close to the pistol, "who are you?"

"Just an old lady, and you won't need that gun," the voice replied.

"Easy for you to say." He observed carefully, still itching for the pistol.

"Look at me," the voice said, as an elderly lady appeared in the fragment of light a few yards away from him. "I'm no threat to you."

He could barely make out the features on the woman's face. She looked to be quite up in her age. She had worn clothes, much like a homeless person he remembered seeing in the subway system before the Scourge. A worn hat sat clumsily on her head. He couldn't tell whether it was a commercial product or something she had made herself.

Staring at her for a few moments, Vincent wondered if she had tried to bait him to lower his guard. He tried to sense whether anyone else was around, but besides a rat minding its own business in the corner, he felt nothing.

"All right," he said, relaxing a bit.

"You said that before. Now relax, but if it makes you feel better to hold your gun, go ahead."

"What are you doing here?" he asked her, amused to see another person in the dark and decrepit building.

"I could ask you the same question. I've been here longer than you," she replied.

"How would you know how long I've been here?" he asked.

"I've seen you before a few times. You're pretty sneaky, he-he," she replied with a short raspy laugh.

"Great," Vincent responded sarcastically. "Why haven't you introduced yourself before?"

"I wasn't too sure about your intentions. I still ain't, but I don't think you're a threat."

She moved closer until they were five feet from each other. He could see her wrinkled face as she looked up to him from her slightly hunched back.

"Okay, now that we got that out of the way, why are you stalking me?" he asked, slightly annoyed he hadn't noticed her before.

"I'm not stalking you." She shook her head. "You keep running into me."

"Okay, well, I'm sorry for running into you, but I had no idea you were around," he said, placing his pistol into the holster.

"I know, son, most people don't," she replied.

"Then what are you doing here? Why aren't you at the campus?" he asked again.

"The same reasons I wasn't before the great collapse."

"Which are?"

She took a brief pause and cleared her throat. "I was what you would call homeless. Then I had a home, and now I'm homeless again."

Vincent couldn't help but feel pity for her in silence. She looked painfully slow in her movements and overall a harmless person, and he wasn't quite sure if she was all there in her mind. It seemed unreasonable for someone her age to be in the middle of a cold, empty, and dark building.

"He-he, don't feel bad, son," she said. "I'm doing much better now."

"You said you had a home, and now you don't." He looked at her with puzzlement. "Why did you say that?"

"I was a drug addict, son, for many years, and I lived on the streets. But thank Jesus, I cleaned up and found a home," she said, smiling. "He-he, but three months later," she waved her hands illustrating an explosion. "Bye, bye to everyone. The Lord works in mysterious ways, he-he."

"Why aren't you at the campus if you're all cleaned up now? That's where everyone else is. They have food, clean water, and a warm place to sleep."

"See, son." She looked at him with her squinty, tired-looking eyes, and then started pacing around. "When I turned to drugs for my problems, people didn't want me. I was messed up. I chose to be homeless, in a way, he-he. I couldn't get a job or pay rent, and no one wanted to hire me. The family wasn't around, and for sure I couldn't kick the habit."

Vincent remembered the addictions he had had and the painful struggles he had gone through.

"But like I said." She pointed her finger up. "The Lord works in mysterious ways, he-he. When I was at the campus in the summer, things weren't going well. People were angry and violent, doing all kinds of things. Then many of us got sick, throwing up and having diarrhea."

"Well, see, son." She came closer to him. "Some of those violent folks decided to blame it on me. I don't know why, maybe because I was different. They thought I had something to do with it, 'cause I was one of the first to get sick. Soon enough, a fool's actions ignited the mob, and they kicked me out, thinking they'd get better, he-he."

He realized she was referring to the traveler's diarrhea many got sick with soon after they moved to the Royal International.

"I see what you're saying," he said, nodding. "So now you're, kind of, in the same place as before. I'm sorry to hear that."

"Don't be sorry, son," she replied. "I'm in a much better place now. If people don't want me, that's okay. See, where before I was homeless 'cause I couldn't kick the habit, now I have peace in my heart."

"Um, I see," he said, unconvinced he understood what she meant by that.

"Do you know what I'm trying to say about peace in my heart?" Her eyes grew wider. "The Lord Jesus has given me-"

"Nah," he cut her off, "not with that Lord stuff. I've seen the world and what it has done. I'm not buying into it."

"But you want peace in your heart, don't you?" she asked, stepping a little closer.

"I want peace in the whole world!" he answered.

"Son, it starts with peace in one's heart," she said, calmingly.

"It starts with us doing something about it," he said, and then pointed to his chest. "That's what I'm doing."

"That's just chasing the wind." She shook her head.

"What?" he asked.

"What you're doing, the justice you're seeking," she replied. "It's meaningless."

"Tell that to the little girl who was about to be raped," he responded.

She stood silent as her eyes turned down. She shook her ahead again. "You did good to help the little girl, but what you did to the man, that's your anger, a fool's food."

"Whatever it is, it stopped that man from harming anyone else."

"But what did it do to you?"

He looked at her silently and then thought for a moment before replying, "It made me happy I could do something about it."

"Hmm, that was then, but you don't look so happy to me now."

"All right," he said, having enough of the conversation with the old lady. "I'm going now. Thank you for the conversation, but I'm going this way to chase the wind. I wish the peace in your heart to continue, and I mean it."

He turned around and started walking away into the darkness of the corridor they were in. She remained standing in the tiny bit of moonlight.

"I wish peace in your heart, too, son. Those who live by the sword die by the sword. And be careful if you come across the old lady again. I won't be causing no trouble," she said, watching him disappear.

"You have my word, ma'am," he replied, having walked some distance away.

"Don't want you shootin' me, too," she could be heard murmuring.

CHAPTER 33

Months passed, and spring blossomed in the city. The snow melted away, and the ever-changing city came to life. Some of the streets and avenues became little streams, while shrubs and other vegetation sprung around it. By now Vincent had well recovered from his injury and delved more into his city patrols.

With this, he also started losing touch with Marcus, Marlene, and Marie. Most of the time they would visit he wouldn't be there. They left him notes, but he was less and less inclined to see his friends. Every time he would, the thoughts of their lives going somewhere normal while his remained abnormal and alone hurt him.

At this time, Vincent found much greater comfort in his patrols. "The Old Wandering Woman," as he called her, didn't come across again. He wondered if something had happened to her or if she was simply that good at camouflaging herself that he didn't notice her.

From what he could tell, the campus had become more and more stable, and there was a real chance that a healthy community could grow into something that its creator had originally planned. The survivors seemed to come there looking for a calm and balanced life.

It appeared that people from all over were making the campus home. Even a few boats had arrived from other parts of the world and helped build the community. At this time, the campus had increased to over five thousand people—almost double the number when Vincent had left. Unfortunately, there was a downside to this. The influx of people also brought more danger.

With greater frequency, Vincent found himself coming across bad and menacing folks in and around Manhattan. The campus seemed much safer due to the more organized campus police, but venture half a mile away from it, and someone would be on his own. That was where uncertainty and vulnerability ruled and also where Vincent did most of his patrols.

In one case Vincent went after a man, perched in the neighboring towers, who was sniping people venturing away from the campus with his high-powered bolt-action sniper rifle. The man killed four unsuspecting campus folks before Vincent found him and ended his hunting career with a single bullet in the back of his head.

By the time July rolled around, Vincent had acted on nine more occasions. The word of his actions spread around the campus. The approval of his actions, however, was more positive than not. They looked at him as some kind of obsessed vigilante taking the law into his own hands and mostly working in the favor of the victims or the campus residents.

Some, however, considered him a mad individual who happened to hate the things most people found morally repugnant, and if given a chance, would become the same monster he was after. Anywhere near or at the campus, however, most agreed he shouldn't act. After all, that's where their law enforcement ruled, not his.

Vincent didn't care where he acted, though. His duty had no boundaries. He saw any action of unjustifiable harm to others as a reason for his reaction. What seemed justifiable or not was a complex subject, but he made an effort to take as much from the various books he read as he could.

Again, this only helped shape his own moral reasoning to a degree and the ultimate judge for his call to action. Much of it still came down to his own perception and understanding and the gut feeling of the situation whenever he would come across it.

Slowly, reflecting back on everything, even Vincent admitted that anger was one of the reasons behind his actions, but he refrained from judging it too quickly as the sole reason. He had meditated on this question before and was beginning to understand its complexity.

Anger, as an emotion, was complex, but it wasn't the justification. It became only one of his drives mixed with the strong sense of protecting the weak and uninvolved from being the victims of the survival of the fittest. He despised that thought as the means for the society to move forward. He thought life in itself wasn't that simple.

Humans were more than animals, he believed, and they possessed a reasoning power different from that of animals. People had to do something about their problems, and in his mind he *was* doing something. Too many people liked to voice problems but refused to do anything about them. They harped on how everything was wrong but then only found excuses when it came to fixing things. He, on the other hand, was doing something.

Whatever people felt about Vincent, they all respected his ability to act. The accounts of the people he helped brought admiration for his willingness to get in harm's way for their sake. Other witnesses recognized his shooting capability and urban savvy. Still, some thought he was a stealthy stalker to be cautious of.

Those people found it hard to trust someone who wasn't a part of their campus, and not everyone seemed so sure that his real motives were good anyway. Regardless, they all accepted the fact that he was deadly when it came to action, and slowly his nickname started to emerge: *The Scourge of Man*, or just *the Scourge*.

"When you hear the harmonica play, you know the Scourge isn't far away," became a saying at the campus.

Midday sun scorched July 28, and Vincent found himself on an overpass in the financial district. He gazed at the West Side Highway below filled with decaying cars, shrubs, and other foliage. Looking up, he saw the majestic wings of the laughing seagull. Unlike the aggressive herring seagull, which he didn't like much, these were much quieter and more pleasant to be around.

They would bask their wings between the rows of tall buildings on either side of the highway that stretched for miles while painting a captivating picture in his mind that he couldn't shake off. It made him wonder what it was like working in one of the towers, having to come there every Monday through Friday, look out the office on the thirtieth, fortieth, or fiftieth floor, and see the swarms of people below.

He wondered if those folks had really found it enjoyable to be in such prestigious places, well above everyone else in most parts of the city. Looking out at the sunset over the city must have been so nice, he thought. It made him think of happy things. Nothing in particular. Just happy.

He thought of himself there, if the Scourge of God had never happened, leaving his office in one of the towers while on the phone making plans with his girlfriend, fiancée, or wife about what exciting things to do that night.

Coming back to reality, he then stood and shook off these thoughts. That was enough daydreaming. It was time for Vincent to head back to his lair. He felt tired this day and could definitely use a long sleep. He could only envision himself in the comfort of his new bed. It was a long way back to 601 Lexington Avenue, the former Citigroup Center tower, which he simply called the "Center" tower.

About a month prior, Vincent had left his old luxurious

apartment and moved into this unique office tower. He'd been visiting it for a while before deciding he liked it too much not to make it his home base. This surprised him since he had always kept a low profile where he had stayed.

This time he couldn't help it. Something about the place drew him in. He knew that it stood out. It was a well-known city landmark with unique columns at the center of each side, and its slanted roof and imposing height would have been too interesting for people not to venture in and check it out, even just out of curiosity. He figured he knew it so well by now that he could make himself invisible in there, even if people came searching for him.

He made part of the fifty-fourth floor his own little sanctuary with all the necessary provisions he needed to be a vigilante outcast. Much like he did at the previous place, he acquired lots of books and training material for his work and practice of Krav Maga. He became so immersed in it that he felt that he couldn't be happier, but then again, he knew that if he was given a choice, he would make a different life for himself.

For now, he felt this was it—his calling. His life couldn't have turned out differently. Many perhaps dreamed about it, but few realized the cost. He was the lion tamer in this post-apocalyptic jungle, and the sheep needed him, or so he reasoned in his mind.

On his way back, he came across a few small groups straddling around. Some were doing something for the campus, some were young and bored folks crazy enough to venture out this far simply out of curiosity, and some were troublemakers and willing outcasts. His senses became so well tuned by now that he could hear any disturbance and pinpoint where it came from, thus avoiding being seen or surprised.

He wondered, at times, if he would ever feel overconfident in his urban savvy, almost to boredom, that no one could spot him, come upon him, or surprise him. He wondered if he would ever feel too aware of his surroundings, making his work tedious. He thought of the time he was stabbed and knew that, in his line of work, excitement and danger walked hand in hand and were never too far away.

Vincent slowly walked along 43rd Street, passing the Grand Central terminal, and saw his tower ahead.

I'm close, he thought. Only a few blocks more.

The satisfaction of finally being in a comfortable place after hours of trekking made him happy.

"Home, sweet home!" he said, excitedly.

He then heard some people nearby. He couldn't see them, but their careless chatter gave them away.

"Damn it." He started feeling agitated. "Why in the world did they have to be around here at this time? Isn't it getting kind of late in the day to be away from the campus?"

As if on cue, Vincent hid behind some cars and watched for those who disturbed his walk. They started appearing behind the building and into his line of sight. They looked like the typical campus crowd. He had no reason to worry.

He then saw Marcus. He hadn't seen him in over three months. He looked good and spirited and was excitedly talking about something with three other guys. He recognized them, as they were Marcus's longtime friends at the campus. He wanted to approach Marcus—give him a sign to step away from the group for a second so he could arrange a time to meet with him. It wouldn't be easy, but he had done it before, and Marcus was good at picking up on clues.

He waited to determine the size of the group, as he still hadn't seen all of them, and more people appeared behind the building. He then recognized Marlene. Good, he thought. They're still together. She talked with another girl he hadn't seen before.

The last to appear was a tall guy holding hands with a girl and talking to her. They looked like a sweet couple, and he admired them. He couldn't recognize the guy, and at first he couldn't make out who the girl was. Then on second look he realized it was Marie.

A quick pain came over him. He stared into nothingness. His heart raced, but he lost the desire to do anything. He realized how much Marie had meant to him, and now she was holding hands with someone else.

Marie wasn't just his former roommate. She was someone he had bonded with quite closely. Now she was bonded with someone else and looked happy. Her face seemed brighter, and she had fixed her hair differently than when she had lived with him. She looked better, which was one of the reasons he didn't recognize her right away.

Vincent felt small and lonely. His duty didn't seem so appealing at the moment. As soon as the state of shock diminished, he felt jealousy. He envied everyone he saw. He was an outcast.

As the group strolled back to the campus, Vincent continued on his way to the tower. The happy thoughts of being in his home disappeared. They were replaced by blandness and lack of desire for anything. It felt like a heavy burden on his hope.

Vincent sluggishly walked into the tower and entered the lobby. He didn't even care to check whether anyone had snuck around. He opened the door of the main staircase and began climbing in the dark. It was a boring pattern he remembered well.

When he reached the fifty-fourth floor, he threw his rucksack and weapons onto the floor and collapsed onto the couch. He saw the sun setting on the other side of the city. It looked nice and soothing, but a little to the right stood the campus. He turned around and went to sleep.

CHAPTER 34

After a couple of days, Vincent's loneliness grew, so he decided to reach out to Marcus. He went down to the campus to Marcus's usual evening hanging spot, but he couldn't see him. Watching the people taking comfort in their companions made him realize all the more how he had none.

He let out a sigh of disappointment and then tried another spot. There was no sign of Marcus there either. He decided to wait there, well camouflaged in his location. Maybe he would appear in the next twenty minutes, he thought.

After half an hour, any folks hanging around there left. He rose, shrouded with disappointment but hopeful of the next day. As he planned to leave, his heightened senses told him of some commotion happening not too far away.

Quietly, Vincent walked around the corner of a large stone building. He could hear something going on farther down. As he approached, he heard grunts, hollering, and cheering. When he came to a narrow alley between two brick buildings, he saw three girls beating and kicking another girl on the ground who cried, barely able to cover herself from the kicks.

They called her all kinds of names and jeered at her. The girl seemed barely conscious and too weak to defend herself. He watched for a second. A switch called rage turned in his head. He approached them.

A butch black girl noticed him. "Who the fuck are you, punk?"

Vincent stopped and then roundhouse-kicked her, as hard as he could, at her midsection. The girl coiled over and fell to the ground gasping for air. The other two girls stood for a second and then went at him. He jab-kicked one in the stomach, while the other girl threw a wild punch at him.

His hand guard caught the punch and responded with an uppercut, which snapped the girl's head back. He clinched her by the shoulders, delivering two knees to her midsection, and then threw her face-first into the brick wall. She collapsed to the ground bleeding from her nose.

The girl who was jab-kicked recovered and went at him. He tried to roundhouse-kick her but missed and hit the brick wall. He felt a sharp pain shoot up his foot and paused for a moment.

The girl tackled him to the ground. They wrestled, throwing punches, and then tried to get each other in a headlock. The girl started biting him, and he responded by pulling her hair back, punching and elbowing her in the nose.

She started bleeding profusely but still kept going at him. He pulled her hair back again and punched her some more. She backed off for a moment, which gave him time to move away and attempt to get up on his feet. As he stood, the incredible pain in his toe made him collapse to the ground. He got ready for another onslaught, but instead the girl rose and ran past him, yelling at the top of her lungs.

"Help! Help! Help!"

Vincent knew he was in trouble now. He was in campus territory, and the campus police wasn't far away. His only solution was to get as far away from the scene as he could. He had to muster all his energy and skill to escape without being noticed.

As he limped away, he could tell that the girl had found some help, and the police approached the scene. He knew he couldn't outrun them, so instead he decided to hide in one of the building's basement entrances and cover himself with readily available foliage. The crowd gathered at the scene and scattered around looking for him.

He heard lots of yelling and running around. The campus police showed up and started investigating. From listening, Vincent thought there were hundreds of them. He heard them say in their shock and anger that they would kill the bastard who did this. He thought he wasn't far from being lynched by the mob. If only one person decided to look in the basement entrance, he would be discovered. Then it would be all over.

As the original victim started telling her story, people's attitudes slowly began changing. There didn't seem to be as much upheaval anymore, but confusion. Yelling quickly followed as accusations went back and forth between the four girls.

For half an hour, the campus police tried to decipher the real story. The crowd started calming their voices, discussing what had happened. After an hour, Vincent could still hear them discussing the events and who did what, and who was at fault.

Being still in his hideout came as a good thing for Vincent's injured toe. Swelling a little, his toe became numb, pulsating with occasional pain as he tried to wiggle it. Fortunately, he was able to move it, and he figured it wasn't broken, but he had stubbed it bad enough to cause soft tissue injury and a sprain at worst. The crowd finally started walking away from the scene. Another half hour went by before everyone had left, and he could slowly head home, too.

Sometime in the middle of the night, after hours of careful and slow hiking, he managed to get back to his lair and investigate his injuries. He had superficial scratches on his face and arms, but his toe felt the worst.

He couldn't do much else but clean the wounds, apply an antibacterial cream, and rest. As he lay there waiting to go to sleep, he wondered what would come out of the event with the girls. Would the campus find the girls guilty of their act, or would they convict him of a crime and send someone after him? Good luck, he thought. There is no one who can beat me in my own backyard.

CHAPTER 35

Two days after the events, Vincent woke up from a nap in the middle of the day. He turned over and saw sun rays, like beams of laser light, pass over his head and paint beautiful colors on the walls and various objects surrounding him. He lay on his back for a while looking for a purpose to get up.

He found napping in the middle of the day the most desirable activity since he had seen Marcus and Marie a few days earlier with their loved ones. Sleep made him forget the disappointment of missing out on love and made the time pass by. He was hoping that something, somehow, would change things for the better, however unlikely that seemed.

Vincent felt groggy, and his throat was sore, telling him he had snored rather loudly, probably giving away his location to anyone within a few floors of him. Getting up, he walked to the wall, where he stared at the panoramic picture of the City of Sarajevo. Then a few moments later he gazed out the window at New York City. He saw the huge concrete wasteland with a well-defined grid of streets and avenues, and birds, of course, dominating the heights. He wondered if there was anyone in the City of Sarajevo staring out the window like he was, watching the birds and pondering their own life.

As he thought about this, he felt hunger pangs, which encouraged him to do something other than think about his life situation. He slowly, leisurely, walked to his food storage and grabbed a box of cereal.

"Mmm, Raisin Bran. Sounds like a winner," he said.

As he stood there eating his cereal soaked in distilled water, he thought it would be nice to have some company. His thoughts turned to Marcus again; he would give him another try. Perhaps not that very day, since his toe still hurt, but maybe tomorrow or the following day.

Vincent missed talking to his friend and felt remorseful about avoiding him the past few months.

Guilt and regret came over him. It was Marcus who had tried to keep in contact. Vincent had squandered those attempts by ignoring him. What else could Marcus do? He risked his own life venturing far off campus trying to find Vincent, but all Vincent did was avoid him and neglect his notes. Now he was paying for it.

Marcus seemed to have moved on, and Marie definitely had. She looked happily in love with the tall guy. Vincent felt so small now, and he desperately wanted to fix the things between them, so much that he forgot the latest ordeal he had there fighting butch girls. He made a promise to himself that he would try to get Marcus's attention and apologize for his behavior.

The next day, well before sunset, Vincent found himself scouting Marcus's usual hangout spots around the campus. After a careful search and some patient waiting, Vincent finally saw him with a couple of his buddies chatting near one of the campus's newly renovated buildings.

He didn't have Marie to grab his attention, so he had to wait for an opportune time. He knew that could be a while, or perhaps not that night at all, but his patience had run out. He wanted to do something instead of just wait.

Vincent decided to try to blend in with the crowd. He left his spot and went to find some clothes. A few blocks away, he walked into an abandoned apartment building, carefully avoiding a few campus stragglers who were completely unaware of him, and half an hour later walked out with a new set of clothes, a hat, and glasses.

Let's see if Clark Kent can really pull this off, Vincent wondered. He felt that he looked silly in the mirror, but he knew it was better to be silly than be recognized. He smirked to himself and headed back to campus.

As he came closer to the campus, he felt increasingly uneasy. This would be the first time he had attempted to walk in there blatantly, without using stealth to hide himself, in about a year. Something prompted him to change his walk and the way he carried himself. He wanted to be a different person. Underneath his disguise, he felt the nerves creeping up on him telling him to stop, turn around, and walk back before it became too late.

As he entered the campus grounds, it seemed that there were people everywhere. He felt like the first time he visited New York City for a job interview and realized how busy it was with people, cars, and all kinds of action. Now he felt used to its buildings, mazes of hallways, stairways, rooms, and birds, but as for people, only at a distance.

It was odd seeing so many people so close and not trying to hide. The first people he walked past completely ignored him. This felt oddly good. A group of girls walked by, glanced at him for a little, and kept walking, minding their own business.

Vincent reassured himself that the experience wasn't so bad and thought maybe he could pull it off.

When Vincent came closer to the spot where he had seen Marcus earlier, he couldn't find him. A gentle wave of disappointment came over him, but the excitement of being around people quickly took over. He enjoyed the opportunity to walk around and feel a part of the campus again.

The glasses he wore blurred his view a little, but he didn't dare to take them off. He felt too good being there unnoticed and a part of the crowd. He strolled around pretending to be on his way somewhere. Vincent slowed his walk to make the experience last longer.

To his joy, the fading light of the day began further concealing his identity. He felt he could have simply walked in, and no one would have recognized him as long as he didn't carry a rucksack and pistols around his waist.

As the night progressed, people started leaving the streets and going to their rooms. He felt the urge to follow them into one of the buildings but held back thinking it would be way too risky, at least for now. Perhaps if he could master his undercover skills well enough, he would.

That day he didn't end up talking to Marcus or anyone else, but he still walked away content. He got to be part of the campus for at least an hour, and it felt good. He was among people. Not an outcast. No one seemed to bother him, and he didn't want to bother anyone either. This felt like a step in the right direction, whatever that direction was.

The next day Vincent woke up early. He looked at the morning rays and got up right away. He ate, stretched, and got cleaned up. He walked around planning his new and better disguise—the kind he would feel more comfortable in and that would conceal his identity even further.

Excitement took over, and he couldn't wait for the evening to come so he could head out. He knew that the campus still kept everyone busy during the day, and he felt too uncomfortable to try his disguise in the middle of a sunny day.

As the evening approached, Vincent dressed up, this time using glasses without prescription strength, and headed to the campus. He felt better about the whole thing than he had the previous day, even though the nerves still played their part in what-if scenarios. He felt excited to see people again.

He walked around in a slow pace, carefully dodging the playful kids who ran around in the twilight phase of the evening. He even got to speak briefly when an older gentleman asked whether he knew if the campus minister had moved the mass time on Sunday. He almost stuttered when approached with the question, but he kept his cool and smoothly responded, "You know what, I'm not sure."

Those six words were the most he had spoken to anyone in over three months, and they felt good. The people around him seemed at ease, as if nothing bad had happened, and it was contagious. He felt at ease, too.

At the close of the evening, as everyone headed back to their rooms, he had over two hours of blending in and feeling the joy of being someone else among the people. This was another good night for him, even though he didn't get to see Marcus again.

Vincent found himself enjoying this so much that he ignored his patrolling duties for the time being. He didn't bother to go on any all that week. Instead, he disguised himself and walked on campus in the evenings, occasionally striking up a quick conversation with a stranger.

At times he would just stroll around, but other times he would sit with a bunch of folks and pass a cigarette between them, talking about random things. One evening, he even was passed a marijuana joint. No law against it existed at the campus, and the folks had worse things to worry about than people getting occasionally high on THC.

Vincent didn't realize it was marijuana until the familiar sweet smell tickled his nostrils and brought some old memories back. He took a whiff and then coughed violently, briefly grabbing attention from the people around.

"Virgin lungs, eh buddy?" one of the guys said, laughing and patting him on the back.

"Uh, yeah," Vincent responded, but it was far from the truth. "I guess it's been a while."

That night was one of the best he had had in a long time. Now he truly felt like part of the campus, and not some vigilante outcast on its outskirts. A warm summer breeze caressed his face, and as his mind eased into its blissful state, everything felt comfortable.

Things seemed peaceful, like the people who stood around him. Everyone enjoyed themselves. They talked and laughed, and he was hanging out with others instead of being alone. He even felt they cared about him. The conversations were mindless and mindful at the same time, yet to the participants, they appeared deep and meaningful. Life, once again, felt worth living.

Walking back to his lair, content with the day, he did his usual zigzagging through the buildings on his way home to offset anyone who could be following. This was mostly a game to him at this point.

The city remained largely empty outside the campus, partly thanks to the Scourge of Man, but mostly because it was much easier living on campus than anywhere else in the city. He smiled, still enjoying the after effects of his companionship as he playfully moved through various corridors and alleys.

All of a sudden a voice came from the darkness. "You look pretty happy today."

"Sweet Jesus!" Vincent stumbled, almost falling down. "You scared the shit out of me!" He recognized the Old Wandering Woman's raspy voice.

"I'm sorry, son." She stepped to the right of him. "I didn't mean to scare you, Mr. Scourge, he-he."

"Hey, why did you call me that?" he asked, while waiting for his heartbeat to calm down.

"I saw some people write it on one of the buildings, 'The Scourge Will Hunt You Down!' he-he."

"Good God, maybe you're the Scourge. You definitely know how to sneak up on people."

"Nah." She shook her head. "God has better things for me."

"Okay, good, I'm glad," Vincent said with sarcasm in his voice. "So, how's life? Still wandering around? You look good, by the way."

"I'm fine, son. I can't complain," she responded. "I'm still standing, and I can walk, he-he. But I was wondering about you. I haven't seen you in a while."

"Really?" Vincent asked with a touch of sarcasm. "I thought you were probably watching me all along."

"Nah, you move too much, he-he," she said, followed by a cough.

Vincent looked at her with that pity he had when they had first met.

"I was actually wondering about you, too. I was a little worried something might have happened," he said.

"Don't worry, son. Nothing can happen to me that matters." Her response was followed with a few more coughs. "I've lived a long enough life. I'm happy and content. The Lord has blessed me, and I have all I need."

"That's good. I'm glad He did," he said, trying to cut the conversation short because he felt in no mood to discuss morality at this moment. Most of all, he was painfully sleepy from the day's activities and desiring his bed more than anything.

"He can bless you, too, if you give Him the chance," she added.

243

"Well, I guess in some way He has," Vincent replied, starting to head back to his place. "I guess in His own mysterious way He has."

"Yes, that's right, my son," she continued, "and He's giving you something else, something you shouldn't refuse."

Vincent had already started walking away and felt guilty about his rude manners, but he also felt too tired to explain that all he cared about was sleep. "I'll have to catch up with you later, my dear ma'am. I have to go now. You be good, all right? Don't be sneaking up on me like that."

"God can give you a new heart." She raised her voice as he walked away some distance.

"Yeah, because you're going to give me a heart attack," he replied.

"He he, you make me laugh," she said as she slowly disappeared behind him. "You know that, too, is a blessing from God."

CHAPTER 36

Two days later Vincent went out to the campus again. He couldn't have cared less about his patrols and his sheriff's duty. That remained far from his thoughts. He passed time with his newfound group of potheads who didn't know who he was or care about his past. He took a hit and enjoyed the aftereffects like his companions had been doing.

At one point he excused himself to urinate and left for the common area where the guys went to relieve themselves. In the distance, children laughed at them. They found it amusing that these adults urinated in the open area.

On his way back he ran into Marcus. Literally. When they bumped into each other, they excused themselves at first, but then they stopped and stared at each other for a moment.

"Vin--Vincent?" Marcus's eyes opened wide as he asked quietly.

"Uh, Marcus? Is that you, man?" Vincent responded, trying to come to grips with what had just happened.

Marcus pulled him aside. "What the hell are you doing here? Why are you wearing glasses?"

Vincent's buzz still held its power and prevented him from answering right away.

"Uh, hey man, um yeah. . . I decided that . . . I was looking for you, man."

Marcus sized him up and down. It seemed strange to Vincent that his friend was viewing him with odd curiosity. Then he realized, in his dazed state, that he had dressed to camouflage with the rest of the campus folks. He must have looked weird to Marcus.

"All right, all right," Marcus said, as if he accepted this state of Vincent. "What's been going on with you? I haven't seen you in months."

"Just give me a second." Vincent grabbed his forehead. He wanted to think clearly. His buzz slowly gave way, but his mind remained cloudy.

"Um, can we talk somewhere else?" Vincent asked. "And, do you have any water? I'm thirsty as hell."

Marcus took him to a more secluded area of the campus and asked him to wait. Vincent stood there spaced out, staring at the park ahead. In five minutes Marcus came back, bringing him a bottle of distilled water. Vincent slowly drank the water as his buzz further faded away. Then he slowly started explaining to Marcus what he had been doing for the last ten days at the campus.

Marcus listened carefully, as a father listened to the admissions of his son caught doing something he shouldn't. Vincent answered likewise, as if his father needed to know the truth of what he had been doing behind his back.

He answered all Marcus's questions—where he had been staying and how he had been managing to come to the campus unnoticed and hang around with his new pot friends. His buzz further slipped away, and any bliss that came with it slowly vanished as well.

Marcus seemed a little different toward him. He acted more serious, and Vincent wondered if the long time he hadn't reached out to him made Marcus resent him a little. After all, it had been a while, but Vincent didn't want to go into the details on his life and struggles. The last ten days were good, and he didn't want them to stop.

After thirty minutes of discussion, Marcus looked away from him and paused the conversation as if he was ready to get something off his chest. Vincent's mood dropped in anticipation that he would say something along the lines that he didn't want to be his friend anymore.

"Hey, listen man." Marcus took a deep breath in his usual manner before continuing the conversation. "I've wanted to see you for a while to tell you something."

Vincent's heart started beating faster, and his fears started surfacing. Anything left of his buzz completely vanished, and his mind got ready for what would come next. Marcus continued.

"I know that . . . I know that you're the Scourge."

Vincent looked at him in confusion. "What?"

Marcus scratched his head. "Marie told us, Marlene and me, that you told her that you-" Vincent didn't listen from that point on. He heard the words, but he didn't listen. He now knew that Marcus was aware of what he had been doing since he had left the campus on that horrid day a year ago, his duty, and something that had become his specialty, regardless of how he had happily ignored it in the last ten days.

He felt partially betrayed by Marie, but that didn't hurt the most. It was the reality of the truth and that his closest friend now knew that he was the deadly figure everyone had been talking about. He felt afraid that he would lose his only friend. He also wanted to know this whole thing about the Scourge.

Marcus continued, "I can't believe I didn't connect the dots this whole time, but I guess I didn't expect you to be . . . I didn't expect it from you. You know? Obviously, I knew about your shooting

Neil, but I guess I never thought you'd be the one people would talk about. I mean, some are thankful for you, man; you saved their lives. That's a big thing, it really is, but I never thought you'd be the one. I'm still struggling to wrap my head around-"

"You have to explain to me, what's this whole thing about the Scourge? Why are they calling me the Scourge?" Vincent interjected, feeling offended he had been referred to that hateful thing.

Marcus shook his head. "I guess you wouldn't know it. How could you? You haven't been around the campus to know."

He took another short pause as if gathering his thoughts on how to tell Vincent. "I'm not sure how much you do know, but this new world is pretty small, man. The word spread around. It didn't take much for people to start talking about you, about what you've done, the shootouts you've had, and the people you've saved. And even if Marie wouldn't have told us about it, eventually the dots would have connected. But it also got around that you were pretty vicious."

Vincent remembered the Old Wandering Woman calling him "The Scourge." Now he understood why. Marcus continued talking. "Whoever came across you said you were pretty darn skilled at killing. Merciless. Like a wild animal. That something wasn't quite right with you. It was like you were possessed—moving through the buildings and streets, hiding, coming out of nowhere. Oh, and yeah, very good at shooting. So, they nicknamed you the Scourge of Man because you're a man, but came out to be nearly as deadly and stealthy as the Scourge of God was. But most simply call you the Scourge."

This didn't make Vincent happy. He didn't enjoy the way people were imagining him. It may have sounded tough, but it was also demented. If anything, he swore to fight demented people and destroy them. The last thing he wanted was to represent the thing he hated. He still thought he had humanity in him, someone acting in people's favor, not some serial killer whose priority was killing and acting tough.

"You might want to lay low for a little bit, though," Marcus said, lowering the tone in his voice. "You know, not come around the campus for a while. Most folks liked you for saving people until you beat up some girls not too long ago. That was some messed-up shit. Now they have mixed feelings about you."

"But those crazy girls were about to beat that girl to death!" Vincent snapped.

"So, it *was* you. We all kind of assumed it was," Marcus replied. "Anyway, you're probably right that they deserved it, but that's not how everyone sees it. They see it more like a guy bashing girls' faces in even though you protected that other girl. Their faces spoke of a maniac."

"But they were animals! They were worse than some guys I've seen! I had to. They were kicking-"

"It doesn't matter!" Marcus cut him off. "To some it's still a guy beating girls, and they don't like it. Not everyone saw what happened, but people choose to believe what they want. Don't get me wrong, there are some who think you did the right thing, but it's a minority. Maybe those girls had it coming. But people still don't like it, and it only reinforced the image that you're out of control."

Vincent got the picture. Not only had they named him the Scourge, the name he wasn't fond of, but the action of saving one girl backfired and the campus approval rating of him had plummeted.

Now his only friend told him to stay away just as he had started enjoying the campus again. This made the evening one of the worst he'd experienced in a long while. He sat on the nearby stone wall with his head between his hands, thinking how it had gotten like this.

Marcus came over and sat next to him. "Hey, listen, man," he comforted him. "Your secret is safe with me, with us. No one knows it was you besides the three of us. I'm not going to lie and say I wasn't shocked when I heard the news. I'm still confused, to tell you the truth. If I could choose it, I wish it had never happened.

"But you made the decision, the commitment, that you would protect or whatever. I just hope that you would find it in you to make the right decisions even when you think you're helping someone or this campus."

The friends remained silent for a while, watching the folks at the square. It all felt unfair to Vincent, but then again, he had gotten used to it. Marcus then broke the silence by telling Vincent how the campus was planning its big move to Parsippany. Vincent listened, gathering all the information on something he knew was inevitable. He just didn't like that it was coming so soon. Now the campus would leave altogether, and he would really be alone in the city.

"Do you know the exact date the campus is moving?" Vincent asked.

"It's going to be more of a gradual move," Marcus explained. "It will take a few weeks, maybe months, to completely move everyone over. It was supposed to happen this spring as Bill Loren had originally planned. But you know how things got out of control last summer. That set us back quite a bit."

"Yeah, I bet," Vincent said, quietly glad the campus remained in Manhattan and close to him. "Do you think you'll move this year?"

"Nah," Marcus shook his head. "I don't think it'll happen this year. There's still much more planning that needs to be done before we can all make an exodus over there. I mean, we're doing well right now. Much better than last year, that's for sure. But I don't see the new place at Parsippany being ready in time before the winter hits."

"Yeah," Vincent agreed. "Who would want to move in the winter anyway?"

"Not me," Marcus responded. "But it'll be safer and better than here. The campus folks recently started heading out there, you know, to scout it out and determine how realistic Bill's plans were to move there."

"Elysie should be there," Vincent said.

"That's right. She should." Marcus seemed surprised Vincent mentioned her name.

"I hope she's happy," Vincent added. "Like Marie is."

"I hope so, too. You never know. Maybe you'll get to see her someday."

Vincent remained silent. He knew that was a long shot, and deep down he felt unsure whether it was such a good idea anyway. If he saw her happy with someone else, it would be too much pain to swallow.

"How many have left for there already?" Vincent asked.

"Not many. Maybe twenty or thirty. One of them is my buddy Jeff. You must have seen me with him. A good standup guy. A structural engineer."

Vincent nodded, vaguely remembering Jeff.

Marcus continued, "He was specifically chosen to inspect the buildings and the reservoir there. This initial group is more like an explorer party doing their detective work before any real work begins on the migration."

Vincent sighed, replying, "Sounds like they have some plans in place. That's good. Better for them to go there. I don't see this island being good much longer anyway. It's going to start falling apart sooner or later."

It saddened his heart. This was his home. He knew it better than any creature living in it. Having the campus there gave him the purpose for someone and something to protect. If they left, it would be different. He became so used to it that thoughts of an open space out there made him feel naked and exposed.

"Oh, and by the way," Marcus added as they got ready to part ways, "I married Marlene. I wish you could have been there when I came by to tell you. I left you notes to let you know about it, but I'm not sure you received them."

Vincent paused, immediately regretting that he hadn't paid more attention to the notes. "Wow, I didn't know. Congratulations, man!" At the same time, he felt genuinely glad to hear that his friend had made something good out of his life that he couldn't. "I'm happy for you guys. I always thought the two of you looked good together."

Before they parted, Marcus patted Vincent on the back, letting him know they would see each other again. He also reminded him that, for the time being, he needed to remain a low profile. Vincent nodded in understanding and then put his fake glasses on and headed back home. They waved, not really knowing when they would see each other again.

That night Vincent walked home with an obvious absence of the excitement he had felt for the last week and a half. The buzz of the last ten days crashed under the heavy thoughts of everything he had heard from Marcus. He carelessly threw the hat away, feeling cheated by his attempts at the disguise.

If he hadn't run into Marcus, perhaps he would have enjoyed his time a little longer. Perhaps a lot longer. He also didn't like the fact that Marie had told on him, betraying his trust. But the more he thought about it, he felt it didn't matter anyway. He was what he was, and denying it wouldn't have made a difference.

When Vincent reached his tower, he looked up and let out a disappointing sigh. He trudged up the long set of stairs to the 54th floor and then slouched onto his couch. He felt exhausted, emotionally and physically. He sat there thinking about how he had enjoyed sneaking into the campus and hanging out with the potheads. Then he laughed at how foolish he was to believe it could have lasted. What a life, he thought. Isn't it something?

CHAPTER 37

Over the next three weeks, Vincent abstained from patrolling the city. He started each day practicing Krav Maga and shooting drills. He designated a few floors of the tower for each exercise he trained for. He had all the space he needed and used it.

The rest of the time he spent reading books, but now he no longer read books on martial arts or philosophy, but adventure. He found the best way to forget the fact that he remained alone was to immerse himself in something. He would sometimes read well into the night supported by the light of the small efficiency lamps, and he had more than enough batteries to last years.

Going over the events of the past two years, he found that at many times his life had been quite turbulent, exciting, and scary. So much had happened since the Scourge, and now he was becoming the Scourge himself—something he could have never have dreamed of.

At this very moment, however, Vincent felt that nothing could replace the excitement of a good book. Books became an escape he couldn't replace. He wondered why he hadn't read more before the Scourge. Perhaps he would have avoided falling into depressions and addictions.

He also wondered what life was like before the Internet became mainstream. He wouldn't have known, but he for sure knew what it was like after. He imagined people reading books a lot more and socializing like he did at the campus.

Taking himself as an example, he didn't remember being as social before the Scourge hit as after it. Perhaps there were some benefits of the Scourge. He remembered how happy he felt with Elysie and the friends they shared, but this time it didn't hurt so much thinking about it. He had books with him.

This solitude with books ended on one hot and sunny day when Vincent noticed someone coming up his tower as he rested from his Krav Maga practice, which remained his daily exercise. This wasn't the first time he had discovered people carousing in and around the tower.

After all, such a big and imposing structure captured curious people's interest, especially the young adventurous ones, but going as high as his floor remained uncommon. Not many people ascended the dark stairs more than the first ten or at most fifteen floors before they turned around.

This time, however, someone came past the fortieth, the floor where he practiced Krav Maga. He went to investigate and could tell by the footsteps that it was one person. Intrigued, he decided to follow and see where the person headed.

The mystery person kept climbing and went past the fiftieth floor. Vincent wondered if the person was trying to get to the roof, like a mountain climber conquering the mountain. But then the person stopped at the fifty-fourth floor. His floor.

This wasn't a good sign. It was too much of a coincidence for the person to randomly select this floor. Did someone see his light from the outside or from the towers across the street and now decided to pay him a visit? He thought he was careful about all that, but maybe he was wrong.

He then heard the door open and the person walking into the main lobby of the floor. He felt certain that someone was curious about him. Taking his gun out, he slid the safety off. Then he heard the person calling out.

"Vincent, Vincent, are you here?"

A huge relief came over him as he recognized Marcus's voice.

"Hey, man, I'm here!" Vincent said excitedly, coming behind Marcus.

"Damn, man, did you really have to pick the fifty-fourth?" Marcus said while resting his hands on his knees while taking a breather.

"Well, this is the prime example why." Vincent jokingly pointed to Marcus's exhausted state. "It's supposed to keep the likes of you away."

"It sucks, but it does work. I bet you don't get many visitors."

"No, they usually give up by the fifteenth," Vincent said while walking into a nearby room to grab Marcus some water. "But I'm glad to see you, though. What brings you? To be honest, I had planned to keep away for a while at your suggestion. I didn't want anyone getting into any trouble because of me."

"Well, man." Marcus took a big gulp of water. "I'm glad to see you, too. And yes, you're right; you did the right thing by keeping away. If someone had recognized you, I'm pretty sure it would have been trouble. But I have to be honest, I didn't come here because of that."

Vincent sat next to him, curious to find out the true reason behind his visit.

Marcus continued. "On the contrary. Well, remember the explorer party I told you about who went to Parsippany?"

"Yeah, now that you say it, I do remember," Vincent replied.

"Okay, well, they got into some bad trouble on the way there." Marcus paused while his eyes gave away worry. "As a matter of fact, most of them didn't make it back."

There was a moment of silence. "What happened?" Vincent asked, intrigued.

"Apparently, they were attacked on their way there by somebody." Marcus paused. "Only three made it back. My buddy Jeff I told you about . . . Well, he didn't."

Silence ensued again. Then Vincent broke it with the only words that could come to him, "I--I'm sorry to hear that."

Marcus nodded.

"Does anyone know what happened to the others?" Vincent asked again.

Marcus's eyes dropped to the floor. "From what they say, nothing good. It seems whoever attacked them, they did it over a period of time. Pounced on them, one by one. They didn't use firearms, just knives. When our guys realized their only way out was running back the way they had come, apparently a real slaughter happened.

"They all became separated, until only three made it back to the campus. One of the three said he saw only one attacker, dressed in some weird shit, wielding knives. But I talked to this guy who was a former crime scene detective, and he told me it's highly unlikely this was carried out by one person; this seemed to be too well coordinated by at least three or four people."

Vincent knew full well that Marcus feared the worst for his friend. He felt especially horrified when Marcus said they were butchered with knives. That was something he had experienced himself, to a degree, when he was stabbed on Christmas night some nine months before. The pain, the fear, and the struggle to make it back home was something he would rather forget. Now this news made shivers run through his whole body.

Marcus continued, "We sent a group of eight campus officers to investigate and take out the killers. These were all tough guys, with plenty of experience fighting crime before the Scourge. All former NYPD, many with SWAT training, they knew how to handle weapons. Actually, it was the same they were debating on sending after you when you had your fight with the girls."

"Oh, I see." Vincent wasn't pleased to hear that.

"But they didn't fare much better. Five days later, only two came back," Marcus said with uneasiness in his voice, while Vincent remained silent and disturbed at this new piece of information. "Yeah, it's pretty messed up," Marcus added.

"I'm not sure what to say, Marcus." Vincent felt the desperate need to console his friend. "I really do wish your friend were still alive and well. It may be hard to believe, but you never know— maybe he escaped when everyone was separated and is now somewhere safe."

Vincent wanted to say more to console his friend because he didn't feel this had done it.

He thought for a moment and then said, "It may sound unlikely to you now, but if you say it's three or four guys hunting a group of twenty or thirty, I think it's more unlikely that they caught all those running away in different directions."

"Well, here comes the part why I'm really here," Marcus said, leaning over to pick up the half-empty bottle of water. "The campus was pretty disturbed by all this. At first they weren't sure if you were behind it. But then they concluded it was too gruesome and savage for you to be the one. Plus, no firearms were used. So instead, the council actually wanted to see if you could do something about it."

Vincent's eyes widened in disbelief.

"I volunteered to find you and relate the request," Marcus

continued. "But don't worry, I didn't tell them anything else."

"They want me to go after the psychopaths?" Vincent asked, still in disbelief that the campus had actually reached out to him.

"Yeah, believe it or not," Marcus answered. "After all, you are the Scourge to them. Who better to send than the one people fear and think is kind of crazy, to be honest. Like those killers, but under better control."

"They think you're the good kind of crazy," Marcus reiterated.

"A good kind of crazy?" Vincent felt disappointed with the word "crazy," and the comparison with some psychopathic killers. He didn't want to be considered "the crazy guy" who happened to be under better control. In his mind he was closer to being sane than most of the hypocrites left in the world, which felt like everybody else alive.

"I don't share anything with those crazy killers you're talking about," Vincent said, "and now they want me to go over there?"

"Yes," Marcus responded. "They're hoping for that. They think you're the only one with 'qualifications' who understands that kind of world."

"But I don't know anything about that area over there," Vincent objected. "I've never been there, more or less take on any-"

"That's the thing, Vincent," Marcus cut him off. "The council doesn't want them to come over here, and on top of that they stand between us and Parsippany, our new home."

"Marcus." Vincent looked straight at him. "I may be better suited than someone from the campus, and I know these streets and buildings like the back of my hand, but over there, I know nothing. I'd be hunting in their own backyard."

"I know, I know." Marcus shook his head. "I'm sorry I'm bringing you into this. I don't want to put you in harm's way. It's just that people are more scared of them than you, and we don't know what to do."

"Great," Vincent responded sarcastically. "First, I have to lay low, and now they want me as their policeman. And let me guess, I get nothing in return."

"Right. Not the ideal treatment, is it?" Marcus let out a sigh. "You don't have to do this if you don't want to. I'm sorry for even asking you."

Marcus took a short pause, gathering his thoughts.

"They're using you. You can see right through that. I get it," Marcus said. "But what the hell are you doing here anyway? Aren't you supposed to be in Parsippany with Elysie? Why are you patrolling this city?"

Marcus stood and raised his voice. "And the real question is, why am I even here asking you to do this? Why are you the one they're sending me to recruit? What have you become? Who are you? I told you the last time why they're calling you the Scourge, but now *you* tell me. Why ARE you the Scourge?"

Vincent couldn't take it anymore. It felt pointless not to open up to his friend. Marie had already started the revelation, and now he wanted to finish it. "Everything changed when I took Neil's life. I couldn't let people like him have their feast on whatever was left in this world. I just couldn't.

"I've felt this fire inside and a duty to make a difference, to hunt them down. Like a sheriff from a Western movie, I suppose. It's been a gift and a curse. I've never attacked a decent human being. Never! Only the filthy scum who deserve to die . . . and I couldn't mix Elysie into this."

Vincent's eyes welled, but he quickly brushed away the would-be tears. "I don't think she would want me after this anyway."

Marcus looked at him with pity in his eyes, and Vincent could tell he hurt, too. He knew Marcus hadn't wanted to come and ask Vincent to put himself in harm's way, but he didn't have a choice. It was Vincent who had put himself in that position by basically advertising himself as the best man for the job.

"Okay, I can't say I get it all, Vincent, but I'll try. It's still all fuzzy in my mind." Marcus sat down. "And don't give up on Elysie that easily."

"I don't want to," Vincent said as his eyes swelled again at the thought of her. "But I don't see how she could want me."

"Don't be so sure about that," Marcus replied. "Love is a powerful thing. If she really loves you, which I think she does, why not give it a chance?"

"Because . . . It's not the same. I'm not the same."

"You may not be," Marcus stated. "But who is? Everyone's different and everyone changes. I'm not the same since last year. I'm not the same since I learned you're the Scourge. Just because you changed from that moment you shot Neil doesn't mean you can't change into something else."

Vincent thought for a while in silence. Marcus was good at reading people, and Vincent knew it. He felt that sooner or later Marcus would figure he wasn't necessarily dead set on being the sheriff forever or living the life that he had chosen for the last year. If he could change this life of a loner preying on gangbangers and would-be rapists for the one with Elysie and him together, then he most likely would.

The one thing Vincent doubted Marcus knew was how powerful that fire, the Scourge, was rooted inside him. It was something he doubted he knew either. Nevertheless, Marcus was good at providing hope to troubled minds, and he knew how to calm them down. As simple as Marcus's words sounded, Vincent thought he did make a good point. The question remained whether he wanted to change or remain the sheriff.

The matter at hand, however, remained the same: who would go out there and take out the knife-wielding killers? If Vincent was best suited for the task, it wasn't right to send someone else. Sacrifices had to be made.

"But here's the thing, Vincent," Marcus cut his train of thought. "If you've made some kind of promise to yourself or God or whatever, and you want to remain true to keeping scum from harming people, then this is something that needs to be done." Marcus made it simple again.

Vincent knew he couldn't debate this. When he made his vow to be this sheriff of sorts, he never once shied away from acting on it when he saw the need to. There was no doubt the campus needed help to take on those killers; otherwise, Marcus wouldn't be there telling him about it.

"Very well," Vincent responded as if he didn't have a choice. "I'll do it."

Marcus looked at him and Vincent felt his pity. It was as if he had just signed a death sentence.

"This time I'm a little afraid," Vincent added. "I actually enjoyed not going on my patrols recently and instead losing myself in books. Now you've snapped me out of it, and I feel like a person who just woke up. I know what I can do. The only thing I doubt is whether it's going to be enough."

"Vincent, I'm sorry I'm pulling you into this." Marcus touched his friend on the shoulder. "On behalf of the campus, all I can say is thank you.

"But consider this," Marcus added, "When it's all over, think about maybe retiring from this business."

Vincent looked at him and gave a quick but reluctant nod, not knowing if he would get that chance.

That was it. Vincent had signed up for a job he didn't want. For the remainder of the day, he gathered as much information from Marcus as he could about the locations and nature of the events that had happened. He wanted to know every bit of data before he headed into the unknown.

He was still surprised that the hunter or hunters solely relied on knives. There was not a single mention of a firearm. This meant close combat, which only the bravest and the craziest would do, and also the most skilled.

This was nothing short of blood-thirsty lunatics enjoying their sick work. Why would they rely on knives when guns were readily available unless they found it more challenging or fun to see their victim bleed up close?

Vincent also learned that the gang used traps, which apparently they could set quickly. Their favorite trap seemed to be a thin thread of an extremely sharp Gillette type of metal they would tie across paths, hallways, and doors, at ankle or waist height.

When people ran into the trap, the thread would cut deep into their ankle or abdomen, immobilizing them or in some cases spilling their guts. Most of the time, however, they would isolate a victim and strike him or her with their knives. Once again, no one counted the killers; almost anyone who was able to see one ended up dead.

It seemed the traps were mostly used to divert the group's attention or split them up. Then they would pick at one or two members of the group who were left behind. All these details disturbed Vincent, but he needed to know them. Unfortunately, instead of making him feel more prepared for the fight, they decreased his confidence further.

Vincent would be going into someone else's turf, against an opponent or opponents who didn't mind fighting up close in some of the most devious ways, and there would be traps. The only thing that made him feel a little better was that at least he planned on taking a gun to a knife fight. Then he remembered what Marcus told him happened to the campus police. Considering that, he didn't seem so sure the gun would make much of a difference.

That night after Marcus left, Vincent chose to study the map of Jersey carefully. He labeled all the locations where the events had happened to the best to his knowledge. He saw a vague pattern and felt happy to at least know the general area the killers were moving around. Vincent planned to avoid the direct route there, which is what the campus police had taken. He planned to outflank the killers, come from an unexpected direction, and then prey on them and hopefully eliminate them in quick succession.

It all sounded good on paper, but he didn't expect it to be easy in execution. He had never been there, and he knew little about the area. He had only spent eight months in New York City before the Scourge hit, and the entire time he was east of the Hudson River. Now he was headed where he didn't want to go, facing something he didn't want to face. One thing he felt confident of was that the killers had never taken on someone like him before. After all, he wasn't new to this game.

He chose not to sleep that night. He wanted to sleep through the following day and then travel at night. He felt more secure this way. Much of the patrolling he had done was at night anyway, and he had become well used to it by now. He felt less exposed then. Just like a leopard hunts mostly at night to avoid detection, he, too, wanted to give these psychopaths the least amount of warning possible.

Vincent packed all the usual stuff into his rucksack, as he would before each patrol, and then laid out all the clothes and weapons he would carry. By the first light of the morning sun, his eyes gave up, and he went to bed. He made sure he got as much sleep as possible because he didn't expect much of it once he left his lair.

CHAPTER 38

The following evening, as the sun slowly set its majesty behind the Jersey skyline, Vincent crossed the Hudson River in a small canoe he found along the coast. He took his time, paddling carefully and making sure the canoe remained steady.

Looking ahead, Jersey looked peaceful. The only movement he saw were the birds flying between the skyscrapers and giving themselves away with the noises they made in the distance. Other than that, all he heard was the slight hum of the breeze caressing his ears and the splashing of the water made by his paddle. It felt serene, almost as if someone were trying to tell him that everything would be fine.

This gave him an extra boost of confidence and let him breathe easier, not thinking too much about the dangers he would face. He started feeling he could do this, that he was good enough, and that he wouldn't give up if it got tough.

He wanted to think clearly, perceive the situation, analyze, and react as best as he could, which he knew was better than anyone else these monsters had faced. He realized that he couldn't count on this current harmonious feeling for the entire trip. It was probably only a calm before the storm. Nevertheless, he felt thankful for it.

Once on land, Vincent walked for hours through the dense array of brick buildings and houses in Jersey City. There was quite a bit more debris and nature in the process of taking over the city than he had expected. To his surprise, the shrubs had made some streets quite difficult to pass through. What was different about this place, he wondered.

Nevertheless, he pushed on through and eventually found himself in the open on the Lincoln Highway crossing a river. Here he stopped to eat, look around, and take it all in. The moon lit the night fairly well, and being in the open helped him orient better.

Behind him and to the east, he could make out the elegant Freedom Tower, rising above the rest over the horizon like a lone soldier refusing to give up and still standing firm. On the right he saw the long bridge that made up the Pulaski Highway. For a moment he felt disappointed he wasn't on it instead because it was much higher than the bridge he walked on. Something about height appealed to him. Perhaps that's why he liked Manhattan so much.

On Vincent's left, the river made a slight right turn before merging into a larger body of water, giving him an unobstructed view for miles even at night. It made him think of the time he would visit Niagara on the Lake, a small gorgeous town on the Niagara River right before it made its way into Lake Ontario.

His parents would take him there when he was in elementary school. At times his friends would come along, which meant his parents were likely to treat everyone to homemade ice cream, which he still regarded as the best he had ever had. He could still taste that chocolate flavor, as if he licked it at that moment on the open Jersey road.

In front of him he couldn't make out anything exciting or that would stand out in the view. The more industrial part of Jersey looked dark and monotonous. He wondered what it must have been like working there before the Scourge, having to drive down there every morning, fighting the heavy traffic, and working in some dirty plant. Now he headed in the same direction to do his own dirty work.

At sunrise, Vincent walked on Interstate 78 passing Newark International Airport. He thought of this as the first stage of his flanking maneuver. Being south of the city of Newark, he bypassed the locations where the campus explorer party and the campus police had been attacked.

He felt this was far enough out of the way where the psychopathic killers operated. He only had a few miles to go before he would head north and hopefully come from the direction they wouldn't expect anyone to come from—at least not from Manhattan.

As Vincent proceeded by the airport, he found himself becoming increasingly tired. He knew he needed to stop soon and have some rest and sleep. By now he had walked over fifteen miles of varied terrain and paddled across the Hudson River. His muscles gave out their plea for a break, and he felt the need to obey.

He got off the interstate and broke into a house nearby. He ignored the dusty remains of its former resident in the living room and went upstairs into a bedroom that looked empty. He felt relatively safe here, which gave him a greater ease to fall asleep without worry.

Ironically, he didn't expect to be sleeping much on this mission, but at this point he didn't care. He took off his shoes and the rucksack, placing them next to a dresser while taking out some mixed nuts to eat. This satisfied his hunger, and within a few minutes he fell sound asleep.

When Vincent opened his eyes he found himself looking out the window at a tree branch. The leaves waved back and forth in the slight breeze at the twilight of the day. On the branch chirped a European Starling, that tireless Shakespearean invader, with its shimmering black color. He figured he had slept for a while and should get up, but he felt hypnotized by the view.

It was so nice to wake up to a nice quiet breeze in the summer evening. He wanted to enjoy it as long as possible before the sun set completely behind the horizon, which meant that he would get on his way.

The night felt warm, and the breeze, once again, was a perfect complement. The moon lit the night, and everything seemed so peaceful. Vincent strolled by various houses, apartment buildings, and brick warehouses. The sleep must have done him good because he felt rejuvenated and ready to walk for many miles like this.

He found it odd that he felt so good at this point in the mission. Yes, the trek was long, but the weather was so perfect, the nights were well lit, no trouble had come his way, and there had been no accidents and mishaps. Even sleep had come at the right time, which was refreshing. His mission remained to find the most disturbing people he had ever come across. How could something so nice and serene lead up to something so awful?

A few hours later the temperature seemed to drop, and the wind picked up. Animal noises could be heard in the distance, giving Vincent goosebumps, and as if on a cue, a cemetery appeared on his left. He felt tension rising and wondered why he felt this way when he should be a veteran at this by now.

He thought about how many times he had crisscrossed various places in Manhattan and encountered assorted criminals while still coming out on top in the end. People labeled him the Scourge; why would this encounter in Jersey make him stiff? Trust your instincts, he thought. This is not your first time doing this.

Half an hour later he came to an intersection. He looked up at the sign that read Sussex Avenue. He knew this meant he had arrived. A few hundred yards away was the spot where the explorers from the campus were first attacked.

From this point on, he planned to be extra careful where and how he moved. No more would he just walk down the streets. This was the stalking game now. He assumed that the killers were likely two miles east of him because that's where the campus police were attacked, but he didn't want to take any chances.

He thought they probably anticipated more campus investigators coming from that direction, but perhaps this time they expected someone more like him—an instinctual killer who was good at battling other human beings for whatever the cause, whether for justice or fun. Either way, the game was on. He wouldn't turn back now. The face-off between the killers had begun.

CHAPTER 39

Vincent took it all in. His already heightened senses picked up on all the information from the environment surrounding him. He surveyed everything, making sure he didn't miss a single thing that could turn out to be a trap.

He listened to every small noise. He smelled the air as if that would indicate clues. He carefully placed his foot with every step. Vincent zigzagged around the buildings, avoiding walking on the streets. He moved from building to building, house to house, each time stopping briefly to investigate the scene ahead.

On certain junctures he waited in the darkness, his senses taking it all in once again, and observed. When he felt satisfied that nothing of danger lurked there, he proceeded farther. He wanted to follow the general path the explorers took when they made their way back to the campus.

Vincent's exploration went on for hours. Each street block took up to half an hour for him to clear. Even then he didn't feel so sure about getting any closer to the killers. He expected this to take a long time, but he remained disciplined enough not to give in to his anxiousness and make a mistake. He gave his adversaries a lot of respect as skilled and capable killers, and he had to be extra careful. He labeled them "the trappers" in his mind from hearing about their methods of setting up traps for their victims.

By sunrise, Vincent found himself crossing a city park, which he checked on the map to be Branch Brook Park. It had grown thick with foliage and trees and resembled a forest more than a park. He had failed to come across a single mark left by the events Marcus had described.

Morning arrived, and Vincent debated whether he should continue with the sunlight coming up or find a place to rest and get some sleep. All the meticulous searching and observing tired him much quicker than the walking of the previous day.

Looking at the map, he realized he had only covered about a mile and a quarter since coming across the Sussex Avenue and officially beginning his hunt. He rubbed his eyes and then scratched his head. All this tension of the hunt wore him down, and he felt uncomfortable to continue. He wanted to feel fresh like he did at the beginning, but the hours had taken their toll.

He glanced to his left and saw a large church not too far away rising above the trees of the park. It looked inviting, and he decided that this would be the place to rest.

He climbed a small hill toward the church, and within a few minutes he was looking straight at it on the other side of the hill. The church stood out from the rest of its surroundings. It had a large open approach unlike other buildings around, and it reminded him of Notre Dame in Paris.

The church was big and gothic in style, with two soaring towers rising well over 200 feet above him. He felt mesmerized by what he saw and for a moment didn't pay attention to his mission at hand. Then he shook it off and approached the church rather carefully.

Vincent felt guilty for giving in to the view and not paying attention to the dangers that may be around him. His eyes darted up and down, left and right, and at the very entrance of what he could now clearly tell was the Cathedral Basilica of the Sacred Heart.

He entered the basilica and soon met the remarkable view of the interior. The beauty made him stop for a moment and take it all in, but this time for pleasure. He stepped in farther and observed all around him. Early morning sunlight came through the windows and lit the wooden pews and white marble, making it all even more majestic.

One ray of light, however, reflected something else between the two rows of pews that he couldn't quite decipher. It sparkled a few feet away about a foot high off the floor between the pews. It looked like a thick strand of spider web. He had seen many before, but perhaps viewing one in a beautiful building like this made it stand out. He wondered if a spider had actually made it and found it rather comical. He came closer to investigate.

The more Vincent looked at it, something didn't seem right. A few inches from the web, he realized it wasn't a strand of spider web at all, but a thin line of Gillette thread sprung between the pews. It was the killer's trap!

At this his heart started beating faster. He was only a few moments away from walking right through it, slashing his shins. Vincent immediately grabbed his gun and crouched. Adrenaline pumped through his veins, and he readied himself for an uncertain battle.

He glanced at the pews to the right, then to the left. Everything looked peaceful and quiet. All he heard was the pulsing of blood in his head. He turned around and scanned the entrance lobby he had come through. The wooden doors seemed dark, but no one was there. Above, the organ section looked like a good place for someone to hide. He carefully observed, but it, too, didn't reveal anything unusual.

He asked himself only one question at this point: was this an active or a passive trap? An active one would have been placed a few moments prior to his entering the basilica and been specifically for him. A passive one would have placed some time ago for anyone who had decided to come to this spectacular church and have a look around.

Vincent slowly stood and carefully scanned all around him with his pistol. He still couldn't tell if this was an active trap. Now his eyes paid a lot more attention to detail. With that, he started noticing other traps. Many were laid out in the pews, which made him believe it had taken a lot of planning and time to be an active trap. The place didn't seem so inviting anymore.

He felt disgusted at the thought of what could have happened if he had run into one of the traps. He started walking back, and to his shock, he noticed a Gillette thread behind him as well. Either by sheer luck or God watching over him, he had managed to step right over it. He also noticed that it laid lower than the others, perhaps to get a victim as he or she raised its foot.

"These psychos are really messed up," he whispered to himself.

Before he managed to get back to the door, he noticed at least a dozen traps. He could have only imagined how many were there in total, but he was in no mood to find out. As he was about to open the door and exit the basilica, he turned around to have another look at everything with his pistol leading the way. Sweat came across his face. "I don't think I'll be resting anytime soon."

Outside the basilica, the morning sun hit Vincent's face, and he felt exposed being out in the open like that. He was nervous. With each step, his heart beat faster. The confidence deserted him, and he doubted he could do this hunt at night. He also had to stop and think whether he could pull this off at all.

A million things ran through Vincent's head, and none of them filled him with confidence to keep going. Then the thought of the Scourge came into his mind. He survived that all alone in his apartment. It felt horrible, but in the most critical moment the will to prevail saved him. It was his will against all the odds.

It felt as if someone had put that desire to live in his mind just at the right time when he thought he couldn't keep going and the only way out was giving up. Now, ironically in front of the basilica, Vincent looked up at the sky, whispering, "Please."

He had no idea which way to go. His anxiety clouded his mind, but he had to choose a direction. He couldn't stay out in the open; he needed to act. Doing this at night was out of the question now; how many traps would he have run into? "The morning is here," he said to himself. "Get to work now."

Vincent took a deep breath, closed his eyes for a moment, and remembered that he was heading east toward the last known place of attack. This time he planned to be even more careful than before when he had zigzagged between the buildings.

As he crossed the street and disappeared among the buildings, he took some time to drink and eat. He also closed his eyes for twenty minutes, resting behind one of the houses. The relaxation was much needed, and he sensed the renewed energy to keep going. However, as he rose and moved between two adjacent apartment buildings, he observed a horrific sight that made him take a step back.

In the alleyway, Vincent witnessed a body lying on the ground with its head snapped back, revealing a wide open neck decomposing in the hot summer day. Without a doubt, he was certain this was one of the campus explorers. The tongue of the unfortunate victim swelled and hung out. The hair on the head had begun to fall out, and the skin was covered with blisters.

The smell was appalling. Bacteria, in the process of devouring the inside, caused the stomach to bloat. The skin and muscle on one of the hands had partly come off, exposing the bone. Above the body was a thin line of Gillette strand.

It wasn't the first time Vincent had seen a dead body. He must have seen thousands of them, but this one felt different. The Scourge left nothing but the grayish dust and bones of its victims— no organs or anything resembling the shape of the victim other than the skeleton. This, on the other hand, was a body mutilation. Everything was exposed and violently cut short by the thin Gillette strand.

This was the first victim that Vincent had come across so far in Jersey, and he pictured in his head how it had all played out. The explorers at this point had been running away from the killers. For some reason they became separated. This particular victim must have been running fast before hitting the barely visible Gillette strand placed about neck height for an average male. The strand cut through much of the throat, snapping back the head. The victim then fell on its back bleeding to death. The killers had placed it there either moments before it happened or a few minutes in advance before chasing the victim toward it.

It would be horrible to die this way. Vincent thought he was a survivor of some disturbingly sick world. Perhaps it would have been better if he had died with the majority of the population. He cut the Gillette strand with the multi-tool he carried and then went on his way.

Two hours later, Vincent came across the Passaic River. The water looked still, dark, and deep. Less than a hundred yards away to his right was a bridge. He assumed that on the other side, not too far away, the campus police had their run-in with the killers. He couldn't help but feel he would find the killers there, too. He wondered how many more decomposing bodies he would come across heading that way.

Soon after he crossed to the other side, proving his feelings true, he came across another fallen victim in the midst of an alleyway he had walked through. This time the victim appeared to have had its shins slashed and then butchered by a knife. The sight didn't look any prettier than the previous victim's. No doubt it was another explorer. Taking a closer look at him, Vincent thought he might have recognized the guy, but with the decomposition well underway, it was hard to tell.

He wondered if it was the guy he met when he was sneaking into the campus about a month ago. He hoped not because he seemed nice.

Vincent cut the strand that slashed the poor guy's shins and kept going. Not too much farther, there lay another victim in a small parking lot between two houses. This one, however, didn't have a trap nearby like the other two. He looked to have been attacked from the front and slashed pretty bad in the abdominal area. The attacker probably left after that because it appeared the victim crawled unopposed for twenty to thirty yards before giving up and bleeding to death.

All this churned Vincent's stomach. At the same time, it brewed fear and anger. He wanted to avenge these victims and stop this evil menace once and for all. He felt the desire to end these killers in the most ruthless fashion, but he also knew he would have to control himself and not give in to his emotions to be successful in this mission; otherwise, he could be their next victim, ruthlessly deposed.

As Vincent continued, he put a lot of thought into doing something to protect himself in case he ran into any of the traps. The easiest to protect and the easiest to injure would be his shins. It proved tough to spot those low-to-the-ground traps, and these trappers seemed to have placed quite a few of them around. He needed something to wrap around his shins.

It would have been great to come across a sports store like he had so many times before and get some soccer shin guards, but he didn't see one around this neighborhood. He then came across a tire shop. There was a small hole in the wall garage with a single garage door. Above it read *New & Used Tires & Rims*.

This could work, he thought.

Vincent walked in and to no surprise found a stack of tires by the wall. He moved around the car that a mechanic had worked on prior to the Scourge and grabbed one of the tires, putting it aside.

"I may not be as good at using a knife as the psycho trappers are, but at least I can cut a tire." Vincent proceeded to cut the tire with his utility knife. After he cut out a few strips, he duct taped them to his shins and moved around a little to test them for comfort. He felt pleased with the outcome and thought that since cutting them wasn't easy, they might work well in the field.

He then thought about making protection for other parts of his body. Since his skills relied so much on movement, he didn't want to restrict himself more than necessary. He figured he should at least protect his abdominal area and maybe his neck.

Vincent figured that wrapping his neck with tire would be a little uncomfortable, but a strip of tire rubber wrapped around somewhat loosely would protect enough. As for the abdominal area, and having experienced stabbing before, he wanted something to stop a knife thrust.

He experimented a little and found that strips of tire wouldn't work well. For this he had to look further.

It was well past noon at this point, and Vincent started lagging behind. He needed to take a break. Carrying the food and water in his rucksack had taken a toll. Vincent also realized that he hadn't drunk much, and only a small amount of water remained in the canteen. He began going into houses hoping to find some bottled water. To his luck he found some right away in the first house.

"At least something is going my way."

Once Vincent sat down and drank some water, he didn't feel like getting up. His muscles were sore, and his mind was tired from all it had seen. He went into a corner of a room and lay down to get some rest.

In front of the door he set up a little trap of his own to alert him to anyone coming. He also had his pistol in his hand across his chest. Within a few minutes of closing his eyes, Vincent fell asleep.

CHAPTER 40

Vincent dreamed he was at his old workplace in Niagara Falls. His father stood beside him, and they walked down the hallway of a building and talked. Then, out of nowhere, his father put him in a headlock. He tried to get away but couldn't. He somehow remembered what he had read in the Krav Maga books and practiced those steps, but it didn't help. His father's grip felt too strong.

After a long struggle, Vincent finally managed to get out of the headlock. He looked at his father, who shook his head and said, "Those self-defense skills are not working out well. They're useless."

He felt disappointed and tried to remember the moves clearly, asking his father to put him in a headlock again. With somewhat less struggle he got out, but his father didn't seem impressed this time either. He still shook his head.

He then dreamed that he woke up in his bed in the Brooklyn apartment as his mom came into the bedroom. She didn't have a smile as she often did, and he felt guilty for it. Soon enough, Elysie came running in. She had tears coming down her eyes.

Vincent asked her what was wrong, and through her sobs she said her fingers were cut. He looked at her hand and saw missing fingers and blood coming out of the wounds. He felt agonizing pain in his stomach. He couldn't bear to see her hurt.

He started crying and leaped out of his bed, carrying Elysie to his car to take her to the emergency room. His mother was already in the car waiting for them. He asked Elysie how it had happened. She cried out, "The claw!" He looked at her in disbelief and fright. His heart started beating faster and faster. Then he woke up.

Vincent now found himself looking up at the ceiling lit by the moonlight. His heart still raced from the dreams, but he tried to calm it down.

"Once you get used to it, the night isn't so dark after all," he told himself.

He then saw a shadow slowly creep up on the floor. At first he felt mesmerized by it, but then he quickly realized someone was standing outside the window. He lay motionless in the corner ensuring the safety was off on the gun. The shadow slowly disappeared, just as it had come.

Now his heart started racing even faster than when he had woken up. He slowly rose and peeked out the window. He couldn't see anyone even though the moonlight was lighting the street well. He listened with intense care for any sound, but he could hear nothing.

"This could be them!" he whispered to himself.

Vincent peeked out the window again, but still there was nothing. He decided to get a look from the other side of the house.

By sheer chance, he glanced out the window as he walked down the hallway to the other room. He saw a dark figure outside a mere few feet from the window slowly moving by. He stopped, raised his gun, and aimed at the figure. He debated on taking a shot but chose not to, thinking he needed more of a verification on who this was. He felt afraid, but he still had the sense not to just pull the trigger at the unknown.

As he aimed and waited to see what the figure would do, it slowly moved away from his view. He moved to another window and then saw it again, walking away from the house. He wondered why it had come so close to this house of all the houses on the street.

Perhaps it was the trapper, he thought, who had spotted his tracks and come to investigate. But then why did it move away? Could it really spot his tracks in the moonlight? As anxiety kicked in, he watched it slowly fade down the street.

Vincent had to act fast: stay or follow? "Follow," he told himself. "What am I here for anyway?"

He walked outside, felt the fresh air caress his face, and started in the direction he had last seen the dark figure. His senses were on high alert, and every step he made was with extreme elegance as not to make any sound. This time he didn't zigzag around the buildings. He knew the figure must be close by, and he didn't want to waste time.

As he came to an intersection, he hid behind a car and looked both ways. There it was again, alone. It was some fifty yards away, up a slight slope to his right, staring at a house. Vincent only watched from his cover.

A few moments later, the figure stepped onto the small ledge in the front yard and slowly crept up to the window looking in. What it was looking for, he couldn't tell. This reminded him of when he used to go on patrols and snuck up to different buildings and offices and poked around out of curiosity.

The figure then moved on up the street, and Vincent moved after it. It didn't take long before he lost the track of the figure once it made a left turn onto a street following another intersection. He had to pause to figure out where it had disappeared.

He hated this. Just as he gained confidence that he was in a good spot, he couldn't see the person anymore. He eliminated the fact that it had gone down far on any street; otherwise, he would still see it. He thought it must have gone between the houses. He waited for a few minutes, and when he couldn't wait anymore, he started walking.

Just then Vincent saw something ahead. He stopped, completely motionless in his tracks. The figure came out of a garage one house ahead of him. The tree obstructed his view, but he could tell that it kept moving up the street toward another intersection.

The figure walked so quietly. It made Vincent think of a mountain lion, as each step was so elegant and effortless. Whoever this was, it moved as well as he did, or even better. Not a single sound could be heard.

This has to be the trapper, Vincent thought. He felt glad that the tree was obstructing his view because it also helped conceal his presence, but he didn't want to let the figure escape him again. For a half hour, as morning approached, Vincent stalked the figure. He would lose sight of it each time it would go into a building or a house, but then he would wait and it would appear back on the street.

He watched it with great curiosity, and as time passed, he became more convinced it must be the trapper. It had the style of a hunter. It was searching for something, but it didn't want to be noticed. That was for sure. It moved lightly and made virtually no sound, as if it were floating. The only thing that gave it away was its silhouette against the moonlight.

Vincent, having spent so much time patrolling the streets of Manhattan at night, had adjusted his eyes to nighttime, helping him see this figure better, perhaps, than other people could have. However, the question remained: where were the other trappers? Could it be that there was only one?

After another half hour, the sun started making its presence known ahead in the distant skyline of Manhattan. The dark figure made its way down a street on the sidewalk. Vincent still followed closely behind but made a decision that it was time to present the trapper with a choice to either show itself with hands raised high or face fire from a safe distance.

The figure then started crossing the street. Vincent followed some fifteen yards behind, but then the figure stopped, and he stopped as well. Both stood in the middle of the street.

Just as Vincent was about to present his demands, the dark figure turned around silently and looked straight at him. A shiver went down his spine as he stood there, surprised that it had noticed him, but he didn't make a sound or move.

Everything had become quiet around them; the birds, the breeze, and even the trees refused to make a sound. It was as if time had stopped. Vincent realized he had made a bad choice of having the sun in front of him, partly blinding his view. On the other hand, he could sense that the figure was a little surprised that someone was following him from behind. They both just stood there staring at each other.

As his eyes adjusted to the scene ahead, he started getting a slightly better image of the figure. The bristling reflection of stainless steel gave itself away on the dark figure's waist and chest. There must have been at least twelve knives neatly strapped in their holders in pairs of three—one pair on each side of the waist and chest. Two rolls of what looked like Gillette strands were strapped to the belt.

Vincent now had full confirmation that, after all, this was the trapper he had sought. More chills went down his spine, but he remained motionless and speechless. The trapper wore all black clothing tight against its agile body. Vincent found it hard to make out the face, but he could tell by the shape that it was most likely a man.

"Raise your hands!" Vincent demanded, as he broke the silence, raising his gun at the trapper.

The trapper looked on as Vincent debated on pulling the trigger.

The next few moments were so tense they could have been cut with a thread. Sweat poured down Vincent's face, and his finger gently felt the trigger on his gun. Out of nowhere, the trapper shrieked an awful sound and with lighting speed threw a knife at Vincent.

Taken aback by the awful noise, Vincent's body stiffened and he pulled the trigger. The knife struck him in the left shoulder, and pain shot through. In agony, he let out a scream.

The bullet also found its mark in the trapper's left shoulder, knocking him a step back. He clutched at it and then peered at Vincent for a moment before he darted toward a parking ramp to his left.

Vincent grimaced with pain and, seeing the trapper running away, frantically pulled off two more shots, but hardly aiming, he missed wide. Gathering himself for two seconds, he then ran toward the parking ramp to pursue the trapper and finish him off.

Ignoring the injury, he arrived there and realized he couldn't get in because it was gated all around. The trapper had somehow managed to get in, and Vincent could see him zigzagging between the cars.

Not wanting to lose him, Vincent shot three more times hoping for a lucky hit. The first two shots missed, but the third grazed the trapper on his right cheek. The trapper subsequently ducked behind a car and disappeared from Vincent's view.

Vincent, unsure of whether he had shot the trapper in the head, carelessly tried to find a way inside to investigate. He desperately wanted to finish him off before the trapper could escape. Looking around, at the same time glancing at the car, Vincent quickly came across an opening in the fence.

Within a few seconds Vincent made his way inside the parking lot, and with much caution, moved up to the car. His heart was beating so fast he could feel it drumming in his head. Unfortunately, to his dismay, he didn't find anything but a small pool of blood on the ground.

Not quite knowing what to do, Vincent felt his anxiety rising. The debate ran on whether he should pursue the trapper further or take a step back and gather his thoughts. A part of him wanted to continue the chase because he took the trapper by surprise, which most likely shook him up, and he had shot him. But Vincent was injured as well, and pursuing a skilled killer in the midst of a dark parking ramp could result in Vincent being taken by surprise instead.

Thoughts and decisions ran a million miles a second in Vincent's head, yet time was running out. Vincent gathered the courage and decided to pursue. Moving around the cars and sneaking up on the stairs leading to the upper floor, he found himself praying for luck much more than reason.

At this point, Vincent wasn't paying as close attention to detail as he otherwise would have, and this scared him. He almost hoped that something would happen and that his quick reflexes would seal the trapper's fate; however, that didn't happen. The trapper was nowhere to be found.

As Vincent came up the stairs to the second floor, he tripped on something and fell forward. He managed to put his hands in front of him to save his face from being bashed against the concrete floor, but the knife lodged in his left shoulder was pushed in deeper, causing an immediate shot of incredible pain.

He couldn't hold it quiet for more than a second before he let out a scream, which then gave his location away to anyone within a quarter of a mile. This caused him to become extremely upset with everything and left him questioning the reason behind pursuing the trapper any more.

"God damn it all! To hell with this damn duty!" he fussed.

Vincent propped himself up and, sitting against the concrete wall, scanned everything around him with his gun. This gave him time to cool off. Then he listened. He heard nothing but his own heavy breathing. Now a new debate started in his head: treat the shoulder or continue the pursuit?

Considering that he was in an unfavorable position in the dark parking ramp and the trapper had probably hidden himself or run away, Vincent decided there was no point to risk it any further and decided to halt the pursuit and get out of there.

He slowly got up and began looking for what had tripped him. He came across a sight that troubled him further. It was another thin Gillette strand about ankle height right at the top of the stairs, and he had completely missed it on his way up. The trapper had set it up, perhaps seconds before he started coming up the stairs. Flashbacks of the victims he had seen appeared in his mind, and the thoughts of how he could have been cut up or immobilized so that the predator could finish him off disgusted him.

"God damn this son of a bitch!" He felt furious at himself as much as the trapper, but deep down he was glad he wasn't hurt more than he could have been. If it wasn't for these makeshift shin guards, he knew it would have been done.

Collecting himself, Vincent started making his way outside. He had had enough of the chase. He was injured and lacked a clear plan to continue. He knew that sooner or later he may be the one pursued. He felt convinced of having no other choice but to get far away from the scene, treat his wound, and ready himself for the next round. He hurriedly went north to find a temporary safe haven, all the while desperately glancing back to ensure no one was coming from behind.

After thirty minutes he came across a neighborhood he felt was as safe as he was going to get. He walked into a family house and immediately went upstairs to look for a bathroom and a mirror. For the first time, he had a chance to clearly inspect the knife injury.

When he looked at himself in the mirror, he could barely

recognize his reflection. Not that he lacked a mirror at his home in Manhattan, but his face looked pale and his hair messier and dirtier than he had ever seen it.

The knife was lodged well in Vincent's shoulder, right through the rucksack strap, and blood covered it. He looked at it, grimaced, and looked away. He knew what would come next—removing the knife. The weapon appeared to have penetrated deep, but there was no way of telling until he took the knife out.

Biting down on a rolled-up towel he found in the bathroom, he started pulling on the knife handle. He wanted to do it in a single motion, but when he tried, the pain immediately made him stop. It was agonizing. After four more tries, Vincent finally managed to get the knife out all the way. Two and a half inches of the knife were blood-stained, indicating the depth it had penetrated, yet it felt like it was triple that. He immediately started controlling the bleeding and bandaging the wound.

A few minutes later he slowly walked into a bedroom and sat on a bed to rest up and think about his next move. It felt good to sit there and do nothing; however, the first thought was how the trapper was treating his wounds. Was he in as much pain? Vincent knew he shot him at least once, but how bad were his injuries?

He figured the trapper would be somewhere, like Vincent, in a safe haven and in agony taking the bullet out his flesh. For an unknown reason, he felt sorry for him for a moment, but then as he remembered the dead victims, that feeling quickly vanished.

"You got a piece of what you deserve, you murdering piece of shit!" Vincent murmured.

The thoughts of everything he had heard and witnessed about this monster started bubbling up anger inside him again, clouding his mind to make a clear plan on how to take him out for good. He wanted to have another chance at a showdown like he had just gone through, but this time he would make sure he didn't stop shooting until the monster was sent to the underworld.

The possibility of that happening in the same fashion as before was far less likely now that the monster had been disturbed. Vincent knew that. The mutual hunt had started; tactics would have to change.

CHAPTER 41

Vincent closed his eyes and slept for about two hours. It wasn't the greatest sleep, since every fifteen or twenty minutes he would wake up disturbed by any sound, whether a creaky door at the house across the street, tree branches grazing the window of the room he was in, or the occasional loud bird gawking.

When he felt he had enough, he stood, rubbed his eyes, and checked the wound. Satisfied that the bleeding seemed under good control, he started planning his next move of the hunt. He decided to go for another flanking move, come from an unsuspected direction and again surprise the trapper.

He assumed the trapper would try to comb the entire area of the showdown looking for him, likely setting up many traps and preying on anything unusual coming his way. For Vincent, the flanking move would require him to move far from the area of the showdown and instead go around, to eventually come up from the south. In this case he would go far east, then move in a clockwise direction with a diameter no less than a mile.

He wouldn't play into the trapper's strengths by hunting him in his own area only to fall into one of his traps; instead, Vincent would let the trapper become frustrated or over-confident, while he would turned up at an unexpected time from an unsuspecting direction.

Vincent ate, drank some water, said a quick prayer, and made his way out.

The sun still had a few hours left in the sky when Vincent got on his way, yet he moved so cautiously that it took almost until sundown to cross a single mile. His trek had been uneventful so far. The pain in his shoulder annoyed him at times, but having experienced something similar, he knew it wasn't life-threatening. His heightened senses masked the pain from time to time as he observed the environment with greater care.

Reaching a certain perpendicular street, Vincent decided to turn south and begin his large roundabout move to surprise the trapper. The fact that the sun was slowly fading didn't bring him joy, but he had confidence that his plan still made tactical sense.

Moving down the street, he came upon a construction area where a fairly large complex of buildings was being built until the Scourge ended it. It was still in its bare structure phase, and all he saw were concrete plates, pillars, and supporting walls. The buildings ranged from four to ten stories high.

A few cranes had toppled over, damaging some of the structures, but other than that there was nothing out of the ordinary about the buildings. As Vincent moved farther into the construction zone, something didn't seem quite right with the area. An unusual number of crows were congregating, and they were especially attracted to one of the buildings.

As he approached closer, he saw that something was strapped to the pillars that the crows were trying to get at. They were behaving unusually wild. To his horror, he realized it was human flesh they were attacking. His heart sank at the sight.

"That evil, evil man," he whispered to himself in disbelief.

Vincent felt stunned once again by the cruelty of the trapper. Coming closer, just below the building, he saw a row of six people tied to the pillars on the second floor facing out with their naked bodies badly cut up all over. Some had their faces carved up. Others had their midsections torn wide open. The mutilation of their bodies was horrendous.

Tears started streaming down Vincent's face, and he was emotionally disturbed. He felt so much for the victims that he wanted to put their bodies back together and lay them in their graves respectfully. He couldn't continue his flanking move now. All he wanted was to take the victims down and drive away the crows.

Climbing the stairs, he openly started to sob. When he reached the second floor, through his teary eyes, he saw various writings on the wall. He couldn't make out what they said since they weren't in English, but he had the gut feeling that the trapper was the author. The print was dark red in color, almost black, the letters written diagonally.

Further on the floor he saw various figurines laid out. They were of people, animals, and various other creatures that were alien to Vincent. Next to them, on the pillars, was more writing, much like that he had seen on the floor.

Approaching the first victim, Vincent's stomach churned. The crows scattered away, leaving pieces of torn flesh on the floor. This was the one that had the midsection open. Unable to look at it for long, he proceeded to cut the strings that held the victim and gently lowered the body to the floor. He tried not to look at the others either, almost out of a sign of respect, but do the same to take them off the pillars.

Vincent did decide to look at the last victim he had come across. It was a young man, and Vincent could tell he was strapped to the pillar while still alive. His face showed agony from the sick ritual the trapper had performed on him. He couldn't shake the thought of what it would have been like going through that ordeal. The cold nausea went through Vincent's veins, and he gently touched the victim's hand. It was small, almost that of a teenager, with many cuts.

"God, what did he do to deserve this?" Vincent questioned. "How could you watch this and not do anything?"

Sick and bothered, he lowered the guy to the floor and proceeded to the third floor, where he found a single victim strapped to the pillar, figurines laid out in the middle of the floor and more strange diagonal writings on the pillars and walls. The victim was a woman, and she didn't seem to be spared any more than the others. Cutting the straps, he lowered her light body to the floor and then went up the stairs.

The fourth floor looked different. Six more victims were strapped to the pillars, but these had their foreheads burned. This time every single pillar had something written on it, presumably by the same author, and in the middle of the floor stood a small altar surrounded by blood-stained knives and swords.

On top of the altar was a wooden chair with writing on the backrest. A few smaller fire pits laid in random locations away from the altar, with one of them relatively fresh, perhaps less than a day old.

After lowering those victims from the pillars, Vincent approached the altar as if drawn to further investigate this grotesque sanctuary. In addition to the weird writings, he saw a number of strange signs that he didn't recognize on the lower floors, giving him an ever-growing eerie feeling.

He believed he had entered evil itself. Everything that he knew about life seemed irrelevant here. This looked like the realm of the disturbed, and it was tough to imagine anything else. The only sign of hope for getting out of there was the diminishing rays of the sun. Night was quickly approaching, and Vincent, as if he woken from a trance, decided he wanted to leave as fast as possible.

Heading toward the stairs, Vincent paused before he entered the stairwell. He then turned around and went back to the altar. He grabbed the chair sitting on top of it and laid it upside-down. Next, he grabbed the blood-stained knives and swords and spelled out "FIN" with them. He wanted to leave his mark and let the trapper know that if he ever came across it again, in spite of all the horror he created, someone would still end it for him.

Descending the stairs, Vincent realized that it had gotten much darker than he expected, and his eyes couldn't adjust well. He told himself he was used to the darkness, and it wasn't so bad.

While giving himself the courage to keep going, Vincent also started debating his next move. He considered just waiting for the trapper here because he obviously came to this place often and probably wouldn't be away for long. Rather than outflanking the trapper out there, Vincent decided to surprise him right here.

He came down to the second floor and found a spot among the construction material left over from the workers. He hid well, covering himself with nylon and other material, while he had a decent view of the stairs. His plan was to ambush the trapper as he came in to investigate the pillars. He didn't have an escape plan, which he knew would constitute for horrible planning, but he felt this was good enough to finish the job.

As he sat in his hiding spot, time wore on. He started pondering various what-if scenarios. They all challenged his decision to hide and wait, while covering a single entrance to the floor. He knew that it was really fear that put him there, and if he thought more rationally he would have done a better job. Perhaps he would have set some traps. Maybe he would have found a different spot where he would cover multiple entrances, or even go to the building across the street to monitor the situation first and then ambush him. All of these seemed better ideas than where he was now.

As the clouds rolled in, the night got even darker. It was one of those murky nights where Vincent could barely see a few feet in front of him. Even though his eyes were used to the night, his only field of vision increasingly became useless, and he could barely see anything coming from the stairs.

This reminded him of the times he walked in dark buildings in Manhattan learning to navigate in complete absence of light. It was solely based on sound, touch, and that sixth sense that something wasn't quite where it should be.

Now what? he thought. He could barely see anything.

Paranoia kicked in, and Vincent itched to do something. Anything. When the night became as dark as his hiding spot, it didn't feel different from being out in the open. Everything felt the same. Fear, uncertainty, and anxiety turned into torment, and he escaped from his hiding spot. He stood in the open and listened. He felt a little disoriented and needed to reach out for something to touch.

Once he felt for the nearest pillar, he approximated his relative location on the floor. He was about fifteen feet from the stairs. Quietly walking up to the entrance of the stairs, he raised his gun.

"All I need is to hear this bastard come this way, and I'll open fire," Vincent told himself. "He can't see me any better than I can see him, but I don't have to make a sound. I'll just stay still."

Minutes passed, and dark clouds slowly passed over the night sky. The moon and stars calmly started displaying their presence. The darkness gave in to a touch of brightness, and various shapes of objects presented themselves shyly. Standing at the entrance of the stairs on the second floor, Vincent remained loyal to silence. He then realized he didn't blend in with the darkness as before and that his shape stood out ever so slightly against the backdrop of dark gray concrete around him. He thought about moving to a different location, but then he heard a whistle.

It came from behind. His eyes opened wide, and as if electricity had shocked his body, he quickly turned around, crouched, and raised his gun in front of him. He saw nothing. His heart pounded. The whistle continued. It was thirty feet to his right! He turned to the right.

A moment of silence passed and the scene remained still. Now he heard it twenty feet to his left. He turned again as sweat fell off his face, but nothing, then ten feet right in front of him!

Two shots rang out as he fired his gun. The silence of the night was broken. Disturbed crows made noise as they flew away from the building. Then slicing pain came over his left wrist, and he dropped his gun. Disarmed, but with a strong fight response, he swung wide with his right, missed, and lost his balance, falling down the stairs, then more stairs, eventually stopping on the first floor.

Feeling aches all over his body, Vincent rapidly got onto his feet. Thanks to the adrenaline, he started running away in an uncertain direction, deeper into the building. He wanted to get away from being finished off. The flight response had kicked in.

Realizing that he had gotten himself farther into an unknown area, he stopped, grabbed for his second gun, and quickly turned around. With his heart running a marathon, sweat profusely coming down his face, and blood dripping from various places on his body, Vincent tried to remain as motionless as he could. The pain slowly revealed his injuries, and his endurance was tested.

This place seemed darker than the second floor, but not pitch black. Light still managed to pass through to show a few features of the first floor. The silhouettes of the thick supporting pillars and the building material made it look like an ancient labyrinth.

Moments passed that felt like centuries; then the whistle came again. It was much farther in front of him, perhaps a hundred fifty feet away. He could actually pay attention to it now and couldn't imagine a more harrowing noise in his life. It sounded like a mystical wave of high- and low-pitched noises, as if an animal were making them.

This made Vincent's blood curdle, and he prayed for a single millisecond of a clear shot to end it. All he heard was the damn whistling. When it got away from him, he wanted to follow it, but when it got closer, he battled the nerves to keep his hand steady.

The bastard is toying with me, Vincent thought. Or maybe he is calling me out to face him and fight, but I'm in no shape.

This prompted Vincent to look around for something he could use to change the present standoff. He then noticed less than fifty feet to the left of him what looked like another set of stairs. He figured there was more than one of them in this building anyway. He decided to go for it, but first he needed to make a diversion.

Keeping his gun raised with his right, he crouched and felt the floor with his left hand. He hoped to grab at something he could throw to divert the trapper's attention, but as soon as he tried to grab at anything, he felt harsh pain in his hand. This made him wince, and he almost let out a scream. The cut he had received upstairs agonized him, but there was no time to whine about it now. He had to hold it in.

Vincent put the gun into its holster and then felt around the floor with his right hand. He felt something like a thick piece of clothing. He thought maybe underneath it he could find something he could throw. He grabbed at it, but when he was about to lift it, he realized it was a rat! It made a squeaking noise and Vincent pulled away for a second but then grabbed the rat anyway and threw it across the floor. The rat, hitting one of the pillars, made a loud screech and fell to the floor.

The whistling stopped, which gave Vincent a clue that the trapper had heard the commotion. At this, he got up, and as quietly as possible he fast-walked toward the stairs. When he reached the stairs, he instinctively turned around to make sure he wasn't being followed, and then he climbed the stairs. Half-way up he tripped on something and fell face-first. He managed to cushion the fall with his hands, but the agony of the pain and everything that hadn't gone his way reached the boiling point. He didn't have to investigate much to figure out it was an ankle trap set by his nemesis.

"God damn it!" Vincent fumed, and while getting up he cussed more inside. "This fall gave me away. He must have heard it. I've got to keep moving now."

Laboriously, Vincent ascended to the second floor and then proceeded to the third. Here it was even brighter, giving him a slight boost in confidence. He moved behind one of the columns and took a breather.

"Dear Lord, will you give me a break and have mercy on me?" Vincent prayed.

His heart still tried to pace itself while he experienced increasing weakness in his legs. He felt blood trickling down his left wrist, dripping to the floor. He still had no idea how bad the injuries were, but the pain told him it wouldn't get any better.

"Brace yourself. Get it together." He encouraged himself not to lose control, while everything else told him to do the exact opposite.

Raising the pistol to his chest, he peeked behind the pillar. It looked clear. Then as he was about to move to another pillar, something caught his eye. He could see the tiny bit of reflection about neck height. It was another trap!

You've got to be kidding me, Vincent mouthed silently in disbelief. He had almost run right into it. Without a doubt, it would have cut his jugular. He would have bled to death within minutes. This was further confirmation that the hell he was in had only gotten hotter.

Vincent carefully moved away to another part of the floor and thought he dreamed all this and the nightmare couldn't be real. It seemed so bizarre that everything had played out the way it had. Only the unrelenting pain in his body gave him the proof that he was awake.

Everything made him feel he was out of his domain. This was completely the trapper's land. It didn't seem like much of a fight anymore, as he was the only one being hunted now. The mountain lion stalked after him. It was hungry, and it wanted to devour him.

He had two choices: fight or flight. Unfortunately, he felt he wasn't ready for either. He just wanted the night to end.

Vincent moved to another pillar not motivated by any strategy, just to make a change. The change made him feel that much better that he wasn't a sitting duck waiting for slaughter. A slight breeze came over Vincent's face, which felt good for a moment, but then he could sense that someone was lurking nearby to his right. Vincent raised the gun and then quickly swung around the pillar to his left.

He saw the figure in front of him now. It appeared to have been taken by surprise that he swung around the pillar the other way, but before Vincent could pull the trigger, the figure ducked and the bullet ended up going over its head. Vincent almost fired the second shot but was tackled to the floor by the shrieking opponent.

For the first time, Vincent was up close with his nemesis. He couldn't see the face clearly because it was too dark, but everything else was visible. The shriek sounded awful enough, but now he heard the grunts, smelled the body and breath, and experienced its strength. All the pain he felt diminished, and complete focus remained simply on fighting and survival. The fighting was dark, dirty, bloody, loud, and intense.

Rolling around, Vincent could feel the trapper's arm going into a wide stabbing motion, striking his backpack two, three, and four times in lightning quick succession. Shocked at the ferocious speed at which the trapper stabbed, Vincent wouldn't let the trapper adjust to strike his side; instead, he delivered two punches of his own and an elbow to the face.

Stunned for a moment, the trapper let go of stabbing and Vincent got up to move away. He reached for his holster only to realize he had lost both of his guns. Within a moment, Vincent fell again as the trapper tripped him trying to slash at his heel. Luckily, the tire rubber Vincent had placed to protect his shins saved him. In the commotion, the rubber slid down and protected his heels instead.

The trapper hurled forward with his knife but met Vincent's foot in his face as he frantically tried to get him off. The trapper fell backward, and Vincent quickly got up. Not wanting to face the knife master without a weapon, Vincent ran for the stairs.

Something in the back of his head told him to stop, which he did right before the entrance. He quickly scanned for any traps, and sure enough, there was one waist high right across the entrance. He quickly ducked underneath it and then proceeded to the fourth floor.

Climbing up there, Vincent saw the reflection of the dark red diagonal writings on the pillars. He realized where he was—the altar floor. The moonlight, as if understanding the importance of the place, shone brighter while the pillars cast their shadows bowing down for the occasion.

The dirt on the floor looked like the moon dust disturbed by his presence, and crows resting on the edges of the floor flew away on cue, casting their own shadows. Vincent kept staring at one of the crows that appeared to fly straight at the moon, and as if hypnotized he stood there silently in the open.

He felt like his soul was carried away by the crow, bit by bit, farther from this existence. Peace at last. It felt inviting. The end. Then, snapping out of it, he quickly dashed to get behind one of the pillars.

Vincent felt defenseless and without a weapon he could trust. Desperation quickly sunk in. Weakness was evident, but now clamminess had kicked in. He felt like he would throw up, but at the same time as if he could fall asleep. He brushed his face to get the sweat off, and everything felt numb—his hands, face, and lips. Only the vulnerability kept him awake. Give in, give up, or give it all; this was the ultimate test.

"God, if you want, help me. I'll do whatever you want." Vincent bargained with the Creator.

Looking to his left and then to his right, he expected to find an answer. Disappointed, he slowly slid to the floor and kept staring forward. Twenty feet in front of him on the floor read "FIN."

It was the sign he had made earlier from the knives and the swords to make his mark for the trapper. He contemplated for a second and then took a few deep breaths. I could use these!

Renewed with an ounce of energy, Vincent scanned all around him and then snuck up to the swords, grabbing the one that made the letter "I," the longest sword there. He then hurriedly maneuvered behind another pillar.

Vincent didn't have any prior experience with sword fighting, but at least it was a weapon he could use. It felt foreign in his hands, but he was glad it had the length to keep someone at a distance. Its blade was almost thirty inches in length, and it didn't seem as heavy as it looked. The longer he held it, the more comfortable it felt. It was a sturdy weapon, and he only wished he had read up on and practiced it before now.

Standing there, he noticed a shadow moving. Slowly, the long ghostly darkness on the floor passed between different pillars. It moved elegantly, as if it danced. Each time it reached a pillar, it disappeared from the floor. The uncertainty and mystery became hard to bear, and Vincent changed his location the next time the shadow moved behind a pillar.

Vincent kept watch for any signs of his nemesis. Soon enough, the shadow appeared on the floor again and then disappeared, causing him to alter his location again. The dance of the shadows felt unnerving, but Vincent pushed on. The weakness and pain didn't register so much in his mind anymore. It was only survival and how to get one step ahead of his opponent. Each of their shadows got closer and closer to each other, until on one of the turns, they faced each other barely ten feet apart.

This time, it was Vincent who didn't anticipate it. The trapper, on the other hand, seemed to have calculated better and stood ready, waiting for Vincent to appear. They could for the first time see each other's face close by.

Vincent thought for sure he was facing a demon in the flesh. The eyes had no pupils. In the moonlight they almost looked silver. The face had a black line running down from its tear ducts, along each side of the nose, to the corners of its mouth. The skin was pale white in color, and the lips were thin, barely present. He wore some kind of a tight hat over his head and overall was about the same height and frame as Vincent.

The moment Vincent showed his sword in front of him, the trapper started wielding his knife in his right hand and moved forward. He slashed the knife so fast in front of him that Vincent could only think of a blender and raised his own sword to fend off.

Every time the trapper would step in, Vincent would step back and make short, quick swings with the sword. They clashed a few times, the knife versus the sword. It quickly became apparent that if the trapper closed in beyond the sword's length, it would be over. The trapper had the obvious skill advantage, and he began moving side to side, then forward, directing Vincent any way he wanted to go.

Vincent went on the offensive trying to back the trapper, cut his hands in the process, or even get a lucky stab, but he quickly realized that the trapper was too agile, countering so well that Vincent had to reel backward.

Step by step in reverse, Vincent tripped, falling backward, with the sword flying away from him. He hit the floor hard and realized it wasn't an accidental trip, but another trap set up for him. The trapper had planned it well, redirecting him and then backing him toward it. Nudging his head slightly to the left, the trapper seemed disappointed to see the protection Vincent had strapped to his legs, but it didn't seem to matter at this point. The trapper was at a huge advantage.

Stepping over the trap he set up, the trapper advanced toward Vincent, who backed away knowing what would most likely come next—a pounce and a lethal stab. This time, however, the trapper didn't pounce right away. Perhaps he remembered Vincent's foot to his face the last time he had tried that, but he didn't seem to want to stab him from a distance by launching his knife at him. It all seemed too personal to end at a distance.

A few short feet back, Vincent felt the cold air under his fingers on the right hand and realized he was at the ledge of the floor. The only way out was fifty feet down, but he wasn't about to commit suicide now. He would join others being strapped to one of the pillars, and hopefully someone would take his body down someday.

He looked over and saw the bodies he had taken down not far from him. He felt closer with them in this moment than anyone else in his life. He was one of them now; he felt their pain, faced their horror, and was about to meet the same fate. As a desperate attempt to do something, Vincent tried to move to the left, then right, to give himself enough space to get up, but the trapper remained right there with him.

One more time Vincent tried to move to the left and away. The trapper quickly stepped to its right, but all of a sudden lost footing and fell on top of Vincent. Immediately, and with all his energy, Vincent bucked with his hips and swung with his left so the trapper wouldn't have an easy stabbing. With this, the trapper flew up and over, then disappeared from his view. Vincent couldn't see anything, and all he heard was the scream and a thump. Then there was silence.

Shaking, Vincent held his hands in front of him as if awaiting another attack. His heart still beat a million miles a minute, his senses tuned to the environment, deciphering its dark code. Terror disappeared from his eyes and left him with an anesthetized feeling of uncertainty.

As moments passed, it became ever more evident that the

trapper had met its doom. It seemed that it was so concerned with Vincent's movements that it had failed to notice the dead body on the floor, tripping on it.

Propped against the pillar, Vincent took a slow, deep breath and then closed his eyes and let out a long sigh. The crows, the spectators of the night, also loosened up, flying and cawing, as if leaving the theatre when the performance was over.

Slowly opening his eyes, Vincent saw the unfinished building across the street basking in the moonlight. It seemed so much brighter than a few moments ago. The grayish color of the concrete didn't seem so cold and uninviting, but the pillars and their long shadows still demanded alertness in his eyes.

Vincent still felt numb to any pain in his body. The adrenaline didn't quite let his nerves wake up from the battle, and he sat there as if awaiting the sunrise. He remained this way and breathed ever slowly, gently staring ahead as minutes went by.

The light of the day gradually casted its own majesty on the building, and the shadows of the night pulled away. Vincent still kept staring ahead, not looking at anything in particular. He eventually blinked and then calmly tried to get up. Feeling weak in his legs, he sat down again. Taking off his backpack, Vincent grabbed the little food and water he had in there and lazily ingested it. He then rolled over and closed his eyes.

CHAPTER 42

Waking up to the crow that came by to investigate him, Vincent felt slightly more energy. The pains and aches remained, but the fear was gone. Looking at his hands and body and feeling his face, he knew the battle of the previous night had been rough. He had plenty of cuts and bruises, but the pain in his shoulder and the slash on his left hand were the most severe.

He bandaged the hand as best as he could and cleaned the rest of the cuts with a cloth. Looking at his feet, he was more than thankful for the makeshift shin guards. If it wasn't for them, he would have been in serious trouble so many times in the last twenty-four hours.

He looked at the victim's body that lay a few feet from him. At the most crucial moment, it saved his life. It tripped his nemesis just before he was about to pounce on him. He wondered if this was God's answer to his prayer of mercy.

Vincent for sure felt he would be finished until the tide turned in his favor in a split second. He thought he saw his own writing on the wall, not the trapper's. Who would have thought that it would be the trapper, not him, who was judged and found too light that night?

Feeling thankful, he couldn't leave the bodies of the victims where they lay. They deserved a lot more. He no longer looked at them as some unlucky and butchered bodies, but as valiant souls who in their own way somehow played their part to end this monster's reign of terror.

Vincent spent the rest of the day taking their bodies outside the building and wrapping them in cloth and nylon he had found at the construction site. He then laid them in one of the pits where the foundation of a new building was supposed to be built and covered them with a modest layer of earth with a shovel.

Since he found a small tattoo of a cross on one of the bodies, he figured at least one of them may have been a Christian. He made a makeshift cross and placed it above the pit.

He then proceeded to dismantle the altar on the fourth floor and throw it, with the knives, swords, and little figurines, down an elevator shaft. Finding a half-empty canister of gasoline, he poured it down the shaft and threw a burning stick.

He then went to the body of the trapper. It lay face down in the dirt next to the street. The left arm was extended with the knife still in its hand. It still looked kind of menacing, but helpless, as if tied in some invisible chains it couldn't get out of. He then wrapped the body in nylon, dragged it to the burning elevator shaft, and threw it down. With this he was finished.

A few blocks from the construction site Vincent found a house to rest in and recover. He cleaned his wounds with soap and water and any antibiotic ointment he could find in the bathroom. Then he proceeded to lie down in one of the bedrooms.

After a short nap, he could barely move his left shoulder. The injured muscle was inflamed, and not given the proper rest after the injury, he was paying for it now. He felt glad to see that the wound wasn't infected and placed more ointment on it, wrapping it with a new piece of gauze.

Vincent took some ibuprofen pills, also readily available in the house, to deal with the pain. For the remainder of the daylight he did nothing but rest and read some books that he found. The ibuprofen did its job, and he found himself drowsy and went into another long sleep.

The next day, feeling slightly less pain in his shoulder, Vincent went back to the Cathedral of the Sacred Heart. On the way back he gathered information on any of the trapper's victims he had come across previously so that he could take it to Marcus. He did this solely for identifying them.

Once at the cathedral, he proceeded with cutting down all the traps. It was too beautiful of a place not to, and he felt obligated to do it. Even though there were many, he didn't quit until he cut and removed all of them. After that, Vincent kneeled in front of the altar and said, "I don't know how to say this but thank you."

The following day he decided to return to his home in Manhattan. He felt there was nothing else he could do. He bore many injuries, visible by the bandages he wrapped them up with, but the job was done. The only thing that bothered him was that he couldn't account for all the traps the trapper might have left behind. Therefore, on his way home, he placed paper signs to warn anyone that may pass through.

Vincent's pace of the walk may have been much slower than usual, but it was also a lot less stressful. Like an old soldier coming home from a battle, he took his time. After he trekked a few miles, somewhere in the Secaucus area, he spotted a traveler. This person appeared alone and seemed without malice. Vincent watched as the traveler carefully navigated through the roughed-up streets going in the same direction as he was.

Vincent followed it from a distance, just to be safe if someone or something else came up. Within twenty minutes he felt confident there was nothing more to the traveler and relaxed. He started closing the distance until he stood some thirty yards behind, and then called out.

"Hey!" Vincent shouted in a raspy voice. "Hey, I saw you. I mean no harm. I wanted-"

The traveler turned around, and Vincent's face dropped. He couldn't believe what he saw. Letting go of the pistol in its holster, he dropped his guard. Now he felt almost certain he had died that night at the construction site and entered Heaven.

"El--Elysie?" Vincent stuttered in disbelief.

The traveler waited for a moment. Then in a tearful voice she responded, "Vincent!"

He still couldn't believe it; it was Elysie! Without hesitation, she dropped whatever she had in her hands, ran to him, and they embraced. Vincent had to restrain himself from hugging too hard, but he wanted to clutch on to every part of her, making sure she was really there.

Vincent started kissing her. The soft skin of her face felt like the sweetest honey on his broken lips. Gentle tears came from her sparkling dark eyes and soon were joined by his. Many memories returned, but all were quickly eclipsed by this very moment. The bliss took him to heaven.

The great surprise was almost too much to bear. It shot a jolt through his heart that seemed to immobilize both of them, and neither could continue the trip that day. Instead, they walked to Candlewood Suites hotel nearby, holding each other's hand and stopping frequently to embrace and kiss. Vincent wanted to catch up on the lifetime that stood between them. They didn't talk much, however, but smiled and stared at each other in amazement.

The hotel seemed untouched by anyone since the Scourge had hit. They managed to unlock the doors into one of the suites and found it neat and ready inside. They took off their rucksacks and then sat on the floor by the bed continuing what they had started on the road. He kissed her eyes gently and then switched to her cheeks with more fervor, working his way to her lips. His hands wrapped around her tightly, feeling her back and sides, while her legs wrapped around him.

It felt too good to be true, and Vincent pulled away. He stared at Elysie's dark eyes, unsure if this was real or a dream. Not long ago he had faced the greatest evil he could imagine, and now he was with the woman he had yearned for so much. He questioned reality, but as the moments passed away, it didn't seem to matter; he was not alone. He felt overjoyed and wanted to make it last forever. His fingers ran through her long silky black hair, while his eyes admired her smooth and flawless face. God, she is so beautiful, he thought.

After an hour had passed, Elysie found herself looking at him passionately while in his arms. She could hardly believe that she was there with him. All troubles over the last year seemed to be an afterthought. With admiration, she looked him up and down and then started noticing his bandages and scars. It started to sink in how different he looked than what she remembered. He looked pale, unshaven, and scarred, with dirty hair. His hands seemed to shake, his arms and body were more muscular but tired, and his eyes appeared exhausted.

Elysie didn't want to ask what happened to him out of fear of finding out something really bad. This felt too good of a moment to ruin, and she didn't even want to glance at his gun holster on the floor. At least that night, she wanted to just enjoy his presence, so she did. That night was theirs, and theirs alone. Nothing mattered as the sun went down, the stars came up, and the moon lit the endless empty roads of the new world.

CHAPTER 43

The next day, when they mustered the will to leave their love suite, they packed their rucksacks and went on their way to Manhattan. During that long walk, Vincent tried to let things out in the open, but it was difficult to start the conversation considering that the last time they had seen each other was right before he blew Neil's and his partner's heads off and ran away.

Slowly, as the city skyline grew bigger in their view, Elysie started explaining her story.

"After you ran away, Vincent," she said, "it became difficult for me to stay at the campus. We didn't know where you were or what happened to you. Neil's guys were angry and started threatening us."

Vincent listened attentively. The time Elysie spent at the campus after he ran away was largely a mystery to him. Marcus never gave him much detail, and he wasn't sure he wanted to know out of fear of learning something horrible.

"They were running around causing all kinds of trouble," Elysie explained. "They tried to assault me a few times, but Marcus and his friends stepped in, basically saving my life. It was hard for Mike to see all this, and he wanted us to leave the campus right away, but we decided to wait, hoping to hear from you . . . When we couldn't wait any longer, we left for Parsippany."

A shot of guilt came over Vincent, and he felt his face turning red. He could only imagine how she felt when, all of a sudden, he disappeared that fateful day, leaving her and Mike in such a difficult position. It was betrayal in a sense, and it had bothered him the whole year, but now shame rolled in that he wasn't there to protect her.

"I wanted to search for you throughout the city, but Mike wouldn't have any of it because it was much too dangerous," she continued. "He said the best thing was to tell our friends where we were going in hopes of relating it to you—that is, if you ever came back to the campus looking for us."

She brushed her long black hair from her face and paused before letting out a sigh. "In Parsippany I waited for over a year, with each day bringing new hopes and disappointments. I looked at each sunrise hoping to see you coming my way, but I went to sleep thinking that something terrible had happened to you. When I couldn't take it anymore, I decided to come back and find out for myself. I left Mike a note and got on my way. I had been travelling for three days when I ran into you . . . It was the happiest day of my life."

Vincent kept silent for a while not knowing how to respond. He wanted to think about it and not just brush it off from his mind. He wanted to find a way to put all the pieces together to explain his actions, to explain how it all happened, and to give it all a purpose.

He looked over at Elysie and noticed that she expected him to say something. He mustered all his energy and started from the moment he had run into the bathroom where Neil and his friend had killed a black man.

"I was overtaken by the shock of what I saw," he explained. "I had a burning desire to do something, but I didn't know what. I was in rage, and I wasn't thinking. All I wanted to do was put an end to Neil. When I pulled that trigger, I had no emotions in me. It wasn't even hatred. I was numb. I saw Neil and his companion fall down, and I felt nothing. Then I turned around and all I could do was run, so I did. I was at a loss and didn't know what else to do."

Vincent glanced at Elysie's expression as she looked ahead. He wanted to see if any of this disappointed her more than he expected, but he found it difficult to read her face.

"When I finally stopped running," he continued, "I struggled with great fear about what I had done and what you would think of me. It was awful. I don't ever want to go through that again. After a couple of days I went back and learned you had gone to Parsippany, so I went that way, too."

He didn't know how to explain what he did next—how he came across Marie and subsequently destroyed the gang on the bridge. He would have sounded more like the Scourge people at the campus had come to know than the lover Elysie remembered. Would she believe him anyway?

"On the way there, I, uh." He paused and scratched his chin. "I ran into a gang. I saw them doing things, and I felt rage and . . . I wanted justice."

He reached for his gun holsters and bounced them off his side as he made another pause.

"I couldn't mix you into this," he said. "I thought that you'd never accept me. Some things about me changed, and I feared it would hurt you to find out. I went back and became a self-appointed sheriff. I went around and saved people from those that were trying to harm them. I became very good at it, and some people, they appreciate me for it."

Elysie remained silent. She didn't see him in this light. That wasn't Vincent in her eyes; he wasn't capable of killing, and he simply just couldn't. He wasn't a fighter, but a lover, and a good one, too. He made her feel so comfortable, like everything around them didn't matter as long as he held her in his arms.

She felt safe with Vincent and couldn't imagine the world going wrong around them while they had each other, but this now explained all the scars and bandages he had, and she realized it could be the truth. Yet, she still saw him as a sweet man, not a killer. He was someone who simply got caught up in it, not actively sought it, and she felt sorry for him.

Vincent couldn't finish on this note. He knew that wasn't the whole truth. There was something more important inside him.

He stopped walking and turned to her. "Elysie," he said, letting go of the gun holsters. "When I saw you yesterday, my heart changed. There's no way I can go back to the way things were in the last year. I could never forget you. You were always on my mind. It's true that I have this fire in me and that I want justice, but who doesn't? I want things to change for the better, and sometimes it's all confusing to me. I need to change for the better, too, whatever that is, but I'm willing to do it. All I know is how I feel and that I want to be with you."

Vincent didn't expect her to feel great about what he'd said, but he had let it off his chest. Elysie knew the truth now. He didn't feel as guilty anymore, even though he questioned whether disclosing so much so soon would frighten her. The last thing he wanted was to realize his worst nightmare—that she wouldn't want him after this.

Elysie looked at him with tenderness in her eyes. "My sweet Vincent," she said and reached out for his hand. "There's a lot more we need to talk about, but I still believe that deep down we can work this out."

He hugged and kissed her on the forehead. Her words were a reward for his revelation. Only Elysie could do this. Things were far from perfect, but she had given him the greatest hope that life would get better.

For the remainder of the trip, they made small talk. A few jokes made their way in brightening the mood as they got tired. When they reached the Hudson River, they searched for the means to cross it to Manhattan. Elysie found it exciting when Vincent reluctantly agreed on a two-person canoe instead of a boat like Mike, Aran, and she had taken on their way to Parsippany.

They struggled paddling together initially, but soon they got into sync, and the crossing turned out to be quite enjoyable. They talked about some of the fun things they had done together around the campus and Manhattan in general. It felt as if everything would be back in its own place and life would move in a happier direction.

As they reached the outskirts of the campus, the night closed in. The only lights in Manhattan showed themselves, and the city looked inviting. Staring at it, refusing to go any further, Vincent's mood changed. Elysie wondered what had made him stop and why his face changed. She suspected something wasn't quite clear between him and the campus.

"I want to talk to Marcus," he said, breaking the silence, "but I can't go in. I hope you understand."

"I understand," she replied in a slightly disappointed tone. "Do you want me to talk to him for you?"

"No," he replied. "Some of Neil's guys are still there, and I don't know what they would do if they saw you. I doubt they have forgotten what I did. On top of that, not everyone is quite comfortable with me since I appointed myself the sheriff . . . or the Scourge as they call me. Don't worry. I have ways of reaching Marcus, but I think it's a little late tonight."

"So, where exactly are you staying then?" she asked.

"In a tower, not too far away," he responded. "It's actually the Citigroup Center tower. I just call it the Center tower. I like it there."

Elysie put her hand on Vincent's shoulders as they stared at the lights of the campus. She knew she was in for a rough ride to learn about this new Vincent. Nevertheless, she wanted to be with him. It became an odd relationship inside her heart, where her love for him and her fear of what she may find out interlocked. The two battled each other, but her love remained stronger, giving her faith that whatever she may face, there was still hope things would work out for the better.

She looked at the campus for a few moments longer and then responded, "All right, sounds like we're going to Center tower then."

CHAPTER 44

The next morning, Elysie arose before Vincent did at the tower. She walked around his large main floor and found it neatly organized. This was quite different from his apartment at the campus when he lived with Aran. It was a pleasant change. He had all his stuff placed in their respective bins, closets, and rooms. All the kitchenettes were clean, and the cabinets were full of all kinds of long-lasting food: corn, wheat, rice, canned goods, powdered milk, powdered eggs, and more.

There were plenty of condiments, and she could tell he placed extra emphasis on iodized salt, since it made up three quarters of all the condiments. In the main kitchenette, she found a gas cooker, which was ideal for frying anything he wanted. He even had a garden in one of the well-lit rooms where he grew carrots, potatoes, summer squash, and tomatoes.

She then came across his armory, where he kept various pistols and ammunition. This room she bypassed as soon as she realized what it was; it was something she hoped they would never have to use again.

Overall, she was impressed with what he had done with his lair. It seemed as if he had prepared it for her. She decided to prepare some potatoes and canned meat to surprise Vincent when he woke up.

A few days later, Vincent reached out to Marcus. When he saw Vincent and Elysie together, he was overjoyed. At first it seemed he couldn't quite believe his eyes; his friend had come back from facing the horrific serial killer, and with him was Elysie. It was a happy moment between them that seemed surreal.

Soon, as the reality sank in, the details started emerging. Vincent didn't go into great detail of what the serial killer had done, but he told them about the dead bodies and where he had discovered them. While it was undoubtedly the worst he'd ever faced, Vincent assured Marcus that it was over now.

Vincent handed Marcus the documents found on the bodies he had come across, and Marcus stuttered with tears when his friend's name appeared on one of them. He seemed so afraid of this moment. Now that it had come, it was painful that it was true but a relief that it was over.

This was the first time Elysie had heard about the trapper. Vincent didn't tell her in detail why he was in Jersey when they ran into each other. He left it ambiguous, that he made sure the passengers to the campus were safe, but not that he faced off with the most diabolical murderer the area had ever known.

No one would ever know the number of Scourge survivors the trapper had killed before Vincent stopped him, and she could tell by looking at Marcus that this was someone they feared much more than the Scourge itself.

Who is this Vincent, Elysie wondered, that they sent him into harm's way to face off with a murderer? It for sure didn't sound like her Vincent, and it didn't seem fair they would send him to do such a dangerous job when they had trained campus policemen do it. His injuries stood out even more now. They told of a turbulent tale.

Marcus noticed the injuries, too, but Vincent refused to go into details. He left that conversation short, and Elysie could tell that it was something he would rather not talk about. This hurt her. She felt bad for her lover, and she wanted to mend his wounds. She wanted to be there for him, share his pain, and help him heal; however, this wound he wanted to lick all on his own.

As Marcus got ready to head back to the campus, Elysie pulled him aside and asked him for his thoughts about Vincent being allowed back to the campus.

"It's possible," he said, "but when they recognize him as the Scourge, I don't know, maybe. It's tough to say right now. At least I think Neil's posse would think twice before they messed with him."

Marcus's words sounded somewhat hopeful, but his eyes didn't say the same. He was probably well aware of the uncertainties Vincent's presence would cause among the people, and Elysie wasn't sure she wanted to find out. In the end, they said a farewell with plans to meet again soon.

The word that the serial killer was dead spread throughout the campus like wildfire. The campus police couldn't quite believe it, and when Marcus gave them the documents of the victims Vincent had retrieved, they seemed astonished.

The police seemed even more surprised when Marcus told them that it was a lone trapper/hunter behind it all. As campus police expressed their skepticism, most of the public embraced it, especially those who had lost their friends and loved ones there. Everyone debated the realities and horrors behind it. Some, still afraid the trapper may be out there, spread an uneasy feeling among much of the public.

It wasn't until ten days later that the campus police sent a group of trained officers to investigate the trapper's sanctuary and discovered the buried bodies. No sign of the trapper could be found—only his writing on the walls and a burned-out pile in the elevator shaft. With this, the debate was put to rest. The trapper was dead.

Vincent, or the Scourge, received a new status in the campus society. The younger folks thought of him as some kind of a mystic but good-natured guardian of their society. He was someone who was a misunderstood defender of the campus—a fearless warrior who acted out of goodness and was more than capable of facing all the oncomers.

They even started playfully talking about Vincent by saying, "I'm going to send the Scourge after you," or "don't be bad, or the Scourge is going to get you." Carefully listening to the stories of those who met or saw him in action caused their fantasy to grow even more.

It didn't hurt that many of those stories painted an even more fantastic picture of the events than had actually happened. To them, even Marcus was a celebrity because he was the one person able to talk to the Scourge in person.

On the other hand, the older folks became much more reserved. In their minds, this guardian could quickly turn into a menacing killer not much different from the trapper. After all, he did some questionable things by attacking the group of fighting girls, and he remained under no one's law. They said that someone like that could easily be acting out of anger, and not necessarily out of duty to help, and those people were dangerous.

They refused to recognize his status as a legitimate angel of the campus; he acted out on his own with no regard to the campus law. They asked, "Why doesn't he join the campus if he wants to defend it so much?"

Over the next couple of weeks, Elysie slowly started getting their new home acclimated to living together. She found the place rather interesting—an office floor turned into living quarters. It slowly grew on her, even though she would have preferred something more comfortable.

Recovering from his wounds, Vincent said he preferred to stay in, which made Elysie happy. Other than doing the general chores, they spent much of their time together, safe in their intimacy, loving each other and looking out the window at the world below. There was so much to talk about, then there wasn't, but it didn't matter to them. They could just sit there and enjoy the view in silence.

Occasionally the two went out for walks, which pleased Elysie because they were venturing to parts of the city she had never seen before. Vincent, on the other hand, seemed to have seen all these places before and knew what to expect.

With Elysie by his side, Vincent experienced each place differently than before. Seeing her get so excited, he relived each place through her. He guided her carefully through each street, building, and park so they didn't run into any unsuspecting people. His knowledge of the environment impressed her, and she asked him frequently how he had come to learn it so well.

One time he pulled her aside, saying, "Listen, and feel."

She leaned her head to the side and whispered, "What is it?"

"There are people in that space over there," he said pointing with his finger.

"How do you know?" she asked.

"I can tell they're there. Maybe four or five of them."

Sure enough, a minute later, four people walked out carrying some goodies they had gathered from the room.

"How could you tell?" she asked in amazement.

He looked up as if looking for a way to describe it. "I sense it. It's like they disturb the flow, the motion, or something. It's like a ripple in the water when you drop a pebble into it."

"That's incredible! So, there's no way to hide from you," she said, smiling.

"Well." He leaned toward her and whispered. "There are still some who can."

Her favorite place was a small park in the back of the building that overlooked the Queensboro Bridge. Vincent found this ironic because not too far away was the place where he had come to cope with his emotions when Marie left for the campus. The place, to that point, had only brought sad feelings in him, but now with Elysie, it had a different feel. It was brighter and livelier, and colors more pronounced.

Vincent could witness in Elysie's eyes how much she enjoyed the small and secluded overgrown park, the view of the bridge, the lazy East River, and the buildings on the other side. It didn't look like a particularly stunning display of beauty, but there was something romantic and easygoing about it, especially on charming, sunny days. They never had to worry about running into any people there. No one ever seemed to come close to it. It became truly their little gem.

On a few occasions they saw Marcus, who told them of the plans the campus had for the big move to Parsippany in May of next year. This got everyone excited there, and the Scourge didn't seem the big topic any more.

This pleased Vincent greatly. Finally, he wasn't the talk of the town. He didn't enjoy that kind of attention anyway. Whereas before he envied those at the campus for having such a large community, having the opportunity to meet friends and being a part of a normal society, all he cared about now was that he had Elysie with him and no one bothered them. Everything else seemed less important.

CHAPTER 45

As another mild winter approached and Christmas preparations were underway at the campus, Marcus and Marlene came to Vincent's lair. This happened to be the first time they were both there, and it was the first time Vincent had seen Marlene in over nine months. This was also the first time Elysie was meeting Marcus's wife.

As they had the year before, Marcus and Marlene brought plenty of goodies from the campus, including a chocolate cake. Vincent and Elysie couldn't have asked for a better Christmas present. Marcus and Marlene watched their hosts eat the cake as if they hadn't tasted one before. They all had a great time talking and laughing as they looked back on the times they had together at the campus.

Naturally through the conversation, the word about Marie came up. Elysie, curious of the details, found out that Marie had spent some time with Vincent. Vincent carefully tried to hint to Marlene to be careful how much she said. Marlene, once she got the hint, changed the subject, but it was too late. Elysie now knew that there was some history between Vincent and Marie.

As they said their goodbyes and Marcus and Marlene returned to the campus, Elysie stood in front of Vincent with a serious look. Vincent could tell something was bothering her, and he had a good idea what that was.

"So, how come you never told me about Marie?" she asked.

Vincent waited to respond for a few moments as he cleaned up the mess left behind in their dining area.

"To be honest, I kind of forgot about her."

"You forgot?" She begged the question. "How could you forget? You saved her life."

"Like Marlene said," he replied. "I found her on George Washington Bridge being held captive by some gang, and I rescued her."

"So, you saved her. Then what?" Elysie gave Vincent a stern look showing how serious she was about the matter.

Vincent noticed, and he didn't know how to explain the situation so the words wouldn't come across the wrong way.

"I helped her get back on her feet," he explained. "She was in pretty bad shape, and I felt I needed to do something, so she stayed with me for a little while until she was ready to join the campus."

"Hmm. How long did she stay with you?"

"Just a couple of months."

"A couple of months?" Elysie looked clearly upset by this.

"Yeah, a few months. Then she joined the campus. Now she has a boyfriend, fiancé, I don't know, and she's doing well." Vincent hoped this would be the end of it.

"Why didn't you tell me about her before?" she asked again to his increased agitation.

"Because it was in the past," he said with a touch of anger in his tone. "I helped her. It's what I do. I help anyone I see who needs it. What was I supposed to do? Leave her to die? No. That's not what I do."

"But you left me," she said with sadness in her voice.

"I--I never left . . ." Vincent tried to tell her the truth he didn't even know. "For a while I thought you wouldn't want me."

"Why would you say that?" She asked with teary eyes.

"You know . . . Because of what I'd become."

Vincent became flustered in his face as anger rose in him.

"I've seen what gangs and people like Neil do." He raised his voice. "I went ballistic, and I killed him, and I vowed to God to hunt and kill anyone who deserved to die! And then I killed the gang who held Marie, and I killed the gang who attacked the campus, then another, and another. Some pedophile I came across—I killed him, too. Anyone I saw who was hurting others for no reason, I killed!"

Elysie stood speechless. Her eyes, already watery, soon shed a few tears down her face.

"How could you kill all those people? I thought you said you just stopped them," she said, sobbing.

"That meant killing them, Elysie!" he responded. "Just like I stopped Neil."

A moment of silence passed. Then Vincent realized how distressed Elysie was. He tried to calm himself down because it pained him to see her cry. "I didn't see them as people, Elysie, but as murderers, rapists, pedophiles, sadists, devils."

Elysie remained silent for a few more moments and then asked him again, "But how could you kill so much? Did you enjoy it?"

"No, never," he responded. "I never enjoyed killing, but I appreciated knowing that I saved the innocent and weak from the thugs and murderers. I wish I never had had to do it. But unfortunately, it's the Wild West out here, and I couldn't stand idle."

Vincent shook his head. "If it wasn't for me, the chances are, you, too, would have been killed by the trapper when you made your way over here. Many more people could have spent their last breath in absolute horror."

His eyes went from looking ahead to gazing at the floor a few feet in front of him. "I faced the terror for them, even when I didn't want to, and I never want to face it again."

The detail of his Scourge days felt too much for Elysie. It wasn't something that she wanted to hear even though she suspected it wasn't pleasant for Vincent either. Silently, she felt thankful for someone like Vincent to have stopped the trapper, but she didn't want this part of life to haunt them anymore, and she felt sorry for him.

Vincent seemed like a troubled man who perhaps may have been called to something unfair. Still, in many ways it was difficult to digest. He was a killer. How else could she describe a *sheriff* who took other people's lives, even if it was for justice? An executioner? This was not an easy thing for her to comprehend or accept about a loved one.

Vincent didn't want to talk about the Scourge anymore. As Marcus suggested to him before, he wanted to retire from this business for good. What pained him was whether it was too late. The nightmare that bothered him from the moment he pulled the first trigger at Neil still bothered him now: was there any future for him and Elysie?

The next day, sunshine rose up with a few patches of fluffy clouds, but heavy darkness loomed over Vincent. When he got up, there was no sign of Elysie. He looked around the whole floor and couldn't find her. At first he felt glad she wasn't around. The argument from the previous night damaged both of them, and not having her around for a bit made him feel better.

In the solitude, he felt he could think and wind down from everything he and Elysie had been going through. He suspected that she had gone downstairs to his makeshift gym or perhaps outside to take a quick walk around the block.

After an hour, Vincent went downstairs to the gym to look for Elysie. As he walked in, he heard no noise. His heart sank a little, feeling disappointed she wasn't there. He still looked all around that floor to make sure she wasn't sitting or lying down somewhere, but there was no trace of her.

He thought that she must have been hurt and angry from last night and gone outside for a walk. Even though it was late January, the temperatures held in the high fifties, and the sun made it inviting to go outside. Vincent went back upstairs and decided to wait for her a little longer.

His heart accelerated with each minute gone by. Another hour passed, yet no sign of Elysie. He felt confused, agitated, remorseful, and everything in between while dark thoughts invaded his mind. Where did she go? How could she disappear like that? I see nothing of hers here. Was this all a damned dream? How could she leave?

The more he questioned, the angrier he became. He felt betrayed, wronged, cheated. He only wanted one question to be answered: where was she?

The campus! Vincent concluded. Where else?

A tear fell down his pained face. How stupid could he have been to lose her like that? he thought. Why couldn't he have controlled himself? How could he be so blind? Elysie had sacrificed herself to cross the path of the trapper to be with him, yet he had failed to acknowledge her feelings. She wasn't a roughed-up soldier like he was. How could he treat her like that last night?

The guilt bore down. What an awful feeling. He felt like drowning himself in a murky lake as the dark clouds rolled in.

"No!" Vincent said out loud. "No more!" Silence shattered in his towering lair. "I'm going to get her."

Vincent's determination was as vicious as his destruction of gangs and criminals he had come across. "I don't care if the whole campus sees me! I don't care if the whole world sees me! Nothing is going to stop me! Nothing!" He grabbed his usual equipment from the table and quickly went to the stairs.

CHAPTER 46

An hour later, as the sun keeled over the highest skies, the campus folks relaxed at Columbus Square. Many more took a walk on the nearby streets or hung around with their companions while kids ran around and played games.

A figure in the distance quickly closed in on the campus. No one seemed to care at first, but as it drew nearer, it slowly became apparent that it wasn't an ordinary visitor. This person looked a little more roughed up, scarred, and tired than the average campus dweller. The penetrating eyes had a harsh stare, and the focus was unrelenting. He seemed not to stop for anything.

As the visitor marched through the square, the noise of the crowd slowly quieted. His sheer presence caught more and more eyes as they focused on him. The guns in his holsters broke the major rule at the campus, and everyone knew something wasn't quite as it should be. He didn't look like any of the campus police officers, so they wondered and murmured among themselves, "Who is this guy? What is he up to?"

Gradually, many started questioning, "Could this be him, the Scourge? Who else would look or walk in like that?"

While the crowd examined their most unusual visitor, Vincent closed in on the courtyard of the building Marcus lived in. He figured that was the most likely place that Elysie would have gone to.

Before he could reach it, however, the murmuring silence at the square was broken by somebody yelling out, "That's the guy they call the Scourge of Man!" but Vincent wasn't fazed.

A few moments later another person yelled, "Yeah, that's the guy! I recognize him now! That's got to be him!"

The murmuring turned into rumbling. This was the guy everyone had talked about for the last year. For some he was the terror from the outside who preyed on the wicked. For others, he was a lunatic with a gun. Either way they viewed him, they all believed that he cursed anyone who came in conflict with him. Even then, for some he was the perfect target to prove themselves among their peers and show off their bravery.

Young, strong, and foolish males grouped toward him, with many others looking on. They yelled at him from a distance, still not confident to close the gap, "Hey! Hey, you!"

The Scourge just walked by them as they kept on yelling.

It seemed only a matter of time before someone recognized his true identity, "Wait a minute. Isn't that the guy who shot Neil? Right here, at the square!"

Soon enough others joined in, "Yeah, you're right, that's him! That's the guy! I remember him. His name is Vincent." Someone even remembered his name.

Vincent pressed on, not paying much attention to the commotion. The revelation of his true identity to the campus was much less glorious than he had dreamed it could have been, but at this stage he simply didn't care. He had one goal on his mind: get Elysie back, almost at any cost.

Vincent wanted to tell her how sorry he was, how much she meant to him, and how they could make their lives better. He didn't know if he could take the rejection, but at least he would try to talk to her. He knew how to respond to all the macho guys ready to bash his head in, but he wasn't ready to be excluded by her.

This made him more insecure than he already was. All the stresses he had gone through over the years boiled in a cauldron of his person and were ready to be served at any moment.

Now, with all the commotion of people around him, all the immature guys manning themselves up to face him, all the peril he would face with another mission he wasn't ready for, his happiness crashed again, and he felt disappointment, fear, loneliness, and pain. Dealing with all this again felt inconceivable. Rage invaded his mind with a blitzkrieg fashion. If anyone tried to step in his way and interfere with his plans to see Elysie, he was ready.

The young and foolish again showed their false bravado by commenting on Vincent's inferior size yet seemed reluctant to approach him. But two of Neil's former members bared their teeth by quickly crossing Vincent's path, getting close to him.

"Hey, asshole," one of the guys belted in his face. "You thought we'd forget! What the fuck do you think-"

An elbow to the face and a left hook dropped the first one to the ground, while a right cross leveled the second. Vincent's reaction came so unexpectedly they didn't seem to know what had hit them.

Neil's posse seemed more dazed by his reaction than the punches, all the while Vincent kept walking on. This quieted the mass of people gathered around and appeared to deter many from proving themselves anymore. It didn't deter all, though.

Less than thirty feet farther, five more guys approached Vincent and circled around. Two crossed his path—one on each side of him, and another from behind. It didn't help that two of them had sticks in their hands. All were Neil's former members.

In Vincent's eyes they were typical dogs. They weren't brave enough to tackle a strong opponent on their own, but teamed together they acted like gods. There appeared nothing honorable about them. Keeping their distance just out of his range, they confronted him.

"So, it's like that, ha!" The leader of the pack pointed to his head. "You think we're going to let you walk in like that? Who the fuck do you think you are, you little piece of shit?"

"Who am I?" Vincent looked straight into his eyes. "Well, I'm the Scourge!"

He quickly glanced at the guys who surrounded him, then at the crowd, raising his voice. "Isn't that what you call me? The Scourge!"

There was silence as everyone looked on.

Vincent continued, "And who the hell are you? A measly slave of that scum Neil? A racist bigot? Still serving him, huh? Surrounding me like a pack of filthy dogs! You cowards!"

The pack leader seemed to change his tactics as the crowd listened. "You're a murderer! We all saw you. And you're a coward who ran away!"

"So that I could come back and be surrounded by you filthy dogs!" Vincent responded.

At this, one of the guys on Vincent's right leaped, throwing a punch. Vincent instinctively kicked to the side, striking the guy in the knee. This buckled the would-be attacker's knee and he went to the ground, clutching at his knee in pain, while one of his comrades struck Vincent on the side of the head with a short stick.

Infuriated, Vincent grabbed at the stick and leaped with a palm strike to his neck. The guy let go of the stick and staggered backward, coughing violently.

At this moment the other three joined the fight. Vincent moved and punched at them one at a time as quickly as he could while trying to avoid being in the middle or tackled to the ground. Taking the punches and dishing a few of their own, Neil's guys slowed down but kept fighting.

Seeing that he couldn't last this way for long, Vincent kicked the closest one in the stomach as hard as he could and pulled back a few steps. Then he quickly took out his pistol, aiming at his adversaries.

"You want to die? Is that it?" Vincent raged while frantically pointing his pistol at each of the attackers.

Bloodied and winded, they froze in their spot.

"Want to go down like Neil? Is that what you want?"

They didn't say a word.

"Put the gun down! Now!" a voice came from behind Vincent. He didn't even bother to turn; he knew it was the campus police. He recognized authority in their voices. Still, he didn't comply.

"Put the gun down!" another warning came. "If you don't put the gun down, we'll shoot!"

"Shoot who? Me?" Vincent fumed. "The guy who saved all your asses countless times? Is that who you want to shoot?"

Everyone became silent.

"It's people like this," Vincent pointed at the three guys across from him, "who need to be shot! These racist, sadistic scum who will ruin your lives any chance they get. Look at them! Look!"

The campus police remained quiet.

"These worthless worms are no better than those I destroyed to save your sorry asses." He glanced at the whole crowd. "All your asses!"

His eyes now bore into those closest to him. "How many of you would be worse off if it wasn't for me? How many? Would your little fragile society even exist if it wasn't for me? Neil would have destroyed you, and none of you dared to stop him, but I did!"

Turning around, he saw everyone appeared lost for words. Neil's guys stood there doing nothing.

"And what about the trapper? Ha?" he shouted. "He massacred you like pigs, and what did you do about him? Nothing!"

Pausing for a reply, he glanced back at Neil's guys and lowered his voice. "Nah, I won't shoot them." He then turned to the campus police and pointed at them. "That's your job!"

"Discard your weapon immediately!" the campus police demanded.

Vincent looked at the gun in his hands and shook his head. "I don't need this anymore. You afraid of me carrying this gun? Here! You can have it!"

The gun went flying out of his hand as he threw it as high and far away from him as he could. The second one followed soon. The eyes of the crowd followed the shiny black objects as they traveled above their heads and landed somewhere on the street behind them.

"There!" he said. "Now you'll have to shoot me if you want me to walk away from what I came for."

Everyone's eyes now focused on Vincent as he continued his walk toward the building Marcus lived in. Silence followed him. Even Neil's guys abstained from doing anything. In front, Marcus appeared, being drawn by all the commotion that had happened. He had a shocked and worried look.

Vincent looked up at him with sad eyes and asked softly, "Tell me, Marcus, is Elysie at your place? I'd like to talk to her."

"No, man, she's not," Marcus responded. "What happened?"

"She left, and I don't know where she is." Tears filled Vincent's eyes. "You wouldn't lie to me, would you?"

"No, I swear, man, she isn't here." Sadness and worry clouded Marcus's features.

Vincent quietly turned around and started walking back, leaving stunned Marcus looking on. The silence got briefly broken by the occasional chatter among the crowd, but for the most part they watched quietly.

As he calmly passed by Neil's former members, he briefly paused and faced them. "If you had anything to do with this, I swear I'll come back and destroy all of you."

They looked at him in bewilderment.

As the Scourge left the premises and his figure faded in the distance, the silence in the crowd quickly started filling with chatter. It grew noisier with each passing moment as arguments took hold between people.

While different feelings were expressed, Marcus grew uneasy. Vincent was exposed, and his chances of coming back to the campus were completely gone now. The campus council would now suspect Marcus was aware about the Scourge's identity, his long-time friend. That would explain how he was able to track him down in the first place. This wouldn't be much short of betrayal in their eyes.

Marcus knew at this point one thing for sure; his situation and that of his fiancé and friends was delicate now. The council would question him and likely ask him to resign, but that didn't trouble him most. What bothered him far greater was that if they assumed him to be an accomplice with the Scourge, it could have dangerous consequences.

Worriedly, Marcus walked back to his tower to look for Marlene and a few of their close friends. He desperately wanted to discuss this with them and then plan their next move.

Vincent, on the other hand, didn't know where to go. He wasn't sure of Elysie's whereabouts, and that's all that mattered. If she'd left him and she wasn't at the campus with Marcus and Marlene, where else would she be? Where could she go?

Vincent's mind seemed as lost as he was in the city that he once knew. He didn't walk toward his home, but north, getting farther away from it. The street numbers climbed up and up: 72nd, 81st, 94th, 107th. By dusk he found himself somewhere in East Harlem.

Vincent had been to this area before, but not like this. His spirits were troubled and desperate for peace, but the only comfort he found was in the falling sun at 116th Street.

Light rain started to fall as night closed in, and Vincent sought shelter in a three-story brick building that housed a restaurant in the bottom. It said "Sandy" on it. It made him think of a beach on Long Island that he had visited a few times before the Scourge hit.

He went inside and sat at the table as if a waitress would come by to take his order. He looked around in silence as if it told him the story of what it must have been like before. His troubled heart eventually tired his eyes, and he lay down by the table and closed his lids.

CHAPTER 47

Elysie got up and walked around their makeshift apartment. She found her note on the floor and wondered if Vincent had read it while pacing around worriedly.

The note read, "I went out for a walk to my favorite place. Don't worry about me. Still love you. -Elysie."

She had been back for hours and still there was no sign of Vincent. She wondered what could have happened. She thought of the worst possible scenarios; he had decided to return to his sheriff's work, had come across a gang, and they had hurt him, killed him!

The light rain hitting the windows on the fifty-fourth floor came down like tears. Looking out, Elysie couldn't see anything but the dark buildings springing up from darker streets below.

"Where is he?" she asked, but the rain kept falling without an answer in sight. Eventually she, too, lay on the floor, refusing to sleep on the bed.

"Maybe I'm overreacting and Vincent just went on a long walk. He's good at this. He'll be fine," she tried to reassure herself. Her half-closed eyes looked at the motionless objects in front and wondered how they now towered over her. With each moment her eyelids closed a little more. Then she fell asleep.

The next morning Elysie woke up with a pain in her back and regretted sleeping on the floor. She looked around the apartment to see if Vincent had returned only to have her heart sink deeper as she found each and every room empty. Her worry grew and then grew some more until she felt she had had enough. If there were no answers here, she would find them somewhere else. She turned to her only friends left in the city. She packed lightly and headed to the campus.

Approaching the campus, she determinedly went forward, encouraging herself not to fear the people who may recognize her. Once in the middle, however, she didn't know where to go. She had no idea where Marcus and Marlene lived. This made her anxious, and she tried to compose herself and find some answers. She approached a small group of girls.

"Do you know where Marcus Laws is staying?" she asked.

The girls looked at each other. Then one by one they shook their heads and said, "No, sorry."

She moved around the crowd, trying to keep her hope up, and eventually came across a group of black guys in the middle of fixing a water pump not far from Columbus Square. Thinking they might know something, she headed toward them.

"Excuse me," she said, catching one of the guy's attendants. "Do you know where Marcus Laws is staying?"

When she mentioned Marcus, they all stopped talking and turned toward her. Their faces became more serious. She didn't like the sign of this.

"Why are you looking for him?" the oldest one of the group asked.

"I need to talk to Marlene, and I thought Marcus would know where she was," Elysie responded.

"See, Marcus isn't around," the guy responded. "But if you need to talk to Marlene, you can find her in that tower." He pointed to a building. "Yeah, over there. Apartment 233."

Elysie quickly thanked him and went straight for the tower as the group watched her leave in silence. She didn't get a good vibe from the conversation and didn't like the feel of the whole situation. As she walked to the tower, she pondered why were they so apprehensive when she approached them.

"Nah, I'm probably overexaggerating," she tried to reassure herself.

Once she got to the tower, she walked up the stairs until she found apartment 233 and then knocked. When Marlene came out, Elysie hugged her.

"Elysie?" Marlene said with a high tone, visibly surprised to see her there.

"Can I come in?" Elysie asked, itching to get in and out of the view of other people. Marlene pulled her in, locked the door behind them, and then guided her to the living room to sit down.

Elysie quickly explained how Vincent and she had had an argument two nights ago and that the next day, after she came back from a long walk to clear her head, he was nowhere to be found.

She told her that it was very unusual for Vincent to be gone this long and that she feared the worst. Elysie fought back tears as Marlene listened carefully. However, Marlene didn't give her much comfort as she started to explain what had gone down at the campus.

"Elysie, I'm sorry that Vincent didn't come back. I know it must be hard for you. Neither I nor Marcus know his whereabouts, but I'll tell you what we do know."

Marlene paused as she went over to the door and looked through the peephole. She came back, sat next to Elysie, and started explaining, "It happened yesterday, sometime past noon. Vincent came by the campus. He wasn't trying to conceal himself as he had done before. From what I heard he walked right through the crowd with his pistols strapped to him, which you know is a big no-no at the campus.

"He didn't seem to care about anyone recognizing him. He simply walked right through. Eventually someone recognized him, including Neil's former posse, and they confronted him, which led to a fight."

Elysie's heart started to beat faster, and she became visibly anguished at hearing this. Marlene seemed to notice as she quickly continued the story. "No one was hurt, though—at least nothing serious. Just scratches and bruises, that's all."

This didn't help much to put Elysie at ease, so she took a deep breath to get ready for the remainder of the story.

Marlene continued, "The bad thing was that Vincent pulled out a gun, and the campus police intervened, telling him to drop it. He did drop it, but not before the whole campus knew who he was—the Scourge everyone had talked about."

Elysie's eyes dropped to the floor. Marlene reached out and touched her gently. "He was looking for you! He came up to Marcus and told him you were missing and asked if you were here. Marcus told him you weren't, and Vincent turned around and left.

"Obviously, this didn't go well with the council. They called a meeting to discuss the whole matter. Marcus told me they would question him specifically because they believe he knew who the Scourge was the entire time."

Now Elysie could see how troubled Marlene was about Marcus and their future as a tear formed in her eye. They had great plans and so much investment in the campus, but now everything could change because of what happened. For the first time in a while Elysie had someone who shared the same anguish as she did. It was painful and burdensome, but now their burden became a little easier to bear as they hugged each other and let their feelings go.

For the next hour they shared thoughts on many things that had happened and could happen in the future. Elysie realized they had much more in common than she had previously thought. Just as easily as some things are broken apart in times of trouble, others are brought closer together.

A few miles northeast of the campus, Vincent started his day with pain, but his was in the sternum because the clothes he slept in bundled up as he lay on his stomach. It felt as if someone had pressed a hot rod against his chest.

As he rubbed his eyes, he looked around disoriented, not quite sure where he was. At first he thought he was at his home in the Center tower, yet it looked so different. A few moments later the memories started coming back. He was still searching for Elysie.

The loneliness of his situation struck him like a spear deep into his heart. His will sapped out of him, yet he still got up and carried on. Walking outside in this unusually warm winter made him think the world had changed into something unfamiliar. Perhaps wiping out a majority of people wasn't enough. Maybe something else was headed this way?

Either way, it didn't matter much. Vincent needed to figure out how to find Elysie. He wondered whether she was still around or if she had gone back to Parsippany to her adopted father Mike. If that had happened, he thought, it would have broken his heart, but at least he would still have an option left: go to Parsippany and find her.

If something else had happened to Elysie and she was gone forever, his spirit would be broken, and there would be no options left for happiness. In that case, he would have to comb the whole island and beyond to find her body and wreak havoc on those who brought her demise.

He debated for a short time and then decided to go back to his tower, the one place he hoped the most she would be. After all, he had already gone to the campus at a heavy cost and not found her. All he had left was hope, and he prayed for the best. He didn't eat anything, but he got himself some water and then quickly went south.

At the same time, Marcus made his way back to his apartment from the council meeting. To his surprise, he saw Elysie and Marlene together. It was a semi joyous moment; he was glad that Elysie didn't look hurt, at least not physically, but the whole situation still troubled him. Without stalling much, he wanted to break the news to them about what had happened at the meeting. Both Elysie and Marlene waited impatiently for his explanation.

Marcus started, "As you probably already know, Elysie, Vincent came over to the campus looking for you, and there was a fight. The campus police intervened, and he eventually left. Everyone knows who he is now, and there's a lot of talk about what to do about it. I was at the council meeting, and the bottom line is that they don't want him anywhere around the campus. They think he's playing judge, and it scares them. If he appears at the campus again, he'll be arrested."

Marcus put his hands together and brought them to his lips. "The good thing is that the council didn't authorize any kind of hunt on Vincent. As a matter of fact, they discouraged it, but what worries me is that there are some folks who have expressed interest in doing exactly that anyway. The council wouldn't be able to do anything about it unless, of course, Vincent turned himself in and they held a trial. Who knows what would happen then. Otherwise, Vincent's left to his own fate out there."

Elysie got up and walked to the window. She looked down at the people of the campus who were carelessly walking around and minding their own business.

"Now I understand how unfair this has been to Vincent, the one who helped make this place much safer," she said.

Marcus came over and put his arm around her. "Even though some want to hunt him down, there are others who want to help him. It's not only me, but other folks at the campus. They don't find him guilty of anything. They think he's actually doing a good thing. I just don't know what they'll do."

"Who wants to harm him?" Elysie asked.

"Some of Neil's friends and a few blow-hards who want to act as tough guys," he answered. "If the council finds out this is getting out of hand, they might actually apprehend these people or kick them out of the campus altogether."

Hearing this seemed to comfort Elysie somewhat. She was at least aware now that Vincent wasn't alone in this mess—that someone out there supported him. The only choice left seemed pretty clear as well, Marcus thought. The time had come for Elysie and Vincent to leave the campus outskirts for good and find a better future somewhere else—that was, if they could find Vincent.

As for him and Marlene, there was still a chance they could stay and have normal lives, but it all depended on how the council treated the situation. He knew that the conflict could turn campus wide. Then they would have destructive divisions like they did when Neil was around. If that happened, Marcus, too, would rather leave with Marlene somewhere far away from there.

Vincent arrived back at the Center tower. Laboriously, he climbed the stairs as hunger pangs tortured his stomach. When he reached the fifty-fourth floor and found it silent and empty of Elysie, he lost the desire to eat.

He sat on the couch looking out the window at the clouds as they slowly converged over the city. He thought about nothing but stared at the gray dust in the sky. Eventually the pain and weakness forced him to eat. He did so without satisfaction, just necessity. Afterward he lay down on the bed and closed his eyes.

After some time, as the night ruled the day, he woke up to the sound of someone coming up the stairs. His senses easily distinguished new noise from the ordinary. He got up, went to his armory, and came out with a pistol. As the noise reached his floor, he figured it was someone who knew about his lair, and his heart fluttered at the thought of it being Elysie. However, he remained disciplined to take on another disappointment and fight an intruder.

As the door slowly opened, two figures walked in with flashlights. Vincent watched from his position, wondering who it could be.

Then one of the figures spoke. "Vincent, are you here?"

It was the sweetest sound he had heard in a long while as he recognized Elysie's voice.

"I'm here, Elysie," he responded as he went toward her and they embraced.

He hugged her tightly, strongly pressing his body against hers, trying to feel every part of her. The flashlight fell from her hand, but he didn't care. All he wanted was to hold her.

"Be angry with me if you must," he said, with tears coming down his face, "but please don't leave me."

"I'll never leave you," Elysie responded. "I love you!"

All the troubles went out the window. They were rejected by the society, yet accepted by one another, and that was all that mattered at the moment. He then noticed Marcus standing aside. He walked over and gave him a hug.

"Thank you so much," he said. "I know how much danger you put yourself in for doing this."

Soon the three lit a lamp and sat in their makeshift living room. Marcus started explaining what went on at the council meeting. Vincent listened carefully as he learned about some people's intentions to hunt him down, thinking that he was too dangerous and that he would inevitably only hurt their society. He felt amazed and sad how, after all the times he had helped them, some people still thought he was the bad guy.

He understood that Neil's friends would want to avenge his death. But others? Why did they find him so unacceptable? Marcus also mentioned that despite all of this, there were still a decent number of people who were taking his side and were willing to stand up for him.

It didn't make a difference to Vincent. He knew that soon Elysie and he should pack up and leave the city. Marcus agreed, with sadness in his voice. The campus was on its own now, without the Scourge or its unlikely hero. Who knows, Vincent thought, it was probably better this way anyway. Elysie and he would get a fresh start.

The rest of the night, they spent talking about what they would do next with their lives. Marcus said he was determined to stay at the campus with Marlene, at least for a period of time. He had enough friends and backing from the pro-Vincent crowd that it seemed possible for them to avoid being driven out by those who were anti-Vincent.

Marcus expressed hope that things would stabilize if the council saw the rift being too destructive to the campus; however, if that didn't pan out and things got dangerous, he would leave with Marlene. In that case they would join Elysie and Vincent wherever they decided to go.

The thought of Marcus and Marlene joining them excited Vincent, and Elysie seemed thrilled by the idea. They fantasized in their discussion about where would they go and how they would make their lives together. It sounded like they had the whole world to choose from, and it brought a sense of adventure.

They talked about how they would travel to the West Coast and find a nice house in a little lagoon where they could fish, grow crops, and have bonfires. The ladies would tend to their chores while the men did theirs, and then in the evenings they would watch the sunset sipping on hot chocolate.

Maybe then, if luck was on their side, they would join some small, peaceful community and watch their children grow. There, everyone would be supportive of each other, in harmony, and full of joy as they learned the trade to live off the land. The Scourge wouldn't be on anyone's minds. It would be just like God intended Adam and Eve to be—in love in Eden.

The ideas they discussed sounded a lot more exciting to Vincent and Elysie than they did to Marcus. He, on the other hand, still preferred to stay at the campus if possible. He had made a lot of friendships, and so had Marlene. He was also accustomed to the life there, which, contrary to Vincent's and Elysie's fantasies, was much more stable, secure, and civilized than in the wild where they were headed.

Seeing Vincent and Elysie get so enthusiastic about the idea of living together, Marcus didn't have the heart to tell them again that he would rather stay at the campus. He let them fantasize, while admiring their childish hope of the new world. It wasn't, however, without benefits to him either. Their dream, too, gave him hope that if the campus didn't work out, life wouldn't be so bad.

They said their goodbyes on the promise that Vincent would let Marcus know, through a secret sign, when and where Elysie and he would be heading. They hugged and shook hands as if it was a temporary farewell. It seemed easier this way at the moment, but deep down Marcus knew the uncertainty of what could come next. His only hope remained that they wouldn't regret it later. He left the tower just before the sun peeked over the horizon, wondering if he would ever see them again.

CHAPTER 48

Over the next couple of days, Elysie and Vincent found a renewed attraction for each other. All of the hurts in the past elapsed, and they became so enticed just by being together. They talked about everything as if no danger would come their way.

They looked at each other differently, with great devotion and warmth in their eyes, and they made love as if they would never make it again. It was a spiritual attraction that transcended their earthly struggles. It seemed as if they already knew everything would work out in the end no matter what that end brought. In their eyes, they had already succeeded.

A week after Marcus left, Vincent heard someone making noise in the lower part of their tower. Quietly coming down to investigate, he found out it was trouble. Five so-called campus hunters had infiltrated the tower and sought their prize, the Scourge. He watched them for a few minutes and quickly realized these guys had no hunting skills. They lacked all the grace of urban sway. They were clumsy, made too much noise, and were spotted easily.

Vincent debated for a moment about whether he should take them out. It wouldn't have been difficult, but he had no desire to do that. They reminded him of mischievous kids trying to prove themselves than some serious threat he had faced many times before. He went back upstairs.

"Elysie, we have to go," he said as he hurriedly packed his backpack. "I think they've followed Marcus and discovered this place."

Elysie stood there with a stunned expression.

He noticed it, and to put her worries aside, he said, "Don't worry, while you were in Parsippany I mastered this city much better than these poor kids. We can easily evade them."

She seemed to think for a bit and then said, "Okay, but promise me you won't confront them unless we really have to."

He looked at her for a moment and said, "All right. I promise."

Vincent made it clear, however, that they would have to sacrifice their lair and leave the place and all the stuff they had there for good. From now on they would be on the run, living off whatever they could find in the city, until they decided to leave the island. The hunters would be behind them, but they would always maintain one step ahead. He reminded Elysie that he knew the city better than anyone else. They grabbed whatever they could in their backpacks and, with Vincent's direction, bypassed the hunters and left the tower without anyone noticing.

For the next month Elysie and Vincent went on the wild city run. They traversed Manhattan left and right, moving from one building to another, from one block to the next, always keeping their distance from the hunters. They zigzagged alleys, hallways, rooms, apartment buildings, office towers, and even the few navigable subway stations.

Vincent was a marathon runner when it came to moving around the city. He had knowledge of many buildings, and even if he wasn't familiar with a building, he knew how to navigate the unknown. He was aware of what to watch out for and which corridors, rooms, or open spaces were safer than others to move around. He always kept his eyes on exit paths and had an innate ability to foresee whether someone else would go down the same way.

As for Elysie, it wasn't always easy, but with Vincent's guidance it never seemed impossible. She learned quickly and soaked up as much knowledge as she could from him, but she still thought there was something that made him special in this case. In her mind, he conformed to some kind of a flow in space. It was something that only he saw, whether he realized it or not. His ability to navigate was like a river that had found its way through a maze of rocks, earth, and caves to eventually end up in the ocean. It seemed Vincent was able to do that with the whole city.

While keeping their eye on the peril they were in, Elysie found this experience strangely exciting; their daily life was dangerous enough to make it an adventure, but she trusted that Vincent would always find a way out. It became obvious these hunters had nowhere as much skill as he did, and she felt secure.

A few close calls did happen, which only increased the thrill, but in the end they always found a safe spot. This seemed like a game, and Vincent and Elysie were always one step ahead, as if someone were watching over them to ensure they were out of harm's reach.

The hunters persisted. Each group tried to outdo the other, occasionally working together. Their bravado didn't seem to make a difference, though; they lacked the skills needed to accomplish their feat, and they had a long way to catch up.

On one occasion, as Vincent and Elysie were pushed by the hunters to make an escape from an office tower, they ended up on the roof of the building at sunset. The blissfulness of the sight immediately had its effect as it calmed Elysie's fast beating heart all the while the quiet and romantic moment took her to heaven.

On the ledge, a pair of doves built a flimsy nest of straw and sticks, and they, too, became quiet and seemed to enjoy the warmth of the moment. Elysie knew they could only enjoy it for a short period of time because the summit of a building was rarely a good spot to camouflage themselves.

She took it all in while joining hands with Vincent and taking deep, slow breaths. The night elevated her, giving her further hope that their life to come would be peaceful. She then looked at Vincent in appreciation of the moment. He returned her gaze, and then together they moved on.

One evening the two found themselves in the northern part of Manhattan, just north of 130th Street. There they looked for a place to rest near St. Nicholas Park. This was once a long, but somewhat narrow, park with many steep steps and recreation areas, bordered on one side by the City College campus and on the other by a wide St. Nicholas Avenue.

Vincent hadn't been this way in a while, so he thought that he and Elysie would get a decent break from the hunters before they, too, came this way as well. Crossing the avenue into one of the side streets, he thought they had found their place.

"Is that my friend Mr. Scourge that I see?" suddenly a voice came from the darkness.

Elysie's eyes widened. Vincent stopped and then smiled. He knew who it was: his friend, the Old Wandering Woman.

"Of course," he said, turning around. "Who else would it be but my old friend."

He looked at Elysie and reassured her, "Don't worry, she's harmless."

"Ooo, I see you have a lady with you. Oh my, she's so beautiful," the old lady said excitedly in her raspy voice as she walked toward them. Elysie smiled at the unexpected guest.

"Yes, she is, my dear ma'am." Vincent felt glad to see the old lady still alive and well. "This is my wonderful, lovely, delightful, and beautiful Elysie."

"Oh, how nice to meet you." The old lady gently reached out her hand and met Elysie's with a shake while the smile never left her face. Elysie seemed pleasantly surprised at the old lady's warmth and couldn't stop smiling herself.

"I'm so glad to meet you, too, ma'am," Elysie greeted her.

The old lady shook her head. "The pleasure is all mine. It's so nice to see two people who love each other. As the Lord said, two are better than one."

Elysie looked at Vincent, but he had nothing to add. The old lady was something else. After a few moments Vincent replied, "We're so glad to see you're doing well, too, and as always, you're the master of camouflage."

"Oh, I didn't sneak up on you, my son," she replied. "I'm too slow for that. But when you're in the right place, people come to you, he he."

Vincent was impressed the old lady always had something to come back with. "What can I say? You always surprise me."

"You surprised me, too," she said. "I've always seen you alone. I didn't expect you with this beautiful lady, but it's a good thing. Two is better than one. Like the Lord said; if either of them falls down, one can help the other up."

"Well, I can't argue with you there. Elysie is a special person to me." He put his arm around his love.

"That's a beautiful name. Did you know it means Paradise?" she asked.

Vincent shrugged, as he hadn't known the meaning before she told him.

"A place stirred in joy," she explained, "and my does it fit the beauty of your lady."

Elysie looked away, seemingly from the embarrassment of the compliment.

"Thank you," Vincent said, "I fully agree."

"It's good that I see this. I was worried about you for a while." She touched his hand. "You needed someone, and now the good Lord has provided you with a partner."

To Vincent's surprise, Elysie invited the old lady to come with them to rest, eat, and sleep. The old lady seemed so happy with the invitation that she gladly accepted while trying to hide a few tears that fell down her wrinkled face. Vincent, on the other hand, felt convicted that he had never tried to be more polite with the old lady before.

Choosing an apartment that faced inside a small courtyard, the three of them lit a candle in the living room and started talking while sharing food. The old lady and Elysie seemed to really connect as the old lady talked to her about how she, long ago, had sung in a jazz band. Elysie seemed very interested in her story and asked questions.

The lady continued to tell them how she had fallen into drugs and despair and become homeless. Her daughter had been taken away from her and put up for adoption, and she had never heard from her again. Her extended time of being homeless actually helped her overcome her addictions because she simply couldn't afford them anymore.

One day someone reached out to her on the street and offered help by placing her in a new kind of homeless shelter, which was also a rehabilitation center sponsored by some not-for-profit organization. The workers she met there told her about a church they were a part of, and she became curious.

After visiting the church a few times, she felt such joy that she decided to give her life to Jesus. Since then she had not lived for herself, but to show love and mercy to others, as that was what Christ had done for her. Soon, however, the Scourge struck and the rest was history, including the fact that the campus had kicked her out during its turbulent years because of fear she would spread some disease, yet she still thought God was good.

Vincent was amazed at her story. Her life seemed turbulent even before the Scourge. The old lady talked about God and His good promise to all those who repented and put their trust in Him. Vincent listened to her testimony carefully. He respectfully acknowledged what faith had done for her, but he had many questions about it. It was a great mystery, and some things didn't make sense. His heart told him to try it out, but his mind held him back.

Perhaps some things weren't meant to make sense to a man, he thought, while his heavy eyelids pulled his body down to a more comfortable position. Elysie, on the other hand, seemed engaged in the conversation, and as the night wore on, Vincent fell asleep while the two of them continued talking.

In the morning, they had breakfast together. When they finished the last bit of food, the old lady said, "You go on without me."

Surprised by the sudden announcement, Vincent looked at her but said nothing.

"I can't accompany you," she said as her hands shook trying to stand. Vincent reached and helped her. "I'm too slow to run like you have to."

This made sense to him, but he felt sad for the old lady. She truly seemed like a nice and gentle woman, and he cared for her, too.

Elysie gave her a big hug and thanked her, while the old lady pulled Vincent aside and told him, "The Lord said; enjoy life with your wife, whom you love, all the days of this meaningless life that God has given you under the sun, he he."

"Okay, so God, too, says it's meaningless," he replied. "That makes me feel better."

"God is the one who provides meaning," she said, then pulled him a little closer. "Make sure you don't stay around here too long. Leave the city and the Scourge behind."

He looked at her and noticed the seriousness in her expression. "Okay, I understand. I just have to make sure my friends are good before we leave."

"I mean it," she said. "It's not good for you to stay here any longer. God showed me."

The old woman kept looking at him for a few moments to make sure he understood. Then she whispered, "Heart is the most deceitful."

He wasn't sure what she meant by that but nodded nonetheless and went back to Elysie. She waved to them as they parted.

"I love you," she said in a farewell. "May the good Lord bless you!"

CHAPTER 49

Another month went by, and Elysie started asking Vincent when would they move off of the island and head west. Vincent thought for a moment each time she would ask, and then he would tell her he wanted to stay a while longer to make sure that Marcus and Marlene were fine. Perhaps, he thought, Marcus and Marlene needed more time to decide if they would join them.

The reality was that Vincent didn't know the right time to move on. He cared about Marcus and Marlene, but he also felt attached to the city. He found it difficult to simply leave. For once in his life, Vincent felt so comfortable in a place. He felt safe in the city, and it didn't matter that others wanted to harm him. The city was his guardian jealously protecting him, granting him special powers to move around unlike anyone else. He felt special.

He did understand, however, that the same protection wouldn't fully extend to Elysie, so he slowly started planning in his mind that they leave and start a new life. After all, she mattered to him more than that special feeling the city gave him. New York wouldn't be easy to give it up, and he knew it.

Elysie could see in Vincent's eyes how much he enjoyed where he was and how comfortable he felt being there. He had truly mastered this realm, and she felt guilty for even asking him to leave. Watching him being a part of the city in such a unique way gave her the will to sacrifice herself, though she did fear that if they stayed there for too long they would never leave.

One day Vincent and Elysie found themselves in a building behind the once-famous Macy's department store on 35th street. They had a little break from the hunters as they converged farther up north. The noon sun had brightened some of the building hallways, and the ever-mild winter kept the temperatures well within the comfort zone. They wanted to reach a spot that would be comfortable to stop at, eat, rest up, and even stay for a few days.

Most of the buildings had deteriorated since the year before, Vincent noticed. He carefully watched where he stepped, as some of the floors had cracks and appeared they could give in at any time. He went first while Elysie traced his steps. He would make a step, make sure it felt sturdy, and in the same spot she would follow.

Early evening rolled in when they found themselves in a hallway where the floor had partly caved in different spots, so they had to be extra careful. All Vincent could hear was the trickling of water down the ceilings and walls. They both learned to remain quiet and listen for anything that could give them a warning about something breaking or falling down.

Vincent made a step and heard a crack. He stopped and carefully moved his foot to another spot and then made a few steps until he felt he stood on sturdy ground. Elysie followed by placing her foot on the same spot. She gently placed her weight on it and then heard a louder crack as the floor gave in a few inches while her foot sunk in.

Elysie's eyes opened wide, and Vincent immediately reached out and pulled her hand. She went toward him as the floor gave out completely beneath her. Part of her body went through the hole, but

Vincent held onto her. The noise of the debris hitting the floor below muffled Elysie's scream as Vincent, even more energetically, pulled her back. Within a few seconds, they were both on solid ground and Vincent sighed, thanking God they were all right.

After a minute of resting on the ground, they stood up, but Elysie cried out and fell to the ground.

"What's the matter, Elysie?" Vincent asked, worriedly.

"My ankle . . . it's so painful," she responded, wincing.

Vincent kneeled and gently took her shoe off. Then he reached for his flashlight, only to realize it must have fallen somewhere on the floor below. Even in the dim light of the hallway, he could tell that her ankle and foot had swollen up.

"I think it's sprained," she said, still flinching.

"I'm afraid you're right, sweetie," he replied.

Vincent elevated her leg to help with the swelling while shaking his head at this unfortunate turn of events. He looked around the decrepit place and listened to the water still trickling down the walls, then down the hole Elysie had almost fallen through.

"We'll need to get out of here," he said. "It's just not safe, and it's too dark."

"Yes, Vincent," she agreed. "We do."

Vincent removed his backpack and started looking for a spare flashlight. Elysie stopped him and reached for his hand.

"Vincent," she said. "We need to leave this city."

Vincent looked at her and nodded. A slight sadness came over him, but he knew that they had to leave the island behind now. She could no longer keep up with him and run from the hunters. At this point it was just a matter of time before they were cornered or gunned down. He took a deep breath and let it out.

"Okay, Elysie," he said and gave her a slight smile. "We'll leave the city."

Exiting the building turned out quite difficult, not only because Elysie hopped on one leg while Vincent helped her, but because every crack caused them to stop in fear of another floor collapsing. They proceeded with extreme caution, and after the sun had long gone and the stars were shining brightly, they got out onto the street.

Looking at the silent towering buildings around them, Vincent felt guilty for not leaving the city earlier, inadvertently allowing this injury to happen. He understood the risks, yet he prolonged their departure. That special feeling he had had anchored them there, endangering her much more than him. He felt selfish now, and the only remedy he could think of was to ensure a safe passage off the island.

"Which way should we go?" she asked, breaking his silent guilt trip.

"West," he answered. "We'll head west. It may take us some time, but we'll get there."

CHAPTER 50

Lying by Elysie and resting in the late afternoon, on the second day since her injury, Vincent stared out the dirty window at the gray sky above. It drizzled rain, and the clouds looked dirty and mean. He felt glad they had made it to a building on the corner of 36th Street and 10th Avenue. Elysie's ankle was badly sprained, and it took them a considerable amount of time to get even this far, especially when they traveled only at night.

They avoided climbing many steps and settled for a small secluded room on the first floor as their resting place before moving on to the river, which was just two blocks away. Elysie was asleep, and Vincent's thoughts were on life itself.

He wondered how much more he adored life when it was closest to death—whether his own or Elysie's. He asked himself how anyone could appreciate life if they took it for granted. Its fragility to end at any moment made it precious, even though it was a bittersweet experience.

"What's the meaning behind it?" he whispered under his breath.

While he contemplated this question, some faint noises caught his attention. Immediately, he snapped out of his thoughts and intently focused on what he had heard. The noise was coming from the outside. He carefully moved to the window and peeked out. He didn't see anything but heard more noises. It sounded like people talking on a two-way radio. Where are they? he wondered, slightly disappointed that his incredible ability to sense and pinpoint things had deserted him.

He moved two rooms over in hopes of seeing who had made the noise. Then he saw them: two guys with pistols strapped to their belts and rifles slung across their shoulders talking on a small radio. They had roguish faces and expressed wildness in their eyes.

"We know he's in one of these buildings," one of the guys said. "Jimmy said he saw the light around here, but the dumbass forgot which floor."

"He said they don't know which floor," the voice came over the radio. "Well, there's only one way to find out."

The guy's eyes widened. "Well, we aren't going in there alone."

"Then wait for us," the voice responded. "We'll be there in a few."

Vincent realized what this meant; the hunters had spotted them, and he had to react quickly. He hastily went back to Elysie and woke her up.

"I have to move you," he said, worriedly.

She looked at him in confusion. "What's going on?"

"We've been discovered. The hunters are out there. I have to move you."

Her eyes opened wide as Vincent pulled her up. He lifted her in his arms, moved her a few steps, and then fell to the floor. She nearly screamed in pain as her injured ankle hit hard. He realized he had no strength to carry her in his arms. Instead, he propped her on his back, awkwardly walked a few rooms over, and then placed her inside a closet.

"Here, take this." He handed her a pistol. "If anyone opens this door besides me, you know what to do."

"But-"

"I'll lead them away from here. Then I'll come back for you and we'll leave this place for good," Vincent promised.

Elysie looked at him in fear as he closed the closet door. He hurried back to the room they had slept in and grabbed his second pistol. He ejected the magazine, made sure it had ammunition, slid it back until he heard the clicking noise, disengaged the safety, and cocked the chamber. His weapon was now ready. It had been a while since he had used it, but he still felt comfortable with it in his hand.

Vincent moved to different parts of the building and observed until he discovered the positions of his opponents. He spotted five in total, sneaking up on the same side of the building. This is good, he thought. I'll make sure they don't go in.

Quickly moving to the perpendicular side of the building he thought the hunters had neglected, he found an exit and then went outside. The drizzling rain hit his face, and a moment later a bullet whizzed past his head. He ducked back in and immediately heard the crashing of the window next to him. He fired two shots wildly and then quickly peeked out to realize he had failed to spot three more guys coming from down the road.

A few more bullets went by, breaking the windows around him, before he peeked again and fired back with aim. Even though they were at least fifty yards away, he managed to wound one, which caused the rest to run for cover.

Vincent stepped outside for the second time and darted toward a rusting car parked on the side of the street. He got behind it and waited for the guys from the other side of the building to make their way before he fired at them as well. The moment the first one appeared past the corner, Vincent pulled the trigger. The bullet struck the hunter in the shoulder, and he let out a cry.

Vincent quickly turned around to make sure the other three, who had run for the cover on the opposite side, weren't sneaking up on him. He spotted two hiding behind a Halal Foods truck and the wounded one behind the corner of the building. Not wanting to be in the middle, he fired one shot at each group and then ran across the street.

After a few seconds, the hunters fired back, but he had already made his way across and was hiding behind a container at a decrepit gas station. Four more shots whizzed by before Vincent realized the gas station, probably with some gas left in it, was an even worse spot for him to be.

A few more exchanges occurred before he snuck away from the gas station and made his way onto the street heading east, and away from the hunters and the building Elysie was in. He ducked behind various cars and thought he could lead them this way without getting hit, as long as he zigzagged behind cars.

Without much hesitation, Vincent started running. Every few seconds he got behind a car. Soon the bullets went past him, hitting the cars and the buildings on either side of him. Good, he thought, at least they are following me.

The hunters chased him as he drew them farther east and away from Elysie. Sweat dripped down his face, and he started feeling lightheaded. He crossed three city blocks and wondered how much more before they tired or gave up. The hunters pursued him for one more city block before he had no more energy to run.

Vincent ducked behind a corner of a building while his heart beat heavily. He peeked past his hideout to monitor their progress. He saw three of them, roughly a hundred yards away, still running toward him. Even though they appeared winded and had slowed down, they seemed determined to chase him. The rest, he assumed, were far behind or had given up altogether.

Vincent aimlessly fired a shot to stop them in their tracks and then laboriously ran north. He felt he had led them far enough east, and now was the time to lose them. Otherwise, he wouldn't have the energy to do so.

As he ran up the street, bullets whizzed past him again. The hunters had already made it beyond the corner and closed in on him. He felt something strike him in the lower backside as he grunted and lurched forward. A burning sensation spread in his back. He knew the bullet had hit him and immediately ran to the closest door and went inside.

"Damn it!" he yelled as he fast-walked down the narrow lobby of the building. "They had to hit me now!"

He walked through the door at the end and then stopped for a moment to catch his breath. A strange sense of familiarity came over him. He looked around a little and told himself, "I know this place."

He brushed the sweat of his eyebrows and then whispered, "This is where I used to work."

A quick thought of irony crossed his mind. He always joked that this place would be the end of him. Now, brushing these thoughts away, his senses told him the pursuers weren't far behind. He fast-walked to the stairwell and made his way up. Turning around to see if they followed, he noticed a small trail of blood.

"That's just great," he said under his breath.

He hiked as high as his legs could carry him and then opened the door to the fifth floor. Walking down the long dark hallway, he went into a large open area. He went past the cubicles where long-dead terminals and laptops remained hooked up to the silent monitors. He stopped again for a breather as exhaustion took over. To the right of him, another familiar detail sparked his memory.

This was his old desk!

"Good God, you've got to be kidding me," he said in disbelief.

He turned around, and as he was about to continue down the area, he nearly fell to the floor. All his energy reserves seemed depleted. Breathing heavy and feeling clammy, he staggered into his old cubicle and slouched onto his old chair. He closed his eyes and tried to control his heavy breathing. When he opened them, everything looked dark at first, but his eyes adjusted well enough to spot his old headphones on the desk next to the keyboard. A few song tunes rang in his mind as he remembered them. He closed his eyes again.

"This is it," he said. "This is where I'll make my stand. The Scourge of Man is finished, whether *I* live or die."

Vincent sat in the chair waiting. He could hear the hunters making their way to the fifth floor and slowly coming down the hallway. Each footstep they made coincided with an increasingly louder beat of his heart. He knew they were close and raised his gun, waiting for the encounter.

Less than twenty feet away, he saw the first one in the tiny light peeking through the window on the far side of the building. He moved slowly past Vincent's view, and right behind him came two more.

Sitting in the darkness, Vincent realized they couldn't see him. He looked down the sight of his shaking gun, trying to aim at them. If I can just steady my hand, he thought, I could take them all out; it would all be over.

As his finger tempted to pull the trigger, he paused. Something in his mind told him to stop. He stared ahead as his chance of gunning them down slowly slipped away, and he felt numb. A moment later, three more figures presented themselves in front of him much like the first three.

"Where is he?" he heard them call out.

"We don't know," the other three replied. "He must have gone farther down this hallway."

"Can't you see his blood?"

"No. It's too dark, and I can't tell against this carpet. Let's move on. He must be farther down."

Vincent sat there in the darkness as his pursuers moved away from him and down another hallway. He heard them open a door that he assumed was to another stairwell and then close it behind them. With that, their noises grew fainter.

All of a sudden, he gulped a big breath of relief and let it out. His pursuers had no idea where he was, and this was his chance to escape; otherwise, he may not get another. Immediately, he got up on his unsteady legs and started walking back the way he came. He struggled down the staircase, but once outside the building, he took another deep breath to gather more energy as pain radiated down his back.

The light seemed to have subsided substantially, and he had a difficult time seeing ahead of him. He stumbled down the streets, making his way back to Elysie. He didn't even bother to check whether anyone followed him. Every fifteen to twenty yards, he'd pause and take a quick rest.

He noticed his breathing had increased and his vision had become blurry. He hoped that closing his eyes during the breaks would help clear his vision. The journey felt incredibly long, but once he made it back to their building, he forgot about his hardship. I'm almost there, he comforted himself, only a few steps more.

"Elysie," he called out as he made his way to the room he had left her in. Then he looked to the left and saw the door of the closet opened. He fell to his knees and shook his head.

"Good God, why?" he said and stared ahead at the empty closet. He closed his eyes and collapsed to the floor. Everything went black.

CHAPTER 51

Elysie's heart struck hard with each beat. She didn't know Vincent's whereabouts and if the danger had passed them by. It was getting dark, and with each moment her heart sank in unrelenting uncertainty.

"What had happened to Vincent?" she kept asking, but to no avail.

She knew nothing more than the little mouse that had hid in the same room as her, although the mouse seemed much less frightened. She couldn't imagine Vincent being gone forever. She risked her life to come back to the city to find him, and thinking that she had lost him again was too much to bear.

It seemed ages since she had moved to another room in the back of the building to avoid being discovered by the hunters. She recalled the series of events after the gunfight receded, presumably when Vincent drew them away from the place. She heard some of the hunters enter the building. They walked around in their clumsy manner, exploring the place, and she felt it was just a matter of time until they searched the room Vincent had left her in.

She took her chance when it seemed they were on another part of the floor and exited the closet, carefully dragging her injured foot, and went out of the room. The feeling of exposure struck her and fear gripped her heart, but she knew she had no choice at that point; she had to find another place to hide.

Her grip on the gun Vincent gave her tightened as she slowly made her way down the long hallway and away from the hunters. She heard them open doors and move around in a room at the opposite end of the hallway. She also heard sliding doors open, which further affirmed that they would have eventually opened the sliding door of the closet she was in.

Turning back every few seconds, she checked on the hunters as she moved carefully and quietly, still dragging her injured foot while hopping on the other and steadying herself against the wall with her left hand. She longed for the walking stick she had used the last two days, but it was somewhere in the room the hunters were in now.

At one point she heard them exit the room into the hallway, and she hurriedly made a left turn into a small, but much darker hallway. There, she saw a single door at the other end and went toward it, but when she tried to open the door, she couldn't.

The footsteps got closer, and she turned around and slid to the ground. She aimed the gun high and waited for what seemed inevitable. Two hunters slowly appeared, one holding a shotgun, the other a pistol. The first one looked into the hallway but seemed unfazed and proceeded down the main hallway. The second looked as well, and he, too, seemed unfazed at first. Then he looked down and straight at Elysie.

She stared back at him as their eyes met, with both of her hands holding the gun and pointing straight at him. Her blood pulsed through her fingers and she started squeezing the trigger. The guy froze. His eyes didn't blink. He looked to be in his late teens with a boyish and naïve look, still hanging on to some innocence. He slowly mouthed to Elysie, "Please."

"What's the matter?" she heard the other guy call some distance away.

"Uh . . . nothing," the young guy responded. "I, I think we should leave. There's nothing here."

Her eyes followed him as he slowly disappeared from her view. She let out a sigh, but fear still gripped her. Did I make a mistake? she wondered. Would they return?

They didn't return, and she was now in a different part of the floor waiting for Vincent. The rain had stopped, but the tears in her eyes slowly began falling. Her throat tightened, and it became hard to swallow. She closed her eyes and prayed. Then she heard some noise. It was subtle, but it called her name.

"I'm here!" she responded, but the tightness in her throat made it quiet and broken.

She went outside the room and down the long hallway, recklessly hopping on one foot. She said "I'm here," again, but without much sound. She moved as fast as she could, striking the concrete wall with her fist, but it seemed to create no noise. She approached the room Vincent had left her in and walked inside. There she saw him lying on the ground, face first, with a dim flashlight in his hand. She came to him and kneeled down.

"Vincent, I'm here! I'm here!" she called to him, but he didn't respond.

She reached to turn him over and felt warm blood on her hands. She looked in horror and shook her head.

"God, please," she prayed. "Don't let him go. Don't let him go."

CHAPTER 52

Vincent opened his eyes ever so slightly and felt someone dragging him. Everything looked blurry, and giving up to decipher what was going on, he closed them again and then fell into a dream.

There stood two trees in front of him. They broke out of the fertile ground and expanded their roots in every direction. They were big and boastful of life with leaf-covered branches reaching high and wide. There were all kinds of birds making their homes in it.

A river flowed between the two trees. It looked as clear as crystal. He felt mesmerized by it and kneeled by its bank. He reached out his hand and touched it. Then he heard a gentle whisper, "Open your eyes."

He opened his eyes, and the blue sky greeted him. He stared at it. He didn't think of anything, just stared. He heard the sound of water and crashing of waves all around him. Lifting his head slightly, he met the rays of the sun and Elysie. She rowed a small boat while gazing ahead of her. He lay in front of her, covered in blankets. He stared at her in disbelief and wondered how he had gotten there.

When she noticed he was looking at her, she stopped rowing and quickly reached out to him with tears in her eyes.

"Stay awake, sweetie. Stay awake," she pleaded with him.

He tried to respond but couldn't. All he could do was look back at her. She hugged and kissed him as tears flowed down her face and onto his. She cradled him this way for a while as the boat aimlessly floated in the water.

When Vincent finally muttered a few words, he asked, "Where are we?"

"We're going to a new and better place," she responded, "and that's all that matters."

He smiled and said, "I'll keep my eyes open," and watched the birds fly over the city skyline.

The End

ABOUT THE AUTHOR

Zoran Obradovic was born in Sarajevo, Bosnia. He moved to Buffalo, New York, when he was a young teenager. Attending Niagara University, he studied communications, international studies, and peace and social justice. He received a master's degree in informatics from the University at Buffalo. Zoran is an avid reader, traveler, and practitioner of martial arts.

Zoran wrote The Scourge of Man in 2014 and in 2017 made the decision to publish it. His inspiration came from a vivid dream he had in June 2012 while going through an emotionally difficult time in his life. Zoran currently lives in North Bergen, New Jersey.